BLOOD ALONE

ELAINE BERGSTROM

ACE BOOKS, NEW YORK

This Ace Book contains the complete text of the original edition.

BLOOD ALONE

An Ace Book / published by arrangement with
the author

PRINTING HISTORY
Jove edition / August 1990
Ace edition / August 1994

ISBN: 0-441-00088-6

ACE®
Ace Books are published by The Berkley Publishing Group,
200 Madison Avenue, New York, New York 10016.
ACE and the "A" design
are trademarks belonging to Charter Communications, Inc.

PRINTED IN THE UNITED STATES OF AMERICA

10 9 8 7 6 5 4 3 2 1

*Dedicated with love
to my parents,
Howard & Eleanor Schmieler,
and to
Margaret L. Carter,
who got me to the finish line.*

*And a special acknowledgment to the American
glass houses—Blenko, Fenton, and Wissmach—
for letting me see and smell and hear and feel
how fine glass is made.*

Blood alone moves the wheels of history

—BENITO MUSSOLINI

Prologue

TWO THIRDS OF the Austra family sat behind twelve long tables, interspersed with other representatives of the global network of firms the family owned. At the podium in front of them Wilhelm Prost, scientific adviser for the firm's Historical Projection Department, concluded his report and waited for the expected barrage of questions. None came.

Prost stood patiently, expecting a dismissal that did not come. Ten minutes elapsed before Stephen Austra asked, "Wilhelm, do we understand correctly? Has your group predicted the end of the world?"

"Yes," Prost said. "Yes, if the weapons we have described are developed and used."

"And you see no possibility of averting this?"

"Only a miracle will save us."

Another long pause. Another question: "What sort of a miracle do we require, Wilhelm?"

Part

One

PAUL

Chapter One

August 1938

I

PAUL STODDARD'S STEAMSHIP chugged into Porto one Thursday in August. It arrived two hours late, and when he rushed to the train station, he found he had missed the last departure for Chaves and there would not be another until Monday.

"But I must be in Chaves tomorrow," Paul insisted in slow, almost correct Portuguese, then added, as if a personal detail might make some difference, "I am there to see about a position."

"Go there," said the old station attendant, correcting him. He looked Paul over. "Are you perhaps seeing someone at AustraGlass?"

"Yes, why do you ask?"

The attendant chuckled. "Where else would a young foreigner go for employment in Chaves? But I ask for another reason as well. AustraGlass has a warehouse on the Rua de Restouracao. A truck drove in this afternoon. It may return to Chaves in the morning." He scribbled a name and address on a piece of paper and handed it to Paul. "Go to this pension and ask for George Samuelson. He is the driver. Possibly he will take you back with him."

Paul looked at the address, then the handbill-cluttered walls around him. "Do you have a map of the city here? I have never been to Porto—or to Portugal, either, for that matter."

The attendant responded with another chuckle. "Ah, young *senhor, descuple*. From your excellent Portuguese I thought you came here often." He reached beneath the counter and pulled out a map of the country with a detail of Porto on the back. "My compliments and *boa noite*."

"*Boa noite. Gracias.*"

"*Obrigado,*" the attendant corrected.

Following the map, Paul found the second-class pension easily. Samuelson was out for the evening so Paul took a room, left him a note, and walked to the Austra warehouse, where, to be certain he would not be overlooked, he left a second note on the ancient truck's dusty windshield. Not at all tired, he explored the streets of the hilly city, deciding the houses were too sullen and the churches too excessively ornate for his moderate tastes.

When he returned to the pension, the driver had already retired but the owner assured Paul that Samuelson would wake him in the morning. "I'm sorry that it will be too early for breakfast, *senhor*, but we will have biscuits and coffee for you."

"What time will we leave?"

"Four-thirty."

Paul frowned. "Then I suppose I had best try to sleep."

The owner asked him to wait and brought him a water glass filled with port. "Our finest and strongest. Enjoy first, then sleep."

"*Gra . . . obrigado.*"

"For a country often noted for being immune to time," Paul wrote his brother that evening, "I continuously alternate between being too early and too late." He described his hurried glimpses of Lisbon and the dull streets of Porto and might have noted the excellence of the pension's wine but his eyes refused to remain open.

The next afternoon, he continued the letter.

I was awakened a few minutes before four by two quick raps on my door, but when I rushed to open it, the driver had already gone. Not wishing to be tardy again, I quickly dressed and found him in the kitchen. Samuelson is a short, barrel-chested Englishman of about fifty who was sporting a thick reddish stubble of at least two days on his ruddy face. When I introduced myself and thanked him for his aid, he replied with an odd look, then the pleasant comment "You'll be too hot" and finished his roll in silence. The pension's owner poured me a cup of thick black coffee and appeared sympathetic.

Later, carrying both valises, I ran to keep abreast of Samuelson, whose short legs are capable of fantastic speed. I had become so impressed with his cordiality that as we approached the warehouse I ran ahead of him, fearful that, were I not sitting in the passenger seat when he started the truck, he would drive away without me.

During the first half of the journey everything was the color of plain baked pottery—the dirt road, the mountains, the trees, the valleys; even Samuelson, with his bronzed complexion, seemed in perfect harmony with the landscape. Samuelson, in one of his rare exchanges, told me this was the dry season and that it will snow on the mountain peaks in the winter and then all will become green in the valleys until summer. I found this no great revelation but did not ask him to elaborate. Talking might have distracted him from the task of driving and, at the breakneck speed he chose to travel, that could have been disastrous.

As we approached Chaves the road began winding steadily higher, curling around the sides of the mountains, then dropping suddenly into the valleys. The lower levels seemed greener than the area closer to the sea but the peaks are higher, sharper, and more barren. I can imagine them in the winter, empty except for the snow and moon.

I fear if I continue, I will either get disgustingly poetic or incurably homesick, so I will tell you a secret instead but you must promise never to repeat it to Mother or she will beg me to come home. Through the first few hours of the trip Samuelson changed gears frequently. Torturing the clutch seemed in keeping with his personality, however, and I ignored the sudden jolts until we made our first stop. Then he shifted into first and ran the truck into the side of the mountain. I looked at him in shock and we had our third verbal exchange. He informed me, quite matter-of-factly, that we had no brakes. Had I been anywhere but nowhere, I believe I'd have

left him and walked, though, to his credit, had he not
volunteered the information, I never would have guessed
it. "Are all the Austra trucks in such good repair?" I
asked.

Samuelson scowled. "This one is mine," he replied
possessively. I believe I should have known.

I walked to the edge of the road and looked down.
We were over two hundred feet above the valley floor,
the drop a steep incline. This was the last time I deliberately noticed our elevation, though later it became all
too obvious far too often.

We arrived in Chaves in the early afternoon. It is a
Lilliputian delight of tidy, narrow streets containing tile-
roofed houses of Arab simplicity in whitewashed stucco.
The walls of nearly all the dwellings are enhanced by
window boxes filled with a multitude of colorful blooms.

We stopped for lunch at a small, dark, empty restaurant (undoubtedly one of Samuelson's favorites) and ate
a huge and surprisingly excellent meal. Throughout it
Samuelson drank copious quantities of the house wine
and for a few moments became almost effusive, asking
me why I was traveling to AustraGlass. I replied I had
an interview for a position in the glass house and became convinced of his intoxication when he *grinned* and
asked where I had worked before. For an architectural
firm in New York, I replied. He returned to studying the
tabletop. When I asked what he did for the firm, he
didn't even look up. "I drive a truck," he said, and
gulped down the rest of his glass. I wished he'd taken
time for coffee, but five minutes later we were off.

In a few miles we made the turn onto the Austra private drive. After dirt roads and worse, the well-kept
macadam, wide enough to allow two cars to pass each
other, seemed a major highway. We soon arrived at a
guardhouse, and an attendant motioned us through. We
drove up a steep grade, then rounded a curve, and I had
my first glimpse of the place.

AustraGlass is built halfway up a mountain and faces
south. It consists of a series of low connected structures,
all with red-tiled roofs and magnificent expanses of dec-
orative glass. I had expected more traditional architec-

ture but the buildings have a modern quality to them. One large building was set away from the rest. Smoke rose from its two tall chimneys and I guessed correctly that this must be the glass house.

Below the glass house is a small cluster of homes, and higher up the mountain, barely visible through the trees, are a number of dark stone houses. Samuelson drove me straight up to the main building and left me . . . dusty, thirsty, and tired; holding my two old valises and standing uncertainly in front of the ornate glass doors while he sat in his truck and waited for me to go inside. The only thing to do was to enter, though I felt less like a prospective employee than a beggar seeking a handout.

Stepping from the hot driveway into the offices of AustraGlass is similar to diving into a woodland pond . . . cool, hushed, and shaded green by the expanses of patterned glass, which made up the entire south wall and slanted at a seventy-degree angle.

With no hint of condescension a secretary managed to correct my mispronunciation of first and last names of my prospective employer by informing me that "Senhor Steffen Ow-stra"—family roots Germanic, it would seem—"is engaged at the moment." She also took polite pity on my travel-worn appearance by pointing out the men's room with no additional comment.

And so, two hours ago I combed the dust out of my hair, washed my face, changed my shirt, and buffed up the shine on my shoes. Returning to the waiting room, I occupied myself with studying the display of Austra family creations.

The firm's lobby contains a stunning assortment of cut and blown glass, as well as paintings, sculptures, china, thick rugs, and tapestries—and, of course, the windows, which, the secretary informed me, are mounted on rollers and changed according to the season.

Finally I pulled out this letter to keep me occupied while I wait and wait and wait.

I will end this page of my letter now. When you read the beginning of the next, you will know whether I will

stay here or return to Boston. Even though your prayer
will make no difference by the time you read this, say
one, anyway, pause in sympathy at how nervous I've
become, and read on. . . .''

II

Paul would spend nearly an hour that evening trying to
recall Stephen Austra's huge office so he could describe it to
his brother. "Sumptuous yet utilitarian . . . a precarious balance" was all he eventually wrote, simply because he could
remember nothing save the huge abstract windows that covered the two sloping outside walls, the carved cherry desk,
and the man standing formally behind it.

In his letter to his brother, Paul described Stephen Austra:

> . . . perhaps twenty-five; with black curly hair; an
> odd but remarkably handsome face that, if sketched,
> could be called a study in triangles; and large, flashing
> black eyes that are impossible to ignore. It's the sort of
> face that would throw Judy into a preadolescent swoon.
> Tell her so and take the bruises for me. He looked com-
> fortably elegant in a loose-fitting deep blue silk shirt and
> black suede slacks. My British tweeds, while new and
> quite the fashion, seemed stiff and shabby by compari-
> son. When he wasn't speaking, he would listen to me
> with an intense stillness, as if he were noting not only
> my words and visible emotions but also my thoughts. I
> felt uncomfortably like a fly buzzing around a frog and
> begging it to strike.

"Are you comfortable speaking Portuguese, Mr. Stoddard?" Stephen asked in musically accented English.

"Not entirely. I find myself lapsing into Spanish."

"A common problem. I see from your letter that you also
speak French and German. A liberal education, yes?"

"A much-traveled family. My father was a diplomat. I was

born in Germany and spent some years in France and Spain.
I have only lived in the United States since 1932.''

"Ah! That explains why your English possesses traces of
a German heritage and your Portuguese a Castilian lilt. Our
staff travels a great deal, so language proficiency is important. Yours is amazing in an American, particularly one so
young.''

"I see." Paul was certain his stab of irritation had not
been overlooked. "I have brought a list of my previous em-
ployers. I believe I have abilities that will be useful to *your*
firm as well." As he spoke, Paul pulled out an envelope
containing his résumé and passed it to his interviewer.

Stephen placed it on his desk unopened. "Mr. Stoddard,
I have already read your résumé, checked your references,
and studied samples of your work. You are here now so that
I may meet you. We will continue, yes?''

They did. In the next hour Paul lost some of his apprehension as they discussed art and architecture and, finally, Paul's
college years. "Track, drama, forensics, and—from your record—excellent grades. Tell me, Mr. Stoddard, did your ef-
forts succeed?''

The question startled Paul. "Yes," he said in reply to what
he believed Stephen meant. "Because of my education
abroad, I was able to begin college at sixteen. The first years
were difficult, but by my senior year I did feel I was accepted." An understatement, Paul thought. For the first three
years his classmates had mimicked his mannerisms behind
his back and laughed at him to his face. He'd been too civilized to fight, and so, he thought ruefully, was a natural patsy.
Paul paused as his eyes focused on nothing but the past, then
returned to the face of the man who would decide his future.
Stephen watched him curiously and Paul felt he must have
endured a similar misery. It seemed an encouraging bond.

"Now, Mr. Stoddard, tell me: How did you feel working
for that genius Lewishon?''

"I was still in school when I worked there. Though I did
no creative work for them, simply being in a place so artis-
tically daring was exhilarating. I had hoped to return after
graduation, but I was born a bit late for them, you might
say." Paul spoke as if the firm's demise had been that of a
close friend.

"So you were employed by the architectural firm of Krohn and Caldwell following graduation?"

"As a draftsman. In those two years I had an opportunity to design only six buildings, and those on my own time without pay. None went past the initial drawings. I gave them notice when I received your invitation to come here. It was a relief."

"Why did you work for them at all?"

"They were the only ones who would hire me," Paul admitted, and added, even more bluntly, "The owner is a close friend of my uncle's."

"I see."

All Paul's ambitions were contained in this valley, but he would not beg to be allowed to stay. "I suppose they would take me back . . . as a draftsman."

"I suppose they would." Austra pressed his fingers together beneath his chin. His look seemed to measure his prospective employee, and Paul began to wonder uncomfortably when the next train left for Porto. "Mr. Stoddard, you have written us a dozen times in the past four years and expressed your desire to learn the art of glassmaking, yet you obtained your degree in architecture. Why?"

"I believe a person should complete what they begin, but by junior year I . . ." Paul paused. Even now this was a difficult admission to make. "By then I knew I had absolutely no talent for architecture." Though the laughter that greeted this revelation was infuriating, Paul's expression did not change.

"So the firm of Krohn and Caldwell has already elaborated," Stephen agreed merrily, then sobered once more. "Now I will be as frank with you as you have been with me. Walter Lewishon wrote that you were 'an extremely likable young man.' He noted they would have been pleased to have you return to the office staff but concluded his letter by stating you did not possess the talent necessary to handle the creative work done by his firm because, and again I quote, 'he possesses no color sense whatsoever.' "

He had come four thousand miles to hear this! Paul began to stand, prepared to take his leave with whatever courtesy he could still muster. Stephen anticipated him and waved sharply like an orchestra conductor ordering an abrupt end to

a movement, then continued as if there had been no interruption. "On the other hand, two of your professors—the
two, I must add, whom I admire most at that unfortunately
bland school you attended—wrote high praises of your tech-
nical ability, your sense of proportion, and your skill at what
one termed 'that outrageous modernism.' I was intrigued
enough to write back to Krohn and Caldwell and ask for
copies of everything you had designed for them. The firm
showed why it has a reputation only for its lack of daring
when it sent me the originals instead. The worth I saw in
those is the reason you are here, Mr. Stoddard—the only
reason."

"I want to learn glassmaking."

"You need not remind me." Stephen hesitated and watched
Paul carefully as he continued. "One point about your brief
architectural career puzzles me. You knew more than enough
to have provided Krohn and Caldwell with plans for buildings
they would have been delighted to construct, yet you did not.
Why?"

"Because if I had designed them as Krohn and Caldwell
had wished, they would not have been mine."

Stephen responded with a tight smile and a penetrating
look. "Mr. Stoddard, have you seen any of the buildings of
Gaudi?"

"Yes. They look like badly decorated birthday cakes."

"Of course. Yet Gaudi will be forever revered as a daring
modernist by persons who would shudder at the merest insin-
uation that they inhabit one of those fantastic creations because he had the ego to build as no one had ever dared build
before, to say 'the world's opinion be damned.' Mr. Stoddard, for what do you dream of being remembered?"

The question was unexpected, yet Paul's reply was quick
and firm. "For glass, as Lewishon and Tiffany will be." He
quickly added, "As you will be."

Stephen waved at the windows around them. "Why are
you so obsessed by this?"

"When I was growing up in Paris, I'd walk past Notre
Dame on my way home from school. Sometimes I would go
inside and sit and study the windows and dream of creating
something that beautiful. Perhaps I have no talent, but I need
to try."

"Very well. You'll have your chance . . . with some stipulations. You'll be apprenticed to the glass house for a period of one year. However, as I am to teach you, I expect you to provide something of value in return. Therefore your hours at the glass house will be from seven to eleven-thirty. From one to five you will report to the architectural studio and work for Alexandre Savatier to earn your education. When the year is over, we'll see where your talent and your inclinations lie."

"Savatier is here?"

Paul could not hide his awe, and Stephen chuckled. "I see you've heard of him. Yes, Savatier and his staff are here. Will this arrangement be satisfactory?"

"Yes."

"Very good." Stephen pulled a printed form out of a drawer and slid it across the desk to Paul. "Now read this and sign both copies, please." Paul scanned the form, then, frowning, read it again. "I can't sign this," he concluded with regret. "I have no intention of staying here forever."

"Any skill you learn you may take with you, Mr. Stoddard. All we ask is that you refrain from providing anyone with information regarding the administration of this firm. Details are on the second page."

Paul read the agreement once more and signed both pages.

"Do you have any further questions?"

"I suppose not."

"Although you do not seem particularly interested, you will be paid the equivalent of thirty dollars per week. Room and board in one of our pensions costs five dollars per week. We're crowded, but I believe Notre Dame has an opening."

Stephen walked around the desk and handed Paul a booklet, a map, and an envelope containing two hundred dollars. "To cover your travel cost here, or, had I not hired you, to pay for your return to America."

For the first time they shook hands, and though Paul had the larger build, Austra's fingers enveloped his hand and Paul felt a sudden, odd sensation, as if the room were too dry and a charge had passed between them. Just excitement, he thought as they said good-bye.

III

As Paul left Stephen's office George Samuelson paused in his conversation with Stephen's secretary to eye him intently. Soon afterward Samuelson walked unannounced into Stephen's office, sank into the chair Paul had abandoned, and lit a cigarette. "Who's the fair-haired child?" he asked.

"Paul Stoddard. He will be working in the glass house and for Savatier."

"Then I assume he's on the up-and-up. He gave me a start when he arrived at the pension in Porto. Young, dreamy-eyed, and bland are perfect attributes for a good cutthroat. When I heard the Spanish accent ringing through his Portuguese, I took back roads all the way from Porto and expected an ambush on every turn. Other than that, my trip was, as usual, successful."

"And the news?"

"Denys reports that two members of Hahn's group have resigned."

Hahn headed a German research team working in nuclear fission. This sudden setback was far better than planned. "And Hahn?" Stephen asked.

"Unreachable, but this loss will delay him for months. Denys and Matthew are finished in Berlin. They're on their way to Switzerland."

"Good. It's best they leave Germany before the war begins, not that anyplace in Europe will stay clear of it. Not even here." He continued on in a tone he might have used to discuss the previous week's weather. "While you were gone, Rachel surprised two Falangists attempting to plant a bomb in these offices. Should this terrorism escalate, we'll have to tighten our security. I fear for the people here."

Those words implied little selflessness, Samuelson knew, but rather some incomprehensible naïveté. Since Samuelson had resigned from the British SIS and began working for the Austras, he'd noticed it often. Usually he ignored it, but now, concerned for Rachel, he muttered, "This firm has built a miniature of a Europe the bloody Fascists never wish to see. The family is a natural target."

"*Nas szekornes.*" The phrase, Samuelson knew, translated

roughly as "we survive," the overtones both amusing and sinister but not confident. Confidence implied failure, and failure was something Stephen could never comprehend.

The phrase also served to remind Samuelson that he need not inquire what should be done with the unsuccessful Falangists. He concentrated on business instead. "Should I put together a package to send to Alpha?"

"Not yet. Hoffman and Wulff are coming from Munich on Monday. The news they carry is always valuable."

Stephen walked to the long worktable at the far end of his office and ran his fingers down the edge of a stack of drawings. "I didn't design any of these. I haven't even looked at them yet, but I will agree enthusiastically when Wulff tells me how perfect they are for the new Reich.

"Last month he tried to commission us to build the windows here," he went on. "I told him I believed only pure Aryans should have a direct hand in rebuilding Germany and was astonished by his embarrassment. I find myself liking him, George, then wishing he was a butcher instead." Stephen leaned against the table and looked at Samuelson sadly. "Ever since Prost presented that report three years ago, I've been playing a role I detest."

"You play it well," Samuelson responded. "But I think you should be more open with British intelligence. Their feedback would be valuable."

"You are correct, as usual. But for the family's sake I will work with only one person and that means someone highly placed. I wish to meet that person here without arousing any suspicion in the Nazi spies who watch me so closely. I will need time and, if the meeting does not go as anticipated, privacy. You can pick someone from their SIS and make the arrangements, yes?"

Samuelson leaned forward, his cigarette held in his mouth at a jaunty angle, the way small men sometimes mouth large cigars. "I can. When you're ready, just say the word and we'll confuse the bloody hell out of everyone."

Chapter Two

I

PAUL WROTE HIS brother that night.

Marvel of marvels. I'm in, though only after being taken on an emotional roller-coaster ride solely, I believe, for the amusement of my new employer. During the interview he alternated between charm and what seemed to be deliberate sadism. Indeed he appeared so convinced of my total lack of value to his firm that when he announced he would not only allow me to remain but would actually *pay* me as well, I didn't know if I should fall on my knees and kiss his aristocratic feet or punch him square in the jaw and get the hell out of here. Of course, I did neither, but I had the unsettling impression that he knew how tempted I was toward one or the other extreme. I suspect my stay here will be similar to my high-school years. I shall grit my teeth, smile politely, and—somehow, by God—see this through!

The sun was still bright when I left the corporate building and walked the quarter of a mile down to the small village, which is also a part of the Austra firm. It has twenty-three stone-and-stucco pensions, a few single-family houses, and a handful of cafés, all privately leased. The booklet I was given notes that the Colony, as it's called, has a population of about four hundred. I walked to the village square, which is complete with a garden and a fountain. I sat on a granite bench and studied the information I'd been given, then

went to the pension called Notre Dame, which Austra
had suggested. The owner showed me to a large second-
floor front bedroom with whitewashed walls, gauzy curtains, and a magnificently curved iron bed. The front
windows give an excellent view of the mountain, and
I'm pleased I decided to pack my binoculars among the
few belongings I brought. He apologized for the clothes
scattered around the room. Apparently the Spaniard who
had the room before me left suddenly. The firm had sent
word there'd been a death in his family and he wasn't
expected to return. We boxed his belongings, then went
downstairs for coffee.

The pension is grandly named Notre Dame. Though
I saw nothing of that great structure in this building
itself, the huge, round dining room table is carved with
the design for the west rose of that cathedral. "Do St.
Denis, Chartres, and the rest of the pensions possess
such treasures?" I asked.

"The residents provided the names and the identify-
ing features. Chartres has the nave's maze carved in the
stones of their porch pillars, St. Denis an entire wall of
their dining room taken over by a portrait of the Abbot
Sugar. I believe I'd get indigestion eating under the scrutiny of those huge eyes." The manager, a retired glassworker himself, laughed loudly. He detailed replications
at Lyon, Ovieto, and some of the other houses then commented in mock exasperation, "There is a rumor that
Chartres will build a miniature window for their foyer.
It's bound to set off another round of rivalry, but I told
everyone that I draw the line at gargoyles and flying
buttresses."

"And do the names have any other significance?" I
asked as I laughed with him.

"*Sim*, they are the names of the churches whose windows were designed by the ancestors of this firm."

I had not known the Austra roots grew that deep,
Brian. Eight hundred years of tradition and I am a part
of it!

II

Dinner that evening possessed all the color of a Gypsy camp on festival night with loose-fitting peasant shirts of conflicting hues ringing the huge carved table. Even the two accountants looked as bright as exotic birds, and only the two women wore more sedate Western dress. Paul recognized Linda Bradley from his visit to the corporate office. The other was newly married to a worker in the glass house and, while they waited for a house to lease in Chaves they shared the room to the rear of Paul's.

Paul sat between a Scottish architect and a French glassworker. Close friends only a few years older than he, they carried on a fast exchange with and around him. When they learned of his unique working arrangement, Mark McCray, the architect, laughed. "So you will have the best of both worlds, Stephen the Stickler in the morning and Savatier the Prig in the afternoon."

"Be fair to Paul," Philippe Dutiel, the glassworker, said in his soft tone. "You tell anyone who cares to listen what a genius Savatier is."

"Among other things, but I warn you, Paul, he doesn't like Americans. Too uncivilized, he believes . . . and then there are the barbaric Scots." Mark's eyes, a startling shade of green, glittered merrily in their deep, round sockets.

"Is Stephen the Stickler Austra?" Paul asked.

The dismay in his voice made a few lodgers laugh. "Of course. How else do you learn except from the best?" Henry Silvas, the newlywed, responded.

A Romanian glassworker added in badly accented Portuguese, "Stephen is a sticker in Mark's department because if walls fall, so fall windows. And at AustraGlass it is still windows that matter."

"He appears too young to be an expert at anything," Paul said in the same moment Mark hooted at the scattered applause the last statement had received from the other glasshouse workers.

Another round of friendly insults seemed about to begin when Philippe stood and tapped his fork on his wineglass to get everyone's attention. "Paul says Stephen is too young to be an expert at anything," he announced then, looked solemnly at Paul and pointing the fork at him for emphasis. "You must understand that Stephen Austra was not born like you or I. After God created heaven and earth and light and darkness, He said, 'Let there be windows.' And then God saw he could not create these unassisted, so he fashioned from silica and lead and assorted Almighty oxides Stephen Austra, who designs windows as God would design them Himself if He had the skill." His words were greeted by applause and laughter.

"Phil, tell him the story given to you," Linda called out.

"Ah, yes! Stephen's descent from heaven in a crystal bubble swaddled in asbestos and carrying a cutter with which he gave himself birth," Philippe replied.

"You are responsible for making up a tale of your own for the next new arrival," Mark explained. "This is a longstanding tradition going back at least twenty months."

Paul was astonished. "You've all been here such a short time?"

"Only to Chaves or to this house," Mark said. "Until early this year I was in Paris with Savatier. Phil was in the AustraGlass house in Moulins. Henry worked for an Austra subsidiary in Germany until 1934, and is lucky to be alive, is that not so?"

Henry nodded, suddenly sedate, and Gianni, a quiet Italian glassworker, squeezed his shoulder in sympathy.

Paul was toasted over a glass of port and the group broke into private conversations. When the meal ended, Philippe and Mark drove Paul into Chaves, where, to the background of a quiet guitar, they exchanged histories. "Tell me," Paul asked Philippe later that evening, "what do you think of Stephen Austra?"

The glassworker replied carefully. "I respect him, and if you have any appreciation for genius you'll do the same. As to a personal opinion of him, I don't know him well enough to have formed one."

Philippe sipped his wine and continued. "I wasn't here when Stephen came, but I understand the glasshouse workers gave him a hard time the first few weeks. The worst mischief makers were discharged and the rest of them learned quickly. Nobody questions him."

"Is he unfriendly?"

"Hardly. Once we met by chance at a tavern in Porto. What a night!"

"Not that he remembers any of it," Mark added.

"I remember enough," Phil countered. "Damn, that man knows how to pick up women! I'd say we both did very well." Phil's wide smile provided lewd insinuations. "But on Monday, when I made some light remark about it, his reply was strangely cold."

"Stephen doesn't drink. He remembered everything you did," Mark teased.

Phil laughed. "I think his only problem is that he's very young."

"How young?" Paul asked.

"He's twenty-two now and has sat in the director's chair for four years."

"Good Lord! No wonder he's so formal."

"And no wonder he confuses the bloody hell out of us all!" Mark exclaimed.

Philippe smiled. "And if you think *he's* confusing, wait until you meet his Cousin Rachel. She supervises glass manufacturing."

"Really! A woman."

"We assume so," Mark interjected with a devious wink, then signaled for another round.

"You'll get a chance to form your own opinion of her," Philippe added. "But let me give you one sobering thought— she's having an affair with George Samuelson. That should tell you something about her."

Paul groaned. "Not him."

"Opposites attract," Mark said, sliding sideways so the waiter could set a pitcher on the table.

As he refilled the glasses Phil asked Mark, "What did you do to ruffle Savatier this time?"

Mark grimaced in mock disgust. "That slimy Austrian, Walter Rosen, was gloating as usual over the rising German star. I told him that with his looks and name he would most likely receive the compliment of being mistaken for a Jew and shot before the war even begins."

"There isn't going to be any war," Philippe mumbled uneasily.

"Let's not go into that tonight. Anyway, there was almost one this afternoon. Walter began to walk away in a huff, then faked a stumble and spilled his coffee over my nearly completed draft. I bellowed an uncivilized highland curse and was dragging him outside to give him the sort of thrashing we Scots will give the Nazi pigs when Savatier stepped in. I'm lucky to be employed."

"Just before dinner Linda told me Walter has been dismissed at Savatier's insistence."

"What! I'm winning battles already?" Mark pounded his fist against his forehead in mock despair. "Oh"—beat—"oh, I take back everything I said about Savatier."

A group of tourists arrived, and Philippe's attention wandered across the room to a slender brunette. After she glanced encouragingly his way Phil turned to Mark, who shook his head, then to Paul. "Excuse this early imposition on our friendship but could I ask for a loan? Better yet, why not come and buy a round? There are four of them."

"And six fellows," Paul reminded him, palming two large bills and sliding them across the table.

"Go be a hopeful fool on your own. Paul and I will be here when you return." After Phil left, Mark explained, "In Chaves all eligible women—the married ones as well—are placed under lock and key after sunset. There is also one posh brothel, but due to Phil's unfortunate lack of budgeting, Amalia's is beyond his reach. A far cry from his wild life in Moulins, I'm sure."

"We could have gone with him."

"Not for my sake. I have the prettiest lass in all of Lothian County waiting for me. And you? Does someone wait for you?"

"More of a some*thing*. You see, someday I will be a proper Bostonian with a proper Bostonian wife, and I assure you *that* can wait."

The conversation continued between the two of them, then the three of them, after Philippe returned bankrupt and alone. An hour after the inn stopped serving, they were politely asked to leave. Humming sections of the night's music, they trudged arm in arm to Mark's car and found George Samuelson leaning against it. "This is the last taxi, I presume. May I ride up with you?"

"Ride!" Mark yelped happily. "George, for all our sakes, take the wheel!"

During the half-hour drive, Samuelson kept his hand on the revolver hidden under his coat, and his eyes on the shadows on either side of the road. He saw no need to ruin the night by mentioning that the Spanish war had crossed the border again.

When they returned, Paul wasn't ready for sleep, so he took a walk through the Colony, finally lying on his back beside the fountain in the central square and staring up at low-hanging stars and a half-moon. His eyes were beginning to close when he heard a high, shrill cry farther up the mountain, and with no destination in mind he began hiking up the road that led past the corporate buildings. Small quartz pebbles trapped the moonlight and glittered before him as he moved on the balls of his feet, trying to maintain the silence enveloping him.

Higher up, the trees grew thicker and closer to the road, and there were only small patches of light to mark the way. Paul heard a rustling in the woods and out of the corner of his eye glimpsed something large and pale running swiftly past. Though he never had time to see it clearly, he seemed to merge with its thoughts, savage and unrestrained. The night played sly tricks. "Go home," it whispered, and he agreed, descending into a town bathed pure by moonlight. When Paul reached his room, he barely had the energy to undress and slip between the crisp, new sheets.

Chapter Three

Banlin, Ireland
August 1938

LONG BEFORE LAURENCE Austra met Kathleen Moore, he'd been charmed by her children. They would wait for her outside the Alpha gates and he would pass them, coaxing their shy smiles into tentative greetings and, finally, an exchange of names. She was Emma; her younger brother Tad. Once he knew them, Laurence could find them easily . . . in crowds at the summer concerts, playing games at the Alpha picnic, or alone in the fields, the girl's golden curls flashing in the sun as she ran, the boy moving less gracefully, his short legs struggling to keep her pace. Their artlessness amused him; their freedom gave him pleasure.

Had the emotion not been beneath him, he might have envied them their life, for as a child he had possessed no such innocence. Before he lost his milk teeth he had learned to adopt only tight, closed smiles; to look down when he laughed or, better yet, never to laugh at all; to speak only vocally outside the family; to stand with his shoulders squared and his arms slightly bent to hide their length; to remain relaxed; and, above all, to move slowly.

He had spent his first few years with his sister and brother, Ann and Simon, in a spacious two-story brownstone in the heart of Manhattan. The toddlers saw no one but their parents and one another and, on rare occasions, acquaintances their father brought home. It seemed to Laurence that he and his siblings were being tested at these times, and the three held their control perfectly through those short, awkward evenings.

24

Sometimes their guests shook hands with Laurence, as adults often do with young children. If they noticed the length of his fingers, they would often suggest that he learn the piano.

If these were close friends, his father might ask him to play. The visitors would smile tolerantly as Laurence placed a book on the piano bench, climbed up, and spread his fingers over the keys. In a moment politeness would turn to rapt attention, for Laurence played the Steinway grand as if he had been born with music imprinted on his soul.

"Genius!" "Prodigy!" "A long, magnificent career!" They would give these or better compliments, but Laurence knew, with the certainty of all children, that fame would never happen. He and Ann and Simon would spend the rest of their lives within those walls, safe from the evil of the world outside.

They were three when the long weaning began. Their parents bought a secluded country cottage, where each weekend the children were free to run and climb and speak as they chose. Watching their antics as he taught them to hunt would make Father laugh, and serenity would flow from him as it never did from Mother. Father showed them how to charm rabbits from their warrens, does from their fawns. And when Laurence first killed, Father understood why that long moment of satisfaction was followed by a wail of such sharp grief that it ripped a hole in the perfection of the night.

In those early years they remained nocturnal, and in the hour before the birds woke to chant in the dawn Mother would sit with them, teaching them the family's language and songs, sharing memories of others' lives, the history of their people. She spoke of the castle on the mountain that had been the family's ancient home; of Francis, the old one, the first of their kind; of the carefree time when the family feared nothing, not even the ignorance of man. As sleep claimed them, they wrapped their arms around one another and took comfort in shared warmth and scent while Mother lay beside them guarding the only things she still valued in this world.

The weekdays in their New York home seemed confining after the country freedom. Laurence would sometimes wake in the afternoon and pour out his music on the Steinway keys or press his face against the thick colored glass of the windows, trying to see those he sensed beyond them. One cloudy day he disobeyed every rule, sneaking out to play in the park with other children. He joined them on the slides, the swings, the parallel bars on which he had swung ever higher, ever faster, until he sensed the awe and fear rising around him. Panicked, he did a final flip onto his toddler's feet and ran back to his house, streaking past his mother, just coming out to look for him. That night, though no hand was raised, he was painfully disciplined. His father implacable, his eyes cold with fear for his children.

Afterward Laurence was sent upstairs to join his siblings, and the three sat, motionless and silent, trying to understand the familiar battle beginning in the rooms below them. They knew it dealt with some old sorrow, some wrong so terrible that the parents spoke of it audibly in languages the children did not know. But the three were telepaths—strong ones, even in infancy—so always there were thoughts of thoughts, regrets unfocused but real.

This time the battle lasted longer, the air sparking with its intensity, then calming as a decision was reached.

—Home— The thought was Ann's, filled with her calm delight, followed by a conclusion he could never forgive her for naming. —You did it, Laurie! You made Father agree. We're going home!—

When they were formally told what they already knew, Simon asked if they were going to the castle on the mountain.

"No," Mother replied, "but to another place where you may live more freely."

"Children?" Ann's inflection of the word implied *family*.

"No. You are the only Austra children in over a century. But, yes, there will be children, and you will not have to hide from them."

They left New York in 1916, on a steamer registered in neutral Spain. The triplets had just turned four.

Whenever he recalled the boat that was to take them home, Laurence always saw the image of New York growing fainter and fainter on the hazy horizon, then the image of their ship, bombed and floundering, growing smaller and smaller as their

lifeboat pulled away from it, away from Father. Both times
the sun had beat down and he had wanted to shriek from the
pain, but he was an Austra and he pressed his lips together
and huddled against his mother for comfort.

The sun attacked him as they floated in the tiny lifeboat
through the high waves of the Atlantic. It cracked his lips and
left him burning with hunger, eyeing the other passengers
with greedy interest. He had sucked down the milk his mother
had brought but it hadn't been enough. His body demanded
more. Later she shared blood with him, the sweet taste of
family satisfying as nothing else could. The hunger subsided.
He slept.

He was still asleep when the sailors threw his mother from
the lifeboat but not when they reached for Simon. He had
clung to his brother, struggling in silence until Simon was
wrenched away from him, a hand covering his brother's mouth
while he was beaten unconscious and flung overboard. Simon
had been alive when he hit the water, but Laurence and Ann
had felt death quickly come to him as they sat clutching each
other as though they could merge and become invisible. The
sailor's hand reached next for Laurence. It seemed huge and
strong, but Laurence looked up at the man, his eyes lightless
hollows, pulled back his lips, and snarled. The hand shook,
then retreated. Laurence did not understand what he had done,
but for the first time he had amplified another's fear.

Through it all he and Ann never made a sound, never tried
to wake the woman who promised to protect them. She had
been the enemy then, though they became desperately attached to her later when she was all they had left. Laurence
had even called her Mother because he knew it pleased her
and because he believed that if he did, his real mother would
return to correct his horrible lie and punish him for ever be-
lieving that she could abandon him, that she could die.

At last he heard the footsteps, the boots clicking on the
walk—too light, too fast for Father's. As they were introduced to an uncle they had never known, Laurence and Ann
remembered the sailor and, quaking with terror, backed away
to hide behind Mrs. Reeve's ample skirts. He and his sister
were survivors, bonded to each other as they had been to
their parents and suspicious of this one, whose mind was so
strong, so brilliant, so unaccountably happy.

Later, there had been children—humanity's children—and he grew up with Savatier's three boys and Alexandre Massier, to whom he developed a slavish devotion. Yet always there was Stephen or Rachel or another member of the family to sharpen the differences. As he aged, the distinction between himself and his human companions became clearer, until he was amazed that the parents of his friends would ever let their children near him. He was pathetically grateful for their tolerance.

Though he grew into happiness, he never learned to dull his past and was forever reluctant to engage in polite handshakes. When he did, those who touched him felt an elusive sadness, as if they had brushed the edges of a dark old dream.

He met Kathleen Moore by chance. She worked in shipping, wrapping the heavy crystal and crating it for travel. He had come to settle a minor billing error, and while he waited for it to be corrected, he heard a soft melody behind him . . . not words, only a soft "la-la-la" of a fast movement by Dvořák. He rarely heard classical music at work and he turned and stared at the back of a woman's head, at a mass of soft auburn curls tied up with a bright green ribbon. Sensing someone watching her, Kathleen looked over her shoulder. She stared at Laurence's face an instant too long before returning to her work, silent and embarrassed by his scrutiny.

"Don't stop," he said. "I was only admiring your voice." Though the compliment was genuine, it seemed wrong—a reminder of their levels.

She looked back at him with reluctant politeness, her round, pug-nosed face like a cherub from some old master's painting. Emma's face. Tad's face. He glimpsed their cottage, fragments of their lives.

"I'm glad you liked it, sir," she said, then bent silently over her order. She found it difficult to avoid looking at him and wondered if her supervisor had noticed how her pace had slowed.

Laurence pulled Kathleen's employment records that evening. She had worked at Alpha nearly a year. The file made no mention of her reason for coming, and he decided he didn't need to know it. He pictured her with her children—

bathing them, dressing them for bed, perhaps telling a story—and the weekend, with all its familiar emptiness, grew suddenly oppressive. Of course, there were possibilities. He could walk the three miles into Banlin for a game of cards at Finnerty's, then later take a brief break outside for the quick use of an unwitting, probably tipsy, acquaintance. He could visit the cottage of a widow who lived alone and slept soundly and never questioned her dreams. These were the best choices, in their way—the choices that forced him to hone his power, to perfect it. But he needed something more than companionship and food . . . he needed the freedom of the forest, the night and the hills.

Two hours after sunset he began the climb. His nostrils flared, trapping night scents, his ears seeking and finally hearing the cry of the great hound . . . someone's pet, run away or abandoned, which had retrieved the spirit of its ancestors, growing to immense size, preying on sheep and cattle and poaching the Austra preserves. He raised his face to the stars and answered that call, the exchange continuing until they found each other and began their run. They had hunted together often, two wild creatures of the hills, but tonight prey meant nothing to Laurence and he held back at the end, letting the hound take the full force of life, sensing that soon the small army of farmers would close in on it, and to sustain, it would need the strength of death given. In spite of its speed and its strength, the farmers would probably win, and one more great beast that could not adapt would die so humanity could maintain its precarious tranquillity. Laurence sensed that this would be their last hunt.

The dog finished and they raced together, splashing through runoffs from the hills, rolling in the grass to dry; wrestling, growling, plunging through the trees and brush, dizzied by the shadows of the moon.

Later Laurence found his clothing, smoothed back his hair, and relaxed into civilization, cherishing memories to sustain his hidden soul.

The moon had set and the world traveled close to morning when he came across a party of hikers camped on a grassy knoll, sitting around a fire, singing well-loved Gaelic songs in discordant harmony. They invited Laurence to join them, one man passing him a bottle of ale, which he declined, instead beginning another tune. One song followed another until everyone slept but Laurence and the group's eldest member. "I've hiked these hills for half a century," the man said. "There is nothing more beautiful than that first touch of dawn. Stay and we'll watch the sunrise together."

The dawn weariness pulled at him. Tomorrow's duties began to intrude. "I can't. I must go."

The man's thoughts were sympathetic and sad. "Ah, I had hoped you'd come along with us for a day or two and we would talk and sing some more. You have a fine voice for the old songs."

Laurence shook his head. His mind embraced the man, who obliged by lying back on the ground. "The ale was too good," the man whispered through a smile. "The songs are all around us like the stars. Can you hear them?" Now, in this place, the question did not seem fanciful.

"Yes. Close your eyes and the music grows."

The man obeyed, drifting on dark wings as the notes poured over him, a torrent of songs he had never heard before, ancient and magnificent. He was an infant swaddled in music, and the bindings felt warm and comforting. The dreams that followed would bring days of happiness, but in the morning his new friend was gone.

Chapter Four

Chaves, Portugal

I

ON MONDAY, RACHEL Austra met with Paul in her Spartan office, peering at him through small round glasses. These, in addition to the severe bun she formed with her hair and the shapeless clothes she wore, made her resemble some spinster librarian of indeterminate age. Noting his "deplorable lack of experience" with the same charming tact as her cousin, she assigned him to tend the pot furnaces, working as a fire teaser in the low-ceilinged cave beneath the glasshouse floor. After an hour of raking out the clinkers and stirring the fire, Paul's skin would begin to vibrate, then pound, as if he had merged with the throbbing coals. He worked alongside Gianni, who kept up a steady stream of conversation, most of it political. Paul answered his anti-Nazi rhetoric with terse comments of vague neutrality.

"When we are finished here, we will go to the Colony, find ourselves a cool table, and share a bottle of wine," Gianni promised. "Then you will see how good you feel."

Paul didn't. Although he had only one glass, the alcohol overpowered his parched body, and later, as he introduced himself to Alexandre Savatier, he felt light-headed.

Savatier greeted Paul in French, nodding once in an impatient aristocratic fashion rather than extending his hand. The architect was in his early sixties, a black beret perched on his balding head, and he possessed incredible salt-and-pepper eyebrows that grew with a seemingly insane will of their own and threatened to blind him. "Whatever hair falls

out of his head he saves and pastes to his brows. Sometimes
the task keeps him awake all night," Mark had told him over
breakfast. Thinking of this, and the rest of Mark's description, Paul pursed his lips to hide a smile.

"Does something strike you as amusing, Monsieur Stoddard?"

"No."

"Bon. This is your desk and your drafting table. And
this"—he pointed to a pile of drawings on it—"is the beginning of the music conservatory for Escotil. I put it together
too quickly, and it is, as usual, cluttered. See what you can
do to simplify it. If you have any questions, please see Michael Dumas or your friend in the skirt." Savatier's voice
rippled slightly as he waved toward McCray, who had sealed
his dubious victory by appearing that morning in full Highland dress.

After Savatier departed, Paul chuckled. Coal shoveler in
the morning and architectural copyboy in the afternoon. His
career was off to a stunning start.

Over the next two weeks Paul's muscles screamed, but he
held Gianni's pace with stubborn determination. Eventually
he grew used to the heat and the exhausting work. After hours
in the hot, dusty cave he would shower, then find a quiet
place outdoors where he could eat his lunch undisturbed. His
shoulders broadened, his round Germanic face became lean
and bronzed, and his hair bleached to a Viking's coloring.
All his clothes grew loose and he drove into Chaves with
Mark and Linda and bought new ones: dyed cottons in colors
he would dare wear nowhere else, a broad-brimmed black
trilby hat, and dark glasses similar to those his employer always wore to protect his eyes from the glaring sun. Though
he felt like a pigeon that had suddenly sprouted peacock's
feathers, he wore a royal-blue shirt and a red cotton bandanna
to work the following Monday. A full-length mirror hung in
the foyer of Notre Dame, and Paul stopped and stared into
it, as if not completely sure whose body and face he saw
reflected.

That morning Paul was assigned to assist Henry Silvas and
learn the art of potmaking. There was a method to this tor-

ture, Paul realized. Had his back and shoulders not been toughened by the work he'd already done, he would have been incapable of hunching over and slowly building up the sides of clay pots, which, when completed and dried, would hold the molten glass. It was simple work, leaving his mind free to wander into the world of struts and foundations and proportions.

Paul had spent his first few afternoons studying Savatier's drawings. They were good but hurried, and had been done freehand. When he passed the architect, Paul noticed that the joints in Savatier's hands were swollen, the smaller fingers already slanting inward in the advanced stages of arthritis. No wonder the aging Frenchman passed on his final drawings. Yet Paul was expected to do more than a draft. Too few changes would be a false compliment, too many a possible insult, so Paul decided to consider Savatier as he would a knowledgeable client. Attempting to preserve the essence of Savatier's design, he began to work. He'd finished Friday, spending his last two hours checking the drawings, searching for flaws. As he left, he laid them on Savatier's desk, then suffered stabs of hindsight all weekend.

"You're making the walls too thin." Henry Silvas's correction brought Paul back to the small room in which he labored. He corrected the error, then added another few inches to the next pot in line. He tried to concentrate on his work, but again anticipation caught him.

How would it feel to have a building he designed move beyond ink and paper, to rise and acquire a character of its own so that he could walk around it and through it and touch its walls and say "I built this. This is mine"? He had hoped too often already, and comforted himself with recalling that it made no difference, anyway. He was here to learn glass and design.

In spite of his rationalizing, Paul's excitement returned that afternoon when Savatier called him into the studio's conference room. Paul's drawings were spread across the table, notes written in the margins in a small, precise script. "I congratulate you," Savatier said. "These are far superior to anything I would have done at your age. I have gone over them with Stephen. His changes are minor."

Paul frowned and Savatier glowered. "I read your face as easily as I do these drawings, *young* man. No, Stephen is no architect, but he does know the stresses glass is capable of enduring. Regard these changes in the same vein you would those of a contractor facing a construction difficulty. If you find that frame of mind impossible, then recall '*le roi le veut.*' "

Savatier detailed the alterations, then said, "I will have Epris draft them. You will have no time." Ignoring Paul's confused expression, Savatier handed Paul a thick folder and continued. "On Thursday and Friday you will visit a building site near Lisbon. Here are surveyors' reports and details of special needs for the house. Elizabeth Austra requests clean lines and a daring style, so you will have an almost free hand. However, this site is difficult, and the angles of the south walls must be precisely as noted."

"I-I'm designing?" Paul stammered.

"You're an architect, aren't you?" Savatier pulled a tied roll of drafting paper off a shelf and handed it to Paul. "You are spending the next two days working with Stephen. He will be pouring two windows for Elizabeth's house and has requested your presence. These are copies of his designs. Like the site, they may be a source of inspiration." Savatier hesitated, then added awkwardly, "I do not praise often, Monsieur Stoddard, but I wish you to know how pleased I am to have you on my staff."

That evening Paul spread the reports on the pension's carved dining table. Though he was tempted to begin the design, he didn't want to consider ideas that later might have to be abandoned because they did not suit the site. He returned the papers to their file, then unrolled the window designs and studied them as carefully.

The bedroom window was in autumn colors, the abstract pattern reminiscent of a pile of leaves . . . orange, crimson, brown, gold, and odd shades of dark jade. The second, to be poured Tuesday evening, consisted of a sunrise over an angry sea, alternating with strips of deep-toned vines, again of the same dark jade. The drawings did not seem complete because, though the leading was noted in the vines, it was absent in the other designs, as if the windows were going to be painted rather than cut.

As he rolled and tied the plans Linda and Gianni walked down the stairs, speaking softly to each other. Gianni pocketed a letter he had been gripping and left. Linda joined Paul at the table.

Paul happily explained his Lisbon assignment. Linda congratulated him on his success, then said, "I have some time off coming. Would you mind if I went with you? My uncle lives in Lisbon and I haven't seen him for months. It is awkward to travel alone. Women in Portugal must always be escorted."

"But you live alone."

"This firm is different from the country. In other parts of it the women eye me as if I were immoral, and the men are so forward that they're frightening. But if I go with you, no one will suspect I am a fallen woman who would ever consider traveling alone on railway cars." She laughed to hide her embarrassment.

Paul had been surprised at how few women were employed at AustraGlass. Now he understood. "Of course," he said, and felt himself flush as she hugged him and kissed his cheek.

II

The glasshouse was stifling when Paul arrived Tuesday morning. Shifts were overlapping and the workers were midway through the pouring of eleven tones of sheet glass, the panes annealed for only half an hour before being stacked and rolled into the storage room to cool completely.

"Is it always so rushed in the morning?" Paul asked Henry as they slid the panes into the gas-fired *lehr*.

"Only today. We'll be shutting down both large furnaces when the pouring is through. This room must be cool by tonight or Stephen cannot work."

"Heat bothers him?"

Henry looked amused. "The two main colors are already

being melted in the small Hermanson, and the complementary tones in the freestanding furnaces.'' He motioned to the oddly shaped ovens, so hot that they appeared to move as the thermal waves rose around them. ''We pour the first window tonight, then begin melting for tomorrow night's work.''

''That's all?''

''All! Ha! You don't understand. He is pouring a *window*. You will see.''

When the last panes were rolled into storage, Michael Austra sent Paul to help assemble the pouring table.

The table was stored on edge along one side of the glasshouse. It measured twelve by eighteen feet and had been lifted into place by pulleys. Its bottom was blackened copper alloy, its top polished tungsten. As Paul helped lower it he guessed its weight at well over a dozen tons. The crew placed it on a wheeled cart, pushed it to the center of the room, and mounted it on firebrick legs over a complex series of individually controlled burners. Standing back from it, Paul decided it most resembled a huge griddle.

Stephen and Rachel clamped inch-thick metal bars along the table's edges, then laid a metal bar inside the frame, dividing the inside into two long rectangles, one twice the width of the other. The dividing bar had rings on either end, which were fastened to steel cables connected to pulleys above the table.

The setup work done, Paul was dismissed until five-thirty, a luxurious three-hour break. He ate and showered, set the alarm, and fell into bed. Sleep came quickly. Hard labor had drugged him.

In contrast to the earlier activity, the glasshouse seemed deserted when Paul returned, only six workers and three of the Austra family on hand for the night's work. Philippe met Paul at the door. ''You and I are spectators tonight,'' he said. ''If you have any questions, you are to ask me; not that I'm sure I can answer them.''

They located an ideal vantage point, a ladder leaning against the wall separating the storage and pouring rooms. Halfway up, they turned and sat on the wide rungs. From there they could look down at the table, a few yards in front of them. Workers bolted a trapezoidal metal framework to the ends of the table, then clamped thick wooden boards across it and mounted an electric blower on the end facing the open door. Meanwhile Stephen and Rachel maintained a vigil over the melts. The creative work had only begun, yet Paul was already fascinated as he watched the confident movements of the young man who was undoubtedly the master here.

Stephen mixed the molten crystal with clay rods, stopping repeatedly to turn the furnace heat down another few degrees, judging readiness for pouring by the feel of the melts being stirred, the clarity of the glowing batter dripping from the rods when they were pulled from the melt, the color of the thin crystal stalagmites growing on the concrete floor.

When the melt neared perfection, Stephen stepped back and ordered the furnaces opened.

"Now the creative work begins," Phil whispered.

Workers ripped down the firebrick from the two main chambers and, using dollies, pulled the clay pots from the heat. After the first was opened and the few impurities skimmed away, it was lifted above the table and its contents slowly poured while Stephen and Rachel used clay spatulas to spread the mix inside the wider rectangle in the frame. The second pot was cracked and blended slowly with the first.

Paul moved up a few rungs and shifted position to obtain a better view. "Why is the table heated?" he asked.

"It keeps the glass molten," Phil explained. "The core is filled with metals that can be heated and cooled according to the pattern Stephen wishes to make."

Another oven was opened. Rachel stirred a white powder into the melt and slowly poured it into sections of the water while Stephen, distinguishing one melt from another by its temperature and sheen, blended the two tones.

Paul tapped his friend's shoulder with his foot and Phil spoke without looking up. "I don't know why she's adding a chemical so late in the process. Family windows always have hints of sorcery surrounding them. I can only tell you that the base for all the tones is eighty-five percent rock crystal and added red lead."

"Lead crystal?"

"Of a sort. It is most stable under varied heat."

As the first freestanding furnace was cracked, Stephen
doused himself with water and slipped on a sort of shirt,
which had a heavily padded front and sleeves and a loosely
laced open back. Leg protection resembling chaps followed,
then gloves and boots . . . all padded asbestos. "What's he
doing now?" Paul asked.

Phil pointed to the boards above the table. "To mix the
colors he must face the pour. If his suit were closed, it would
trap heat like an oven, or so he tells us."

Paul gaped down at the table, watching the pot from the
first small furnace lifted into place while Stephen stretched
over his creation, pouring ladle after ladle of the glowing
liquid, one shade of heat puddling into another, his hands
and arms silhouetted in the glowing creation beneath him.

Though the crew had no way of knowing, the heat would
have blistered a normal man. Stephen's body merely protested, but the pain was insignificant compared to the rapture
of creation. Stephen had worked in this manner only twice
before (creative narcissism, Rachel called it) but those had
been the necessary displays on which he had built a solid
reputation while building pieces so incredible that they
astounded him. Now he kept a vow he had made to himself,
trying the method on a far grander scale.

He descended only long enough to turn down the burners
below the sea, splash some water down his back, and take a
long drink before returning to work.

The next melt added would become the ruby of the sunrise.
Rachel poured it carefully, then began slowly lifting one end
of the center bar while Stephen swirled the sea into the sky.

Below the glasshouse floor, four workers tended the fires,
creating the steady stream of producer gas necessary to fuel
the burners. Gianni directed with careful diligence, hiding
nervous anticipation. He had acted his part well, and tonight
. . . tonight was the end of weeks of deceit. When word was
sent that the fires could be damped back, he sent the fire
teasers upstairs for air, then took the inside stairway to the
glasshouse floor to risk a hasty glance at the activity. The
burners beneath the table had been turned down, and Stephen
was centered above it, his knees gripping a board while,

holding clay forks in both hands, he swirled thickening melts together for the final cloud patterning.

Gianni would never have a better opportunity! He rushed back to the cave and sent a flow of raw gas into the storage room. He'd just opened the series of lines below the work-table when he heard the voice behind him.

"I came to help you," Henry began, then "What are you . . . ?" A metal bar smashed across the side of Henry's head and he crumpled onto the sooty floor.

His execution only moments from completion, Gianni stepped over the body and rushed up the stairs, weaving between the buildings to a waiting car.

In the glasshouse the burners beneath the table continued to provide their even heat, but beneath them the open valves poured out streams of raw gas that ignited with a murderous roar. The explosion shook the platform and severed the wiring to the blower. As his knees lost their hold Stephen tossed his tools clear and caught the board next to him. The flames formed a lethal wall around him, making it impossible for any on the floor to see his struggle or come to his aid. He cursed the protective gloves that interfered with his grip, wishing he had done this work without an audience. The lack of oxygen had begun to make him dizzy and he considered probable miracles.

From his spot high on the ladder, Paul watched Stephen's struggle. Michael Austra had gone. So had Rachel, and the workers were immobilized by her order to do nothing and uncertain of what course to take should they disobey. For an instant Paul shared their indecision. It ended when he saw something that made him understand how hot the platform had become—the back of Stephen's shirt ignited, pieces of it ascending in the updraft created by the flames.

The pain must have been horrible, yet Stephen made no sound even when he lost his grip on the far board. "He's falling!" Paul shouted, leaping over Phil and running toward the table. "Help him!" When Paul was a few feet from the table, an explosion in the storage room behind him thrust him forward, toward the flames and molten glass. In the instant he believed he would die with his employer, someone hit him head-on and he landed on his back.

Paul found a breath to replace the one knocked out of him. "Help him!" he cried, trying to push away his rescuer. His hands burned from the other's body, and by the time Stephen said "I'm all right," Paul knew it to be true.

Stephen slipped off his headgear, stood unsteadily, then rushed into the storage room. Before anyone followed, he removed his protective vest and slipped on a torn shirt to hide the burns on his back. "Open the windows," he ordered those now entering. "Check for fires, and when you are certain the room is safe, go home."

Michael Austra waited for him in the pouring room. "We found Henry lying beside the furnace. The doctor has been called." The next, spoken mind-to-mind in the private way of the family, —Gianni is missing. Rachel has gone for him.—

—My office. I will be there when she returns.—Stephen studied the table for a moment, then added audibly, "Michael, have those below check for gas leaks and keep the furnace on a slow burn. We are going to salvage this if we can." He turned to Philippe. "Please go with Michael. And you, Paul, stay with me."

In an astounded, silent daze, Paul watched Stephen turn down the heat and study his creation as if waiting for it to answer some significant question. At last, satisfied with the unspoken reply, he turned to Paul. "What did you think to accomplish when you ran toward me?"

Paul had been prepared to demure thanks; instead he detected disapproval in Stephen's tone. "I saw you falling. If there had been any chance, I would have pulled you out."

"I see."

"It's a miracle you're alive."

Stephen seemed oddly amused. "I've been the recipient of miracles before. But I thank you for what you would have attempted." He studied the glass on the table once more. "I cannot continue until the temperature falls. Will you wait for me here, then stay and watch me finish?"

"If I may."

"Good! I will return within the hour."

Chapter Five

I

GIANNI LET HIS car gain speed as he wound down the steep road to the front gate. If the barrier was down, he could drive through it. If his luck held a little longer, he'd make it safely over the border.

—You are leaving?— The question formed in his mind, as clear as if it had been spoken by someone in the seat beside him. His own thoughts, he decided, though the voice seemed feminine and somehow familiar.

He laughed at the suggestion. How could he stay now?

—You thought to take a life, perhaps more?—

Of course. The Fascists had killed his father, would have murdered the rest of the family had they not fled Italy. Of course he would follow his orders, and gladly.

—Why?—

Speer, Galini . . . how can Austra ship to men like those and call himself neutral?

—Turn around. Go back.—

His mind tricked him. He accelerated.

—STOP!—

"No!" he screamed to the empty darkness, flooring the pedal.

—Slow down. Go back. Go back.—

Voices . . . voices. He never should have hit Henry so hard. Murder your friends and you'll go mad; die unabsolved and go to hell. He drove, barely in control, down the steep mountain road.

You're going to kill yourself, Gianni. His first logical

41

thought, and a correct one. As he maneuvered a sharp curve he saw a figure in the middle of the road, a woman facing his car. She crouched, one palm flat against the pavement, as if she were planning to spring.

—Stop!—

He braked, but he might as well have had his foot on the gas. He swerved and the car went into a full skid over the edge.

It wasn't a long drop but the car hit a tree head-on. Gianni's door broke open and he fell sideways onto the ground. In the beam of the single burning headlight he saw a woman—a vision—walking toward him. Her plain black cotton blouse was ripped at the shoulder. Her dark curly hair formed a halo around a pale, magnificent face. Through the blood that flowed into his eyes, through the pain that kept him conscious, he stared at her too perfect body, at her expression of pity and concern. "Rachel?" he whispered, astonished by the beauty she had hidden.

With a low, convulsive sob that might have been grief, Rachel knelt beside him. The light hit the side of her face and he looked up and saw that the tips of her back teeth were longer and sharper than they should have been, her eyes too dark and huge to be human.—Tell me who duped you into playing assassin, Gianni?—

No! He wouldn't speak, not to her or to anyone. He tried to move, to back away. His broken body ignored him. He lay waiting, frightened as much by this woman as by death itself.

—Tell me who sent you.—she repeated. Her will bored into his, trying to pull the answer from his fading mind.

She tried too late. As his heart pounded its last, he heard her high, impossible shriek of rage, a sound no human throat could make. He died with an unspoken word on his lips. *Vampire.*

II

Alone in the empty pouring room, Paul studied the table and frame overhead, wondering how Stephen had survived. The distance between the boards Stephen had been grasping was over five feet, a difficult reach. He picked up a fireproof glove that had fallen on the floor beside the table, looked down at the blood-red tabletop, and saw the blackened print of a hand near its edge. When Stephen returned, Paul wanted to ask a multitude of questions, but, as Stephen's hands were not badly burned, he settled for asking Stephen how he'd escaped the flames.

"I swung out just above the table. I was about to be broiled, so I moved very fast. Fortunately I landed on you. You are the only person who saw any of what occurred on that table. I ask that you keep it confidential."

"I don't understand."

"The flames were no accident." He explained what Gianni had done, blaming the Italian's death on his own reckless speed of escape. Noticing Paul's sorrowful expression, he added, "Save your condolences for his friends, and tell no one how close to success this attempt came."

Paul looked up at the metal-coated boards and thought of ways the structure could have been sabotaged. "As you wish."

"Good." Stephen walked around the window, studying the sheen on the surface and noting the temperature of the table. "It's time to continue here."

In the next few hours Paul saw glass manipulated in ways he'd never believed possible. When Stephen had finished, the sea appeared so lifelike that it seemed to move, but, though Stephen had worked diligently with the sunrise, it still looked flat and ugly. "Perhaps I am being optimistic," Stephen said. "Tomorrow we will strike the ruby. Possibly I have learned a new technique." He looked at Paul. "It's nearly dawn. Are you tired?" he asked.

"No."

"Good. I want you to see the effect I hope to achieve here. I wish to show you the windows in my house. You will come, yes?" Paul felt unaccountably uneasy, as if the low stone wall on the mountain were a barrier that, once bridged, would imprison him forever; yet he could think of no reason to refuse.

They followed a narrow path through the woods, Stephen setting a quick pace in the waxing light. Beyond the stone wall the trees grew thicker, the ground beneath them more barren, until the path ended and they walked over earth spongy from years of fallen leaves. The air was crisp, hinting of the winter to come. Neither spoke until they reached a clearing. There Paul saw a house resembling a modest fortress, its sharp, vertical lines broken by huge expanses of glass. It appeared to have risen from the bare rock beneath it, resting for centuries, weathered by the same storms that had shaped these peaks until some intelligent creature had found it, seen its merit, and added the windows as a mark of ownership. "Savatier designed this after he completed the buildings below. Come."

He led Paul up a narrow stairway to a widow's walk on the roof. Beneath them stretched the valley, the forest at the top thinning and acquiring more ordered patterns farther down the slope. Paul saw the office buildings, the glasshouse, the Colony . . . Stephen's domain.

"We offered Savatier land on which to build. He declined, saying he preferred to live among his children rather than above them. The sun is rising, let's go inside."

Descending, they walked through wide, carved wooden doors into a huge open space divided not by walls but by function, the overall effect one of candid intimacy. The walls rose high above them, dominated by a series of tall narrow windows on all but the north side. That was taken up by a huge stone fireplace, and on either side of it were doorways: one dark and closed; the other open and glowing in the dawn light. There were bookcases, empty save for a few uncracked volumes; suede-covered furniture of an indeterminate style, designed primarily for comfort; and a series of steps rising to a loft. The north wall was devoted to closets and a bath; the east and south walls and a slanting skylight all of deep-toned windows.

Resting in the center was a platform covered with a huge feather bed encased in deep blue satin. On it were a multitude of contrasting pillows, all glowing rich violet in the altered hue of the morning light. It was a bed made for lovers, and with that thought Paul's earlier uneasiness returned and intensified. He did not belong here, yet now it had become impossible to leave.

Stephen sank wearily into a chair. "Lie on the bed and face east."

Paul did and waited. In a few minutes the sun struck the top of the window and the room was filled with light . . . not the tones of the glass but rainbows of all colors moving with each minute change in the angle of the rising sun. "If you manipulate solidifying glass in the manner I did tonight, this is the result," Stephen said in a pronounced cadence. "These windows have another property as well. Concentrate on the warmth where the rainbows touch your skin."

Something brushed against Paul . . . like dappled sunlight in a shady glade. He closed his eyes and the feeling intensified as Stephen moved behind him. Looking down at his guest, Stephen held out his arms to absorb the rays of the docile sun, feeding to Paul the warmth it imparted. Paul moved close to sleep, the trace of a smile on his lips. "It's wonderful," he murmured. "Who made them?"

"I did. Savatier and I designed this house together twenty-three years ago."

"That's impossible," Paul whispered without real protest. He believed himself asleep, dreaming the pleasantly fantastic.

The answer was subtly given mind to mind. —No. Later you must forget, but for now know that this, as well as all below, was built for me.—Stephen lay perpendicular above Paul, their heads nearly touching as he concluded. —You have entered my reality. One day you will see it with your eyes open, but for now, dream of the future as I will it to be.—

And Paul saw the sea, the sharp cliffs rising from it and, slowly forming, a house in Lisbon of plain white stucco with a red-tile roof and terrace decked with sweet-scented night blooms like those in Chaves. In its center was a fountain, slow bubbles barely marring the glassy surface of its pool. The woman entered—the one for whom his house would be built . . . petite, dark-haired, with a wide, heart-shaped face and huge ebony eyes—and, seeing her, the house dissolved, the site dissolved, and before he could touch her, she vanished with the rest. . . .

But no, a suggestion of her remained . . . her scent, her hand brushing his hair, her lips brushing against his temples. "Who?" he asked, struggling to wake.

—Elizabeth. You build for her.—

On the edge of sleep, Paul whispered, "You frighten me."

—I challenge you.—

Paul woke to find himself alone, sprawled impolitely across his employer's bed. From the adjoining bath came the sound of running water. He began to stand, then sat back down, feeling oddly light-headed, his stomach burning with hunger. As he fought the vertigo his host appeared briefly in the doorway. "There's some fruit and fresh bread on the table in the main room, and wine on the sideboard. Then please explore Savatier's creation."

Paul devoured half the loaf, washing it down with a glass of burgundy. The food and spirits revived him and he roamed the living space, marveling at the simplicity of the design and the beauty of the glass, one swirl of color growing out of another, spectrums from the windows moving through the room with the sun. He recalled that earlier there'd been an elusive warmth to the colors, but now the sensation was gone.

The kitchen was well equipped but bare, as if it had been added as an afterthought. The guest suite and servants' rooms were furnished but apparently unused.

The workroom seemed the most fascinating. Over a thousand small squares of glass hung from metal rods on a north-facing window. They appeared to be arranged by color, though some were indistinguishable from their neighbors. The pieces weren't labeled and Paul wondered how their places would be found if the hangers fell. The room also held a small furnace, a kiln, a potter's wheel, a dusty loom, and—stored in glass-doored cabinets—a variety of paints and brushes and vials of unlabeled powders. The space spoke of optimistic ambition and too little time. It seemed somehow depressing, and Paul walked back into the colorful main room where, picking up a well-used guitar, he began picking out a song. Stephen joined him and added three verses in a pleasant tenor, then, taking the guitar, played a quick canzone. The music reminded Paul of Gianni. The Italian had been a Communist but that explained nothing . . . certainly not why Gianni, or anyone, would want to kill the artistic young man now playing so magnificently for him.

Later Paul leaned beside Stephen above the table and watched the sun rise . . . its sanguine shades of wine, vermilion, ruby, and rose merging with the now more vivid blues of steel, aqua, cerulean, and tones for which Paul had no precise names. In the room behind them, men were sweeping up the wreckage of the shattered glass, ruined crates, and tables but Paul heard none of their clatter or their loud conversation. He had moved into a private space, bewitched by the joy of creativity.

He didn't need to ask why he alone had been chosen to view this; he had been told. Nor did he question why he, so young and so new to this place, should receive such a difficult commission, only that, though he might never create another building, he would design the one to hold this and it could be the most important work he would ever do.

The confidence stayed with Paul, and during the long train ride from Chaves to Lisbon he responded mechanically to everything except Linda's understandable curiosity about Stephen's attempted murder and her friend Gianni's death. With these he was more careful, recalling Stephen's warning. When Linda's uncle met her at the train station, Paul was relieved to say good-bye to his traveling companion. He wished no one else's plans to interfere with his own.

He picked up his small bag and walked to the address included in his itinerary. There he obtained not merely directions but a horse and guide as well. When he reached the uneven plateau, Paul dismounted and walked to the edge of the cliff, admiring the magnificent view of the sea, his mind lost in the creative void between data and conception.

"Shall I remain, *senhor*?" his guide asked. Receiving no reply, he repeated the question in a louder voice.

"Stay . . . ah, no. Return at eight to the inn we passed, and if I am not there, wait for me. And please arrange a boat for me for tomorrow morning. I will need it for at least half a day."

After the guide left, Paul hiked to a pinnacle above the site that afforded him a good view of both the plateau and the cliffs. Opening an artist's pad and pastels, he began to sketch.

In Lisbon, Linda Bradley also worked in the field she knew best, relaying to her uncle a string of failures and their one piece of good fortune: Gianni had not survived to be questioned. "They are treating this attempt as if Gianni were a madman. Are you sure Austra is a British informant?"

"Yes, and I want you to contact me the moment you hear of any plans he may have for visiting Lisbon."

"That may be months. We're very busy."

"But he will come. He is, after all, building a family house near here. He did nearly die creating the windows for it. Do you think he can resist the temptation to visit that secluded site? When he does, I will take him alive and provide the Gestapo with proof of their imbecilic mistake."

Ernst Bradley looked out the window across the Calcada da Ajuda and squinted against the afternoon sun. "If you brought something suitable to wear, it would be wise for me to introduce you to Lisbon society. There is a gathering at Elizabeth Austra's tonight."

"A relation?"

"Yes." Linda looked intrigued and Ernst added, "I suspected her as well, but I have decided that the woman, for all her intelligence, is no more than a harmless dilettante. To be certain, I sent three agents through her bedroom doors, and all have reported delightful experiences—nothing more. Now she has formed a playful attachment for Heinrich Schoofs, and I play the role of aging uncle; a role made for me, was it not?"

Chapter Six

Banlin, Ireland
August 1938

I

LAURENCE WAS DRIVING home from Cork during a sudden squall when he passed the Moores walking quickly down the road toward their home. Emma's thin cotton dress whipped around her legs, threatening to trip her as she dragged an old picnic basket. Kathleen carried a flapping brown blanket and tightly held Tad's hand.

Laurence pulled over and called out, "Do you always go picnicking in the rain?"

"It wasn't raining when we began," Kathleen responded. "We were optimistic."

"Would you like a ride?"

Laurence Austra had a fine reputation, and were he not her employer, Kathleen would have accepted in an instant. Now she looked at the threatening sky, then indecisively at the expensive ivory Delange and its owner.

"Take it, Mum," Emma piped up, then smiled at Laurence like the good friend she had become.

Kathleen agreed and spread the blanket over the leather seats before lifting up her children. They did not speak— Kathleen because Laurence's looks and position made her self-conscious; Laurence because he was lost in the fantasy that this was his wife, his children, his family out for a weekend drive.

In the few miles they traveled, Tad, tired and warm, dozed against his sister's shoulder while Emma stared at the back of Laurence's head, fascinated that her friend from the factory should own such a grand motorcar. By the time they arrived at the cottage, the rain had turned to a downpour. Covering Tad with the blanket, Laurence carried him inside. Acting on some sudden impulse, Kathleen invited Laurence to stay for tea.

She started the water heating on the peat stove, then dried off her children. As she did, Laurence studied the room, noting the mended lace cloth covering a pedestal table before the window, the bowl of violets resting on it, the delicate Wedgwood cups on a wooden rack beside the stove. Kathleen used the cups when she served him, and he sipped his tea slowly, finding the effect of the aromatic blend of chamomile and lemongrass odd but not unpleasant.

"And what brought you to Alpha?" he asked.

She glanced at the children playing in the corner, no longer concerned with adult conversation. "My husband was no family man. He deserted us after Tad was born. Perhaps it was a blessing." She recalled a few words too late that she shouldn't share family secrets with a stranger and moved the conversation in a different direction. "This cottage was my aunt's. She willed it to me."

"Where were you before you came here?"

"I worked in Manchester as a spinner." She remembered the grueling hours; the dust that had filled her lungs; and the woman who had lost her husband, her son, and her health to a textile factory. As long as she had strength to lift a baby, she had watched Kathleen's children and had come close to dying with Tad in her arms. Kathleen had gone to the funeral and seen her future resting in that coffin. Her inheritance had not only given her children a home; it had given her hope.

She must never know how much she had revealed to him. "So tell me why you were singing a melody by Dvořák?" he asked in a falsely bright tone.

"I was raised in London. My parents were able to allow me one inoffensive vice. I'm sure the London Symphony sounded just as sweet in my seat in the balcony as in the boxes below. I believe I could list every piece played my final season because I knew it would be my last.

"My father was ill and we spent a great deal of money in the last two years before his death. Afterward my mother moved in with my brother's family and I married a sailor. Now I am here." She spread out her hands, emphasizing that all these treasures belonged to her. "This is a good place to live, and Alpha treats its staff well."

Uneasiness grew in those last few words but he wouldn't allow position to stand between them. "Do you play the piano?" he asked as he looked at her strong fingers beating nervously on the tabletop.

"I do, but the only available piano in this town is in Finnerty's and I don't go into pubs."

"I have one, and sheet music as well. Would you like to play it . . . and bring your children to hear?"

An irresistible temptation! "Oh, yes."

"Tomorrow? Could you come at one?" He sensed she was about to decline and added, "I have servants. You'll be chaperoned."

He had pushed her too quickly. While she contemplated how to change her mind gracefully, Laurence turned to watch her children with such a wistful expression that she accepted instead.

That evening she laid clothes out on her bed . . . first for her children, then for herself. Of her two Sunday dresses only the brown one fit her well. She had gained weight since coming to Alpha but, she thought, consoling herself, the dress that fit was the better of the two and this was only an afternoon of music . . . an afternoon with a man she could not help but find fascinating. She placed an iron on the stove to heat and set up her board. Their clothes might be worn, but they would look their best tomorrow.

II

Laurence's music room had stark stone walls and high curved ceilings that made it resemble a monastic chapel. The Steinway grand sat in the center like an altar. Neither gave Kathleen any reason to relax, and she approached both the piano and her music cautiously.

She began with simple songs, gradually building to more difficult pieces. When Emma and Tad lost interest, running outside to play hide-and-seek among the hedges, Laurence became her patient audience, his attention building her confidence. She reached her limits with a slow Polonaise by Chopin, then asked Laurence to play. He chose pieces she had not heard, modern works by Gershwin and Stravinsky, while she sat beside him, enthralled by his presence, the music, and his skill.

The following Sunday, Laurence came upon the family picnicking in a shady glen.

"You told him we were coming here, didn't you?" Kathleen whispered to Emma while Tad puffed out his cheeks trying to blow into a six-reed pan flute Laurence had given him.

Emma shook her head and clapped as her brother made his first sound.

"That's right," Laurence said. "Like blowing into a bottle." He slipped Emma a pennywhistle and the two children began a discordant but enthusiastic concert, Laurence setting the rhythm with a pair of stones.

The concert reached ridiculous proportions. In spite of her uneasiness Kathleen laughed. "You need more practice," she said when they paused.

"No, more players," Laurence pulled out another flute and, following a series of birdcalls, handed it to her.

Later the children ran off to collect wildflowers, and Laurence moved deeper into the shade, watching Kathleen pack her basket, her strong, tanned hands shaking slightly as she worked. He knew she was fighting his attraction, thinking of ways to discourage him, and she was right. No matter. He was in exile here, with no family except Ann, and he needed the things these people could give him—laughter, friendship, perhaps even love. He began helping Kathleen, deliberately letting his hand brush hers. His touch seemed to move up her arm and over her body, and she sucked in her breath and pulled back, looking toward the sunlit field and her children, reminding herself she should be sensible.

I am a fool, she thought. *And I cannot help it.*

The discreet relationship grew over the weeks until, one Saturday night, an Austra servant looked after the children while Laurence drove Kathleen into Cork for a fall concert. Amateurish compared to London, he'd said, and though she agreed, she said she'd cherish every near perfect note.

She wasn't surprised when, rather than taking her home, Laurence drove her to his house. He slipped off the cloak Ann had loaned her and led her upstairs to a bedroom nearly the size of her cottage. A fireplace heated the room, sherry and glasses were arranged on its mantel. Kathleen stood in the center of the room, looking uneasily at the luxury around her. Laurence poured her some sherry, but instead of taking the glass she walked to the door.

"What is it?" he asked, convinced he had frightened her and not certain why.

When she turned back to him, there were tears on her cheeks. "I'm a married woman. I have two children."

"If your marriage concerned you, you would not have gone with me tonight." His voice was harsh. He wanted her, and his nature was not easily denied. "What is it?" he repeated more gently.

"I had thought I could stay with you, but, Laurie, I can't. My life shows in my face and in my body." Her chin rose in honest courage as she continued. "I wish I were beautiful. Perhaps then I could ignore the differences between us. I cannot remain here when all I will feel is shame when we are done." *Take me home,* she thought, and was about to say the words when he spoke.

"I have been empty, Colleen." He deliberately used the nickname her father had given her. "I find myself counting the days until I see you and your children again and you lift that burden from me. Please, don't leave me now." She watched him closely, understanding for the first time that this would be no hasty affair. "Do you care for me?" he asked.

She turned full circle, taking in her surroundings without really seeing them. "I have tried to separate who you are from what you own, and I'll answer honestly: I don't know, Laurie. Please give me time. Take me home."

In two long steps he stood in front of her, his hands on either side of her face. "I want you now," he said, "and we do not have the luxury of time."

Something about the chaste way he kissed her made her back up a step, wishing to ask him if she was the first. But no, that would be absurd. He was too sure of himself, so sure that he replied with a sad nod and said, "In one way you are," then let her desire for him push away thoughts of Ann and how determined she had been when she told him they had grown too old for such childish pleasures.

Kathleen was not one of his own, and he touched her with exaggerated tenderness, turning her around, undoing the buttons of her dress and slipping it off, then the rest. In the firelight he saw that the spattering of freckles on her face extended to her shoulders and arms and, though paler, over the tops of her breasts. She bore little resemblance to Ann, who was tall, lean and flawless, but Kathleen's body would be comfortable and healthy. Even now that extra reward enticed with its promise of a kind of monogamy, an escape from the constant seeking.

His clothing made her blush and she moved back, preparing to slip beneath the covers and wait for him. "In a moment," he said, pulling her to him and giving her a kiss that was far from chaste. She pushed away, her brows rising, troubled, trying to touch each other, as if by touching they could answer the strange question forming in her mind. He kissed her again, running his hands down her back, and her confusion vanished.

Sometime tonight she must learn the truth, and he was filled with dread that he might have misjudged her and she would have to forget what they did here. He recalled tales of how badly this revelation could be taken, and his hands shook as he reached for the buttons on his shirt. Kathleen undid them for him, staring at his face all the while, at the indecipherable emotions etched so vividly on it, trying to recall what she had wished to ask.

He loved her first as any man would love a woman, then lay holding her as he revealed the truth about himself and his family—how they lived, how they might never die. He paused after each sentence to follow her thoughts. She felt wonder and disbelief but no abhorrence, no fear. He hinted at his powers, then concluded his story with words spoken only to her mind. Though her eyes grew wide when she sensed them, they only added another score of questions to the hundreds she longed to ask. Since she did not know where to begin, she moved closer to him and said, "So there can be nothing between us but love?"

"It is all I can give you."

"I had prayed it would be enough."

Laurence rolled onto his side and looked down at her face. "There's more. So many things I must tell you."

"Enough," she said, and kissed him.

Since coming to Banlin, Laurence had taken what he needed by stealth. But now a woman had given herself freely to him and he used his power more boldly than he ever had before. He judged Kathleen's needs first by her reaction, then by her unspoken requests. As her desire grew, he reached for it, exciting it with his own, sending it back. The cycle continued, reverberating, until passion acquired a presence, swirling around them as they moved.

He waited, waited until her nails raked his side, pulling him deeper into her, before his teeth, long and sharp and painless, sank into her neck just above the shoulder.

For an instant he paused, frightened, waiting for her to understand what he had done and begin to fight. Instead, willingly, she tilted her head back, one hand on the nape of his neck, inviting him to take.

He drank slowly, the warmth of each swallow exploding in him and through him into her, each deep spasm of her body echoing his. He could have gone on forever, killing her with his love, but he thought of her and tomorrow, untangled his mind from hers and pulled away.

Kathleen touched the mark on her neck with one finger and rested it on his lips. "I think I understand how I'm the first," she said. She didn't expect or receive a reply and, after a brief silence, snuggled closer to him and closed her eyes.

Laurence lay awake, thinking Kathleen was right. She had been his first. With other human women he had noticed nothing beyond their vitality, their ability to be controlled. The others had been food, nothing more. He stared at the fire, wondering if ever again he could survive without this deliberate, perfect ecstasy.

Laurence drove Kathleen home the next afternoon to the accompaniment of curious eyes. Banlin was a one-industry town, and by Monday afternoon, news of the scandal flooded

Alpha. Kathleen's friends divided into two camps . . . those
who no longer acknowledged her presence and those who
defiantly sought her company. She affirmed nothing and denied nothing but did welcome her friends' support until one
commented indignantly, ''You have a family and no man to
protect you. How would you live without a job at Alpha?''

So his honor had been ruined as well as her own! Kathleen
bent over her food, too miserable to say a word. Though
Tuesday was dark and cloudy, she ate her food outside, alone.

From her office window two stories above, Ann Austra
looked down at Kathleen's slumped shoulders, then turned to
her brother, her expression fierce. ''This is Ireland, not Moulins or Paris, and you're not on some lark with Alex. You've
ruined her, Laurie, and the most honorable thing you can do
is to speak to Uncle. He can arrange a position for her in
Chaves or with the new branch opening in Canada.'' When
she sensed only anger in him, she added, ''You don't love
that woman; you love the thought of acquiring her ready-
made family.''

''It isn't true,'' he whispered, and added honestly, ''Maybe
it was. Not anymore.''

''Do you think you can hide your loneliness from me when
I am lonely too? Do you think I don't mourn the loss of our
parents?'' She tried to embrace Laurence but he moved back
a step, unwilling to take comfort from her. ''For your own
good, send her away.''

''Why the advice? What does my life matter to you?''

''Laurie!''

Through her shock he thought he sensed the truth. ''Why
did you come here, Ann?''

She hesitated, trying to understand what he meant, but
every time her mind tried to touch his, she found it shut
against her. ''I didn't want to return,'' she replied carefully.
''Uncle sent me.''

''To keep an eye on me?'' She shook her head. ''Admit
it!''

''No! I have work here, and you know how important it
is!''

''Work that my mind isn't strong enough to share. Work
that I don't even understand.''

''Someone has to run Alpha now that Robert is in Chaves.

You're good at it, Laurie; much better than I could ever be. You know that.''

He rested his hands on her shoulders and she let her mental defenses fall. He detected her reluctance to say anything that might hurt him and her love. "I'm sorry," he said more gently. "But when you write to Stephen, you do tell him about me."

"He asks. Of course I answer. Stephen is concerned about you, Laurie. That's all."

"And what does he write about Kathleen and me?"

Ann's hands were stiff at her sides. "He believes that you are fortunate."

"If he doesn't disapprove, why do you?"

"Because Stephen doesn't know, or maybe he just doesn't have time to see. I'm your sister, Laurie, and I sense that Kathleen will bring disaster to you. And you to her. Feel it, Laurie, look inside yourself and see. . . ." Her voice trailed off because, as she'd expected, his mind had already been made up.

Chapter Seven

Ireland
November 1938

I

IF HARRY BLACKWELL had possessed less self-confidence, he would have found his abrupt meetings with Ann Austra more unsettling. However, after the first few occasions he grew accustomed to the idea that it was somehow possible for him to travel from Britain to Ireland and, once there, to acquire the correct mode of transport to take him to a crossroads, an abandoned cottage, or, less frequently, a fine country inn, always without a conscious destination in mind. Although he'd sometimes been tempted to ignore phone calls at odd hours, his intelligence duties took precedence over whatever social obligations he had acquired; and he would pick up the receiver, hear a distinctive combination of syllables, and leave.

When he met Ann, he would be given a message he couldn't recall until he returned to London and faced his superior. Then the facts would spill out—valuable, accurate information none of their usual sources ever could have discovered. In exchange for her help the British Secret Intelligence Service agreed to leave the Austra family alone. No SIS agents collected data on them or infiltrated their firms to spy on the employees; no demands were made that AustraGlass stop their heavy trading with the Germans.

Though Blackwell found Ann Austra's odd arrangement nearly flawless, it created personal problems for him. He'd had to apologize to Lady Julia twice—once for not attending one of her summer socials, and the second, never forgiven, for failing to escort her to Edward Grey's dinner party. Business, he'd explained, but she would accept no vague excuse, and the truth would be thoroughly unbelievable were he able to break security to relate it. He consoled himself by deciding he had been more enamored of marrying into royalty than with the far too independent lady herself, so the dissolution of their engagement had been for the best. Actually Ann Austra caused this ambivalence as well, for she was as deucedly fascinating as she was remote.

And, he thought ruefully, after nine visits to Banlin he should have expected danger along with infatuation. Still, it was unpleasant to be only partially in control with an enemy dogging his heels.

Blackwell had first spotted the sandy-haired young man in Cork while he was arranging the use of a motorcar and, from habit rather than suspicion, had noted his face. He noticed the man again in a town a few miles west of Banlin. Had Blackwell been in control of this meeting, he would have canceled it, but his mind responded to only one message and he continued driving north, the roads growing rougher as he neared some destination. In his rearview mirror he detected the distant cloud of dust raised by his follower.

Any defense he might have taken was frustrated by his obsession, and he pulled his car to the side of the road and ran a quarter of a mile up an ill-kept path. When he reached a dilapidated cottage, he skirted it like an animal sniffing an unfamiliar lair, entered through the door, and exited immediately via the shell of a rear window. Following a line of shrubs, he backtracked, with sufficient time to see his pursuer pull out a gun and crouch down beside a rock fence to wait, no doubt, for the arrival of Ann.

"Good evening," Blackwell said. "Please hand over that weapon." He wasn't surprised at the vehemence of the refusal.

When Ann arrived just after dark, the man was trussed hand and foot and blindfolded with strips of his own shirt. He lay close to the small fire on the cottage's old stone hearth while Blackwell sat beside him contemplating this new problem, seeing only one logical conclusion. It had seemed wisest first to discuss the situation privately with Ann, but she ig-

nored his motion for silence, demanding in an irate tone,
"What are you doing to this man?"

"I caught him hiding in the bushes."

Ann knelt beside the prisoner, examined the welt on his
head, then spoke fiercely to Blackwell. "Just because someone is curious about our affairs is no reason to maul him,
Harry."

"I thought you wanted secrecy," Blackwell protested.

"My uncle would not spy on me! Now who is this?"

"He was carrying a Krupp revolver. I assume he's a German agent."

"What!" Ann gripped the prisoner's shoulder and asked
in a low, resigned tone, "Is that the kind of British civil
servant you are, Harry?" Without waiting for a reply she
added, "What are you going to do with him?"

"Whatever's necessary," Blackwell replied, falling into his
sinister role.

"You intend to kill him, don't you?" Ann's voice rose,
and the hand resting on the prisoner's shoulder began to shake.
This was low melodrama, yet she had planted the suggestion
that the captive believe every word. It had been so simple
because he desperately wished that somehow she could save
him from . . . from . . . ? She sniffed his private fear and
pantomimed it to her partner.

"He was prepared to kill us," Blackwell countered, then
added derisively, "I suppose what I do depends on what he
tells me."

They argued until Ann, apparently unable to move her
lover, slapped him and stormed out of the cottage. After some
minutes of silence broken only by the quick breathing of both
men, Blackwell dragged his prisoner closer to the fire and
ripped off the blindfold. "Well, my young friend," he began
in a voice taut with rage, "thanks to you, I've lost my delightful excuse for visiting Banlin."

He rubbed the livid palm print on his cheek, then pulled a
stick from the flames, blew on the end until it glowed, and
held it close to the prisoner's face. "If we were in Britain,
I'd let the experts deal with you. Here it's up to me to obtain
your information by whatever means are at my disposal." His
mocking expression implied the man beneath him would provide greater pleasure than the woman who had left.

He gripped the captive's chin and blew on the stick again. "You fancy yourself quite the dandy, don't you? Well, we'll see who looks at you if we spend too much time together. Why not keep that pretty face intact and tell me who ordered you to come here." When the man didn't reply, the stick grazed his temple. His scream came more from anticipation than from actual pain.

"I'm paid," the prisoner said, fear constricting his voice so the words came out a broken squeak. Blackwell loosened his grip, allowing the man to catch his breath and continue. "My name is Timothy Cummings. I work in a factory in Cork. I met a fellow in a pub one day. We had a few drinks and—"

"Who pays you?" Blackwell tightened his knees on either side of the man's head.

"I don't know." A hand held his chin again. "I don't. I swear it!"

"Ah, but you do—and I think it's high time you told me."

From the concealing darkness Ann watched through the window as the questioning continued. If she hadn't shared Blackwell's cause, the emotions she sensed in him would have been loathsome. But now they, combined with a mind more predatory than she had seen in any other human being, created a heady attraction. The desire to postpone the conclusion of her sham became almost irresistible, particularly since, when she had not immediately returned, Blackwell had decided to conduct the questioning in earnest. With effort she unwound her mind from her ally and moved to the captive, a shudder and quiet moan escaping her as she shared his torment. He alternated between pleas and sobs, past hope but still claiming ignorance, held back from his breaking point only by a more pervasive fear that once he gave his information he would be killed. Her hand closed around a rock. —Now, Harry . . . finish this now!—

Blackwell moved back, one hand gripping the captive's neck, the other brushing his bare chest. "The coals are at their hottest, my young friend. You will tell me what you know and perhaps you will live—or I assure you, what I do next will make what I have done seem no worse than the slap that bitch gave me. Now, damn it, who pays you!"

"All right! The money comes through Portugal. The man who provides—'' He never completed the sentence. Ann's hand swung down, the rock she gripped opening Blackwell's temple, and he fell sideways onto the hearth. She began to untie the prisoner, apparently reconsidered, then picked up the gun before freeing him. Holding the weapon in two dangerously shaking hands, she ordered, "Get out!"

The man needed no second invitation, though he did risk a quick look back. Ann had fallen to her knees beside her unconscious lover and raised Blackwell's head into her lap. "Oh, Harry!" she cried, "I think I've killed you!"

She continued to whimper softly until she knew the agent would not return, then tapped Blackwell on the shoulder. His first words were far from pleasant. "Blast it, Ann! You could have waited one more minute.''

"Now he's all the more certain I've been duped. Besides, I know everything of value.'' She untied the scarf from her hair and began blotting up the blood running down Blackwell's face. "His name is Timothy Ryan. He is a member of the IRA, assisting the Germans against a common enemy. His contact in Cobh sends information to an American living in Lisbon. . . .'' She continued to provide one detail after another, making no attempt to judge what might be significant, concluding with a tight, patronizing smile that created two long hollows down the side of her face.

Blackwell was astounded. "How do you know all this?"

"All you need know is that I do.''

"The same way you knew how to break that young man?"

"Don't inquire further. How does your head feel?''

"You hit me rather hard. Things could not have gone better had we planned it.''

She acknowledged the praise with a quick toss of her head, then said, "We're alone for the moment but I'd better not abandon you. Have you a motorcar?"

"Two miles south of here.'' He handed her the key, then slid into the shadows, cradling the revolver. His mind must have wandered, for Ann seemed to have been gone an unusually short time. Afterward she bundled him in her own cloak, solicitously adjusting the fabric to keep him warm as she drove toward home. She sensed when they passed Ryan and reached out to touch Harry's head with a broad, loving gesture.

When they reached the house, Ann made a pretense of helping Blackwell inside, then pulled the car around to the back before returning to pour her guest a glass of brandy. "We can't have you making too miraculous a recovery. Can you stay the weekend?"

"Of course. But won't my presence cause difficulty for you . . . your reputation in particular?"

"My reputation doesn't concern me. Disappointing Mr. Ryan and the others who will be watching us so carefully does. Besides, tomorrow is Saturday. Only the spies will note that I spend the entire day nursing you."

Lifting the carafe of brandy, she led him upstairs to a large guest room, set the bottle on a butler's table, and said good night. The room was sumptuous, its ceiling slanting down to an outer wall containing three dark-toned windows before which stood a square, Spartan-style bed of grand proportions. Along one wall was a fireplace, the hearth already laid, and in front of it a thick Ispahan Oriental rug and dark leather Chesterfield chair. The adjoining bathroom was as luxurious, the tub resting beneath a huge skylight of smoke-shaded glass. But for Blackwell the hot water and fine Wood's soap were the most pleasant discoveries of all. While he soaked out the night's chill his revolver was on the ledge beside him and the connecting door open. He was always listening; certain locks would not keep out intruders. The addition of tea, biscuits, and pâté aux truffles on a butler's table was therefore an ambiguous blessing, the crackling fire even more so.

He slipped on a robe that had been left for him and sat in front of the fire eating the pâté (tinned but of excellent quality), sipping tea laced with brandy, feeling vaguely bewildered and lonely. The door clicked open. He grabbed his gun, then lowered it when he saw Ann, now wearing an emerald velvet dressing gown—high-waisted, modest, and becoming.

She laughed as if he held a child's toy. "We're in no danger of invasion, Harry. Actually this seemed an ideal opportunity to complete what should have been this evening's purpose."

"As you like." He concealed his disappointment, sitting

back in the chair with his hands resting on its arms, prepared to be thrust into that receptive state he'd learned to attain easily.

As Ann relayed her message she moved her hands to cover his. When she'd finished, she knelt in front of him and studied his face.

His black hair was touched lightly with gray and one of his brows was set a slight distance above the other. That flaw—combined with an aquiline nose, thin lips, and colorless gray eyes—gave him the cultivated look of an aristocrat, civilized, waiting to be sensual.

Curiosity triumphed and she began kindling one emotion after another, fanning the strongest until they flamed. His breathing quickened, he was nearly awake. "Quite some message," he mumbled.

Ann pushed her control to it limits, then sat back on her heels, watching his expression move from confusion to rapture. Downstairs, she heard the click of the bolt on the servant's entrance, the soft footsteps on the stairs. Her timing had been perfect! She slipped off her gown and, pulling Blackwell to his feet, slid the robe off his shoulders to land beside hers. —Kiss me, Harry.— she ordered as she wrapped her arms around his neck.

That was how Ann's maid found them. Sarah Donoho's hand flew to her mouth to stifle a cry of embarrassment and she flushed and fled in quiet panic. As she ran from the house to relay her discovery Ann felt Sarah's conscience protest, then lose the battle in the face of her devotion to Timothy Ryan, her rage at how he had been brutalized and her contempt for the sinfulness of the lovers.

Only a dauntless ego could allow such complete surrender. It was this ego that made Blackwell a perfect courier and, as Ann discovered as she kissed him, a man who faced passion as superbly as he did danger. The self-protective distance she had placed between them vanished. She backed away, startled at her response, then studied his body as she had his face, letting the cold use of her power restore her balance. No, she decided, there were too many risks to loving this man, though she was not above using him. Indeed, after poor, virginal Sarah he'd be a feast.

Ordering him back into his chair, she knelt in front of him, running her fingers across his neck and shoulders, feeling his slight shudder at her touch. Though he was not asleep, Blackwell dreamed of holding her, of her holding him, of every wonderful thing they could do to each other. His body fell forward. Her lips brushed, then covered, his wound. As she fed, his desire soared up and up until he flamed and fell with dizzying speed into the present . . . to the brush of fabric against his thighs, a brief glimpse of Ann with her gown swirling around her bare legs. His pulse raced as he sat weak and baffled, the robe in his lap his only cover. Blood dripped down his face and he staggered into the bathroom and placed a cold washcloth against the wound. When the bleeding stopped, he slipped beneath the covers and slept.

II

The morning light streaming through the windows transformed the bed into a multicolored cloud. Blackwell had an illusion of floating, a sensation that brought back vague images of the night before. What little he recalled might have been a dream caused by the blow to his head or the bewitching presence of that woman, but he didn't believe either. No, somehow Ann had ravished him. His curiosity stirred and he wondered if this had been the first time.

The butler's table had been moved beside the bed, and without rising, Blackwell reached for biscuits, washing them down with a quick swallow of cold tea before dressing and going downstairs.

Though he'd been in the main room before, he'd never really studied it. Now he noted the quality of the artwork . . . the glass by the family, the paintings (most unsigned) speaking of taste and, when he recognized works of famous masters, wealth. Deciding to explore further, he walked into a barren kitchen, then risked a look out the back window. His car had attracted a small boy who bobbed on the front seat. A girl wearing loose riding slacks came out the back door of the older house and walked across the courtyard, swinging a crop as if she'd been born with it in her hand.

* * *

Blackwell settled in the library where he paged through
back issues of *Punch*, finding an article on the Irish Rebellion, followed by a selection of poems by Yeats. He was
reading "Byzantium" when Ann arrived. "Good morning,"
she said, "you're looking well."

The utter cheek! "I suppose I'm well enough considering
my confusion," he began in a sportive tone. "I'd like to
know what you did to me last night."

"*To* you? I don't understand."

"Then I recall far more than you, and I warn you that if
you ever attempt that trick again, be prepared to accept the
consequences." His words were accompanied by a long, li-
centious look implying he would relish the opportunity to
provide them.

Blackwell had expected embarrassment, possibly anger,
certainly not laughter. "Last night one of Mr. Ryan's inquisitive friends came to call. My reputation has now been thoroughly ruined."

This was only part of the truth; nonetheless, he said
sincerely, "I'm sorry."

"Whatever for? Now we can meet in Cork or even London
from time to time. That's preferable to long walks in the
damp Irish hills, is it not?" She spoke as if she had settled
all their problems, and he thought her naïve until she added,
"Of course they'll still suspect me, but also a great many
others."

"Your family in particular. Are they aware of what you do?"

"Some are."

"And they allow it?"

"I am an adult. As to my family's feelings, they are not
your concern."

"You are right, of course, and I apologize again." A door
slammed and Blackwell stiffened.

"That's Kathleen," Ann told him. "She's undoubtedly
prepared a feast for you."

"Is she your inquisitive spy?"

"Hardly. She is my brother's mistress." Ann's tone revealed dislike, and Blackwell wondered if it was directed at
the woman, her brother, or the arrangement in general.

Kathleen brought a plate of sausages, biscuits, hot soda

bread, and a steaming pot of tea. She wore a loose-fitting work dress. It did not seem like the sort of clothes the mistress of a wealthy man would wear, but the deep heather-green fabric set off her hair and rosy complexion. Though they exchanged only a few words, Kathleen charmed Blackwell. He thought her outgoing geniality would be an ideal complement for Laurence, who seemed rather shy.

When she'd gone, Blackwell asked Ann, "Were the children I saw hers?"

"Yes." She briefly explained Kathleen's situation.

"Perhaps an annulment could be arranged."

"No matter. Nothing can come of this relationship." Ann spoke as if the woman were a servant existing only to be seduced and abandoned.

"Is your brother's future so predetermined?" Blackwell asked carefully.

"I don't expect you to understand."

Blackwell thought her meaning clear and changed the subject.

Ann was absent all day. Kathleen delivered a lunch tray to Blackwell and later invited him to the old house to share a late supper with her. "I hope you don't mind the informality," she said as they sat down to their meal in the mansion's vast kitchen.

"Not at all, and the food has been excellent. You may give my praises to your cook."

"Thank you. I *am* the cook. There are no servants in Laur—our house." She seemed embarrassed by her mistake, even more so at the correction.

"It must be a great deal of work for you."

"I like taking care of my family. Besides, Laurie and I don't entertain, and two of the wings are closed off."

"Someone must have had a large family at one time."

"Or a live-in army, or so one of the legends tells. The house is over two hundred years old."

"Are there any ghosts in it?"

She feigned being shocked. "I hope not! I've barely learned to tolerate the echo in some of these rooms." She watched Blackwell devour what was on his plate, then passed

him the serving bowl again. "I'm pleased you like the stew.
Some people don't like venison."

"It's delicious, but I didn't know there were deer in Ireland."

"There are in these hills."

"And someone hunts them?"

"Laurie is an excellent hunter. We have venison often."
She seemed amused, as if she had alluded to a private joke.

Near the end of the meal the music began. First a series
of complex scales breaking abruptly into a prelude by Rach-
maninoff, a pause, then another far more difficult piece.
Blackwell stopped speaking in mid-sentence, straining to hear
the strange rhythm, the incredible contrasts in the chords.

"Who's playing?" he asked.

"Laurie."

"And what piece?"

"His own. Shall we have dessert in the music room?"

"Please." She led him down a long arched hall and into
the white-walled music room. They sat in a pair of chairs
near the fire. Blackwell finished his meal quickly, then closed
his eyes and listened, certain he had never heard composition
or playing skill to equal this!

Bits of Irish whimsy merged with a heavy pagan beat, as
if leprechauns blithely dodged the huge sandaled feet of Druids in their oak groves. The music continued for an hour,
concluding with the lyric Irish theme, which grew softer and
softer, so that Blackwell had to strain to hear the final notes.

Laurence acknowledged Blackwell's praise with a tight,
quick smile. "The firm is my livelihood. Music is my life."

"Music could be both," Blackwell suggested.

Laurence shook his head.

"Composition, then?"

"My music is private. It will always be private."

He spoke as Ann had earlier, as if he were a crown prince
and his life ordained and this incredible talent no more than
an escape from his obligations. And what an escape, Blackwell thought as he leaned back in the chair, lost in the contrasts of another piece that might, miraculously, be more
magnificent than the first.

Later Ann found Blackwell in her library reading one of
the antique volumes, a collection of work by a Spanish ro-

mantic poet. Apparently it had been a gift because Blackwell had noted above the author's portrait an inscription that read, "To Steven, who I hope will understand and forgive this major indiscretion. Charles."

Blackwell turned back to that portrait and commented to Ann. "The poet bears a remarkable resemblance to your brother. An ancestor, perhaps?"

"Distant," she replied mechanically, staring down at the picture a moment longer. "Do you like poetry, Harry?"

"Yes, it seems to restore a proper sense of balance."

"And you have need of restoration now?"

"Yes, I don't enjoy torturing young patriots, however deadly they may be."

Her reply was tinged with smug satisfaction. "But you did. I know you did."

"At the time but not now. I don't feel guilt. I simply feel . . ." He paused, seeking the proper word.

"Unsettled?"

"Precisely." He closed the book and returned it to its place on the shelf. "I suppose what occurred must have seemed barbaric but . . ."

"Not barbaric, necessary." She motioned to a chess table beneath a window. "Would you like to play?"

They did, and he bested her two games out of three, then received permission to take some books upstairs. He picked the one he had been reading and two more from the specially bound collection . . . one of sixteenth-century French verse, the other a thin volume by a little read Italian poet.

He lit a fire and settled down in the chair, reading selections by one poet, then by another. Although the form and subject matter differed, there were frequent similarities in phrasing that astounded him. Soon he lay stretched out on the carpet, the three books open to works he was certain had been written by the same person. He compared the inscriptions, all in the same hand, though two were signed Charles, the third Edward.

He decided to go downstairs and study other volumes on that shelf when a sudden weariness overcame him and he lowered his head to his arm and slept. When he woke in the morning, he was in bed, and his interest in the books, like the books themselves, had vanished. Though he spent the

night in deep, dreamless sleep and was certain he had not
been disturbed, he noticed Kathleen's private smile as the two
of them ate an unusually hearty breakfast.

III

On Sunday, Emma went to the stables and found Laurence
discussing the spring races with Jake Finnerty, the county's
most respected horse breeder. She said she'd come back later
but Laurence asked her to stay. "We'll only be a moment,
Em. Saddle Henna and show Jake how well you ride. Then
he can go back to Banlin and tell everyone that you'll be the
main contender in the junior races."

Jake waited until the girl was out of earshot and asked,
"You'll have her ride this spring?"

"She's ready."

"I wasn't thinking of her skill, Laurie."

"Neither was I." Laurence stared at his friend for a moment, then turned the conversation back to the race until
Emma returned with the bay.

Soon the girl was circling the pen, jumping hurdles of increasing height. She cleared four easily but on the fifth lost her
balance and fell, tearing the knee of her riding pants. Laurence
rushed to her, his speed and concern looking for an instant like
anger. Emma paled and slid back, covering the rip with both
her hands. "I'll sew it, I promise!" she blurted.

Laurence glimpsed someone huge, red-faced, bellowing
with rage. Horrified at her past, he froze while Jake asked,
"Em, are you all right?"

"I . . . I . . ." Emma jumped to her feet and, clutching
Laurence, began to cry.

Jake studied the two, then walked over to Henna and short-
ened the stirrups a notch. "Let's try again, girl?"

Emma sniffed and nodded, and Jake swung her up in the
saddle. "There are things Laurie hasn't taught you, I see.
Now, if you just lean forward a bit more . . ." He continued
giving pointers as Emma returned to her practice.

Jake sat beside Laurence on the top rail of the fence and

watched her jumps. "She's good. She just might take a ribbon at Banlin Fair." With hardly a pause Jake asked, "Forgive me for prying, but does Kathleen ever mention her husband?"

Laurence smiled sadly. "You'll stop prying a week after your wake, and, no, she doesn't. She's afraid even to inquire if he's dead. Now let me ask why you're asking."

"I was just wondering what kind of man would leave so fine a family in limbo. I think, if you offer, I'd like a cup of tea, Laurie. It's been too long since I've seen your Kathleen."

IV

Timothy "Cummings" Ryan knew religious fervor when he saw it. His mother had been afflicted; so had two sisters. In the same way he'd ingratiated himself to the women of his family he gained the perfect devotion of Ann's maid, Sarah Donoho. He never touched her except to plant a chaste kiss on her cheek or to take her hand. "We'll wait to marry," he told her. "We've more important work now."

Convinced of the worthiness of all Tim's causes, Sarah had conveyed her information to him without question. But last night's scene troubled her soul. Oh, their evil had tempted her before, but she'd resisted—resisted the sinfulness around her and the strange things she dreamed. Tonight she had prayed for guidance, and the Lord told her clearly what she had to do. Ann Austra's liaison with that Englishman was despicable, but Laurence's with the little children in the house was a mortal sin that must be stopped.

With no remorse she wrote a lengthy letter addressed to James Stimpson Moore, care of the British Navy. She sealed the envelope and mailed it with a cover letter explaining this concerned the seaman's family and was of the most serious nature. She sent it with a prayer, never doubting the righteousness of her act—or that God would aid her.

Chapter Eight

Portugal
January 1939

I

IN EARLY JANUARY, Paul sat on the train returning him to Chaves and wrote an apologetic letter to his brother.

I'm sorry I wasn't home with you for Christmas. I have made excuses to Mother and Father but I want to be honest with you. I had no desire to be assaulted by cousins, uncles, aunts, three screaming infant nephews, and the suggestion that one or another excellent position can be found for me in Boston or New York if I will only abandon my foolishness and come home. I am too weary to fight them now. Rest, Brian! I needed rest.

So I have spent the unheard-of three weeks we are given with Philippe Dutiel's family at their dairy farm in Brittany. Their house is tiny and Phil and I shared an unheated room in the loft of their barn so his grandparents could use his room. After the first night I was thankful we shared a bed because the temperature outside (and in!) fell below freezing. The family made me feel quite at home, and I can now add milking cows to my list of accomplishments.

Philippe and I toured northern France and took a train into Belgium, then, briefly, to Germany. The Germans seem more prosperous than when we lived there but I sense a frantic quality to their lives, as if they were all passengers on some sinking luxury ship who had determined to make the best of the hours left them by ignoring the sea. We saw wealth without freedom, comfort

without security. Though I passed for a native, we sensed
danger to Phil and stayed only long enough to pay a
quick call on the Stronheims before going back to
France. Irene sends her love to Mother and promises to
write.

Now I am returning to work. My hours have switched
since I wrote you last. I work for Savatier in the morn-
ings and Stephen in the afternoons. Stephen has more
time to teach me later in the day, and if he is in the
middle of explaining something, I don't have to go rushing off to Savatier. I admit Stephen makes me uneasy,
but I'm awed by his skill and he's a patient teacher.
There are even times when we step out of our roles and
behave like friends.

I wish I could be as hopeful about my work. Both my
jobs are fascinating, challenging—and so maddening that
just before shutdown I dreamed I popped both Stephen
and Savatier into one of the huge Hermanson furnaces
and locked the door with relief, as if I were Gretel and
they a pair of witches. The dream was so vivid, I woke
shaking. I was still shaking when I met with Savatier,
who gave me a structural problem best described as how
to build a skyscraper on quicksand. It was so similar to
the other site problems I have been given I have become
certain Savatier pulls them out of some horror file he
keeps to torment fledgling architects.

That same afternoon Stephen placed me in charge of the
melts. Though the work went smoothly, I didn't understand why. I asked him if there were formulae for the pro-
cesses and he replied curtly, "We have a library. Pull a
book and tomorrow tell me what you've learned." I confess I stayed up half the night reading, then discovered
Stephen had not been serious at all.

Adding to my frustration is the mystery of the vanish-
ing house plans. I suffered over every inch of the placement of the doors and windows. I brought them home
with me, to roll and unroll and reroll time after time.
But after demanding I submit them, Savatier said nothing at all for weeks. Just before shutdown, I asked what
had happened to them and Savatier told me to be patient.
Three months and not a word! I would ask him what

happened to the plans, but he's been away so often I
hardly have a chance. When he leaves, he places me in
charge. I get along well with the staff and haven't made
any mistakes, so I suppose the appointment is an honor.
Honestly, I don't know. Oh, Brian, box up some of your
abundant confidence and mail it to me. Perhaps it will
arrive before what little I possess slips away.

II

February 1939

The handbill proclaimed Rosalia the greatest *faudista* in
all of Portugal, and Henry, who had heard her performance
in the Colony two years earlier, said every word of it was the
truth. And so that Saturday all of Notre Dame took their
evening meals in the largest Colony café and, by arriving
hours early, managed to hold the finest table. When the café
began filling for the evening, Samuelson, Rachel, and a number of other members of the Austra family claimed the smaller
reserved table behind them. A short time later Stephen and
Savatier, both of whom had returned that afternoon from
Stockholm, joined them.

Paul glanced up as the two men came through the café
door, then self-consciously back at the stage. After days of
nonstop work they had discovered him here! He considered
this injustice while Stephen exchanged quick greetings with
a number of patrons, then sat at the reserved table beside
Rachel.

The guitarists began with a flourish, using the conflicting
notes as weapons to battle for the singer's favor. She chose
neither, preferring to pine with her own melody for her departed love. The lyrics were so melodramatic as to strike
anyone but a native Portuguese as hilarious, but Rosalia used
voice and gestures to give them dignity they did not deserve.
By the end of her first set there were a number of moist eyes
in the café.

* * *

During her break Rosalia accepted a glass of wine from Michael Austra, then said a few words to Henry before moving on to speak to other admirers. Stephen took the opportunity to pull his chair next to Henry's and ask about his recovery.

"Is there going to be another church in Sweden?" Mark asked him later.

"Definitely! And the changes you made in the plans will make the construction much easier."

"I hear Sweden is beautiful in the winter," Philippe said.

"It is if you enjoy arctic cold and near constant darkness."

"You sound like you did," Mark commented.

"It wasn't entirely work. I also went hunting."

Here was something to interest the Scotsman. "Bear?" he asked.

"Wolves."

"Really! With a bow or a gun?"

"I'm better with a bow," Stephen replied, and immediately turned to Paul. "Everything went smoothly in Savatier's absence, yes?"

"Yes. It seemed an unexpected . . . honor." And the work! Good Lord, the work!

"Deserved."

The music started again, saving Paul the problem of deciding on a reply.

In her next number Rosalia abandoned fado and sang a soft Spanish love song and, in response to the applause, another that was somewhat faster, then a piece of her own creation . . . a hybrid of fado and flamenco. "Didn't I say she was brilliant?" Henry whispered to the table as her voice rose and fell, wild songs in civilized spaces, and abruptly ended. As the applause died, Rosalia took a guitar and pointedly extended it to Stephen.

Stephen shook his head. "I am here to listen."

She raised the guitar higher. "Please." There was a scattering of polite applause.

"A duet?" he asked, conceding.

She laughed, the sound as husky and expressive as her voice. "Of course. The one we did together in Baraganza."

The music was quick, the lyrics lighthearted; not fado, the

antithesis of fado . . . no sorrow, no self-denial, only the joy
of spring after a long winter. As Rosalia sang, she began
clapping, urging the audience to do the same, moving the
beat faster as Stephen's fingers flew over the strings. Paul was
mesmerized by the suggestive lyrics, her soprano and Stephen's tenor merging exquisitely.

Paul's vision blurred at the edges, the shouts of bravo and
wild applause dulling as well. In front of him, Rosalia, her
head tilted defiantly back, flung herself into Stephen's lap.
Paul saw him whisper something in her ear, his dark hair
brushing against her bronze shoulder, his pale hand covering
hers, and he imagined them later pressed together, the blankets flung back. She was talented, fiery . . . so right. . . .

Paul felt a sudden rush of envy so sharp and shameful that
he flushed and bolted from his chair into the scented night.

Phil began to follow but Mark held his arm. *"Fou!* And
he won't welcome your help. Besides, we're about to get another duet. Who would have thought the monarch was so
multitalented, hmm?''

Paul returned to Notre Dame, pulled a bottle of wine from
the kitchen cabinet, and took it upstairs, prepared to get disgustingly drunk in private. He placed it on the night table,
considered it sadly, then, instead of uncorking it, took his
valises from the closet and laid them open on the bed. He
had no reason to drench the loss but merely to leave as quickly
as possible, and a hangover would only make his train ride
more miserable in the morning.

As he reached into the lower drawer of his dresser, he
heard the door to his room open and close. Knowing who
stood behind him, he took a deep, slow breath before turning.

"You are leaving." Stephen's words were not a question.

Paul's response was fierce. "I can't stay here any longer."

"What will you do at home?"

"I have my experience here. It will count for something."

"If you leave now, you will get no references from us, not
even the simple acknowledgment that you once worked here."

"Why are you threatening me?"

"Because I will not let you ruin your future out of foolishness."

"Foolishness! It isn't that. It's . . ." Paul flushed again and backed up a step. He could never admit how he felt.

"I know precisely why you want to leave, so, you see, there's no reason why you need go."

Stephen's honesty was brutal and Paul glared at him. "You left that singer to come here and force me to stay. Perhaps I do understand."

"I doubt it. No, I came to tell you that starting Monday you will begin learning glass design from Marilyn and David."

"I won't be working with you?"

"No. But on the Friday after next I want you to go with me to Lisbon. Afterward, if you still wish to leave, I'll provide the references you deserve."

"We're going to Lisbon to discuss the house?"

"Yes."

"Very well, Senhor Austra. I will remain for two more weeks, and now, though you own it, I pay for this room. Please leave."

His valises had been thankfully returned to the closet when Paul felt a tap on his shoulder and turned to see Linda behind him, her expression solicitous. "Too much wine," he explained with a flustered laugh.

"Oh. Well, if that's all, I'll go back, I suppose."

"Must you?"

He sounded as if he were making a pass but didn't know how to begin. "No," she said, leaning against the edge of the door, "not if you don't want me to."

"I don't." She closed the door behind her. "Would you care to lock it?" he asked.

Linda had seen Austra leave, and now this unapproachable man had become abruptly forward. Hints of danger made her passionate.

For Paul, an hour that should have been savored was filled only with shame at how thoroughly he believed he was using Linda. He had no illusions that he could ever love her, and to discourage her he told her he was considering taking a position in New York and must make a decision soon.

"Is that why Austra was here?"

"No . . . well, yes, in a way. He wants me to stay. We're going to Lisbon in two weeks to see about the house."

"I hope you stay," she said, and kissed him. Then, to fill

in the silence, she asked, "It's only midnight. Would you like to go back?"

He didn't, but it seemed the easiest manner of parting. "Of course."

When they returned to the café together, Stephen glanced up from the table, Paul's scorching look telling him that what had occurred in the last hour had been of the greatest importance and, on the other hand, of no consequence whatsoever.

III

During their long train ride to Lisbon, Paul intended to apologize to Stephen but didn't know how to begin. He stared uncomfortably at his employer, lying sideways on the seat across from him in their private compartment, his wide-brimmed hat pulled down over his eyes. Sensing the scrutiny, Stephen looked up and returned Paul's gaze. "You wish to tell me something, yes?"

"I want to say I'm sorry for everything I said that night in my room." He could go no further toward admitting the truth . . . that he dreamed of Marilyn constantly; that David, always aloof, was unsettling to be near; that he had begun to notice all the Austra family with the same intolerable attraction.

"I understand," Stephen responded. "I intend to explain a great deal to you tonight, then ask you to accept my apology." He pulled down his hat and went back to sleep.

They arrived in Lisbon late Friday afternoon. Stephen slipped behind the wheel of a waiting automobile and drove Paul to the building site. When they stopped on the rise above the site, Paul saw his house, already standing. Without a word he left the car and walked alone down the rough gravel drive. The major structure was complete . . . the doors, fixtures, windows, and decorating all the work that remained. Unfinished, yes, but the unadorned walls made its daring elegance all the more obvious. As he had expected, Paul did walk around his creation—moving slowly, touching it often, recalling the lines he had drawn on paper. It was exactly as he'd pictured: terraces jutting impossibly out above the sea; the walls behind them rising cleanly; and, inside, the floating staircase to the second level, the stage for the woman who would give life to these walls. He climbed those stairs, traveling slowly from room to room, and returned to sit on the top step, tears stinging his eyes.

"Does the man who designed this house have 'no talent whatsoever for architecture'?" Stephen leaned against the empty doorway leading to the terrace, his expression as serious as his tone.

"No, damn it! But why didn't you tell me?"

"I'll answer after you explain why you wished to abandon your profession."

"You know that already, don't you?"

"I do, but say it."

"Because architecture is the most egotistical of art forms. It's the only creative endeavor in which the artist sells his piece before he completes it, and if the design is wrong, it's not his to destroy. Instead it will stand as a monument to his greatness or folly . . . a monument for all the world to see."

"And to laugh?"

"Yes." Paul's assent was barely audible. "I'd had my fill of that."

"And if someone saw this house and laughed, what would you feel?"

"Nothing. I wouldn't care."

"Now I will answer your question. I did not tell you the house was being built because, had you been here since the ground breaking, you would have worried over the placement of every joist and strut. You would have questioned every aspect of your design not once but a hundred times, and you never would have felt as certain of your talent as you do now. You'll watch the next one rise, and the next, and the scores that will follow."

"God! You tempt me!"

"Absolutely, and I assure you I've hardly begun. Now I will leave you alone with your masterpiece."

As Stephen turned to go, Paul called after him. "I suppose you know precisely how I feel at this moment?"

Stephen looked up at him with an unreadable expression. "Precisely? I suppose. When you're ready come out on the terrace and I'll show you the plans for the interior. Take your time."

In the sketches Stephen spread across a rough worktable, Paul saw fragments of his own concepts, a design made stark by the absence of color: walls rough white plaster; floors gray serena stone; the windows, skylights, and doors to the terrace pale topaz glass to screen the harsh rays of the sun without obstructing the view. On the interior walls of the huge, multipurpose lower room were wide ledges concealing lighting, as well as providing ample space for whatever display Elizabeth would wish to create.

"My cousin collects pottery and her taste runs colorful," Stephen explained. "Given what she owns and her needs for the windows, white is the only choice. This seating arrangement"—he pointed to a large sunken circle ringed with pillows—"is her design. The center of the circle will be as padded as most furniture, so a guest need only take a pillow and find a spot on the floor."

"It seems so informal."

"Elizabeth delights in making stuffy guests ill at ease with simple comforts." He gave brief details concerning the sketches for the dining room and kitchen, then flipped to a plan for the upper hall and stairs.

As Paul had hoped, the stairway remained untouched. "It would be a sacrilege to adorn something so dramatic, yes?" But in the open hallway Stephen had added long planters of white tile and concealed lighting to augment the narrow, slanted north-facing windows, which provided ventilation as well as light for the upper halls. Stephen mentioned the servant and guest rooms, the baths and kitchen, then concluded with the master bedroom.

The room was the antithesis of everything Paul had seen before . . . color upon raucous color beginning with the autumn-leaf window, the bronze-framed platform bed resting beneath it, the patterned terra-cotta floor, the abstract multicolored carpet.

Paul studied the sketch for some minutes, then said thoughtfully, "If one were to tour the finished house, this room would seem the most significant, as if the guest had suddenly discovered the many brilliant facets of the owner's soul." After one final glance at each sketch he rolled and tied them. "I'd like to meet my client. Is that possible?"

"Tomorrow. Tonight we have much to discuss. Would you have any objection to a night in the country. The family has a cottage farther up the Tagas. I use it often and there is an inn nearby known for its excellent food. You are hungry, yes?"

"Of course," Paul replied, thinking he should be hungry but captured once more by his creation. He looked over his shoulder often as they climbed the hill to the car.

A few yards from it, Stephen heard faint breathing and sniffed the unmistakable scent of danger. "Walk to the crest of the hill," he said to Paul. "I want to show you the view once more."

Without breaking the rhythm of his pace Stephen moved away from his body, studying the space around them, then spoke in a low conversational tone. "Pretend we discuss to-night's dinner and do not question what I tell you. There are eight armed men surrounding us. They intend to kill you and take me alive."

Kidnapping! The blood rushed from Paul's face and he was thankful it was nearly dark. "So what shall we do now?" he asked with a magnificently contrived chuckle.

"When we reach the rise, you'll see a pile of rocks to your left. When I tell you, run and crouch behind it."

"And you?"

"I'm going to the ditch on the other side of the road. Can you shoot?"

"Yes."

"Good. I'll toss you a gun."

Paul's fear grew with every step, but he felt an irrational confidence as well. Fate would not be so callous as to let him die now. Near the top he heard Stephen's order: "Run!"

Paul never had a chance. The move had been anticipated and a line of bullets ripped across the backs of his legs. He fell first to his knees, a perfect swaying target, until Stephen kicked him facedown in the dirt. As Stephen whirled toward his closest attacker an explosion not meant for him hurled him back on top of Paul. Fighting became impossible. Defense narrowed to survival.

Consciousness returned in layers . . . first a smell, dank and ancient, then words muffled by a ringing in his ears, last his body and its pain. Paul choked back a moan and listened.

"The one we wanted is as good as dead. The other won't survive long."

"Are you sure we shouldn't shoot them?"

"Don't bother with Austra. As for the other, the one who hired us may wish to question him. After a few days resting beside a corpse he'll say anything to get out of that hole. If he doesn't . . . '' The man laughed. The crunch of boots against stones grew softer. When Paul was certain he was alone, he opened his eyes to impenetrable darkness.

"God, no!" he said with a sob, recalling the agony when someone had rolled him over, the brush of cold metal against his neck . . . how pain had jarred him awake during the bumpy ride . . . and worse, far worse than the rest, how he had seen Stephen beside him, shreds of flesh on his hands and arms and, most horrible of all, his face. Blind, deformed, it was better if Stephen was dead or as good as dead. The last thought was too close to despair and low in its implication. "Stephen," Paul whispered to the darkness, expecting and receiving no reply. He moved an arm out hesitantly, fearful he would touch something or, alternately, nothing. He flinched when he brushed Stephen's sleeve, then moved his hand back out to find and softly cover his friend's . . . cold, sticky with blood, lifeless.

As if he were comforting a corpse, he squeezed that hand. Perhaps it was the shaking of his own that made him feel a faint response, but with uncertain hope he moved his fingers to Stephen's wrist and found a pulse . . . unnaturally slow but strong. Ignoring his own pain, Paul slid closer to Stephen and whispered his name.

As the body repaired, the mind held it deathly still, and both resented this interruption. Yet this creature must be warned; part of him cherished it and would prefer to not destroy it. It was dark here. He had not lost an alarming amount of blood. Perhaps . . . perhaps there was another way. His greed rose stronger and Paul sensed the mental command. —Don't touch me now.—

"What!" Paul pulled back and cried out in pain, his eyes straining to see in the blackness.

—I am deadly to you now. Move away from me.—

"I don't hear you!" In response Paul felt a stab of pain between his eyes, its intensity making that in his legs seem a minor irritation. "Stephen!" The word was broken, more a sob than a name.

—I am sorry.— A pause. —I am hungry. Move away from me.—

Paul bit his lips to keep from screaming, and the tears rolled down his face as he pulled quickly back. He could only retreat a few feet before he reached a damp stone wall of the cell.

—Silence!— Stephen's order; his own thought. Paul tried not to breathe, certain that had he lungs full of air he would scream in panic as his skin began to tingle from invisible charges whirling about him. Then he heard it, a faint rustling blasting the silence. He wrapped his arms around his head, wishing he could press his legs against his chest as the room filled with a nauseating reek of life . . . scurrying over his feet, gibbering, waiting, then squealing, as one by one they died. It ended as quickly as it had begun, the quiet broken only by a beat, impossibly quick, Paul's heart pounding in terror. His breathing became a ragged pant as the fear magnified in him—louder, faster, stronger—until, when hands closed around his arms, he screamed and made no sound.

—What are you! What in the name of God are you!—

Crystalline laughter filled his mind.—All you have ever feared.—

The hands moved, ripping open the collar of his shirt. Paul tried to struggle but his body was no longer his to command. "Please," he managed to whisper, "please."

No reply except the brush of fingers over his temples. —Twenty-six tiny lives were not enough. I need you, Paul.—

Paul turned his head sideways and back, his body obliging where his will would not.

—You will be a part of me. We will be together forever.—

Hours ago the world had been waiting for him, this demon attacking him had been his friend, and now . . .

—A part of me.— Lips brushed his cheek, the side of his neck. —Your ambitions are beautiful, your genius immense. I will build as a monument to you.—

Paul's will faded, then roared one final protest.—No! Damn you, no!— And a thought surfaced in the fear, a final cry for help . . . a name . . .

—Scream it. Scream it with me. Her name.—

——Elizabeth!!——

Chapter Nine

I

In a small coastal town near Nazare, Elizabeth Austra looked up from her dressing table, met her own eyes in the mirror, and tried to build another's face around them. "Stephen?" she mouthed anxiously, then shook her head. No, he was with that architect in Lisbon, too far away to touch. This wasn't danger, merely apprehension. Tonight had to go well for her.

A knock on her door interrupted her reverie, and without waiting for a response Melanie West popped in. "Are you ready? Oh! You look ravishing in that shade of blue . . . and the neckline! Hank would never let me be that daring! Ian will be speechless."

"I trust not."

Stephanie giggled. "Well, for a moment, anyway. I hope you don't mind a blind date?"

"Blind too?"

"How silly of me. Of course you haven't heard the term. It means an escort you haven't met. I think you'll like him. If you don't, you can say you have a headache and Hank and I will see you home."

As she walked downstairs with Melanie, Elizabeth studied the man standing in the foyer beside Hank West. An Adonis, this young American . . . this traitor . . . no, not a traitor, an imbecile like the rest. He was thinking he had to see the German ambassador later, carry the message of neutrality—and aid—from the American embassy in London.

When their eyes met, she began the game. Ah, yes! He was arrogant, experienced, demanding . . . all she preferred her lovers to be. Later he would suggest a discreet tryst, and she, with proper reluctance, would yield. She did not possess the full measure of Austra mental power and could not practice public espionage, but she had her own tricks and they rarely failed her. The American paid her some quick compliment and she laughed, thinking how fortunate she was that this one's messages were not written on paper . . . and that duty would hold such pleasant compensations.

He came straight from his meeting to her, slipping into her unlocked room. She poured him sherry, and as he stood in the center of the room he felt awkward and impatient.

"You meeting is done, *oui*?"

"Yes." He was prepared to explain he could reveal nothing but she asked nothing. Instead she blew out the lamp and pressed against his back, her hands unbuttoning his coat. He began to ask a question. "Shhh, *ami*. Don't speak. Sip your wine."

As his clothing fell to the floor, one piece after another, he focused on the meeting he'd just left, holding back his passion by recalling every small detail. "It will be over before we begin," he growled when he could not longer think of anything but the places her hands moved.

"No, *ami*. We have all night. And perhaps tomorrow?"

"Meetings," he mumbled.

"And tomorrow night?"

"You told me you were leaving."

"I've cabled Lisbon. I'm staying another day."

"I don't know. I'll have to . . ." The American's voice trailed off as she fell on her knees in front on him. And one more night in Nazare did not seem nearly long enough as her lips closed around him and her hands slid down his thighs.

II

Painful spasms in his legs roused Paul from a fitful sleep. His eyes opened to blindness, to the feel of someone leaning against his back. Bare arms enfolded him, legs pressed against his to hold them still; warmth flowed into him to battle the lethal chill. He brushed the hands and the top of the head resting on his shoulder and relaxed. Stephen's injury and what followed had been delerium, though too much of the rest had apparently been real.

Trying not to disturb Stephen's sleep, Paul ran his hands over his legs, feeling the strips of cloth binding his bullet wounds. He touched one spot too hard, hissed in his breath in pain, and caught in it a foul scent, the return of dread.

He silently endured the agony, until Stephen woke and moved away from him. Then he shifted his weight and moaned.

Stephen gripped his shoulders, a gesture of confidence in the dark. "You will be all right," Stephen said.

"Do you know where we are?"

Stephen's flat reply masked his own panic. "We are in the ruins of the D'Oscuro Fortress, in one of its lower dungeons. The space is approximately a nine-foot cube. The walls are stone. The door is a grating overhead. I have tried to force it but do not have the strength, and so we wait for someone to open it for us. As Stephen spoke, he automatically began to pace, then checked himself and knelt next to Paul.

"I heard a man say someone might be back, but that could have been a dream along with the rest. It must have been a dream because afterward you . . ." As Paul spoke, his hand moved to his shirt collar, to the empty place where the top two buttons should have been, and his mouth formed a silent *oh* of understanding.

"It was no dream, Paul."

"Even your attack on me?"

"A necessary lie." —We called for help, remember?—

To forget became impossible. "The rats?"

"All too real." Stephen shuddered, not from their memory but at what would have occurred had they not inhabited the fortress in such abundance. When injuries were so great, need could not be ignored . . . not for friendship, not even love.

Paul stared into the darkness, the next question seeming the greatest absurdity and totally unavoidable. "What did you do to them?"

"I took their lives, drank their blood so that I might live."

Paul swallowed hard, thankful his stomach was empty.

"Your disgust is natural, but consider: The rats were preferable to you, yes?"

If Stephen meant that as a joke, Paul missed the humor. Instead he said with reluctant awe, "They sat and waited."

"Of course. Had it been you rather than they, had you been able to run and the means to escape this place, you still would have done the same."

So Paul remembered—and more. "At your house that morning after Gianni died, you used me, damn you!"

His hand shot forward and Stephen caught it palm to palm, gripping it as friends grip hands while he replied, "I did that so today you would know I am no monster. I gave you more than I took, yes?"

Paul rested his head on his outstretched arm. Challenge, confidence, inspiration; only the swiftly passing vertigo had been unpleasant. Curiosity overpowered his anger, and drawing Stephen closer, Paul ran hands over his face. "Your eyes . . . they were gone, and your chin . . . Oh, God! It's as if the wounds had never happened."

An impossible conclusion began to form, and in response Stephen said anxiously, "No, I am no vampire, no demon . . . nor am I the man you believed me to be."

"Let's have the discussion you promised, Stephen," Paul said with volatile calm. He sensed Stephen's presence as a faint current in his mind, questioning endurance and resolve, and though he felt neither, he knew he'd go mad if he didn't learn the truth. "Why not? It's what you planned to do tonight, isn't it?" Paul managed a hoarse chuckle. "We'll never have a more opportune time than the present."

"Or worse surroundings." Feeling Paul's natural protest, Stephen quickly added, "Claustrophobia is a family curse, and for you there's the darkness and the pain." He hesitated briefly, then reached the only conclusion. "My mind cannot remain here. If you yield your will to me, I will show you my world and we can escape this nightmare for a little while.''

"Dreams like we shared the morning after Gianni died?"

"Yes, though not all will be so pleasant."

Such vivid illusions; so almost-real.

—And this will be the same.—

"Please. That way."

Paul had made the right choice, not from bravery but from a passion to understand. Stephen debated how much to tell, deciding to be more candid than he'd planned. If Paul was here when the assassins returned, he must be prepared. "I will sit behind you. Touching simplifies our merging."

Paul detected the deceit. "Admit the truth. You're keeping me warm, aren't you?" He heard Stephen's whispered assent and a feeling of unquestionable optimism filled him, banishing all doubts. Stephen's arms circled his body, crossing on his chest, hands meeting hands, twining as if in shared prayer.

"Close your eyes.''—Quiet your thoughts, as if you were preparing for sleep . . . perfect . . . perfect . . . yes! I move within you. . . .—

It began as a gentle floating, then a wind roared through Paul's mind, tearing away memories . . . years, centuries, millennia gone in an instant.

In the beginning there was emptiness, then a presence . . . life giving death, marveling at the delicious beauty of the night, surprised by the burning of the angry sun . . . that first clash of intelligences astonishing, the inevitable bloody outcome instilling no horror, for Paul's thoughts were Stephen's thoughts, soft-focused visions of visions known in the wordless way their history flowed one to the other.

Paul pressed tightly against Stephen, seeking some anchor as century upon century rolled past. Scenes sharpened at Stephen's birth, and for a time he saw the world through a child's eyes.

Then the history of the family merged with that of the world: persecutions dangerous, sometimes deadly . . . retaliations glorious . . . all interspersed with the pure ecstasy of creation, of cathedrals rising as monuments to God and to those who built them. They tumbled from that dark and golden age into the present, the conclusion obvious before Stephen spoke the words. "Mankind has made us more than we were. Your race has given life to our souls, your visions are our creativity."

Paul considered how patiently he'd been taught, how eagerly he'd struggled to compete, and what little experience could be acquired in a human lifetime. He felt joy, as if an unjust burden had been lifted from him. "All those pensions, they're named after the churches you helped build, aren't they?"

"I and my family, yes."

"You are so human."

"And so forever separate. Our aspirations have changed, but our natures are immutable and deadly. We are not so different from the vampires of your legends, yes?"

Paul stopped the automatic denial. "Yes," he said, and unwound his fingers from Stephen's with exaggerated care.

"I know your thoughts, Paul. Don't be concerned with gestures."

"And if my thoughts were filled with fear or worse, what would you do?"

"Once we left here I would take this memory from you, and we would go back to Chaves. There I would teach you with meticulous civility, looking through you and mourning you as if you were dead."

"I don't want that."

"So I had hoped from the moment you walked so timidly into my office."

The preparation for this day had proceeded so carefully . . . one test flowing naturally into the next, his talent only one trait to be considered, his discretion and loyalty of equal importance. He considered the way Stephen had manipulated him and asked, "Why have you made such an effort for me?"

"I admit I ignored you at first because you kept applying for a position in the glasshouse or in design, and you had no experience with either. But when an unforeseen difficulty arose, I remembered your persistent correspondence, as well as the letters others wrote on your behalf. All revealed your integrity, and in your own I noted a rare sense of wonder. I sent for your drawings and after Savatier and I studied them I sent for you. It appears I was not wrong."

"I'm still confused."

Stephen sat beside him. "Were we at my cottage on the Tagas, I would pour you a glass of wine and say 'Congratulations, Paul. Savatier is retiring at the end of this year. His position is yours if you want it.' "

"What!"

"I said I'd tempt you."

"I can't. I . . . I'm too young."

"There are whole weeks when you run the studio. You're ready, and should you take the position you'll have time to grow into it. A world at war hardly thinks about building. Afterward the survivors will have little taste for busy granite monuments. The lines of buildings will be stripped bare of all but function, and few designers will handle that simplicity well. There will be a need for your talent, Paul."

Dreams of the future were held in check by the present. "It's absurd to discuss anything when I may not be alive tomorrow."

"Would you prefer to contemplate the absence of water or the sudden dearth of rats?"

At that sharp reminder Paul swallowed, tasting grit and thirst, and paid full attention to Stephen's next words. "What you heard the men discuss was true. They'll be back to question you. I want you away from here before they arrive. The next battle belongs to me."

"Will you kill them?" Paul asked with obvious distress.

"Stephen Austra was dead; now he lives and is unharmed. I have no choice, even if I wished to make one. And I don't. That's a part of my nature too." He laid a hand on Paul's shoulder. "The explosion that injured me was meant for you, and the only reason you are not lying here with a bullet in your head is because I prevented it."

And Stephen wouldn't be here if he hadn't paused to push Paul out of the line of fire. "I told you I know how to use a gun. If I'm strong enough to help, I will." He hesitated then, trying to hide the fear in his voice, asked, "Are you sure they're coming?"

"They will come and I will win. If I had any doubt of this I would not have let them lock me in here, not even to save your life. In a thousand years my instincts have never failed me. Yes, they're coming."

"When?"

"Today, tomorrow, a few days at the latest. Compulsions require subtlety, and in the meantime there are your legs."

Stephen's reminder made Paul's pain intensify. "Tell me how they look."

"The bullets are out and the wounds bled well. I think your right leg will heal, but the joint on the left has been shattered. I'm no doctor, but I think that even with the finest reconstruction it will always be stiff. I'm sorry."

Stephen's sincerity was infuriating, but before Paul spoke, the anger—envy, only envy—dissipated. Paul stared into the darkness, the absence of sight sharpening his intuition. "You haven't finished. Go on."

"Scraps of my shirt are a poor substitute for antiseptics and bandages. If an infection occurs, and in this place it's likely, you may lose both your legs or worse. Then we must add the hunger and thirst . . . yours and mine."

"The rats weren't enough, were they?"

"No."

Days! Paul hugged his elbows for comfort. "Do you suppose we should send a second call to Elizabeth?"

"I was about to suggest it, yes."

"Then pick whatever unpleasantness you wish and get on with it."

"Very well. Lie against me." His fingers circled Paul's wrists.

In a moment Paul was screaming. Agony, like fear, carried well.

III

Four times they joined and soared, the first remembered, the pain of the others discarded in the memories that followed them. Paul became lost in places he'd never seen, conversed with men he'd only read about. Their voices! Their thoughts! He watched the vaultings rise at Notre Dame, saw the west and north roses as they had looked before time destroyed and man rebuilt. He saw it all with heightened intensity . . . Stephen's memories, as perfect as his senses.

* * *

At other times he shared his friend's watchfulness, caught
in a point not up but out, flowing through his surroundings,
feeling rather than seeing every rock, every tree. They had
sensed life, too small for anything save voracious panic, and
once larger prey, but the gates to the fortress had been closed.
Yes, there was hunger . . . accept, control . . . dissolve, dissolve.
—Do you think of me?—
—Always and never, Paul.—

On Saturday afternoon two children were playing the fields
well beyond any ordered summons. Stephen pushed, and too
young to be intrigued, they ran home in fright. Later it rained,
the slow drizzle turning to a steady downpour, but by then
Stephen had retreated, sparing them both the torment of
touching what they could not have.
When Stephen wearied of his mental wandering, Paul slept,
caught in dreams of his own devising, waking often to the
sound of footsteps around him . . . padding from one corner
to the next, soft and confident in the dark. At times Paul
could disregard them, at others he would dwell on the fact
that his friend could see while he was blind; had healed to
perfection while he sat wounded; would live . . . no! Don't
think of that, not yet. As he grew weaker he stopped thinking
altogether and slipped back and forth between sleep and un-
consciousness.

Chapter Ten

I

SAMUELSON ARRIVED IN the capital late Sunday afternoon. He stopped first at the building site, then at Elizabeth's. Finding her house deserted, he began making inquiries. Two hours later he was playing poker with the three likely assassins, drinking and losing heavily.

"He pays me a bloody fortune to handle security, then wanders off alone with some American who's only been on the staff for a few months. I don't trust that innocent type, especially since his father is a government man. Used to be a vice-consul or something."

Tomas Alvas paused, feigning concern over his next wager. "Why would the Americans have any interest in Austra?"

"He doesn't pay me to know a damned thing, just to keep an eye on him and that bloody firm. Then he disappears, the stupid fool." His disgusted look mirrored precisely how he felt, and waving his cigar, he signaled a waiter. "Another round?" Without waiting for a reply he bellowed the order.

"I doubt anyone would want to kill him, though there's plenty who'd think about trying for a ransom, or so I hear," Alvas said. "Wait. He'll either show up or you'll get a note demanding money." Samuelson listened intently, his stare glassy and his mouth hanging open as if he planned to swallow and digest every word without any mental effort. "Have you been out to the building site?"

"At dusk. No sign of a struggle by the car. I decided to wait until morning for a good look around."

"That's wise. You might have missed something."

Not your interest or your relief, Samuelson thought as the game continued.

Edmundo Costa dealt the next hand, and by the time they'd finished it the drinks had arrived. As they played, Samuelson appeared increasingly worried. "I suppose I ought to tell Elizabeth Austra her cousin is missing, but I can't even find the bitch."

"There's a reception at the American embassy. She might be there," Alvas volunteered, hoping Samuelson would leave.

"You don't say?" Samuelson downed his drink in one gulp and threw in his cards. "I forfeit. Thanks for the tip, though I don't enjoy being the one to break the news."

"He makes me sick," Jão Rables said after Samuelson had left.

"Of course. But he's useful. Consider all we learned." Alvas lowered his voice and turned to Costa. "You might be right about the architect, Edmundo."

"*Sim.* I was thinking he must be getting lonely. Perhaps we should ride out later and inquire about his health."

"Let him die," Rables said. He had no taste for torture.

Costa laughed. "We would have gotten five thousand dollars to take Austra alive, but only two for his corpse. Suppose the architect is as valuable, eh? Maybe we could start our own network . . . a steady flow of information and income." He waved toward the door. "Here's Manolo, we can take his car."

Rables collected the cards. "I'll go, but I want you to kill the man when you're through."

"You're too merciful," Costa said, "but I promise you he'll be dead when we leave, if he's not dead already."

II

The uneasy feeling that had plagued Elizabeth all weekend intensified when Ernst Bradley entered the embassy ballroom, walking toward her as if she were the only person in it. As he politely took her hand she touched his mind, her gay words masking her concern at the wisps of thought she detected, the reek of triumph that hung around him, and the sinister twist to his fatherly smile.

Later she would arrange time alone with him, but now there were a number of new arrivals she was anxious to meet. The crowd around her thickened; the two Americans who had flown in from New York were vying for her attention when the butler led her aside and informed her George Samuelson wished to speak with her.

"Tell him to come in, then." Her voice, though not loud, carried and held a hint of distaste.

"He wishes to see you in private."

"Very well." She turned to her escort. "Come with me, Henny. If it's important, you may be able to help. If not, we will make George come in for champagne. The British are so amusing when they are drinking, *oui*?" The group around her laughed and she turned and said to Bradley, "Excuse us, Ernst. When we come back, you can tell me why you look like the cat who swallowed the tiny bird."

"You see right through me, Elizabeth," Bradley said.

Samuelson met them in the lavish anteroom, holding his hat in his hand, anxious to be off once more. He greeted Heinrich Schoofs, then addressed Elizabeth. "I would prefer to speak with you alone." He added privately,—A damned German agent. Get rid of him!—

Elizabeth gave no indication that she'd heard his mental comment. Instead she rested a hand on Schoofs' arm. "Don't go, Henny." As she spoke the words she asked Samuelson, —May we speak around him?—

—We can try. — "This is quite serious."

"If this is serious, you must have a drink." Samuelson began to protest but Elizabeth ignored him. "Henny, they keep brandy in the cabinet. Would you pour poor George a glass?"

As Schoofs moved away, Samuelson explained in a low tone, "Stephen came down to Lisbon on Friday with that architect, Stoddard. They seem to have vanished."

"Vanished?"

"Stephen's car was found near the site of your house. Two jackets were in it but there was no sign of either man."

—And a good deal of blood on the ground, some of it Stephen's, shells and signs of an explosion.—

Schoofs handed Samuelson a glass and laid a hand on Elizabeth's shoulder. Elizabeth covered it with her own and looked back at Samuelson. "Do you suppose someone is holding him for ransom or could this be the Communists again?" She said the last words reluctantly, as if the thought were too horrible to consider.

Samuelson looked ready to strangle her. "Leftists?" Schoofs asked. "Why would those fanatics have any interest in him?"

Elizabeth waved her hands in an expansive gesture of frustration. "They think he's a Nazi sympathizer."

"That's preposterous!"

"They're not the only ones, Henny. SIS had the whole family investigated. Is that not so, George?"

Samuelson nodded.

"I am sorry to hear this, Elizabeth," Schoofs said sincerely. "Would you like me to take you home?"

"Yes. Thank you, Henny. You are a help already."

As he went to retrieve Elizabeth's cape Schoofs stopped to whisper a few words to Bradley, who then waited for her at the front door. "Are you leaving us so soon, Elizabeth?" Bradley asked.

"My cousin may have been kidnapped."

Bradley held out his arms and she melted into them. "I am so sorry, Elizabeth," he said.

"Your presence would be a comfort tonight, Ernst."

"Of course I'll come." He held her like a daughter, only an instant too long.

Bradley and Schoofs shared Elizabeth's open car while Samuelson followed in the American's consumptive Ford. As he drove, George hummed bawdy Navy songs. By the time they arrived at Elizabeth's she'd know a great deal more about what had occurred. But as she said good night to him outside her door and told him what little she'd learned, he found he'd been optimistic.

As expected, Schoofs knew nothing of the abduction. As for Bradley, most of his conclusions were clearly wrong.

George decided to follow up on his earlier lead, but when he got to the tavern, Costa and the others were gone. He returned to Elizabeth's a little after midnight and waited in the shadows. After the two agents left, he joined her in her library, where she paced anxiously.

"I stayed last night in Nazare. If I had been here . . ." She sank into her desk chair. *"Na'szekornes."*

"Where he survives is the question, Elizabeth."

She folded her hands beneath her chin and looked down at her empty desk. "He was seriously hurt and is near where he was captured. There is no one guarding him and he is in a remote location. Stoddard is with him."

"How do you know they're together?"

"If Stephen could fight, he would have killed them all. If not, they wouldn't have bothered to lock his cell door. If Stephen had a guard to control, he'd be free. Simple logic, *oui*?" She pulled a map from her desk drawer and spread it out on a table. "There are isolated ruins—here, here, and here—with intact cells beneath them."

Samuelson leaned over her shoulder, catching as he did the scent of her straightened, bobbed hair, so similar to Rachel's. "This one," he suggested. "It's not as close to the site but the area is the most remote. I'm driving out there."

Elizabeth pushed herself to her feet. "I'll go with you."

III

Paul's body shook him awake, and he licked his lips, his tongue unable to moisten them. The footsteps stopped and a hand brushed his forehead.

"Why didn't you tell me your fever was rising?"

"You're going to do something about it?" Paul attempted to laugh and coughed instead. "Besides, I didn't want to interrupt your eternal constitutional." He began to push himself into a sitting position but, when he raised his head, decided to lay back down. "Have we reached Monday yet?" He held up his arm so Stephen could see his watch and was frightened at how terribly it trembled.

"It's an hour after midnight. I'm glad you're awake."

"Let me guess. We're going on the air again."

The assent was filled with apology.

"I can't."

"We meet the morning; today is given us."

You said that yesterday. At your age you should have acquired a better stock of clichés."

"Today you're leaving here."

"I know."

Stephen slapped him just hard enough to startle.

Paul turned toward where Stephen had been sitting. "Show some respect for the dying." The next slap came from a different direction. "Listen, you damned immortal . . ."

Laughter. —Too weak, did you say?—

Paul tried to hit back, screaming as he jarred his shattered leg.

—Too weak?—

Paul swung again. Stephen grabbed him, pushing him down. "Your anger at me is trivial. Consider those who left us here. Consider those who would—"

"You, damn you! They would have shot me but you stopped them, and I know why. I feel you staring at me in the dark, circling me like a scavenger. Only I'm no good to you dead, am I? I'm only good if you kill me, so why don't you just get it over with, you damned bloodsucker! Come on, devour me!"

—Thank you, Paul.—

Their anger burned through the walls and flared into the night. . . .

—Stop!—

Samuelson barely had a chance to brake the car before Elizabeth gripped his arm, sending a crude response that left him with his head resting against the steering wheel, panting and weak with panic. Elizabeth was composed and thoughtful. "D'Oscuro," she said.

"That's . . . twenty-five . . . miles." Samuelson caught his breath and swung the car around. "The trip must have taken at least an hour."

"N'importe." Elizabeth stared absently at the passing countryside. "The architect. What is he like?"

"Remarkable discretion for a child. He follows Stephen about like a puppy."

"Did you see the house he built for me?"

"I walked through it."

"No child built that."

They worship talent, Samuelson thought. Any talent would do, even his own.

Elizabeth caught wisps of his thoughts. "My apologies," she said when he glanced her way. "I spend too many hours with my mind stretched to its limits to retreat completely, even with friends. You think of Rachel, *oui*?"

"And Stephen and you. Also of Denys in Greece, Phillip in Vienna, all of you."

"We do only what we choose."

And pay the price. Samuelson concentrated on his driving, contemplating how, for one so cautious, Stephen had been capable of such stupidity.

IV

Tonight there were no visions. Paul returned to the darkness, leaning against Stephen. "I'm sorry. I didn't mean any of it."

"I asked for your anger, Paul." In response Stephen felt tears moisten his chest. "Elizabeth heard us. She and George are coming."

"I know." Paul began to sob openly, tried to stop, and found it impossible. "This is ridiculous."

"This is hope. Yield to it. You can afford to lose the moisture now."

"You're so practical. I know, *szekorny*. No, that's wrong."

"Too desperate on the final rise. That's unavoidable, I suppose." They sat together without speaking until Stephen pulled back and stiffened.

"What?" Paul exclaimed as a loud clang sounded above them. "They got here so soon?"

"No. Four of our jailers have returned. You know what to

do.'' The sound of voices descended through the grate. Paul nodded, thankful their speed gave him so little time to think.

Stephen moved into the corner of their cell, hooking fingers and feet into cracks on the wall and ceiling, hanging facedown above the floor. He'd planned this retaliation well, piling the rats and what rubble he'd found in a corner and covering all with a thin layer of dirt to make it appear Paul had buried him in a shallow grave. The precautions were probably unnecessary, but Stephen would take no chances. He relaxed his control and let his hunger rise. Paul, feigning sleep, marveled at how anyone could venture within the fortress walls and not feel death waiting.

A soft light danced across the walls of the corridor above them, and when the lantern was lowered, Paul moaned, then opened his eyes, quickly shutting them against the blinding glare. ''Help,'' he mouthed.

At the sight of Paul's bandages and the mound in the corner, Costa whistled in admiration. ''A real survivor you are.'' He pulled the lantern back, undid the lock, and lifted the grate. When his feet were a few inches off the floor, he heard a low, lethal snarl and saw a flash of motion. His ribs were crushed before he slammed against the side of the cell, then he slid to the ground, where, still conscious, he fought for every breath. Costa's hand inched toward the gun tucked in his belt. ''Who?'' he asked.

''You didn't kill him,'' Paul said triumphantly. ''You can't. No one can.''

—Here.—

A revolver was tossed to Paul with painful accuracy. He aimed it at the man dying in front of him. ''Don't move.''

Costa ignored him, his hand closing around his weapon's handle, drawing it out slowly. ''Don't move,'' Paul repeated.

Costa raised his arm. His motion seemed infinitely slow to Paul; his face, lit from above, a mask of hollows and ridges of hate and pain. He was aiming when the screams began above them. Both started. Both fired, two shots merging into one huge blast. With no interruption the screams continued. . . .

V

Elizabeth remained in seclusion all week but held her Friday evening social as planned. Only Bradley and Schoofs knew of Stephen's abduction. Both came . . . Bradley to observe and Schoofs to offer what comfort he could. The two arrived together, each attempting to have a moment alone with Elizabeth and finding it impossible to separate her from the lively group she always attracted. The quick movements of her arms under the flowing sleeves of her silk kimono made her resemble some exotic butterfly in flight. Schoofs beamed as he listened to her provide the group with a description of her new house. All must be well, he decided. After Bradley disappeared into her library, she took him aside and confirmed this.

Bradley closed the library doors behind him, expecting to meet Elizabeth and learn the sad news of no news. Instead Stephen Austra entered by the rear door and held out his hand.

The American's recovery was immediate, but his palm was cold and moist. "I see you have come to no harm," Bradley said, looking down at his fingers, resting against Stephen's ruby ring. Bradley guessed it cost more than he could earn in half a decade.

"Money purchases a great many things." Stephen motioned Bradley to the seat in front of the desk. "I promised my would-be abductors that no word of my release would be given to anyone until today. I believe that, as your movies say, they wanted to skip town."

"I'm surprised you didn't break your word, considering it was given under duress."

"They might have escaped in any event and, were they to ever abduct another of my family, might recall that I broke my promise. No, the Austras have an established reputation for honoring these agreements, and I would not wish to see it besmirched merely for petty vengeance."

"I see. And did you ever discover who paid them to abduct you?"

"I asked, of course, but they would not say. Wise men, yes?"

"Infinitely." A momentary hesitation. "But why are you telling me this?"

"I believe the time has come to be blunt with each other. You are the head of an independent and highly effective group of German agents. I am apparently suspected of being a Nazi sympathizer, so it seems wise to ask you to find the one desirous of killing me. I will pay you for that service." He pulled an envelope out of the desk and extended it to Bradley. "Will five thousand dollars be a sufficient advance?"

Again Bradley was struck by Austra's aristocratic manner of flaunting wealth. The assassins must have been well paid . . . doubly paid, Bradley thought as he stared avidly at the envelope, still not certain he should reach for it.

Stephen's laughter was intentionally grating. "If you wish to deny your position, I could use Osten or Hemmit or even Schoofs, but you are their superior. You will succeed where they might fail." He laid the envelope on the table in front of Bradley, his fingers beating on it, the ruby ring flashing as he continued. "I have only two stipulations. I wish to be given proof and to have the person responsible for these attempts delivered to me in Chaves, alive and unharmed."

"Alive?"

"And unharmed. Vengeance may be petty, Ernst, but it is wonderfully satisfying."

Only a quick recollection that he was not the quarry kept Bradley from paling. "And the payment?"

"Ah, better! Negotiable, of course, but let us say this advance is ten percent. And I am prepared to be generous with you in other ways as well, but I will pay nothing for damaged goods and I will deal solely with you. You understand me, yes?"

Bradley nodded and pocketed the money. When they joined the party outside, he felt for the first time that he belonged in Elizabeth's palatial home as he savored with private delight the benefits of the bargain he'd just struck.

This plan would require all his skill, small pieces from a multitude of contacts. Alive and unharmed would mean nothing then. The victim could scream whatever truths or lies he wished and they'd be ignored. Sensing the possibility of a trap, he knew he must be certain those he had paid to abduct Stephen had lied to Stephen, as well as to himself.

Elizabeth stood in her foyer waiting for him. "There you are!" she said happily when he walked over to her from the library. "Have you been to see my house yet?"

"No, but I've heard it's as magnificent as its owner."

"You flatter me, *mon ami*." She kissed him on the cheek and said, "The architect is so ill. He was shot, you know."

"Stephen didn't mention that. Will he be all right?"

"Perhaps. It was fortunate for him that Stephen was not harmed."

"I don't understand."

Her voice fell to a whisper. "Stephen says I am not to say, but I will tell you. The assassins held a gun to Paul's head and asked if he had any last words. Of course he could think of none, so Stephen supplied them."

"What did he say?"

"Fifty thousand dollars." She laughed and patted his hand. "They didn't think to bargain."

And he had paid three thousand dollars for Austra's death! He consoled himself by thinking such a large amount of money would make the assassins easy to trace. His eyes shifted to the main room, and as he watched Stephen circulate through the crowd, his hunter-green slacks and vest elaborately beaded in jade and garnet, Bradley considered the irony of plucking the peacock who had played him for a fool.

Chapter Eleven

London
February 1939

I

LONDON NIGHTS WERE dreary in late winter, with fog so thick that Blackwell walked to nearby destinations. Arriving home from an evening with his mother at the opera, he was shaking the water off his hat and reaching for the hallway light when, with an awareness stemming from the constant expectation of danger, he sensed he was not alone.

He moved away from the front door and into the shadows, his right hand slipping beneath his coat to the revolver he now carried constantly. In his study a light switched on. "Blast it!" he swore when he saw Ann. "One of these days I'm going to shoot you."

She wore a deep bronze gown beneath a hooded cape of red fox. One of her hands rested on an abstract sculpture by Stephen Austra, which he had purchased for far more than he could afford because its exquisite delicacy reminded him of her and because he'd expected she'd be pleased to see something from her family in his possession. However, this was the first time she gave any indication of noticing it, and that only in how her tapering fingers caressed its fragile turns. "How is the admiral, Harry?"

Though his superior's injuries were a well-kept secret, he'd long since learned the futility of denying anything she knew. "Recovering. The men he surprised were thieves, not killers."

"I'm glad to hear it."

"Is he why you came to London?"

"No. Earlier tonight I represented the firm at the dedication of the new wing of the British Museum."

"I thought your uncle planned to attend," he said petulantly. The empty seat beside his tonight had been meant for her, and the grilling his mother had given him in Ann's absence hadn't improved his disposition.

She looked past him to a sun-washed landscape by Corot, preparing for a lengthy reply, apparently thought better of it, and answered, "It would be difficult for him at this time." She gave Blackwell a long, penetrating look. "You and the admiral have kept your end of our agreement, haven't you?"

Shocked by the doubt in her voice, he declared, "We have."

"I believe you, Harry." Her next words were spoken quickly, as if she were embarrassed by her question. "I hadn't intended to disturb you tonight, but I discovered something you'll want to know immediately." She handed him a sheet of his own writing paper. "Here are the names of the men who arranged the theft of the admiral's files. Below them are the thieves hired to commit the crime, what they were paid, and a few additional details."

Three names headed the list. One Blackwell had expected. Another was the admiral's nephew and the third a baron well respected in the House of Lords. When he scanned the other names on the list, his only surprise was that the attempt had failed.

"It's an awkward situation, Harry, but I assure you the facts are correct."

"Awkward indeed!" he muttered, staring down at the paper and considering the consequences should this information ever be made public.

"May I stay the night?"

"Of course," he said mechanically, still looking at the sheet.

Ann picked up a book from the desk, noting the page before closing it. "Good night, Harry." She kissed him on the cheek and he watched her back as she left the room and climbed the town-house stairs, her heels making soft clicks on the wood floor. He stared at the empty foyer until he heard the opening and closing of the guest-room door, then returned to the information, memorizing it before depositing the paper in his safe. He believed her. He might be the only one who would.

He made a final check of the window locks, fastened the dead bolts on the doors, and went to bed. Sleep eluded him, the names of the men on Ann's list occupying all this thoughts. He began plotting a subtle assault until, hearing the clock strike two, he got up and poured an inch of brandy in the bottom of a snifter. Returning to bed, he sipped it slowly while he contemplated Ann.

Though rumors of their alleged affair had spread throughout London, in private she was far from the mistress he wished she would be. But every time Ann slept here, or he at Alpha, he would wake the following morning, vaguely disoriented and ravenously hungry. And there were the dreams . . . at times vivid images of the war, at others visions so erotic that he would wake hot and trembling and convinced the woman meant to drive him mad. If it hadn't been for the marks on the back of his neck (scratched from her nails, no doubt), her musky perfume lingering on the pillow, and that one night at Alpha, he might have dismissed these occurrences as frustration or a nightly purging from what had become an increasingly dangerous profession. In more peaceful times her actions would have disturbed him. Now they seemed an amusing diversion from the approaching war.

Curious, he'd gone so far as to arrange an appointment under his usual alias with a noted psychiatrist. After hearing the story the doctor had said with a smirk he didn't try to hide, "You are describing a succubus."

"I am describing a woman," Blackwell had retorted coldly.

The doctor adjusted his bifocals and recovered his professional demeanor. "Then let me give you some advice. She cannot hypnotize you if you are asleep, so if you wish to cease your participation in these nightly . . . ah, acts, simply refuse to cooperate after she wakes you."

"I would if I had the opportunity."

"Mr. Harris, did you ever consider that not recalling what you do with this woman alleviates a great deal of guilt?"

"There is nothing to be guilty about," Blackwell had snapped, aware that the appointment had been an embarrassing mistake. But the doctor did provide him with a list of books and articles, excellent though not particularly enlightening, about his situation.

Now Blackwell looked down at the amber liquid in his glass and recalled what he had read. Intoxication, one of the articles had noted, made it more difficult for a subject to be hypnotized. Might it have been the factor that made the encounter at Alpha more memorable than the rest? Heartened, he finished the remnant of liquid in his glass, gulped a quarter of the bottle as quickly as he was able, and soon fell genuinely asleep.

He sensed the hall light turned off, his bedroom door close, bare feet padding toward his bed—then, for a time, nothing.

As they had that first night, his emotions flared and he became lost in an unfocused, rapturous dream. He felt a pleasant vertigo, as if he had broken free of his body and was floating happily above it. He traveled back to it by the sound of its quick breathing, the palpable waves of passion flowing from it. He imagined his bed and it took form beneath him. He imagined his fingers and felt the sheets. He imagined Ann, her hair brushing his chest, and he returned to his body with a tangible snap. He startled her, and as her confidence faded, so did her mental control.

Twisting her around so she was pinned beneath him, he gloated over his first triumph in this puzzling affair. "I warned you," he said with sinister good humor, "but you didn't listen. Now it appears you have two choices. You can admit it is more pleasant to be in bed with a man who is awake, or you can fight. Either way the ending will be the same."

No, Ann thought, the ending might be far worse than Harry could ever imagine. Rachel could stop this absurdity with a word or a painful mental thrust, but it would be years before Ann matured into that power . . . perhaps centuries, perhaps never. Her arms tensed instinctively, preparing for the fight and the kill. She forced them to relax and considered that, after all, she had invited this. With Harry's guard raised, she didn't know if he was serious, but for his sake she dared not test him. Instead she turned her head sideways and said with obvious distaste, "You're drunk, Harry."

"Deliberately."

So her only choices were to agree or to give him up. Could

she make love to him without him noticing she was not an ordinary woman? The darkness encouraged her. She decided to try. "Let me take off my dress. I promise you, I won't leave."

Ann was standing beside the bed undoing the buttons on her bodice when she saw Harry reach for the light. Her hand closed around his wrist. "Please leave it off."

Her body was invisible beside him. "How did you know what I was doing?" he asked.

"I heard you move." She undressed quickly, slipping into bed and running her hand up his side. He tried to kiss her, but she turned her head sideways and said, "I don't drink. The taste of brandy is unpleasant to me."

His lips brushed her cheek. "I'll have to acquire some vodka."

"You won't need it anymore."

He stored the comment for later inquiry. Now he was too busy exploring her; finding the skin on her arms, her legs, even her hands, as smooth as that on the underside of her breasts. If he had frightened her, she gave no indication but lay passive instead, giving permission to him but not to herself. He almost wished she'd push him away or say some word of negation, anything to end this farce. When she didn't, he ended it as quickly as possible and afterward reflected that the dreams had been a far greater delight.

II

Blackwell's investigation began with the most inconsequential information Ann had provided. During the weeks that followed, he meticulously assembled proof that the thieves Ann named were guilty, but he could find no evidence linking the three most powerful men to those who had carried out their orders. As he worked, he became aware of an unavoidable conclusion—someone was watching him, someone close by.

Papers were missing from work files, orders he should have received were lost, and once someone ransacked his office desk. Of course there were spies in the SIS, but the information stolen from him made no sense. This new problem only heightened his preoccupation with the admiral's case.

Ann visited him in March, remaining anxiously in his foyer. He hadn't seen her since the night he'd caught her in his bedroom. He walked toward her, intending to embrace her and apologize, but she shook her head and backed up a step. "I can't stay. I came to ask you to go to Lisbon and find George Samuelson. Tell him I sent you, then ask him what has happened to my uncle. . . . No, I can't explain, only to say that whatever occurs, please believe I am still your ally." She handed him an envelope and left before he could question her.

The envelope contained a brief angry letter to Ann, written a month earlier by her uncle; and another, dated a week later, ordering Ann to cut off all contact with the SIS. Blackwell requested a leave of absence and flew to Lisbon, where he arranged a meeting with Samuelson at a local café.

When Blackwell arrived at the café, he found Samuelson sprawled at a prominently placed table, playing cards with three other men, including Ernst Bradley, whose activities were well known to the SIS. After being introduced to the table and, through the volume of Samuelson's voice, to the rest of the café's patrons, Blackwell suggested they speak somewhere in private, perhaps the next day.

"So it's like that, is it?" Samuelson turned to the men with him. "Excuse us. I'll be back."

At a more secluded table Blackwell ordered coffee and cream for himself and another drink for Samuelson and explained why he had come. "Ann is not to see me, to phone me, or to write me. She suggested I ask you why."

"Well, it's clear, isn't it? You've been screwing the girl. Maybe someone doesn't like it." Samuelson's expression was smug, as if this were far from the reason and they both knew it.

"Listen, it would be better if we talked. . . ."

"Devil take it! You'll speak here and now!" Samuelson's voice had risen once more, and Blackwell noticed Bradley studying them from behind his cards.

Blackwell decided his wisest course of action would be to leave. He started to stand but Samuelson gripped his arm. "Listen, Mr. Harris, or whatever in the hell your name is, I've nothing against you, so I'll give you a warning. If you look too closely into the actions of my employer, you'll find yourself floating facedown in the Tagas." He leaned forward in his chair, as if he were about to supply something confidential, but he spoke no more softly. "Just don't expect any Crown loyalty from me. The bloody SIS gave me a fine choice . . . resign or be let go. Fifteen years of service, wounded twice, and barely a pension. But now I get, and in return I give. You remember that."

Samuelson took a large swallow of his drink, spilling an equal amount when he slammed it down and rose unsteadily to his feet. He pulled back his coat to reveal a narrow leather sheath and the handle of a knife, and said in a softer voice, "There are wolves all around you. I suggest you leave before you're bitten." He spun, his hand pushing momentarily against the table for support, then, after a fast word to Bradley, he left.

Blackwell stared after him, hiding his admiration. The SIS had lost a damned good man eighteen years ago because, Blackwell was certain, Samuelson was completely sober and this act had not been intended for him.

Blackwell was paying the tab when Bradley motioned him over and invited him to sit in as a fourth. In the next few hours he learned enough about Stephen Austra to understand at least one plausible reason for his apparent change of loyalties. He pocketed his small winnings and said good night, taking a circuitous route back to his hotel. He expected to find Samuelson waiting there, but his room was empty.

III

Early the next morning Blackwell bought a bottle of whiskey and a box of chocolates and began making rounds of Lisbon clinics and hospitals, searching for Paul Stoddard. It

was not luck that made him pick the correct facility on his
second attempt. "He was here," the clinic's administrator
told him, "but only for three days."

"I came all the way from London to see him. Do you know
where I might find him now?"

The man's eyes shifted away uneasily. "I can't say. If you
wish to wait in the lounge, I'll check my records. The doctor
who treated him is not in, but if Miss Ames is on duty, I'll
have her speak with you. She was his nurse."

The woman who sat across from him a few minutes later
was young, British, and obviously upset. "I'll always remember him," she said. "He was too fine a man to have deserved
such an ordeal."

"Paul didn't say very much about what happened to him
in his letter," Blackwell said carefully. "I don't think he
wanted to concern me, but he asked that I come. Will you
tell me how he was injured?"

"I'm surprised he was able to write anything at all." Miss
Ames covered one of his hands with both her own. "He'd
been robbed and shot in both legs, then dumped in a remote
spot to die. When he was found, his cousin was contacted
and the man brought Mr. Stoddard here."

"How was Paul?"

She shook her head sadly. "Someone had taken out the
bullets and crudely splinted the broken leg, but the infection
was massive. He was too weak for an operation, so we ad-
ministered sulfa. The drug had a beneficial effect on the left
leg, the one that had been broken. The right, however, did
not respond to any treatment."

"So what did the doctors do?"

"They requested permission to amputate, but they didn't
get it."

"Paul always was the brave one," Blackwell commented
with a fond expression, recalling a friend who would have
made precisely that gamble.

"It wasn't him. He would have gone ahead, but his cousin
would not allow it. I was in the room when they brought Mr.
Stoddard the consent form. He was lucid enough to understand what they wanted, and he must have known how close
to dying he'd been because he seemed almost relieved to hear
that he would survive.

"If his leg came off?"

"Precisely. But his cousin moved close to him and whispered something extremely odd. He said, 'I am intimate with death and it will not claim you. Trust me now.' Then he said a word, or words, I had never heard, *'Say-ka or na-I.'* " She inflected it carefully, as if trying to speak Japanese. "Then Mr. Stoddard mumbled something similar in reply and handed the form back unsigned."

"He let his cousin make that decision for him?"

"Worse. He let his cousin check him out of here, and now he's dead. I'm sorry . . . but he has to be dead."

Blackwell's hands shook and he turned his head away, as if to hide his strong emotion. "I should have heard if that were true. Which cousin was with him?"

"Steffen Anthony, I believe. You'd have to look at the record to be certain."

"Paul has such a large family, I'm not sure I know this relation. What did he look like?"

"Handsome." She gave a description of a man who could easily be Laurence Austra, then concluded, "It was difficult to be in the same room with him and not stare." Miss Ames's hands fluttered in embarrassment.

"Did Mr. Anthony appear to care for Paul?"

"Definitely. I wasn't here when they arrived, but I understand that he carried Mr. Stoddard in, and with the exception of a few hours that first night when his sister sat with the patient, he never left Mr. Stoddard's side. No one saw him eat or sleep; but once, when Mr. Stoddard was delirious, I went into his room with a pitcher of cold water and saw Mr. Anthony leaning forward in his chair with his head on his cousin's chest. He was apparently sleeping, but with the oddest expression on his face, as if he were lost in the patient's dreams."

"Did you wake Mr. Anthony?"

"I wouldn't have dared. We were all . . . very much in awe of him."

She looked past him nervously and Blackwell decided not to inquire further about Paul Stoddard's counterfeit cousin. "Did the police speak to Paul?"

The question startled her. "No, I don't believe so."

"Doesn't that seem unusual?"

"Yes . . . that is, no, not really. You must understand that this is Lisbon, not London, and violence is the norm as of late." She stood. "I must get back to work, but one favor please. Would you call and tell me what happened to your friend?"

"Of course. I'll try to call today." He held out the chocolates. "Please take these as a gift." She began to shake her head, and he added, "For your patients and the rest of the staff as well."

When she smiled, she became quite attractive. After she left, the administrator returned to tell Blackwell the records were incomplete. "Mr. Stoddard was never officially released so I can't say where he went, but the bill was mailed to his employer's Lisbon offices."

"AustraGlass?"

"Yes. Perhaps if you visit them, they can tell you where . . ." His voice trailed off and he asked with obvious reticence, "Miss Ames was frank with you?"

"Yes. I pray she is wrong. Thank you for your assistance."

After leaving the clinic Blackwell visited the site of what Bradley had told him had been the assassination attempt. He took a moment to walk around the deserted house, then began searching the area, seeking clues as to what had occurred. At the crest of the hill he found pieces of shrapnel speckled with what he believed was dried blood, though it was of an ashy gray color rather than brown. Stoddard had been shot and Stephen Austra had not been harmed. Had one of the would-be assassins been wounded?

An automobile gave enough warning so he could crouch down in the sparse grass just before it passed by on the road. Samuelson was driving and there were three passengers. He used his binoculars in an attempt to get a better look at the group but their backs were to him, and before they turned, they went inside. One important fact had been obvious. The young man was on crutches and both his legs were bandaged. Miracles, he thought, sometimes did happen.

The sunrise window was not as dark as Paul had expected, and it imparted a soft rose tone to the white-walled room. The expanse of glass, broken only by stylized lines of leaves, gave the illusion of looking out to sea through a summer arbor, a magnificent effect.

He sank awkwardly into a chair, his broken leg extended in front of him, the other bent though still in pain. But Paul felt none of it, for the house had once more bewitched him. And the woman! Yes, this was hers, not his, and never had a giver felt as rewarded as he did at this moment, watching her roam gracefully through the lower rooms, inspecting the work to be done. She broke the silence only to ask if he would like to go upstairs.

"Please." Paul's better leg had stiffened. As solicitous as she had been throughout his illness, Elizabeth helped him to his feet.

"Shall we take the inside stairs?" she asked.

He nodded. "I want to stay in these rooms as long as possible."

"You don't have to leave with Stephen tonight."

The attraction he felt for Stephen, for all of them, was bearable now that he understood it, but this woman . . . From the moment he'd seen her through half-delirious eyes as he lay on the grass outside D'Oscuro Fortress, he had loved her . . . every gesture, every tinkling laugh, every color rippling on the edge of his vision. At night he would sometimes lie awake thinking of all the obscene ways he wanted to use her. And she'd let him—he was certain of that—if only he'd begin.

The consequences terrified him.

Of course she understood, for she moved away from him as soon as possible and agreed when he said that work would be better for him now. "And you must return soon. I'll be having the house party in a few weeks. That is tradition for an architect, *oui*?"

"Hell for this architect." He looked at the tile flower boxes and pictured them filled with green leaves and bright blooms. He looked over the wall at the gray stone floor below, softly colored by the windows. "I hear the orders are already com-

ing in, special requests for Savatier's 'new architect.' Are
those orders really mine, Elizabeth, or do they come because
of you?''

She rested one hand over his, squeezing with him the padded grip of his crutch. ''Stephen told me how much you
admire Notre Dame. Is it any less magnificent because the
enthusiasm for its building came from us?''

''That isn't what I asked.''

''What you are asking, Paul, is if you are good enough to
deserve the enthusiasm. You are.'' She walked ahead and
opened the bedroom door, then stood back to allow Paul to
enter first. The rooms and adjoining bath had both seen use.
There were towels untidily arranged on hooks in the bathroom, and across the foot of the bed lay a man's robe.

Paul felt a sudden sadness and hobbled to the doorway
leading out to the upper terrace. He saw Stephen standing
beside George, looking at the sea. ''Considering the lecture
George gave Stephen, I'm surprised he isn't sitting on the
roof with a shotgun in his hand.''

''His lecture was correct.'' Elizabeth looked sadly at the
crutches, thinking that even George was not aware of how
carelessly Stephen had wooed the attack.

Sometimes she was so easy to read. ''They're both still in
place, thanks to you. On the bright side, I won't be requesting
a leave of absence to play pawn on some general's battle-
field.''

''And you are thankful, *mon ami*?''

''I killed someone, and though I don't regret it, I have
learned that killing is quite the opposite of *my* nature.'' He
smiled ruefully as he shook his head and added, ''Your family has a strange ally in me.''

Her laughter rang like bells in empty churches. ''You are
the sort we prefer. You civilize us.''

In the distance an automobile engine coughed its way toward the building site. ''That is Ernst. I have promised him
a tour. Shall we go down and meet him?''

The two outside had already descended the terrace stairs.
''You go,'' Paul said. ''I would prefer to be alone for a little
while.''

''Of course. I won't let anyone disturb you.''

She walked across the hallway to a north window and detected a flash of sunlight against moving glass. She sent a silent warning down to Stephen, who in turn met Bradley with a greeting more cordial than usual, an act for their well-equipped observer.

On the hill above them Blackwell adjusted the focus on his binoculars, wondering if the gathering were social, business, or a bit of both. He sat patiently watching the house until, an hour later, both cars departed and he began the long trip back to Lisbon, using the solitude to form some theories about what he'd seen.

V

An apologetic clerk called Blackwell a little after six the next morning to announce a visitor. "It's Mr. Bradley, and he says he must speak with you. Should I have him wait?"

I'd like to tell him to go to hell, Blackwell thought as he replied, "Ask him to meet me in the restaurant. I'll be down in ten minutes."

It took Blackwell longer than he'd expected, and when he arrived, the waiter was refilling Bradley's coffee cup. Blackwell requested a cup as well, and at his insistence the waiter left the pot. Bradley eyed him with amusement. "My, you look beastly this morning, as you British say."

"I was rather late."

"So was I, but then I seem to require less sleep, one of the compensations for age, allowing me to pack more waking hours into my life before my final demise." Bradley smiled pleasantly and spread a thick layer of jam on his toast.

"I hope you didn't wake me merely to discuss your advancing years over breakfast," Blackwell replied as he stirred the cream into his coffee.

"Not at all. I came to ask what you found at the building site yesterday. Oh, don't deny it. Stephen Austra has remarkable eyes. He spotted you on his way in. You should have come up and introduced yourself, Harry Blackwell, then you could have seen the inside. It is far more interesting than the exterior, but that's true of most things, isn't it?"

"Usually," Blackwell replied, not surprised Bradley knew his name.

"Unfortunately it is also true of government. Geopolitics, for example, grows increasingly complex. We will soon be caught in the middle of a global war."

"Your understanding comes rather late."

"That's true. I never expected my own country would be involved. You see, I taught history for twenty-five years. My pupils were young men with high social standing, languorous intellects and jingoist attitudes. Those years did not make me wealthy, but they did make me wise and, I admit, avaricious. Now I am a businessman, nothing more, and the Germans have always been the highest bidder. However, I do not wish my country to view me as a traitor when the war ends."

"So you want to abandon the German cause?"

Bradley did not reply directly. "Could we go somewhere more private to discuss this?"

"This is private enough."

The surroundings were apparently satisfactory to Bradley as well, for he leaned across the table and began providing a wealth of details on the operation of a German network in London, including damning information concerning the admiral's nephew. When he'd finished, Bradley asked, "What would your government pay for proof of what I just told you?"

"I'll have to see your documents first, then I'll make arrangements to negotiate the fee. It will be high—though, to be honest, far less than it's worth."

"I understand, but in this instance money is not my need. Now, of course, things get awkward. We will simply have to trust one another. As the provider, I am willing."

What Bradley offered far outweighed any danger. "So am I," Blackwell agreed.

"I could visit you this evening?"

And he could have a change of heart. "Now," Blackwell said.

"Have you objections to a drive?"

"Not if I can take the wheel."

"Fine. My car is parked in front." Bradley began to stand, then leaned forward across the table and spoke softly. "I am not armed, Mr. Blackwell and I trust your honor enough that I will not ask if you are. Shall we go?"

The morning sun scorched Blackwell's eyes as they drove. Within a few miles his head was pounding, and for their safety he pulled over. He remembered opening the car door, wondering how he'd been duped, then nothing.

Chapter Twelve

I

THE LIGHT BLINDED. . . pinks, reds, corals . . . a dream, another vivid dream. "Ann," Blackwell whispered, and as his sight cleared, he saw he was alone and this wasn't Alpha but Elizabeth Austra's new home, the colored light streaming through the sunrise window. He studied the room, focusing with difficulty on one bare wall, then another. He tried to move and found his hands were tied behind him, and though his legs were free, he was unable to stand. As he rolled sideways all the colors enveloping him merged into a gray, nauseating haze. He swallowed hard, his saliva tasting of the drugs he'd been given.

The doors were open and he pushed his body through them and out onto the terrace. The sun burned away his endurance, and the stones ripped at his shirt and arms as he inched forward. Reaching the outer wall, he managed to kneel and look down at the long drop into the rock-strewn ocean. Sure death and stupid. It was late afternoon. If he'd spoken, it was already done.

The corner of the ledge was rough, and he began sliding the rope across it when he heard Bradley say with mock delight, "There you are. I believe it's time to go back inside."

"Go to hell!" Blackwell muttered, too drugged to care what Bradley did to him. He would have continued chafing the ropes, but Bradley pulled him upright and led him toward the house.

Near the doors, Blackwell broke free and managed to run a short distance before Bradley tackled him. He fell hard, breaking the rope around his arms and, kicking out, scored a satisfying hit. Bradley grunted and retreated while Blackwell took off in a staggering sprint around the side of the building and into the arms of George Samuelson. "Not so fast, chap," Samuelson said as he shoved Blackwell back through the terrace gates and onto the ground. "Is this the one you will take to Chaves?" Samuelson asked Bradley.

"Yes."

"Your word will mean nothing there."

"I am taking more than my words," Bradley retorted, his dislike for the Englishman obvious.

Samuelson's eyes flicked over Blackwell. "Alive and well, remember?"

"He put the scratches there himself. And I wasn't told I couldn't grill him before delivery."

"That's true," Samuelson admitted.

"And I am too old to carry on a constant battle from here to Chaves."

"That's true as well."

Bradley pulled a metal cigar case out of his pocket and extracted a syringe. "Then you don't mind, do you?"

Blackwell crouched on hands and knees, his gray eyes moving from one man to the other, then locking with Samuelson's in a plea for support. Samuelson shook his head and Blackwell rushed him, an effort that ended when, pinned helplessly, he watched the needle enter his arm.

Afterward he recalled nothing of the drive save their numerous stops along the way and the times when the drugs made him exquisitely sensitive to the pain of touch, nowhere near a violation of the word *well*. Hours later he was wrenched back to consciousness with his heart setting the staccato rhythm of a powerful stimulant. Before he had time to consider escape, Bradley drove up to a guardhouse. On the door Blackwell saw a familiar symbol, the combined alpha/omega symbol of AustraGlass.

Samuelson slid into the backseat. "Sure took you a while. Did he ever sing?" When he received no reply, Samuelson chuckled. "Well, even a greedy bastard like you can't expect to get it all. Take a right when the road divides or you'll drive through the Colony, a damned clumsy mistake, even at this hour. I see you trussed him up again; wise, I suppose, since your drugs barely held him.''

Samuelson began giving directions: past the lower building; up a narrow, unpaved road; through a second gate; finally stopping near a thick-walled granite structure . . . a fortress to hold back a multitude of enemies or to keep the prisoners within.

Scents of spring hung in the air—lilac, wild rose, chives, and thyme—Blackwell's feet breaking the new shoots on the herb lawn as he walked toward the carved wood doors.

Blackwell might be the victim, but as they crossed the threshold of Stephen's house he was more curious than concerned, taking in his surroundings and being the first to notice their host as he slipped out of the concealing shadows. Stephen's clothing was dark and austere, broken only by the ruby pendant around his neck. When their eyes met, Blackwell recalled his words to the admiral. ''A firm run by children,'' he'd said, yet with this one, age was irrelevant and he had the irrational idea it was likewise deceptive. No one so young could be so perfectly poised, so completely in control. Blackwell's quick appraisal evolved into a long, mental exchange during which Blackwell realized that he was an important piece of a much larger puzzle, a piece now carefully set in place.

Stephen motioned them to seats in front of a long wooden table, then switched on low-hanging overhead spotlights and the space took on the quality of an interrogation room, the two men bathed in light, the table before them likewise revealed, the inquisitor standing motionless behind it. Samuelson stood in back of Blackwell's chair, apparently in the role of bailiff, and at a signal from his employer he freed Blackwell's arms and firmly gripped his shoulders.

''Is this the one who ordered my execution?'' Stephen asked Bradley.

''It is.''

Blackwell's pulse raced so quickly that the revelation had little effect on it. ''I perceive you have been drugged,'' Stephen said to him. ''Perhaps we should postpone this discussion for a few hours.''

''Then he will most likely fall asleep,'' Bradley interjected.

"I see." Stephen turned toward Blackwell and the agent felt a power invade his mind as he sometimes sensed Ann studying his thoughts, but this merging had more subtlety, greater depth. "You understand what we discuss here, yes?"

"Enough to know we've both been deceived," Blackwell retorted.

He's going to fight, Bradley thought, and for the first time since they arrived, he felt confident. When Stephen requested the proof, it required effort not to smile as he laid a thick yellow envelope on the table. "It's all here. Every important detail."

Blackwell's amazement grew as piece after piece fell into place . . . notes from the admiral, orders to subordinates, bank drafts, steamer tickets, minor points that added credence to the rest, all coalescing into one irrefutable conclusion. When it was his turn to speak, he merely said, "It appears I have vastly underrated Mr. Bradley's abilities."

"But Mr. Bradley's abilities are not the issue here, are they?" Each man reached a different conclusion from this statement. Both relaxed. "Do you deny your guilt?"

"The evidence is damning."

"He can't deny it," Bradley added.

"These documents could be forgeries, yes?" Stephen suggested.

Blackwell had been allowed to examine them. "My signature is, of course, forged. The rest appear genuine."

"Even these notes from your superior?"

"Taken out of context."

"I see." Stephen studied the documents for some time before asking, "Mr. Blackwell, if you were in possession of this evidence, what would you do?"

"If I were able to determine who had stolen this information, it would 'be sufficient to assure trials for some on charges of espionage and treason. Some would most likely hang."

"A complex procedure for such a simple end. In any event, the documents will be yours if you leave here."

Bradley leapt to his feet and pointed an accusing finger at Blackwell. "I give you proof of the guilt of this man and you ignore it on the basis of his word!"

Stephen's reply flowed with cloying mockery. "I don't re-call him ever giving his word. No, I ignore it with the abso-lute knowledge that he tells the truth. Sit down, Ernst. You've kept your part of our bargain. You brought the man who ar-ranged my assassination to me alive and well. Sad that you will never claim your payment."

"This is absurd," Bradley protested in a calmer tone. "I would have stayed clear of this investigation if I were guilty."

"On the contrary, you found a scapegoat rather than risk the chance someone might bring you here drugged and bound. Then, of course, there was the money . . . what I offered you and what I paid to the men you hired. You have proof I paid them, yes?"

Newly opened accounts made by men meeting the descrip-tions of Alvas and Costa in Cadiz, another for Jão Ables in Porto. The rest were too stupid to handle their money wisely. The letters from Stephen to his niece had been reassuring, but even without them Bradley would have gone ahead with this scheme . . . betrayed by his own stupid greed. He sank back into his chair. There was no use in denying the obvious any longer. "What happened to Costa and the others?" he asked.

"They are dead."

"If you didn't pay them, why did they lie to me?"

"They never lied. They had every reason to assume me dead."

Taking advantage of a silence broken only by Samuelson's chuckle, Blackwell asked, "Will I be taking Bradley to Lon-don with me?"

Bradley interrupted, his eyes on Stephen's as he spoke. "He said he wishes vengeance. Let him claim it here with me."

"Thank you, Ernst," Stephen said. "Now I will tell you how it will end. You were seen leaving the Prado with an Englishman whom Lisbon authorities suspect is a British agent. Neither of you will return. In a week a man meeting your description will go into a Geneva bank and withdraw fifty thousand dollars from an account recently opened in your name. Afterward Ernst Bradley will leave the field in which he had so remarkably excelled to begin a reclusive retirement. An air of mystery will suit your end well, yes?"

Bradley rested his head on his arms, a posture of defeat. "It's far too early for sleep, Ernst. You have a great deal of work ahead of you tonight."

"Work?" Bradley asked without looking up.

"Of course!" Stephen continued in a buoyant tone. "First you must write a letter to Heinrich Schoofs explaining that you have retired due to declining health and providing him with a list of your Lisbon contacts."

"Never!" Bradley bolted for the door, stopping so abruptly, it appeared he had collided with an invisible wall.

"You will do what I ask either simply or painfully, Ernst. Which do you prefer?"

Bradley did not reply. Instead he continued to will his body forward, convinced he had been hypnotized and certain all he need do was find the correct mental posture to break the spell. He moved dangerously close to hysteria when Stephen walked around the table and, placing an arm over his shoulder, led him back to his seat. "Schoofs is an idiot," Bradley mumbled, more concerned about who would inherit his position than his imminent departure from it.

"At times," Stephen said in apparent sympathy, "but we will see that he does an extremely thorough job." He pulled the chair up to the table and helped Bradley into it. "Here is your writing paper, a pen, and ink." Bradley stared down at the sheet, finding it impossible to begin. "Do you need help composing something appropriate, Ernst?"

Bradley stared at the blank sheet of paper. These men had, after all, made espionage their profession, and most of them would be known to Austra already. He picked up the pen and began to write. Midway through the second page he paused and said, "I will go no further unless you promise me that no one save Schoofs will read this."

Stephen glanced at Blackwell, then more pointedly at Bradley. "I give you my word. No one will read it."

Bradley continued, the scratching of the pen often the only sound in the room. When he'd finished, he slipped the letter into an envelope and sealed it. "This cannot be mailed," he said.

Stephen took the letter from him. "Elizabeth will tell Schoofs you left it for him. This should be enough to allay his suspicions."

The response was a barely audible "Of course."

"Now, Ernst, I want you to tell me the names of those who provided the evidence you presented tonight."

No! These were his special contacts, men whose trust had been cultivated over a lifetime. Austra would have no knowledge of them; no one would. "I will not . . ." Bradley began, then, with a cry of pain, locked eyes with Stephen and began to obey.

II

The homecoming party for Paul started downstairs and, when the guest of honor became tired, moved to Paul's room so he could stretch out on his bed. There, for the benefit of a tardy arrival, he had to relate once again the fictitious account of the robbery near the building site.

"To think they nearly killed you for a few hundred *escudos*," Philippe said, disturbed that poverty afforded so little protection from thieves.

"They came close." The lie troubled Paul and he began talking about the house.

"How you carry on!" Mark exclaimed. "You act like this is the first thing you'd ever seen built." He grinned. "Brag away! I did the same myself."

"So are we to lose the great architect's presence in the glasshouse?" Henry asked as he poured another round of sparkling Borges.

Paul rapped on his cast. "For a while. Then I will be back, though, like you, I doubt I'll be tending furnaces."

"I tend them now and I never thought I would consider *that* a blessing," Henry said. He leaned over Paul and asked Linda, "More?" Receiving no reply, he tapped her on the shoulder.

"Ah . . . no thank you. I think I'm going to go to bed." She pushed back a stray strand of hair and kissed Paul good night. She had ben sitting on Paul's bed, in the narrow space between it and the window. As she stood, she stared for a moment out the window, certain she'd heard her uncle's old car. She went upstairs and, pulling out a pair of binoculars, managed to see the back of it disappear above the corporate offices, the lights dancing through the thickening trees of the mountain. Waiting until the pension was quiet, she stole down the stairs and began the long walk up the hill to the Austra estate.

Paul had also noted the distinctive-sounding motor and was puzzled by Linda's sudden exit from the party. Now, hearing her leave, he moved to the window and looked down, barely able to make out her dark-clad figure. Earlier that evening she had been wearing white. The inevitable conclusion angered him. Moving as quietly as he was able, he climbed the stairs to her room, sat down in a chair behind the door, and waited for her to return.

Chapter Thirteen

I

IN THE BEGINNING Blackwell had taken notes, but as the effects of the stimulant wore off, he passed the pad to Samuelson and only attempted to follow Bradley's statement. Soon afterward he dozed.

Dawn was breaking, and a single, full-throated scream woke him. Stephen knelt in front of Bradley, their eyes riveted on each other. Bradley swayed, fighting for control, and Stephen's body followed, maintaining always the same distance, like a snake dancing with its prey. "What in the hell is happening now?" Blackwell asked Samuelson.

"You're watching Bradley die."

It must have been the drugs that had created the illusion Blackwell was part of this act . . . both executioner and victim . . . savoring the terror and anguish as it grew to unbearable proportions . . . staring into those eyes, huge, ebony, flashing bright as a hawk's and filled with an impossible power.

He tried to rise, to go to the aid of the one who had drugged him then brought him here to die, but Samuelson gripped his shoulders and hissed a warning.

Blackwell never cried, but tears, Bradley's tears, ran down his face and he broke when Bradley broke and would have fallen forward into nonexistent arms had he not been held back. "Watch it now," Samuelson whispered. "Feel it and understand what you see."

And he did . . . certain finally that he was going mad, that he would die from no reason except that he believed it. In that instant his perspective shifted. He became the victor savoring the bittersweet triumph of destroying an enemy nowhere near his equal.

For Bradley, life became a dull, throbbing pain borne on his blood. The one who held him had no need for thought, no concern for his helpless struggles, and so Bradley's mind was free to observe his own end, his body capable of limited motion. And he remembered! Even now victory was within his grasp! His hand dipped into his pocket, then, while he hung on the edge of shock, he willed it out and down. "Look out!" Blackwell shouted, too late. The needle emptied into Stephen's shoulder, then Bradley pulled it out and reeled back, waiting for the final satisfaction of seeing his enemy die.

But Stephen didn't. Instead he looked thoughtfully at Bradley, then at the needle in his hand. "If that could kill me, it would have done so by now. The rest, Ernst, is for you."

Samuelson's whispered exclamation was drowned out by Bradley's laughter, the sound quick and hysteric. "I underestimated you in so many ways. Sad I will never understand what you are. With incredible precision he emptied a second syringe into his arm and folded forward, dead by the time his head touched the table.

Afterward, weakened by emotions not his own, Blackwell was led to the house's guest suite. He began to ask the first of a multitude of questions, but Samuelson turned and left, the click of a heavy lock providing the first answer.

II

As Linda pushed open the door to her room Paul's hands shot out. Gripping her wrists, he pulled her down to her knees in front of him. Though she did not cry out, she looked surprised as she asked, "Paul, why are you here?"

"To ask where in the hell you've been."

"For a walk . . . ouch! Please, let me loose." She struggled, but his grip, hardened by months of labor in a glass house, tightened.

"Oh, no. If I do, I'll never be able to catch you again.

You and your uncle saw to that, didn't you . . . didn't you?''
If his hands had been around her neck, he would have strangled her; her feigned helpless expression only fueled his rage.
''Where were you?''

''I thought I heard my uncle's car.''

''And he is with Stephen?''

''Yes.'' For the first time her fright was no act. ''I have to get out of here.''

''What did you see?'' Her expression hardened and she looked away, refusing to answer. He shook her roughly and added, ''If you want any help from me, you will tell me. Damn it! What did you see?''

''My uncle, Stephen, George, and someone else. My uncle was talking and Samuelson was taking notes. If he mentions me, they'll come for me.'' She tried to wrench away and almost succeeded. ''Please, Paul. I didn't want anything to happen to you. I'm sorry it did.''

''You called your uncle and told him we were coming to Lisbon, didn't you?''

''Yes. But he wanted Austra, not you.''

She only admitted what Paul had deduced as he had waited in the darkness. Linda's trips to her uncle, her solicitousness about his project, the voices he'd heard that afternoon in Gianni's room. Even on the night she'd made love to him she'd been following Stephen . . . no desire for him, only professional curiosity. Love someone. Use someone. Kill someone. So easy. So damned easy. The fury he'd been too weak to vent in D'Oscuro roared in him now, and he let go of one of Linda's wrists and backhanded her as hard as he could. His arm flew back to strike again when a soft voice said, ''Stop it, Paul.''

Paul pulled Linda to him, wrapping his arms around her.

''You claim her as your victim?'' Stephen asked.

''No.''

''Then give her to me.''

Even though her fear was an act, Linda's shudder and tears made Paul hold her all the more closely. ''Hasn't there been enough killing?''

''Yes.'' The answer startled Paul. ''I won't harm her, I promise you. Now will you leave us?''

Paul let Linda go. She bolted for the door but Stephen was

faster, swinging her around to face the dim dawn light, frowning when he saw the cracked lip. "Something must explain what she will see on her face in the morning. You understand why it must be you, yes?"

"It's only what I deserve. Do what you have to do." As Paul hobbled to the stairs he heard her softly cry his name. He never looked back.

Paul went to his room and lay on his bed. In a few minutes Stephen joined him.

"Is is over now?" Paul asked.

"Yes. Avoid her if you can. In a few days she'll receive a letter from her uncle and will go to Lisbon to watch his house until he returns."

"Will he return?"

Stephen shook his head, pleased he could answer with the truth. "He tried to kill me. When he failed, he used the poison on himself."

Paul buried his face in his hands. "I have to leave here," he said when he looked up.

"Wouldn't you prefer to know why you should stay?"

"Even now you would try." Paul sighed. "All right, do what you refused to do in D'Oscuro: Explain why we were attacked and what happened here tonight. Tell me what I nearly died for."

Stephen locked Paul's door and sat on the windowsill, staring out at the dawn. And somewhere, between his eyes and the distant light, the history unfolded. Though Paul knew no effort was made to control him, he felt the horror of those centuries disguised in Stephen's toneless words.

"Men were destroying one another when I left my father's house. I and my family skirted the battles, picking our way past the dead rotting on the plains. We watched brave young men march proudly off to fight for others' causes, thinking how sad it was that lives so short should be so wasted. We saw Napoleon's soldiers return defeated from battle, and as they marched through the streets of Paris we smelled the gangrene on their feet and hands. And we said, 'This is war. This is humanity.'

"When the weapons changed from swords and cannon to bombs and gas, we hired experts to tell us how to avoid the destruction, men who were paid to determine years in advance when the political tide would turn. We retreated often, and sometimes, as in Germany, our experts made mistakes.''

Stephen described his few months in the Reich . . . the terror, the fanaticism, the constant fear of arrest and torture, the impending genocide; none of it new, all of it modernized to assembly-line efficiency. Then he detailed the horror that would be unleashed on the world if the war lasted more than five years.

"This is our world as well as yours, and we are not prepared to idly watch humanity destroy it. For the first time we take a side in one of the endless human conflicts, and by doing what we do best, we may shorten it enough that the development of the weapons will be postponed. Ernst Bradley saw through our professed neutrality. No one believed him, so with his own meager funds he paid for my death and now he is dead in my place." Without his glasses the morning light began to blind him and he moved to sit beside Paul on the bed. "He tried to destroy me and he failed."

"Like the assassins?" Paul countered.

"I was attacked, and, when attacked, as you know, my instincts make my defense lethal. As for those who died afterward, there was justice done."

"I have tried to understand but . . ." Paul shook his head. What had happened tonight sickened him, his small part in it most of all.

"In my long life I have been robbed, imprisoned, assaulted, and worse. And in all that time I have never requested the aid of any authority. Consider our situation. Could I have gone to the Lisbon police and said, 'Ernst Bradley paid to have me killed. I was attacked and left for dead'? Look at me. Who would believe me and what would be the result if someone did?"

The vulnerability, Paul considered; the constant need for caution.

"Our way of life is vulnerable, Paul. That makes us independent," Stephen responded. "In one matter you must trust us: When we take vengeance, there is no question of innocence or guilt."

"There's something more," Paul challenged. "When the

time comes to destroy an enemy, you enjoy it. This is what I cannot understand or stomach.''

"In need I could destroy a friend and enjoy it." Stephen paused, letting Paul consider the full implications of the remark. When he continued, his voice was softer, as if the words were difficult to say. ''You know my nature. I have told you it is not just the blood that sustains us but also the life and the emotions that are part of it. The strongest are the most attractive, and fear of death is the most potent of all. That is why we left Germany so quickly. You understand me, yes?''

"To keep from becoming a part of the killing?"

"I could forget everything I have worked for centuries to become.''

"Is that why you support the British?"

Stephen shook his head. ''We support them because we know they will win. But I am pleased we can support them. You understand me, yes?''

"I think so."

"And there is one more thing I must tell you. Before I revealed the family's secret to you I tested your discretion. For a reason even more important, Savatier tested your skill. Should we fail in our goals, we will ask you to build us a new Colony, buried, secret, to protect us from that future our experts predict.''

"I would build it if it were needed, no matter where I go." Paul hesitated, then asked, ''If I decide to leave, will I remember all that's happened to me?''

"Yes. And I hope that from time to time you would welcome a visit from someone who places great value on your friendship.''

Paul rested a hand on Stephen's shoulder. ''I can give no less than I get. I ask you again, is it over?''

"For Europe it has barely begun. For us the siege is ended.''

He was wrong.

III

When Blackwell woke, he saw his host standing at the foot of the bed, one hand on each of the high foot posts. That pose, with his long arms fully stretched, invited Blackwell to note one obvious difference between them. "You are well, yes?"

The annoyance of small bruises; the disquieting, vague, focused memories; even the shudders of cold and weakness were inconsequential. "I am. Bradley showed great restraint, but you arranged that, did you not? Just as you arranged the rest?"

"Your admiration should be directed to Samuelson. I merely implemented his plan. And I complement you on your remarkable endurance. You revealed nothing in those extra hours it took you to arrive here from Lisbon."

"Would that have made any difference?"

"A great deal. On the table beside you are your notes and a report I wish you to study. The evidence Bradley brought remains with me until we reach some agreement about how we will work together in the future. You understand, yes?"

"What choice do I have?"

Though only a hint of Blackwell's anger was conveyed in his voice, Stephen felt the full measure of it and replied in kind. "That is not the attitude that will allow you to leave this place."

A question occurred to Blackwell, one too personal to ask and too important to be left unanswered. Before he found the words, Stephen answered, "No. The only orders under which Ann acted when she went to your bed were your own, so I understand. I regret her actions. In many respects it makes your decision more difficult."

"I have a great many questions."

"I'm sure you do. I've brought you something to eat, as well as a pot of coffee. This time the cream isn't drugged."

Blackwell managed to get to his feet unassisted, and by the time he reached the main room, the color had returned to his face. The fire still burned. A tray of food had been placed where the table was closest to it. Blackwell sat on the stool in front of it. The heat against his back felt wonderful.

Stephen perched on the end of the table, one leg up with his bare foot flat against the top. His head rested on his knee and he watched Blackwell with calm curiosity. "I wasn't sure if you'd be ravenous or fasting," Stephen said. "I don't know what Bradley stuck in you. I suppose you got whatever he'd intended for me. In the end, so did he."

Blackwell poured himself a glass of wine and fixed a thin sandwich. When he'd finished, he slid the plate of bread and meat closer to Stephen.

Stephen shook his head. "My nourishment comes from a different source."

Blackwell put down his food and stared at his host. "I said I had some questions. Would you start by explaining why you're still alive?"

Stephen replied with a fleeting grin, held just long enough for Blackwell to notice his long second set of canines glint in the firelight. They were set back in Stephen's mouth, far enough that they would only be seen if Stephen wished it. "Very well, I will be direct," Stephen began with some amusement. As he continued, Blackwell's expression grew skeptical. "Believe it," Stephen concluded. "Your acceptance will make our agreement that much easier."

"And my decision must be to guard your family secret?"

"Yes, and to make your pledge a matter of the highest honor. If the admiral, Chamberlain, or even King George himself demand that knowledge, you will refuse to supply it."

"And in exchange?"

"A kind of cooperation far more valuable than Bradley's documents, I assure you."

"Cooperation?"

"Cooperation. Once you read the file, you'll understand why I am taking this risk. When you reach your decision, I will know. If we will be working together, the outside doors will be open to you."

"And if we're not?"

Stephen paused, then asked, "Do your superiors know you are here?"

"The admiral knows but no one else. I had to tell him or it would have been sticky to leave the country. Travel for those in my occupation is becoming difficult."

"Ann had written that you and the admiral have been curious as to whether or not our mental constraints can be overridden. Sadly, Mr. Blackwell, they can."

After Stephen left, Blackwell tested his status. Though he could roam through the inside rooms at will, he found he could not even approach the door, let alone leave the house. He retrieved the report from his bedroom, stretched out on the leather couch and began to read.

The report was labeled "Repercussions of the Next Great War" and it had been prepared by the AustraGlass Department for Historical Projection in 1935. Blackwell thought the title audacious, but after the first few pages he became engrossed by the addition of fact upon irrefutable fact and the logic of the conclusions. At the end were terse notes regarding AustraGlass holdings: divest of this stock, close this firm, move another, expand, relocate. He considered what he knew of the history of this family, always ahead of political upheaval, always maintaining their wealth in spite of the world's disasters. But if this file were correct, the future might best resemble the Dark Ages. Blackwell recalled what he knew of the laboratories of the Reich, the development of heavy water by Norwegian scientists, the tenacity of the Soviets, and accepted a world half slave, half almost free on the brink of annihilation.

Hours passed. It had grown dark by the time Blackwell finished. He closed the file, stared up at the wood ceiling above him, and thought of the future that concerned him, the one he would not live to see.

"I understand," he whispered to the empty room. "I'll do as you wish." As he spoke the words he felt a weight lift from his mind. His jailer had heard. The doors were open to him, Stephen had said, and Blackwell was thankful. He had a sudden need to see the pure night sky.

He walked up the outside stairs to the roof and looked down at the valley below him, at the lights glowing tranquilly in the gathering dark, and found himself recalling the night flights of the last war. The whistling of bullets and the droning of the engines masked the soft footsteps on the stairs, and he started when, sensing a presence, he turned and saw Ann standing behind him.

Her eyes mirrored his concern that he might be unkind then; far worse, she sensed his regret for all he had dared dream that would never come to pass. She was about to speak some word of apology when he shook his head. "The mistake was entirely mine. You gave me no reason to expect anything from you." When she said nothing, he asked, "Did your uncle send you to me?"

"No. But he wished me to be here when you made your decision, so, should it have gone badly, I would understand and your death would not come between us. Our minds . . ."

Summoned to be a witness at the execution of her lover? "The barbarism!"

Ann continued, a slight quickening of her voice the only sign she had heard. ". . . are open to one another. Even to conceal builds walls, and when these grow too high, we become isolated in desperate loneliness." Her voice betrayed a constant sorrow as she abruptly said, "I only came to be certain you were all right. Good-bye, Harry." She turned to go.

"Wait!"

Ann whirled and faced him. "For what! For more of your pity? Though we are few, we are closer to each other than you can ever hope to be with a woman you would cherish for a lifetime. And you? Shall I pity you your loneliness? Shall I pity you because, a century from now, you will lie rotting in the earth while I will look no less perfect than I do at this moment?"

He held out his arms. "Will you accept my apologies and some small pathetically human scraps of fear?"

She clasped his hands for a moment, let them go, and stepped back. "Think about me, Harry. Make a decision outside of my presence. . . ." He moved toward her and she motioned him away. "No! It is no conceit to admit my being close to you is an impossible temptation."

He persisted. "My decision regarding your family secrecy has been made. Now I ask you to help me reach a personal one. Do you wish to be my lover, Ann?"

She whispered, "Yes."

"I am aware I cannot help but be honest with you, and so

I ask you to be as honest with me. I look at you and see a woman of incredible beauty. I look at your uncle and see an equally handsome man who at will seems to drop a civilized pose and become . . . something more than human. Help me to understand, Ann. Let me know you and love you and remember.''

Ann gripped the iron rail and looked down at the forest beneath them. ''Do you understand how I have used you?''

''Yes.''

''Your passion, your blood? You will allow me to take these?''

''Yes.'' God, yes!

Even in the dim light he was certain she had not spoken, yet he heard the words —As you wish, Harry.— He did as she silently requested and followed her to his room, where she lit an oil lamp and began to undress as naturally as if she were alone.

When she reached for him, it required all his will to keep from flinching back, not because he feared her but rather because to touch her condemned him to some future sentence of holding another woman, any other woman, and remembering the perfection of this moment.

Chapter Fourteen

Banlin, Ireland
August 1939

I

LAURENCE AUSTRA'S BAY held the lead until the last quarter of a mile, when Jake Finnerty's deceptively short-legged mare made her final effort and thundered past. "Told you this was my year, Laurie," Finnerty said when they reined in. He patted his mare's neck and appraised Laurence's stallion. "He'd make a fine sire for Little Mary's first foal."

Laurence chuckled. "Wait until you see the one I ride tomorrow, Jake. Afterward we'll discuss a trade. I'm considering your Precious for my Tidy Bit."

"Tidy Bit?"

"Tad named her. I bought the mare for him but she has too much spirit for a child and enough to be a fine contender tomorrow." He scanned the crowd and found Kathleen, Emma, and Tad. The girl waved her second-place ribbon while her brother held out bits of apple for the horses. Jake trotted over with Laurence and scooped up the boy and the three circled the dusty track, cooling down the horses.

"You've got a fine family, Laurie," Jake said, brushing the top of Tad's head.

"Thank you," Laurence said stiffly. After months of isolation, even this cordiality was suspect.

Finnerty appeared not to notice. "We've a party at my brother's after the races are over."

"Another time. The children have been up since early morning."

"Let them stay with the rest of the little ones. The boys at the stables will see to your horses. You'll all be welcome."

139

Jake had been delegated to say this, Laurence knew, and this first community gesture should not be ignored. He searched out Kathleen, finding her standing alone with Patricia Finnerty, listening to the older woman with intense interest. "You're coming, aren't you?" Patricia called out when she saw Laurence.

—Are we?— Laurence asked Kathleen privately.

—Please!— Her enthusiasm only heightened what he tried so often to ignore. Outside of shopkeepers and tradesmen and the tutor he had arranged for the children, no one spoke to Kathleen.

Laurence felt Kathleen shudder as they walked into the noisy tavern, but the social thaw seemed to extend beyond the Finnerty family. Emma and Tad disappeared into the noisy pack of children in the pub's back room. A few people left when they saw Kathleen, others snubbed her, but Patricia Finnerty and a few other women stayed close to her, protecting her from any open insult. Later Kathleen took a turn at the piano while Laurence found himself pressed into a smoky corner with the county's most serious horse breeders.

Exaggeration was a bigger sport in Banlin than racing, and as Laurence listened to each man extol the virtues of his Sunday mount he considered his own speed and began to wonder what sort of odds he could pull on his first time around: *And the first-place ribbon goes to Laurie Austra by twenty lengths, now favorite contender at the Cork Races, ridden by. . . .*

He'd carried the thought too far! Jake eyed him merrily. "Been at the tap when our backs were turned, were you, Laurie?"

Laurence shook his head. "There's good black tea in this mug, so perhaps its only the smell of the stout that's got me tipsy . . . or confidence, hmm?"

This initiated another round of betting that continued until the band began to play. Laurence was walking toward Kathleen to ask her to dance when a cry and a crash sent parents rushing to the back room.

Tad stood over Sean Gallagher, his knuckles bleeding though not nearly as much as young Sean's nose. Sean's sister stuttered only one word, then all the youngsters fell silent, their guilty expressions telling everyone what had prompted the fight.

The parents formed a circle around the pair, their silent approval telling Laurence what his mind had not dared determine. Ann had been right, he thought. In this single-industry town he was master. And though his alliance with the owner of the town's only tavern could not be defied, his mistress would never be accepted.

He stared across the circle to Kathleen and sensed her pain. —Shall we go?— he asked.

Kathleen shook her head. "Tad, you will apologize," she said sternly.

Tad looked to Laurence for support. Seeing none, he blurted, "I'm sorry," then stared down at his feet and tried not to cry.

Laurence directed his mental power to Mary Gallagher, who made a quick, unexpected decision. Laying her hand on Kathleen's shoulder, she said to her son, "And you, Sean, I want you to apologize to Tad."

"But Father said . . ."

"Father isn't here, I am. Do it! Then shake Tad's hand and say this will never happen again."

All eyes were on the boys when Kathleen glanced at Laurence. —We must not retreat, Laurie.—

As if on cue, the music continued and Laurence turned to Mary Gallagher. "May I have this dance?" he asked.

Mary blushed as she accepted. Jake Finnerty immediately moved in and made the same request of Kathleen and the painful moments, while not forgotten, could at least be ignored.

On their way home Laurence held the carriage reins loosely, letting the team set its own pace. In the surrey's rear seat, Emma and Tad giggled, then fought briefly before drifting off to sleep. "It's a beginning," he said to Kathleen.

"Were they sincere?"

"The farmers were, as well as some of the younger women." His hand closed over hers.

"Jake and Brian had a hand in this, didn't they?"

"Yes," he admitted, thankful she hadn't asked about his own part in this. "The Finnerty's campaign would not have

worked without you. Ye must be a well-loved woman in Banlin, my *maevoreen*.''

"And ye a well loved man.'' She snuggled closer, and
wrapped in each other's warmth, they sat silently, the only
sound the creaking of the carriage wheels and the soft click-
plop of hooves on the hard dirt road.

The air held an unnatural hush as they approached the
house, and Kathleen commented, "It seems so empty with
Ann gone, though I hardly see her when she's here.''

"You are beginning to sense the presence of family. I was
twelve the first time I was away from all of them and terrified
by their absence. Now I'm happy we're alone.'' He helped
her down from the carriage and ran his hands slowly up her
sides. After they'd sent the children upstairs to dress for bed,
Laurence went to tend the horses and Kathleen to the kitchen
to prepare their tea.

She smiled as she took down the periwinkle-blue teapot
and cups from their rack in the window. Her mother's tea set
was one of her few treasures in daily use. A shared pot of
tea had become their evening ritual, a ritual she'd learned
from her parents. Knowing how much it meant to her, Laurence learned by trial and error which herbal blends his system
could tolerate, hiding the pain from her when he found he'd
made a mistake.

The door opened behind her. She picked up a cup of tea
and, smiling, turned. "Laurie, take . . .'' The china fell to
shatter on the floor in front of her. "James,'' she whispered.

Her husband sauntered into the room and leaned against
the table, using the knife in his hand to clean his nails. "Look
at my wife, dressed in such finery and in a house so grand.
I never thought you deserved this much, Kathleen, but then
I could not have given it. Perhaps you gave more in return to
this lord I hear you live with.''

She willed herself into a frigid calm as she listened to his
clipped words, thinking she understood what it was he
wanted. "We can pay you then—''

"Shut up!'' He walked toward her and she backed up until
she reached the cupboard. When he'd moved close enough
that she could feel his breath on her face and smell his un-
washed clothing, he held up the knife in front of her eyes.
"Shut up or I'll cut out your tongue before I'm through.''

Years of nightmares came rushing back. Kathleen closed her eyes before James could see her tears, then swallowed hard and forced them open. She felt a horrible guilt for ever having allowed this man to touch her, and only the unreasonable hope that she could somehow make him leave before Laurie returned and gave her the bravery to speak. "What do you want?" she whispered.

He reached into his jacket pocket and pulled out a stained, wrinkled envelope. "I received word you've been living in sin. Giving scandal to our children. I have come to take them away from this evil place."

He was insane, he had to be. "Where will you take them?"

"Ah, you think to know, so you can find them later. I tell you they go to my aunt's because it will make no difference. I'll be the only family they have, you see, and no court would dare find me guilty."

He held up the knife and her eyes were fixed on the flashing of its blade. "Ah, yes, I frighten you, but don't worry. Before you die, you'll see your lover die, then you can travel to hell together." He used the blade to move her sideways, then pushed her down into a chair and stood behind her, one hand tangled in her hair, the other holding the blade to her throat.

That was how Laurence found them, infinite heartbeats later . . . Kathleen, her breathing ragged, her eyes wild with fear for him and her family —It will be all right— he told her, and sensed only a mute scream for a reply.

The intent was clear from the moment his eyes met Moore's. "Ah, a pretty boy," Moore crooned. "I'd expected someone older. No matter. Come here!"

"He—"

"Quiet, bitch." He pressed the knife tighter, breaking the skin.

—. . . wants to kill you first.— Blood flowed from the cut on her neck and Laurence stood, watching it in fascination. His instincts were strangely silent and he tried to avoid the fight, but the man's mind was too full of alcohol and delusions to be controlled.

Moore jerked Kathleen's head back. "Come here, boy. Come here before I kill her."

Laurence fought back the tumble of emotions—uncertainty, shame, anticipation—but the rage he needed to save

them both still eluded him. Desperate, he made one final
gamble. With all the contempt his mind and voice could convey, he said, "If you plan on killing an unarmed man and a
hysterical woman, do it the way a coward prefers. Begin by
stabbing me in the back." He spun, ignoring Moore's oath
and Kathleen's inaudible warning.

Laurence's hands were held at his side, his fingers curling,
hardening, waiting . . . waiting as he fanned Moore's anger,
drawing it out, amplifying it, and feeding it back, as if it
were comfort or desire. A quick thought was directed to
Kathleen. —When he lets you go, run. Don't come back until
I call you.—

Kathleen had no time to argue or agree. Moore flung her
aside and attacked. At the last moment Laurence whirled and
the knife sank into his shoulder. He brushed it away, four
bleeding slashes and a broken wrist making Moore's right
arm useless.

The sound of death—half snarl, half screech—rattled the
cups on the window. Kathleen covered her ears and slowly
backed away.

—Please, Colleen. If you love me, go!—

She obeyed, fleeing through the door into the darkness,
escaping the sight but not the screams. She'd run only a few
yards before she remembered her own and, circling the house,
entered by the front door, scooping up Emma, who stood
trembling at the top of the stairs, clutching a fireplace poker
in her hand. They retreated to Tad's room and found the boy
sitting up in bed, his eyes white-rimmed with fright. "We
heard a banshee, Mum," he said, and flew into her protective
arms. Clutching her sobbing children, she leaned against the
door and tried to listen only for the sounds she must hear and
dared not consider . . . the sounds of heavy feet ascending
the stairs.

Once Kathleen had gone, Laurence let the last of his will
merge with his instinct and moved slowly toward his victim.
Moore retreated, clutching his arm, blood dripping from his
fingertips. Every step made him wince with pain and his eyes
were fixed on the hands of the one he had planned to kill.

—Look at me. Look at my face.—

Moore pulled in his breath, a long "Ahhh," then exhaled,

the same sound louder, broken by fear. "Ah-h-h-h. Demon," he whispered, and tried to pray and discovered the words were long forgotten.

—You brought the demon with you, now it demands your life. Give it to me.—

The reply less than a whisper, hardly a word at all. "No."

—Then I must come to you.—

In one long step their bodies touched and all thoughts of the woman and children he loved were swept away by the compulsive drive to consume this enemy, this death-fear, this final magnificent terror. The knowing screams aroused him as no cry of any animal had ever done. He lowered his head to his victim's neck, his lips seeking, finding, instinctively biting . . . not too deep, sucking . . . not too fast. He would savor. He would learn. The part that was Laurence—that treasured music and dancing, the woman and her children; that thought it understood its nature from those long, satisfying woodland hunts—that part looked on and mourned.

The sounds of fear grew fainter, the begging faded, and still they remained pressed together . . . body to body, soul to soul . . . until death claimed one and the other returned to stand and contemplate with dark, glazed eyes the blood and the corpse and the broken teacup on the floor.

Much later he sensed movement and turned to see Kathleen, a revolver in her hand. "Someday I must teach you how to fire that," he said.

"Laurie, thank God! The children are asleep. I . . ." Her calm ran from the sight of the blood smeared across her lover's lips and chin, her husband faceup on the floor, the horror of his death etched forever on his face. She sank to her knees, hugging her elbows, pressing her arms to her stomach, doubled over, keening "Laurieeeee, Laurieeeee," as if it were he who had died.

Grief. This was grief, and grief must be allowed. He knelt before her, his arms open to comfort, and was flung back by the force of her attack. She could not hurt him. She did not mean to hurt him. He concentrated only on this as he pulled her against him, pinning her flailing arms at her side.

"Let me know what it was like, Laurie. Let me know how it feels to rip something apart with your body as your only weapon. Share it all with me, Laurie. Share it all . . . do you hear? Do you? My God, all those nights! Show me what it was I loved?''

He held her, unaware that his wound was bleeding, that her mouth covered it, that she was sucking, that . . . ''No!'' He pushed her away, spun her around, and held her as her tardy tears began to flow and he wished he could cry with her in anguish for that moment when their life together ended.

When the hysteria dulled to sorrow, he carried her up the stairs and slipped her between the covers, then returned to the kitchen to begin his work. In the morning the body was gone, the blood washed away; the only reminders of the night's tragedy were the wound on Kathleen's neck and the missing space on the sun-drenched display rack.

They went to Banlin as planned. Tidy Bit, skittish at her first formal race, came in fourth, impressing Finnerty enough that a trade was arranged for consummation in the spring. Through the day Laurence watched Kathleen moving with contrived cheerfulness, her emotions dulled by shock. They waited the week—and the next and the next—but the constable did not come.

Though it gave him little comfort, Laurence hunted every night, often stopping at the grave of the man he had killed. He felt no remorse for what he had done, only a silent anger that happiness once again had been such a cruel hoax. He doted more than ever on the children, but Kathleen—her smiles, her tentative touches, her private tears—he ignored.

Eventually he wrote his uncle a long letter explaining what had happened. He sent it to Chaves through Ann's mysterious channels and received a reply within the week. Ann delivered it, passing the letter to him, then resting her hand on the side of her brother's face. —We understand.— she told him, speaking for herself and the rest of the family. She felt something surfacing within him, something he quickly fought down. ''Laurie, what is it?'' she asked. When he would not reply, she added, ''You cannot be blamed for this?''

''No,'' he said woodenly. ''No, not for this.''

* * *

He waited until Ann had gone before opening the letter. As he read it he pictured Stephen writing it—sitting at his desk, calling up his vision of a savage past—and he understood the love that had gone into each word.

When I was a child, my father kept slaves in our house: servants who taught us to speak as humans speak, to move as humans move, to think as humans think, for even in that age such deceit was useful. But one night when we were twelve, your father and mother and I stood in the tower of the great stone keep and watched different kinds of creatures driven into our cellars by the el--ders of our family.

These were dark men, bound and strung together, and the elders deliberately made little attempt to control them. Like all the family, my body had the strength of thin, forged steel while these men had the power of muscle and weight. Indeed they were the hugest creatures I had ever seen on those desolate peaks, and their minds were savage, for they had been plucked from some Magyar horde pillaging the plains below. I looked at the two standing beside me but nothing passed between us save a shared foreboding.

The next night our father ordered the center of the great hall cleared and the family formed its ring. We three were led in, and six of the prisoners. The weakest prisoner was pushed into the ring and tossed a knife and a short sword. Not knowing what was to come, he tried to bolt and found the mental barrier around him a stronger confine than any wall could ever be.

I was chosen first. My father unclasped the tunic from my shoulder. —If rage does not come, let him have you.— With that frigid advice he thrust me in.

Here was the silence of ritual; no cheers greeted me, no cries, nor even any thoughts of support. The family watched me, yet when I looked for them, I saw only darkness surrounding me and the eyes of the one who would kill or be killed. I saw his expression change to surprise as my father's thoughts touched him, and I knew what had been promised, when, without warning, he sprang.

I reeled back, a deep cut in my thigh and a roaring

in my head. He let his hands fall too low and I leapt, wrapping my legs around his arms and chest. His back arched. He lurched from side to side, trying to shake me off. My grip only tightened, my fingers digging into the soft underside of his chin, forcing his head up. Our eyes locked, and with the realization of what he faced, his dull rage turned to terror. As he sank to his knees my fingers found his eyes. I will not describe how I felt as I killed him. You know.

Your father was chosen next, then your mother. More men were brought in, and we faced them—two, then three to one—until we could think of them as any other beast. This was how we learned to kill men in my father's house.

What I write must seem barbaric, yet I believe the family showed me a greater kindness than I did you. Had I been wiser, I would have remembered my past and not let the peace of the years in which you grew to manhood lull me into postponing this inevitable understanding. I would have had you and Ann with me in Germany when I avenged her lover's death; or here, patrolling our little world with Rachel and Marilyn and the rest; or walking some dank waterfront street in Porto or Lisbon, where death is easy and easily justified.

My given son, you write words and defend them with more words and so manage to avoid saying what is in your heart. Though you write otherwise, I believe you are closer to the woman you tell me you care for than ever before, and I grieve with you that you must lose her. Chaves is safe and, I would guess, will be far more pleasant for her and her children than Banlin. If she wishes to come here, there will be countless positions opening soon and the only difficulty will be the travel. There is a house in the Colony waiting for her. Assure her of the friendship of our family and those close to us.

You have asked to join us here but I would prefer you remain in Banlin until this war is over. For the safety of you and Ann, and Kathleen and her children while they share your house, I have asked Ann's contact for protection for Alpha. I hope the extra security will not be necessary, yet you and your sister are our youngest and so the most vulnerable. I caution you to be careful, and, should any mishap befall you, ignore logic and consequences and trust instinct. Though it often chooses the most difficult path, it chooses the one that leads to survival.

The following morning Kathleen found Stephen's letter on her bureau. She read it, then burned it as Laurence's note requested and spent the first half of her day compulsively cleaning, for if they were to leave, everything should be as it was. Later she opened drawers and closets, sorting what they had brought from what had been given, thinking they would go to Chaves carrying only what they truly owned. She dared not consider the loneliness or how she would answer her children's questions but thought only of practical matters until the grief she had held back broke free and poured over her. She locked the bedroom door and lay sideways across their bed, racked by deep, empty sobs that stopped as abruptly as they had begun. It was not over; it could not be over until she faced Laurence and apologized.

That night she set a fire in the parlor and sipped a glass of sweet white wine, hoping to find in such a simple pleasure the strength she would need to accept the new grief when their conversation was over. The gown she had chosen was white satin, its high neck trimmed with lace and ribbons, and it and her loose auburn curls gave her the innocent guise of a child preparing for an adult ending.

He sensed her resolve and entered, startling her as he sometimes did with the silent way he moved. His hands and bare feet were caked with drying mud. Pieces of it stuck to the carpet as he walked over it to sit in a tapestry chair close to the fire, flexing his fingers over the hearth and letting the dirt flake off. He did not look at her as she began her carefully planned speech.

"When I came here, I asked you to dismiss the servants because I wished to care for you as I do for my family. Yet now I feel like the servant, and I have stayed only because this is home for my children and because you appear to need them very much. I was hysterical the night James came. I don't remember what I said or did, but whatever it was, I ask you to accept my apology."

He stared at the fire, sitting so still, she wondered if he was listening. No matter.

She took a deep breath and continued. "I had considered asking for my old position with Alpha but that's impossible, so I want you to do as your uncle suggested and send me to Chaves. I would also ask that you sell my cottage and post the money to me afterward. Understand, Laurie, that I do not wish to go, but I will if there is no other choice left me."

He looked up at her, his expression one of frank amazement. "You could leave me?" he asked.

"Of course I could! You are not so irresistible now, Laurie!" The joy in his eyes first confused her, then made her more angry. She began to stand, but he rested his hands on her shoulders to stop her, then sat beside her.

He spoke gently, soothing the harshness of his words. "My uncle was right to apologize. I did not understand how different we are until I killed James and perhaps even that could be overlooked for love. But afterward I feared you had fallen victim to a most terrible slavery. I thought I had stolen your will."

She shook her head, her look questioning.

"Our blood is as invasive as our minds. It flows in you now and binds you to me. To touch you now would be to force myself on you, and I cannot do such a terrible thing. Do you understand?"

She reached for his hand. "Love has already bound me, and it would be love that would force me to leave. Understand, I cannot stay here if I am repulsive to you."

"Repulsive! Kathleen, I frightened you. I frightened myself." His face mirrored her joy, then he sobered. "There is more. The small part of me that is in you seeks life. We could have a child, Colleen." He continued on more quickly, sensing her savoring that unexpected idea. "You could die in the birthing. Our own usually do."

"And the child?"

"I don't know. Twice there have been children born of such a mating, outwardly human and later altered to be . . . a part of our family. But it is rare that such a child will have the physical or mental power to survive in our world, and so we must abandon it to a human fate." He shook his head in frustration and stared into the fire. "I know so little, only that I have been told never to contemplate cross—this."

"If we have a child, I will raise it with my own, and if it cannot have the gift of forever, it will have the lifetime any human child is given. Laurie, I assure you that for us it is enough."

"You risk your life, Colleen," he reminded her.

"*If* we are blessed and I conceive, there are hospitals, transfusions. You told me your mother survived that way. Why not me?"

"Yes, she lived. Drained of everything but life. I can't ask that of you."

"I had two children, Laurie. They didn't destroy me. You said it yourself. There are differences between us."

He had visions of Emma and Tad and a small dark-haired child toddling along behind, and he shook his head quickly as if to disperse their temptation. "What you offer me is more than I had ever hoped to have, and I find myself concerned by the thought of family censure. You humble me." He paused, then said solemnly, "Kathleen Moore, whatever the future holds for us, I promise I will never abandon you or your children. And I wish that for as long as we are able, you will stay with me . . . as my wife."

Kathleen nodded but looked at him sadly, her thoughts impossible to follow. "What is it?" he asked.

"I was remembering the horror of my marriage and considering what the world would think of you if they knew what you are."

"And the night I killed James, what did you think of me then?"

"I was terrified, but had you been less than you were, we would be dead."

He pulled her upright and brushed away the few tears left in her eyes, the dirt from his fingers leaving smudges on her cheeks. Then he kissed her, his hands dirtying the satin gown. Had he been a pessimist he might have seen an omen in this— a body dressed in a shroud, covered with earth . . . an image waiting for reality.

II

September 2, 1939

The band that had played at Elizabeth's reception broke before midnight, and most of the wealthy of Lisbon departed soon afterward. But some of Elizabeth's close friends, along with the lively group from the Colony, still sat on the terrace, surrounding Paul, laughing, keeping him sane with their good-natured insults. As was becoming common in Chaves, some-one handed Stephen a guitar.

"You ought to be a musician someday," Paul said softly.

"I was a singer once. Perhaps one day I'll sing again." Stephen adjusted the strings and asked, "Requests?"

One was immediately called out, then another, and the few still capable of carrying a tune began to sing along. Some time later Samuelson came outside, caught Stephen's eye, and nodded. Stephen paused, took a slow, sad breath, and began to play a plaintive version of "The Mademoiselle from Armentières." The meaning was unavoidable; the war had begun. Philippe lowered his head to the table and cried, while around him Mark and a few others raised their glasses in a grim heavenly toast and downed them.

Paul scanned the terrace, seeking Elizabeth. She sat against the outside wall, holding Schoofs in her arms as the reluctant German agent fought for composure. He had three sons in the German army, Paul knew, and if this war was similar to the last, perhaps one would survive.

Stephen's song increased in tempo, then merged into a series of French peasant dances, Polish mazurkas, rounds from Britain, pieces from Sweden and Norway. When the medley included a Spanish song, a few people looked puzzled. At Italian and Russian ones there were some who whispered quiet profanities, but when Stephen concluded with a few bars of a popular German drinking song, Phil and a few others jumped to their feet, prepared to rip the guitar from Stephen's hands.

Stephen stopped playing, laid the guitar aside, and said solemnly, "I did not play for causes or for soldiers but for

Europe, for the places and friends we have loved and will lose.

"We have all expected this news. I know many of you will not be in Chaves on Monday, but I hope that each of you will return once the war is over. I promise there will be work for all of you."

He picked up the guitar once more. "I will play anything you wish to hear. Shall we be Europeans one more night, my friends?"

"Another czardas!" someone called out, and the music resumed. A few hotheads left, but the rest stayed to sing or hum along with the foreign lyrics. Just before dawn the music quickened to an impossible pace, and the few who remained and were awake enough to notice, watched Stephen's hands fly across the strings. He mouthed the words, not daring to sing them.

"I can't place that," someone called out when Stephen finished.

"That last was for my own."

Paul left the reception long before the night ended, soaking the pain from his legs in a hot bath. Afterward he was pouring himself a glass of port—just one final glass to numb his body and his mind and allow him to sleep—when Elizabeth entered the guest room.

He hadn't heard her come. He had his back to the door, so he had not seen her, but still he knew. That rich scent of musk and flowers, the sudden tingling of his skin, were enough. He looked over his shoulder and tried to smile.

She had not changed but her gown seemed more revealing now, and he wondered how anyone could fail to notice that she seemed formed from the finest white porcelain. "This should have been your triumph, Paul. It was until the end."

Even in that simple statement he sensed a difference. The pitch of her voice had changed, the lilt becoming more pronounced. If he looked into her dark eyes, all his strength would be gone. So instead he studied the wine in his glass as he replied, "The news was no surprise."

"No, I suppose not." She paused, then said, "I came to thank you."

"Did you? It's late, Elizabeth, and as you so often remind me, recovery takes time."

She began to turn toward the door, then looked sadly over her shoulder. "I would have given you a gift, Paul."

Go back to Schoofs, he wanted to scream. Go screw all of them. But he didn't say it, because jealousy was only a fraction of the truth. Instead he simply said, "I'm not strong enough for you, Elizabeth."

The change in the air vanished. "Not yet," she replied, and kissed his cheek and left.

III

As the Reich turned its productive resources to the necessities of war, its citizens looked elsewhere for luxury. In conveniently neutral Chaves the glass was poured; orders were taken for silver and china and fine fabrics. Suggestions were given: Buy steel from this firm, use this one as your builder. They're the best and, of course, good German firms so no one will question your loyalty, Frau Mueller. . . . Oh, the war, Herr Kieffer, such an inconvenience for builders such as yourself! Can we ship through the Channel? A direct route would save so much time. . . . Fraulein Wulff, how pleasant it must be in Berchtesgaden. No, I have never met Herr Himmler. Perhaps you will dine with me this evening while your Papa studies the contracts, yes?

Elizabeth was in Paris when France surrendered. Marilyn opened the doors of her palatial estate near Lyons to a new French government. Sebastian remained in Norway when it fell, purportedly on business. Mark and David were in London working quietly with Blackwell, ferreting out the spies in the SIS.

Laying aside his balance sheets, Stephen sat with Samuelson and contemplated the information received and the subtle compulsions sent: Go east, conquer Russia first, then, when Britain falls . . . what a perfect, final victory!

Two months later all family communications ceased, but by then, thanks to Blackwell, they were prepared.

Part

Two

GREGORY HUNTER

Chapter Fifteen

Romania
March 1941

OF THE TEN men who had dynamited the bridges over the Szeda River, only five survived to cling stubbornly to life. They might have sought shelter. Even now there were some who would have given it gladly, but concerned about reprisals, they dared not stop.

At night they stole potatoes buried in the straw in barns and, twice, milk warm and rich from accommodating cows. As the farms thinned and disappeared, hunger and winter became the more deadly enemies, followed by the relentless German and Romanian troops that had picked up their scent once more. The mountains were their best hope, and they headed for them first in a stolen German truck, dressed in uniforms they had stripped from the strangled driver and his passengers before tilting the bodies into a convenient ditch. When the roads became too dangerous, they returned to peasant dress and continued on foot.

As they approached the mountain passes the snow became a mixed blessing, sweeping away their tracks and forcing reconnaissance planes to the ground. Plodding along, they speculated whether the planes were searching for them or if they were approaching the German supply camps. There was no way of knowing. The radio had stopped working even before they had followed their last directive and set their explosives, and since the storm had howled down on them the night before, they had been lost.

The snow was knee-high, swirling around them and diminishing vision to less than a few yards as they began moving up a path so narrow, it appeared to have been forged solely for mountain goats. When they had climbed for the greater part of a day, they found a rocky outcropping and huddled under it. Once the storm ended, they had a view of the valley below.

When they saw the pass into which they had wandered, Aden and Karl began to mumble to each other, then demand they travel back down the mountain. "There are Germans below us and you want to go back?" Gregory Hunter exclaimed, astounded such levelheaded men should suddenly become so suicidal.

Karl Resik towered over Hunter, his thick frame, wiry red-blond beard, and frostbitten face making him look like some huge mountain beast. He stamped his feet to warm them and spoke patiently, as if Hunter were an ignorant child. "We have gone too far already, Gygory. The Mountain Lords know we are here. It may already be too late to retreat but we must try."

Resik's bravery was incredible, yet he quaked at folk tales! "Will superstition do to us what the Nazis have not? Will we be destroyed by myths you learned at your mother's knee?" Hunter challenged.

Resik huffed in anger. "They are not myths, Gygory. Remember the old woman in Tirgu and what she told us. Even Swiss doctors have interest in the powers of the ones who dwell here."

"Which proves nothing, except that the rumors are true about that so-called Dr. Baivie!" Hunter laughed. "Lords? In a place such as this?"

"We do not come here," Resik answered solemnly, "and in return they leave us in peace. It is an agreement we have observed in these mountains for centuries." The huge Romanian beat his fists against his shoulders, as if to break loose the ice coating his veins. "Come, it is almost dusk. We must go back."

Insanity, Hunter thought. There was no place for the group to take cover below, and if they divided, there would be a greater risk of capture. He tried a different approach. "If these lords have been here for centuries, Karl, perhaps they will not welcome our enemy. Perhaps they can be made to understand we fight for their futures as well as our own. I am an American and have made no pact with them. Would you agree to wait in this place while I go forward to explain why we are here and the horrors we oppose?''

Resik looked at his comrades, sitting close together for warmth, too exhausted to travel without rest. Even Aden sat wearily, unconcerned about the discussion's outcome. ''You are a fool, Gygory. But the war has made fools of us all. Go. Take your chance. At least with the ones who live here we may die less painful deaths. I will pray, and maybe God goes with you.''

God might be needed just to insure he survived at all, Hunter thought as he climbed. But he had forgotten how to pray, just as he had forgotten how it felt to think in English, to be warm, to sleep without dreams. He had lost all sensation in his feet hours ago. His fingers were beginning to follow, and the rest of him was hot and sticky under the layers of clothing. He stopped frequently to catch his breath, certain it was not only the thin mountain air that made his lungs labor so hard. If he was at home, he would turn up the heat, mix up some whiskey and cider, and stay in bed for a day or two, sweating out the fever. Here, alone or with the others, there was only one step, then another.

The path grew more treacherous, at times nearly ending completely, and once he slipped and found himself staring over a precipice that fell to the devil. Afterward he was thankful for the accident. His fear of heights gave him the adrenaline necessary to keep his exhausted body moving.

The mountains were deserted, and his best maneuver would be to find the first available shelter and in the morning descend and tell whatever lies were necessary to keep the small band together and in hiding. But what lies would he tell? Was he supposed to meet with creatures resembling Neanderthals? Vampires? Abominable snowmen? And when they met, what language would they speak? With no concrete information he allowed his mind to wander past that tenuous barrier separating the real and the fantastic and imagined some Shagri-la with food and drink and warmth for himself and his comrades. Rounding a bend, he was confronted by the reality of a rock slide covering a wide point in the path. Unpassable, but the only other choices were to stay where he was and

freeze by morning or return to his friends and admit he had
failed.

Hugging the mountain as tightly as he could, he began to
climb. Midway to the top, his numb fingers lost their hold.
He tried to twist and land on hands and knees but instead fell
on one side, dislocating a knee and, far worse, fracturing an
arm. The bone punctured his flesh and the blood that flowed
felt hot on his icy skin, giving him an odd, quick thought of
how pleasant it would be to drown in it.

He forced his leg to straighten, rearranged his jacket for
use as sling, and considered his dwindling possibilities. It
was useless to attempt to stand when he would only fall over
with his first step, so instead he began sliding back the way
he'd come, using his good arm and leg for leverage. The cold
was an anesthetic, the first small pile of stones an insur-
mountable obstacle. He took a deep breath to call for help,
then exhaled with a sound midway between a sob and a grim
laugh. Even if he did contact his friends, what then? Help
was miles away. Long before they reached it, he would die
of shock or exposure. Better in peace . . . here, alone.

The sky overhead had become a deep crimson, the moun-
taintops above him touched by the same color. He looked out
at the valley below, vowing to absorb every nuance of this
magnificent sunset, before the final sleep claimed him. . . .

"Death has a way of being elusive, even when we await
her kiss, Gregory Hunter."

Hunter had not heard his name for months. Since his arrival he'd used an alias and spoken the language of his mother,
and yet, halfway up a deserted mountain, someone addressed
him in English in a voice that convinced him angels were
real.

As he looked up he heard a flow of high, clear laughter.
"No, Gregory Hunter, I am not here to take you to your final
rest, though death may come to you yet—and soon. I am
Charles and I have seen to it that you will obtain your interview with . . . the Lord of the Mountain. A droll term, don't
you think, but accurate and one the master of this place finds
to his liking. Can you walk?"

The young man speaking to Hunter had pale skin and dark,
loosely curled hair. His features were radiantly handsome and

he was wearing elaborately tooled leather pants and a black, thinly woven shirt. No demon—quite normal, actually, except that his feet were bare and there were no tracks leading to the snowy spot on which he stood. In response to that last observation the man pointed to a ledge thirty feet above them. "Angels float. I jumped."

"Sure . . . sure you did." Again Hunter heard the laughter, as cold and clear as the water that flowed down the mountainside, harmonizing with its echoes off the ice-covered peaks. If a chamois could laugh, Hunter thought, this was the sound it would make.

"First you decide I am an apparition, then, like most Americans, you disappoint me by becoming so dismally concrete. But I am sure we will have more comfortable places to discuss American stolidity than here. I ask again, can you walk?"

"If you'll help, I'll try." Hunter began struggling to his feet, and as he swayed, Charles caught him and pushed him back against the boulder. "You are quite persistent but . . ." Charles looked up. A moment later Hunter also heard the whine of an aircraft, then saw a German plane flying low.

"Get down!" Hunter exclaimed but Charles held him upright and stared at the sky. "If you take pleasure in watching your enemies die, Gregory Hunter, observe this."

The tiny Messerschmidt passed them, then circled back lower and lower, again and again, until it hung less than fifty feet above the valley floor.

"He's killing himself!" Hunter whispered in astonishment.

The man beside him watched the plane with a displaced look of rapture. When it crashed, there were multiple explosions. "The soldiers following you were foolish enough to park their trucks too close together. They're now on an equal footing with your friends, so to speak."

Hunter gaped at Charles, who responded with a sly smile, as if the crash had been nothing more than a practical joke. Hunter whooped with a joy impossible to contain, and slumped unconscious against his rescuer.

It might have been hours or days later when Hunter woke and found himself in a small windowless room. The fire had been laid to burn too fiercely and the heat was stifling. His arm was splinted and supported by a sling, and he lay on a low, wide platform made comfortable by a huge feather mattress and a multitude of pillows piled atop it. His clothes were gone; someone had bathed him and shaved him. He recalled consoling whispers, tentative and gentle touches, the hint of a face but no more. On a carved wooden table beside his bed he saw a glass, a pitcher of water, an open bottle of wine, and a plate of cooked meat. Hunter sat up with difficulty and began to reach for the food, then pulled his arm back in suspicion.

—Take it, Gregory Hunter. You will need your strength when you are summoned.—

Hunter's eyes darted through the room. He was alone, yet someone had spoken.

—Only to your mind, Gregory. Now eat and sleep. You will know when it is time.—

"What happened to the men who were with me?" Hunter yelled.

—If you must speak, have the decency to whisper. As for your comrades, they toast your audacity with fine red wine. Good day, Gregory.—

The meat was too salty and smarted where it touched Hunter's chapped lips. It was burned black on the outside, raw near the bone, and it was the finest food he had ever eaten. He devoured it, washing it down with half the bottle of wine, and slept.

No one nudged him, no one spoke his name, yet Hunter woke knowing he had been called. His clothes were stacked neatly in the corner, and resting on them was a soft wool robe and a walking stick. He slipped on the robe, tying it as best he could, then limped down a narrow hallway, so lightless that he moved only on faith toward the archway ahead. When he crossed the portal, he stopped, transfixed by the glory of his surroundings.

The hall was over a hundred feet long, the ceilings vaulted high above it. Its sole illumination came from deep-toned glass windows . . . two roses at either end and a series of small rectangles near the ceiling along one side. The roses had a Moorish quality to their design but there was no form to the smaller ones, save that they filled the room with patterns and colors so vivid that they held substance. The tones enhanced the tapestries and paintings that softened the rough stone walls and the thick intricately patterned carpet that covered the floor; sculpture sat on low, carved, hand-rubbed tables. There were piles of pillows arranged on narrow benches, and all was shining and orderly and empty.

At the near end of the hall hung a life-size painting of a woman rising naked from a forest pond. The drops of water clinging to her pale skin were so realistic, Hunter was certain that if he touched her, his fingers would come away wet. She was standing in moonlight, and the light that fell on the canvas from the windows above had the quality of moonlight with the intensity of the sun. He was bewitched by the skill of the artist and the beauty of the subject, and all concerns vanished as he stared at it.

—My fourth chosen and the mother of my most troublesome and best-loved children.— The chant poured directly into his mind, the melody sung in a language Hunter did not recognize but somehow understood. Surprised, he whirled too quickly and, catching himself before he fell, looked up and saw a man sitting on a pillow-covered dais in the center of the room. Like Charles, the man's hair was coal black, his face bloodless, pale and captivating in its flawlessness. His wore only a pair of loose black trousers and a multitude of intricately worked wide gold bracelets on each wrist. The light that touched him turned his skin to white gold, and he sat cross-legged so still, he might have been an idol rather than a living creature.

"I'm sorry," Hunter said, his voice betraying little of the uneasiness he felt. "I thought I was alone."

"I do not think it rude of you to be enticed by beauty such as hers. Indeed, as the artist, I am complimented. Come forward." The order was whispered in Romanian and in a manner so natural, Hunter knew this was the lord whose hospitality he must request. He walked toward the dais, amazed at the youth of its occupant, until he felt that ancient soul move out from its long gaunt body and into his. Those brilliant eyes of undiluted darkness promised fulfillment of his every desire and every nightmare as the power flowed through him, touching his weakness and his strength. Hun-

ter's steps slowed. A few feet from the platform he stopped
and, for the first time in his life, bowed low and sincerely in
homage to another living creature.

"If all Americans have such impeccable taste, Captain
Hunter, I have been remiss in not visiting that land." Hunter
detected satisfaction in that whisper but no nod of the head,
no gesture to break the elegant stillness of that body, no
change in the unreadable intensity of the speaker's expression.

"How do you know my name?"

"In the same manner that I know you were born in . . .
Des Moines in . . . 1912 and received your first military training at Annapolis. You arrived here via . . . Belgrade and your
contact was . . . In Xanadu did Kublai Khan a stately pleasure dome decree. . . ." The fragments of the poem were
given in English, then the speaker chuckled low and quickly,
with a sound like a soft purr. "You learn at a remarkable
rate, Captain, and I am pleased you thought of that poem in
this place, for I am Francis and this is my pleasure dome. As
to my decree, tell me why for the first time in three hundred
years I should grant sanctuary to one of humankind?"

The words were intoned so softly, Hunter had to strain to
hear. When the question ended, it took Hunter a moment to
begin the rehearsed reply he had never anticipated giving.
"Because those with me fight for the country around you,
and if they fail and the Germans succeed, their people will
be enslaved and their masters will observe no pact, no ancient
beliefs. Your existence"—he paused, understanding he faced
a power he dared not belittle—"will no longer be peaceful.
You will have to fight for your lands." Hunter sensed approval of his wording, his speedy acceptance of the unbelievable, but his words had been spoken quickly and, in contrast
to his host's musical whisper, sounded strident and ugly.

"I am not ignorant, Captain Hunter. Romania and Hungary are both German allies, and these are not your people.
So tell me, Captain, why do you fight?"

"These are my mother's people and they have been betrayed. As to my own country, it will eventually be drawn
into this war. I am impatient to do my part."

"Are you merely suicidal or do you also claim to be a patriot?"

"I believe only that when madness threatens the world, it is my duty to respond."

His host's arm rose, pointing up and out, beyond the thick walls into the past. "I was a patriot once, I think, with dreams and ambitions for another race and time. And though my struggle and my life have been forgotten, I know I failed and this world is my condemnation. Once I wondered what my cause might have been; now I have long since ceased to care. As to man and his impatient ideals, I tell you, Gregory Hunter, I have found few whose souls equal those of the beasts that inhabit these peaks." He lowered his hand and smiled at Hunter, a serpent's smile of anticipation. "And are you brave, Captain?"

"My bravery has never been tested." Even before the reply came to him, Hunter knew and blanched.

—You have said it.—

". . . tell me your name and your contact and your assignment," the voice demands in German.

"No," he replies, the one thousand and fourteenth no to the one thousand and fourteenth time they have asked this same question. No one has touched him since his arrival, except to chain him face down in this lightless cell, his arms behind his back, a collar attached to a ring in the floor so he can only lay pressed against the damp stones, shivering and waiting for the door to open, bringing death or food. In the beginning he didn't care, but now life is his only passion, all that remains.

Whenever someone enters, a bright light comes on, blinding him so he can see the silhouette of boots but no more. "Your contact and your assignment, Captain Hunter." They have learned his name since they last questioned him, and their voices are polite, seemingly sympathetic to the level to which he has fallen. Sometimes they ask the question hundreds of times, hour after hour; at other times only once, and then the darkness comes and he is alone. At last he feels the toe of a boot brush down his back, and he swallows a cry and shakes so the chains rattle. They hear and he knows. *Tonight, tonight is the rest of my life. . . .*

They come for him, pushing him down the hallway. He is flung into a shower, the water first scalding, then icy cold. He manages to swallow some before they drag him down the hall to a tiny room and fasten his hands above his head. They wait an infinity of minutes, watching him, never speaking a word. They begin.

". . . talk to us, Captain, and we will dispense with any more of this. Tell us, Captain, tell us."

His future shrinks from days to minutes, to his next breath of air. The pain grows so intense, it acquires the substance of dreams and he wonders if he is alive . . . or tortured or in chains. "How in the hell do you know all this! How do you know what to do?" His words, then his screams, echo in the tiny, crowded room.

"Your contacts and your assignments, Captain." Their voices and their faces blur but the pain is real; they must be real, and the other—yes, the impossible other—must have been the dream. He is mad. He is certain he is mad.

"Talk to us, tell us and we will stop."

"No!" One thousand and . . .

He sits alone, unbound. Before him on the table is a re-volver. They give their own this simple way out. It seems a compliment, an admission of their defeat. As he reaches for it his hands shake and he wills them steady. He has survived this long, and his end will serve one more purpose. He picks up the weapon, cradles it like a newborn child, and waits.

When the door opens, he sees no uniform, only eyes . . . his enemy's eyes, reading the responses, the words on his soul. He holds out the gun in two shaking hands. "You god-damn beast. Get the hell out of my mind!" He fires. The chambers are empty of all but hope. A fist shatters his jaw, the first time something has broken, but its pain and all that follows is not real or true any longer. He remembers. . . .

It is an ancient mariner and he stoppeth one of three
'by thy long grey beard and glittering eye, wherefore
    stoppest thou . . .

Scraps of verse vanish in a final act of impossible power, pain returning as unfocused agony. It surrounds him, engulfs him, and with a frantic surge of will Hunter surfaces to reality. "I don't know any of this. You can't even guess. It's over, do you hear? You can't make it real anymore. It's over!"

Hunter fell slowly to the floor as the rain of blows softened and the walls of his cell moved up and out. . . .

His tormenter sat quietly in front of him, his head tilted, his expression of detached interest unaltered. "What in the hell did you prove?" Hunter yelled, then quieted to a whisper as he remembered what he faced. "Just tell me. Please . . ."

"Better, Captain. Now say no more until you have thought about what you have experienced in the last few minutes and what we both have learned."

Few minutes! Hunter took inventory. His body was untouched. "Thank you," he said.

Francis nodded in acknowledgment. "I have created similar illusions in different men with different fears. The majority chose death and so they died. Other sought refuge in insanity, but only three surprising times have any faced their deepest horror and returned to this room unchanged.

"You believed your life over. Self-destruction would have been the logical choice, yet you chose to destroy an enemy instead. Your mind is as easy to manipulate as any animal's, yet your will is magnificent . . . one worthy of family.

"So now we both understand that you are brave, Captain, but I tell you, such bravery is futile. When this war is ended, Britain, France, and your own nation will be the victors but it will be too late for this country. It may never taste true freedom again."

"Can you be so certain?"

"I can. The gift of prophecy has come with my millennia. So you see, there is no need for you to fight."

"And if everyone knew this and laid down their arms, would your words hold true?"

"Only you know. Only you have this choice, for I perceive your part in this conflict will make no difference on its outcome. Indeed I see you chained and shaking in that damp stone cell. You have lived through one path of your future, Captain. Reality may not be so merciful."

Hunter frowned and shook his head, not in denial but rather as a request for time, a request Francis refused to grant.

"Now I wish to offer you an alternative to that almost certain death."

. . . A cloud swirls around him, and when his vision clears, he is lying in a high four-poster bed between crisp sheets. He is propped up with pillows, a glass of wine in his hand, a leather-bound volume of *Moby Dick* open on his lap. A fire burns low on a huge stone hearth, and the room's walls are dark-paneled, decked with prints of old masters. He rubs his legs together, then flings back the covers and looks down at the green satin pajamas Amy had given him. They had been her gift; a luxury, she had said, to see him through the hard times. He had kissed her windburned cheeks, pushed back a strand of her pale brown hair, and thanked her for coming to see him off, though not sincerely. He had already told her good-bye when he'd hinted of the danger and asked her not to wait.

He knows this room. It is in the manor house, where he'd stayed while the British trained him for this assignment until the work became more physical than mental and he'd been transferred away. Perhaps he has returned because the war is over.

Only one facet of the room has changed. Before him on the wall hangs the picture of the woman bathing in the moonlight. He studies it, wishing she were real and here with him or, better, he in the woods with her. As he stares at it the frame loses its substance and the canvas expands, the forest circling him. He breathes deeply, smelling earth, scents of greenery and flowers. She turns and looks at him, her eyes slanting upward, her skin pale, glowing with the moon. She swims to the edge of the pool and steps up to the land. Water drips from her hair, down her high, small breasts, and she shakes her head, droplets flying as brilliantly as diamonds in the colorless light. She walks forward to where he lies naked on the soft pine floor, her legs straddling his as she kneels and pushes him back. For an instant he sees his body . . . hairless, luminous, his penis longer, narrower as it hardens in a desire more than physical, a desire not confined but surging through his body, pounding in every cell. He does not question his transformation; it is too great a pleasure now to feel.

His hands burn where they touch her while her nails scrape

his chest and hips. He hisses, strokes her, kisses her. His tongue is harder, rougher than he knew, her teeth long and pointed where molars should be, and both are no surprise. She balances on her knees, and lowering herself onto him, they press close, chest to chest, mind to mind. It is the ritual of dryads and satyrs . . . silent, immobile. His teeth in her shoulder, hers in his .. mind to mind, blood to blood. They share . . . they drink. . . .

Something rustles in the leaves and she looks at him standing beside her, gives a wordless challenge, and is gone. He follows, hand and feet springing lightly on the spongy earth, leaves whipping against his shoulders and thighs.

The fog closes in. He smells wine and wood smoke. He is back in the room with the picture on the wall.

Through the illusion the offer is made.—I live with my memories and I will share this past with you. You are free to stay here, safe from the storms that sweep across those cluttered lands below. No! Do not answer quickly. Think of all you have seen and felt this day.—

Hunter sips the wine, then places the glass on the table. He pages lovingly through the Melville book before closing it and setting it atop the nightstand, then shakes his head and replies sadly, "I thank you, Francis, Lord of the Mountain, but my place is with my people when they leave."

Walls dissolve. He lay naked at the foot of the dais in the great hall, his knee throbbing with pain, semen wet and sticky on his leg. For a moment he smiled then mouthed in silent rage, "You!"

"No. Illusions bring their own satisfactions." For the first time Francis stood. He was incredibly tall, well over seven feet, the height more in length of his legs than in his body, and his hand, resting on Hunter's shoulder, was long and thin, almost transparent in its delicacy.

His power lay in his mind, Hunter thought, and in reply Francis held up those hands spreading the fingers wide, curling them to reveal their impossible power. "I am a perfect instrument of death. Yet I have ignored your kind because it is convenient and because they have kept their promise and left me to my peace. I will not have that pact broken. You shall not leave this place until I have your word that what you have seen here shall never be revealed.''

Hunter's thoughts swayed between perplexed and furious, but fear held him silent.

''I understand, Captain Hunter, so I will speak for you. I summon you to this hall, and though you have no scars to show for it, I torture you and tempt you, then ask you for your oath. You have no reason to wish to give it.''

''And if I refuse?''

''You will die. Slowly but painlessly, for I admire you. Do you wish time to consider?''

Hunter shook his head. ''I agree. You have my word on it but—''

''But no, Captain Hunter, they would never think to ask, and if they did, I assure you, you will not speak. Now I extend to you the freedom of my home.''

Hunter looked up first. Another aircraft approached, its sound a reminder of a different savagery beyond these walls. The droning of the engine grew in volume until, a moment before Hunter believed it would crash through a window, it veered off. His host shook his head and sighed. ''They are such a persistent irritation. This one carried bombs. I suggested to the pilot he drop them on his own airstrip instead, so perhaps we shall have peace for a while. This hall is filled with memories. Feel free to explore them all. Good day, Captain.'' As suddenly as he had appeared, Francis vanished.

Hunter would have circled the room, but the visions had taken the same toll as their reality. He sat on the edge of the dais, marveling at the warmth of the the golden light, then slept and dreamed of the woman once again.

. . . He still sits on the dais but the hall is altered. There are no windows. Instead torches light its space. The painting is missing, the room filled with dark corners. He knows the woman's name now, Aiwe, and he whispers it as she walks toward him. He is young, the number thirteen comes to him; too young to be called! Shaking with awe and fear, he clutches a pillow and watches her approach.

Her clothing is of loose Turkish design, a short vest and long, side-slit skirt descending from a golden braid low on her hips. Fastened to the hems and strung on chains around her neck are a multitude of tiny golden bells that ring like child's laughter as she comes to him. The clothes accent her grace, and the white fabric from which all is cut is so gossamer that he sees the body beneath it outlined in the fires she passes. When she stops uncomfortably close to him, he breathes her scent, musky and enticing, as he thinks of all the magnificent terrible legends.

She kneels beside him and picks up a lute. "I have learned the song, Zoti. The one you murmur as you drift to sleep. Sing it with me." She begins in notes he can reach, "Why have you come here, girl of the night, your hair braided with wildflowers, you body clothed only in the first leaves of spring? I drench you with water that the earth may be kind and bring forth her fruit. Why have you come here, girl of the night, your breath with the warmth of the first breeze of spring. . . ."

When the song is done, she places a hand on his. "There is no need to fear me, Zoti," she whispers.

With great effort he replies in his own voice, "My name is Gregory and I will live this dream as myself." He expects her to vanish, but instead she holds out her arms, and though he hears the echoes of another's laughter, he does not care. . . .

From the concealing shadows of the catwalk high along the north side of the hall, Francis studied with frank interest the reactions of the man sleeping below him. He felt his son's presence behind him and said with thoughts tinged with sadness, —This world had altered my children in ways I could never understand. You, your brother, all of you have been seduced by it, yet I have never found a reason to care. Tell me why you have courted the danger and exposure?— "Tell me why you have died for them."

The last words were spoken, pitched low for emphasis. Below them, Hunter woke for a moment and would have looked up had Francis not forced the dream to continue.

—Think of how this vision should have ended, Father, and you will know that though you are an infinitely more skillful lover, you never could give Aiwe what that child did . . . the lust, the impatience, and the frank worship of her magnificent body. And when she killed him, she savored the finest feast of all . . . not only the fear but also the anger, the sorrow and the regret of unfulfilled hopes even old men have. The most unfeeling of them is more alive than I with my centuries, and you with your millennia, can ever be. You have grown cold, Father, yet even now their fires could warm you if you wished. Forget your promise. I give him to you. Go down, use him as you will, and let his body and his death recall for you the pleasures of your past.—

Charles laughed, but below them, Hunter had ceased to listen, lost in the vision, raised to a passion he had only imagined. In the end he cried out with her, and these were sounds Hunter had never expected to make or to hear on a frozen mountaintop somewhere too close to hell. . . .

Then, below as above, there was silence. Hunter slept a natural dreamless sleep. Francis shook his head and turned away. The desire he felt was the strongest he had experienced since Catherine had left him. He waited for some comment from his son, then realized he was alone. His mind expanded to the limits of his domain.—No— he wished to call, but Charles was correct, and when he returned, the gift he brought would be accepted.

Chapter Sixteen

I

KURT SCHMIDT MISSED the fur-lined boots he'd worn the previous winter in Bonn. Although he'd been allowed to bring them to Romania, they were not regulation, and his sergeant, in a fit of imperious rage, had ordered Kurt to destroy them. "Discipline and order," the sergeant had barked while Kurt labored with a dull knife, carrying out the wasteful command. Some days later the sergeant had been killed by insurrectionists, his dark uniform making him an easy target against the moonlit snow, and warily men began wearing sheets over their jackets when they were on guard duty. Even the most meticulous leaders turned a blind eye.

After his boots were gone, Kurt wrote and asked his mother to send his thick wool socks. He wanted spares, he told her, not wishing to concern her by saying he would wear three pairs simultaneously if he had them.

That letter, like those preceding it, was deceptively light and short because he could think of no good news to convey. "The mountains are majestic," he wrote, "and cold, endlessly cold."

But their wild beauty cleansed him, helping him forget the eyes of the farmers, of their children, staring at the convoy as it rolled through village after village in Austria, then Hungary, commandeering what supplies they needed and leaving barely enough for their reluctant allies to survive. And they dulled the memory of the one time he had seen action, shooting down a group of boys, some younger than his brother, trying to sabotage the train tracks near Aba. He made the mistake of looking into their faces. Later he could not sleep, until he cried.

After the sergeant was shot, conditions improved. His replacement was a seasoned veteran and a practical man. Their lieutenant, Eric Ruthinedt, had a reputation for caution . . . a perfect leader to follow into battle. For the moment they guarded incoming shipments of supplies, but once the fighting began, they would be called to the front. Perhaps it was the inevitability of that horror that made them so lighthearted on today's mission.

When he heard they'd be climbing today, Kurt had rejoiced. Although only seventeen, he was an experienced mountaineer and had always wanted to study this range. The night before, he had labored to make his uniform more practical, scoring the soles of his boots to give them better traction in the snow, then lining them and the legs of his pants with strips of cloth cut from an old blanket. The small modifications had been a success. Outside of the lieutenant, who had brought a walking stick, he was the only one who had not fallen, though, he admitted to himself, he was not as warm as Abert and Boch, who, bringing up the rear of their group of ten, were quietly sharing a flask of schnapps.

Discipline appeared to last only as long as the lieutenant was watching, Kurt thought, and today Ruthinedt was too preoccupied with peering into the distance ahead to keep a close watch on the troops behind. Their orders had been vague . . . to seek and destroy an undetermined number of insurrectionists, and, rumor said, Ruthinedt had argued with his superior about bringing such a small group of men. Still, the heights seemed deserted and the only danger came from the path that had narrowed until they were forced to travel single file. Although it would be practical, Kurt was loath to suggest they string a rope along their company, for he had no desire to be attached to the two behind him, nor to be the one to reveal they had been drinking.

As they rounded a bend Kurt lost sight of Abert and Boch. When the path straightened, they were no longer behind him. "Lieutenant," he called out anxiously, "we've lost two men."

Ruthinedt signaled a halt, then, in apparent irritation,

walked cautiously around his squad and looked over the side of the cliff. The bodies lay halfway down the mountainside. When he called their names, they didn't move.

"One might have tripped, and the other fallen also when he tried to help," a corporal suggested.

"I didn't hear anything," Kurt said. "Shouldn't they have cried out?"

The lieutenant agreed as he studied the bodies through his field glasses, then angrily snapped them shut. "Damned fools!" he muttered to himself then, louder, to his men, "They're dead. Keep close together and be careful."

"Sir," Kurt persisted, "I could climb down."

"It isn't necessary." Ruthinedt stared at the ground as he continued. "We'll discuss what happened after we've rested."

Kurt glanced at the spot that had fascinated the lieutenant a moment earlier and saw the small drops of blood on the snow. This had been no accident. Their mission was more dangerous than anyone other than the lieutenant had known. For safety Kurt stayed as close to the mountainside as possible as they continued up the narrow path.

In a wide place where they could see some distance in either direction, the lieutenant called a halt. Guards were posted above and below, and the rest of the men set down their packs and rifles and wearily dropped beside them.

"Cigarette?" Hans held out a pack to Kurt.

Kurt shook his head and reached into his pocket for a peppermint, slipping one to Hans as well, ashamed that he had no wish to share with any save his friend. Hans chuckled. "I'd forgotten how young you are, but they recruit children now, don't they?"

In the past weeks Kurt had grown used to the teasing. "You can always refuse to partake of such a childish vice."

Hans winked, then popped the candy into his mouth. "Too bad about Albert and Boch. Drinking, weren't they?"

Kurt nodded absently. He'd hardly known the two, and from what little he had observed, he hadn't liked them. He watched the lieutenant study the sheer sides of the cliffs above them, looking perplexed. *We chase shadows,* Kurt thought, and looked up at the threatening sky. It would snow again soon, and they would be trapped here.

"Ten more minutes," the lieutenant called out.

Kurt leaned back against his pack and put a fingerful of fresh snow into his mouth, its coldness amplified by the taste of the mint. Were it not for the uniforms, the weapons, and the deaths, this would have been a fine winter outing. He lay back and listened to the voices speaking quietly around him. The sudden tragedy had sobered them all.

He felt thoughts brush his mind as melodies would sometimes replay in his memory until he was almost certain he truly heard them. He looked up and saw a face leaning over the cliff above him, a beautiful face, so beautiful that he knew his mind played games with him. Daydreams, just daydreams. He sighed, returned the apparition's smile, and closed his eyes.

"What! Gott! Where did . . . Who are you?" voices exclaimed as they stared at a young man wearing only leather breeches who seemingly had fallen out of the sky. Kurt sat up, stared in astonishment, and said nothing.

The man addressed Ruthinedt. "You have violated the borders of a sovereign state, Lieutenant. The penalty is death. I am here to carry out that sentence."

Ruthinedt's surprise lasted only a moment, then he bristled and ordered, "Take him!"

The two men closest to the intruder rushed forward to carry out the order. Instead of preparing to fight, the intruder held out his hands palms out at his side, the gesture down to his beatific expression a replica of plaster images of much-revered saints. His eyes were locked with Ruthinedt's but on either side of him the soldiers walked past him and, with no falter in their somnabulant pacing, with no sound of protest, over the edge of the cliff.

"*Sechs,*" the young man said, and grinned. Then, as they stared at the long extra set of upper canines, the youth made a motion Kurt could only compare to a cat unsheathing its claws. His fingers curled, his muscles tensed, and with a demonic shriek he lashed out with one foot, catching Walter in the stomach, pulling back with his toes hooked to steaming entrails. Walter screamed and fell forward, his blood pulsing bright red onto the pure white snow.

The remaining soldiers stood as frozen as the peaks around

them while the young man tilted his head and whispered softly, *"Fünf."*

The spell lifted and the lieutenant bellowed, "Shoot him!" and pulled out his revolver only to find he could not raise his hand. Kurt, trying to grab his rifle, could not move at all. Two more were caught before they reached their weapons. One died as Walter was dying, but instantly when a hand ripped him open and severed an artery. As he scrambled for his rifle Hans slipped in the snow. "Hurry!" the lieutenant bellowed as Hans turned and aimed.

Their enemy flung another over the cliff. *"Drei,"* he said then, too fast for any to see, dodged the bullets and wrenched the rifle away from Hans. He hesitated then and, with an expression of arrogant and deadly anticipation, grabbed the lapels of Hans's coat, ripping it and the shirt beneath open. Hans's eyes were locked to his attacker's and he said nothing until he fell forward into those deadly arms. Then screams, more terrible by contrast to the earlier silence, began. The sight and sound and the agony he was forced to share became more than Kurt could stand, and he fought the grip on him, managing to roll his body sideways to vomit what little remained from his last meal onto the snow.

Long after the cries had ended, Kurt heard the soft sucking sounds becoming louder and slower until death claimed another victim. Then the victor dropped the body and stretched gracefully. Each limb was covered with the gore of a different life ended, and his face was bloody from the remnants of his feast. He licked his fingers. *"Zwei."*

He straddled Kurt next. Kurt tried to avoid his stare, and when he could not, Kurt returned it with what small boldness he could muster. He was touched by hints of all his possible ends until his bravery faltered and he begged, "No."

His captor moved, standing inches away from the lieutenant, who waited with a stoic expression that masked a multitude of smaller emotions. With a silvery laugh the killer exposed them.

Ruthinedt's reputation was one of the best in the division, yet how easily he broke, Kurt thought. The lieutenant tried to turn the revolver on himself but suicide was denied him. He fell to his knees. "Please . . . do it quickly, please!"

Kurt was ashamed of his fascination, yet he watched until

the young man, who was something far more than a man,
turned to him. "It is fortunate to have a coward for a commander. Follow such a one into battle and there's a good
chance you'll survive." He turned back to the lieutenant.
"You disappoint me. I had expected some endurance. Nevertheless, your life is in my hands and it is not for you to say
how it will end. One of you shall deliver a message to the
commander of the troops below and the other shall stay with
me. Which, Lieutenant, shall you be?"

II

With empty darkness and disconnected memories for companions, the one men had called Francis for these last thousand years sat in his private chamber and waited for his gift.
When it arrived, he would feel the changes in the texture of
the air around him, and should he wish, he could know a
great deal before he ever saw the man, just as he had felt first
the pain, then the prehensile determination that was so much
a part of Gregory Hunter.

When the fearful fluctuations began, he was relieved. Here
was one with a conscience already so black, death terrified
him. Francis had destroyed that kind a thousand times, and
while he had hoped for an easy conquest and an easy kill, he
had expected greater subtlety from his son. Francis bowed
his head until the call found him.

—He is in Hunter's room. I have prepared him and he
awaits your pleasure.—

The still air swirled around Francis as he traveled the length
of the corridor. At the doorway he felt the warmth flowing
out through its thick wood . . . the heat of the fire and the
passions of the man beside it longing, as all creatures do, for
freedom, happiness, hope. He reached for the door handle,
then pulled back, desiring nothing more than the crisp mountain air, the starlit snows, and the vacuous life he used so
carelessly.

Laughter, followed by thoughts from a distance. —You may

refuse my gift, Father, but I recall you saying you did not care.—

Words spoken in haste had condemned him to this moment. He unlocked the door and stepped inside.

His first impression was that the Germans sent children to fight their battles, for the face that stared at him was a child's face. But as the soldier stood and tensed for this final conflict, Francis saw it had a man's growth and its body was strong and healthy. The soldier was warm from the fire and from the dregs of the bottle of wine Hunter had left unfinished. His eyes were round with terror and he clutched a letter to his chest, as if it held some treasure more priceless than life. The soldier sprang to his left, and when he landed, Francis was facing him. He tried once more and Francis moved closer. In a last heroic effort the soldier grasped the neck of the wine bottle and broke it against the fireplace stones. "I will betray no secrets!" he screamed, and held it out protectively.

The doubt in Francis departed. He had let first impressions deceive. "I have no need of your knowledge. You are alive only so that I may have the pleasure of killing you, and how mercifully I consummate that final act will be determined by how much of yourself you are willing to surrender to me." He reached out an arm toward his victim. "Now put down your weapon and take my hand."

A blood-soaked demon had dragged Kurt up the mountain, then ripped the torn and soiled uniform from his body, feeding it piece by piece to the fire while Kurt had stood unable to move or say a word of protest. Only when his shirt was held up to the flames did he begin to tremble so pitifully that he was allowed to plead, "There is a letter in the pocket. Please, don't burn it. . . . Please." His captor returned it and Kurt clutched the thin envelope to his chest as his uniform dissolved into smoke, then fire.

Afterward he was left alone, and as he waited for some fate to find him, he drank the wine and watched the buttons of his coat melt into bright metal coins atop the coals. There was no glory left, no cause save his dying, and he prayed for the strength to face it with nobility. Now that would be denied him as well. His will fled as he looked at the tapering fingers reaching out to him, up the long arm to that bewitching, beautiful face . . . to the huge black eyes glowing in the fire-light with understanding and compassion and love. Slowly he lowered the bottle, let the envelope fall to the floor, and grasped that hand. . . .

In the hour before dawn the door opened. Across from it, Charles sat with his legs pulled tight against his chest, his head resting on his knees. When his father emerged, he looked up with an expression that held the weary challenge of a fencer making a final, furious onslaught in a duel that had lasted far too long.

"There are monsters below us and you brought an inno-cent to me! Why?" The intensity of Francis's emotions rang through the empty halls.

"Because the other would have been an insult. I wished you to recall their worth. Did I succeed?"

"There was no worth save what he might have become." He threw Kurt's letter at his son's feet. "This letter he begged back from you was no note from a sweetheart but one to be mailed to his mother should he die. But we are never uncer-tain when one of our own is lost, are we, Charles?" He looked toward the great hall in the first glow of morning. "Once these walls were filled with the sounds of a family. Soon I shall be the only one of our own that remains. When Hunter is well enough to travel, leave with him. We are too alike to live together any longer."

"So you have told me a thousand times, Father, though never so bluntly. Very well, I will go with Hunter. The war will be a heady sustenance and provide, perhaps, an end to the charade that has become my life." He felt the purity of his father's astonishment, then the expected wrath before the words began.

"Once I longed for such an easy accident, but the only ones destroyed were the ones I loved. Guard your soul jeal-ously, Charles. If the world grows too oppressive, go to your brother and confess your sins or return to me. For the family's sake, I will never close these halls to you."

Charles's look apologized for a multitude of transgres-sions. Finally he said, "I will remove the body."

"There is none. It has been centuries since I killed a man solely for pleasure, and I did not choose to begin once more with a child merely to prove something we both know. No matter, it is unlikely he will leave here alive, so that letter is as good as true. Send it after you leave."

"Of course."

"One final request. See that Hunter doesn't strangle this child should they pass in the halls."

He departed with long catlike strides, leaving his son staring at the closed door. After a moment Charles stood and entered the room.

Kurt slept, sprawled across the bed. There were no marks on him; nothing had been taken, not even innocence. Ordering Kurt to a deeper sleep, Charles lay behind him, one arm cradling his head, as his mind began its delicate probing . . . childhood, father, mother, the family, the easiest memories those so soon replayed. Through loneliness his father had found mercy.

Charles withdrew to his own past, fighting back a desire acquired more from experience than from inclination . . . from the years when women had been sheltered and dangerous and men so approachable, so ready to satisfy. Oh, humanity, how unpleasant there were so many he could not help but love.

He held Kurt tighter, counting the years since he had possessed such innocence . . . but no, let Francis claim this one, should he wish, unsullied by his touch.

Without waking, Kurt rolled sideways, pressing his body against his captor's, attracted by the warmth. Charles wished he had brought the other one, shaking, screaming, hysterical with fear. Yes, his father could have played with that, devouring it without care. He carefully slipped away from Kurt, retrieving the blanket that had fallen to the floor, covering the young man. Then he crouched beside him, forcing Kurt into a lighter, more receptive sleep. Brushing a hand over Kurt's forehead, his mind began to speak

—Listen to me. Should you wish to survive, listen now and I will tell you what you must do.—

And later, far later, a thought daring in its implication.

—When this is over, if I am able, I will come for you and

take you home. Remember . . . remember . . . let my promise be your hope.—

III

The singing woke Hunter, crystal-cold notes rising and
falling, a soprano of rare power.

> "I am dark, I am light,
> I am the consummation of the night
> Come to me.
> I have lips, I have hands,
> I have a mind to dream your private dreams,
> Speak to me . . .
> Love me . . . Yield to me . . ."

Hunter followed the music, traveling toward a flickering
light that spilled from an open door at the end of a long,
narrow hall. The singing stopped as he entered an artist's
studio, large and functionally furnished, its clear glass windows coated with frost feathers. An oil lamp provided the
light, a low fire some small warmth. He saw Charles holding
a palette and studying the canvas on the easel. He waved
Hunter over, then held the lamp close to his creation. "What
do you think of it?"

Hunter flinched, then replied, "It's horrible."

Charles laughed. "The execution or the subject?"

"You have a good eye for detail. What is it?"

"The Children's Crusade."

Hunter studied the face of the Saracen victor, the stance of
his body as he stood above the carnage, his lance descending
to destroy the last adversary, a boy half his size who had
fallen to one knee, his broken sword held high, his expression
one of fearful resignation. Hunter's gaze returned to the victor's face, and he saw in it the guilt the man would carry for
the remainder of his life. Hunter did not believe he had ever
seen anguish and duty so perfectly portrayed.

"A friend lost three of his sons in that battle. The oldest was fourteen."

"I . . . I see."

Charles laughed. "I suspect you finally do. And did you have a satisfying afternoon?"

"Spotty." Hunter moved closer to the fire.

"He had his reasons for what he did," Charles said.

"When we go through training, we are subjected to Gestapo grilling, but only I am prepared for the pain. I thanked him sincerely. There are many who would envy me the experience I was given." The words sounded hollow but they were the truth.

Charles looked intently at his guest, then commented, "Perhaps he is wrong about your future. His gift is not flawless, and sometimes, I suspect, he lies." Charles waved the brush at a shelf behind Hunter. "You'll find something more substantial than dreams over there."

Hunter glanced over the assortment of food and took crackers and cheese. "German rations?"

"The ones who carried them have no need for them any longer." Hunter studied the dried red streaks on the box. "Yes, it is blood."

"I'm still hungry."

"A realist who quotes Coleridge. I'll relish your company when we leave here." He laughed at Hunter's obvious dismay. "Yes, Gregory, I will leave with you. I've been asked to take a sabbatical from the ancestral nest, so to speak, and I will be an admirable addition to your group, will I not?" His eyes hinted at the depth of his scrutiny. "Of course, I am a damned aristocrat, but even aristocrats are penniless today." Charles appeared to shrink in stature, in the length of his arms and legs. His eyes became smaller, filled with peasant suspicion. "You will find my talents useful, Gygory; more than you know."

"Maybe. I haven't agreed."

"You will. Look in the cupboard behind you."

Hunter did. "A radio! Where did you get this?"

"From the same platoon that has no need of food any longer. Can you send a message with it?"

Hunter opened the case and began checking the transceiver. "Farther than I'd ever thought we could go."

"Send your allies this." Charles handed Hunter a scrap of paper. "One of their ciphers, I think."

Hunter looked up at Charles in frank astonishment. "How do you know it?"

"I am my father's son, Gregory."

And his assets were irresistible! "Can you follow orders?" Hunter asked.

IV

Concentrating solely on the placement of one icy foot in front of the other, Eric Ruthinedt plodded back to his camp, intent on concluding his mission. The afternoon sky darkened, the snow fell once more, and the hungry wind devoured his strength. He was on the edge of lethal exhaustion when a search party found him, yet he struggled to break free, needing to be reassured repeatedly that they would take him directly to his superior before he would cease the struggle.

Once there, he stood before the colonel, swaying and shivering. His commander, feeling pity for his subordinate's devotion to duty, walked around his desk and offered a chair.

Ruthinedt shook his head and forced his stance to become as formal as a gun barrel. "I act as courier with a message for you." His language switched to musically accented Romanian. "The penalty for trespass into the Varda Pass is death. Should your assault on our borders continue, we will have no choice but to destroy your base. So speak the Mountain Lords. Heed them." Ruthinedt wilted and leaned against the colonel's desk. "Heed them," he repeated in German. "My men have been ripped apart . . . devoured . . . all dead. I must join them." He paused, his final compulsion held back by a rush of natural dread, then he began to raise his gun to his open mouth. The colonel, noted for quick deduction, lunged for the weapon while bellowing for his guards.

The next afternoon a disarmed, sedated Ruthinedt woke to find himself sitting beside a sergeant on a train heading west to his new assignment with a squad near Paris.

"Did they discover the bodies?"

"Boch and Abert. They'd been shot through the necks, apparently by a crossbow." He snorted with contempt. "The resistance is so primitive."

"And the others?"

"Lost in the storm. This spring we'll look again."

"You'll never find them," Ruthinedt said, and looked out at the snow-covered farmland. No amount of distance could separate him from his fear. He would be haunted by every small detail of that bewitching face, and he knew that someday his suicidal compulsion would return. He consoled himself with thoughts of revenge. Should that unlikely opportunity arise, he would savor every pain-filled moment.

Chapter Seventeen

I

THE WINDOWLESS ROOM holding Kurt a prisoner had been built specifically to contain human hostages in an era when such hostages were valuable. Though he had no way of marking time, Kurt remained there for four days, and while he slept, someone left food and fresh firewood. Finally his unseen jailer brought slacks and a shirt, which, when cuffs and sleeves were rolled, were a fair fit.

He was asleep when the unexpected touch of a hand startled him.

Though Kurt did not remember their first meeting, this creature's resemblance to the one who had brought him here was obvious, and Kurt rolled quickly onto his feet on the far side of the bed, realizing too late that he had placed himself in a corner.

Francis sat on a stool, absorbing this fear for some time before trying to soothe him. —I have come to say you will not be harmed. You have been given to me and I have spared your life. Now I wish to offer you the freedom of travel within these walls.—

Kurt understood only part of these thoughts. "Who? Who gave me to you?"

—You could not speak his name but you may call him— "Charles."

"Charles . . . gave me to you?"

—Yes. If you obey me, I will care for you.—

Kurt turned his face to the wall, determined to ignore this

mental conversation; nevertheless, he stiffened as he felt the hard slap of anger.

—Like it or not, you will remain here and you will obey me.—

Kurt shook his head and moved toward Francis, preparing to attack or escape, but a few feet from him he could advance no farther.

—Your attitude will cause only your death, do you understand?—

Kurt clenched his teeth, prepared to have an assent wrested from him, but Francis only stood and walked toward the door.

—Very well. When you are ready to yield, I will know.—

He locked the door and departed.

The fire died for lack of wood and the cold winter draft crept in beneath the door. Kurt rolled the feather mattress sideways and huddled in it—shivering, hungry, and thirsty. His body was young and made demands. He surrendered.

Francis brought water and wine, food, wood for the fire, and a robe and boots for him to wear. Perhaps Kurt should have been grateful and it certainly would have been wise to give some thanks, but all he saw when he looked at Francis was the one on the mountain, that bewitching, blood-soaked face. Kurt held his breath each time Francis moved too close, finding it impossible after a while not to stare at him, caught by the grace and strange feline beauty of his almost human captor.

He expected some commands, but Francis left without a word. Kurt contemplated the open door for some time before walking through it.

For days he explored the cold, deserted halls, seeing none of their beauty, knowing only that they were his prison and he must be familiar with them. Finally he found a staircase leading to a tall open tower overlooking the mountainside. Pulling himself onto the parapet, he leaned over it, staring at the moonlit snow beneath him, thinking not of suicide but of how easily he could achieve it should that desire ever come.

Below him, someone meditated on his thoughts and answered them. —It is easy to contemplate what you do not wish to seek.—

"You!" Kurt screamed, an echo the only audible reply.

—Should you ever pursue death, recall my promise.—

Kurt crouched in the darkest corner, staring at the staircase, waiting for that monster to come for him, quaking with the terrible dread of insanity. "I belong to no one but myself," he bellowed.

The laughter enveloped him. —To whom did you belong when you wore that uniform?—

"Leave me alone!" Kurt demanded, then winced, waiting for a response both unfathomable and unpleasant.

—Child, tonight I leave this place. You need only fear the other beast.—

Kurt sat watching the moonlight pattern the stone floor. When he grew sleepy from the cold, he descended to grope his way to his cell and build up the fire. As he dug in his dwindling cache of food he spied a peppermint, half hidden by the stones of the hearth. The taste brought memories of home, and he lay facedown on his bed in a despair too huge for tears.

He sensed the touch in his mind, the loving, deceitful concern of his jailer, and dared not move as that body lay behind him, arms circling his chest, a body pressed against his back. Rash confidence was Kurt's first response. *I am asleep; he cannot wake me.*

—Child.—

I am asleep. He cannot wake me.

—Child.—

You cannot wake me, such a simple affirmation failing to a plea.

Francis pushed him onto his back. —Child, look at me.—

Inevitably Kurt obeyed and fell into the calm, inviting sleep of his captor's eyes.

. . . He is at his grandmother's, in the vinyards on a sun-drenched October afternoon picking grapes for the wine presses. It is his favorite week of the year, this week he is near Katya, and he watches her working farther up the row, her long blond hair brushing against her white cotton blouse.

He loves her with all the fervor of a first love, but she is his aunt, born twenty years after his mother, and he dares not speak. To be near her is enough . . . to brush against her bare arm is enough. Her box is full, and he offers to carry it to the cart at the end of the row. There he looks down at the dusty mounts of purple and, shining like undyed silk, is a single strand of her hair. He winds it around his finger, watching it catch silver highlights from the brilliant autumn sky.

When the work is done, Katya's brother steals a bottle of wine and the three sit side by side behind the house sharing it, watching the sun set behind the gold linden trees. He leans close to her and imagines how her kiss would feel, her hands brushing back his hair . . . a vision so vivid, he knows she must sense it, and he flushes and looks quickly away so she will not see.

Too late. She laughs and kisses him with all the passion he'd imagined her kiss would hold. He responds and feels the warmth of her skin against him, the soft brush of her hair on his shoulder. "I love you," he whispers.

"Of course," she replies. "Of course."

He has never felt such happiness, such perfect desire. He holds her head against his chest and, lost in the touch of her lips and hands, raises his face to the paint box blue sky and closes his eyes. . . .

When he opened them, Kurt saw the gray stone wall of his cell, the embers of a fire he had set hours before. For a moment he smiled at the memory of the dream, then recalled that earlier he had not been alone. The side of his neck tingled and he brushed the spot and looked in horror at the blood smeared across his fingertips.

If this was the beginning, how would it end? What old dreams and desires could this creature touch when it wished? And once his mind no longer amused, would it use his body too? But no, there was another path open to him. Pulling the blanket from the bed, he began ripping it into long, narrow strips.

II

"I tell you, Gygory, I have never felt such fear but I could not disobey, so instead I walked forward so stiff-legged, I fell over the things that had been left for us. Food, wine, wood for a fire . . . such wonderfully simple treasures. Then the next day we were led to this." Resik gestured at their small stone cottage. "No words were used but we knew where to find it."

"I prayed for you," Dimi added to Resik's account. "God listened."

"The lords listened," Mikel corrected. "Had they not, we would all be dead." From Hunter there was no response, not even denial.

"I hear their skin is as pale as new milk, their hair black like the wings of a raven, their eyes as brilliant as ripe blackberries," Resik said.

Hunter laughed. "Do you think I don't know my own heritage? You describe Rusalii the Satyr."

"And their minds soar like swifts in the twilight sky and their voices ring as high and as pure as notes played on the finest old violins. It is said that to share their love is to grasp a piece of paradise," Aden added.

"Blasphemy!" Dimi exclaimed with practiced anger.

"No, fantasy." Hunter snorted. "Just pretty fantasy. A few days ago you expected monsters to rip you apart."

"Two weeks ago," Resik corrected. "And why should we not contemplate the finer tales of those who have proven to be such perfect hosts?" When Hunter only looked at him blankly, Resik pointed to his splint. "Someone tended to your arm, Gygory. Who?"

Hunter's expression hardened. "None of you would break your oath. Now, shall we go there while there is still some light to travel?"

They departed, walking single file, Resik supporting Hunter when the path grew too steep for his injured leg. They halted at the same overhang where their good fortune had begun two weeks earlier, and looked at the sky, thinking of the irony that after days of perfect weather they would have another storm in which to travel.

* * *

Noticing motion on the path above them, Resik pointed out the traveler to Hunter. The clothing and the speed made the man's identity obvious. Hunter had been warned not to harm the young German, but certainly that warning did not hold if the man was attempting an escape. "Stay here," he whispered to the rest, then scrambled up the path, clutching a revolver.

They met at a wide place in the path. Kurt's slacks were ripped and a welt had formed on his forehead. He'd tied the ends of his flapping robe together, then wrapped the make-shift rope around his waist. When he saw the figure in front of him, his first expression was one of mute terror until, realizing his adversary was only human, he relaxed.

"Go back," Hunter ordered in Romanian. Kurt did not understand the language, but the meaning of the gun pointed at him was unmistakable. His eyes widened and he shook his head and continued walking forward, his expression a plea for mercy.

"Go back, I said." Hunter accompanied this with a clar-ifying gesture and, when ignored, aimed and shot at Kurt's leg. In that moment Kurt sprang and Hunter rolled sideways, his feet lashing out, kicking the young German over the edge. Kurt fell without any cry, still fearful that his jailer would hear and seek.

Shaken, Hunter walked as close to the drop as he dared, then slid forward and saw Kurt lying motionless on a snow-covered ledge some twenty feet below him. Resik rushed up and knelt beside his friend, then called back a reassurance for the rest.

"Let's go," Hunter said.

"We leave him?" A high-pitch cry descended from the mountaintop.

"And fast. Come on."

The cry came again, louder and closer and seemingly an-grier. With one last look at the man lying below, Resik ran after his retreating friend.

The five reached Hunter's destination at midnight, hiding in a small stand of trees near the crossroads, waiting for the American contact Hunter had told them to expect. When the man arrived, they exchanged first names and he fell in behind the rest.

The wind increased and snow was beginning to fall when they finally stopped for sleep in a barn beside a burned-out farmhouse. Their new ally declined to share their food, evading questions about his past. His Romanian held no trace of an accent and his gestures spoke of one born to wealth or title. Dimi and Aden watched Charles suspiciously while Mikel slid to sit beside Karl Resik. "He does not look like an American," Mikel hissed, the anxiety in his tone saying more than he had spoken.

"You think of the tales of the ones that serve?" Mikel gave a quick nod, his eyes on Charles as he spoke. "He will be loyal only to his master. We can't trust such a one, Karl. I say we leave him."

"Silence! If the devil declared himself Romanian, I would welcome his power and call him brother." Resik walked across the barn and sat beside their new ally, giving Charles a heavy clap on the back. "Now that here is a chance to speak, welcome, friend."

Charles did not move from the blow of that huge hand. Instead his dark, colorless eyes met Resik's, and after a moment he responded, "I am pleased to be among such courageous men as you, Karl Resik. We fight for our country, yes?"

The word *our* fell like a bomb, followed by silence. All eyes were fixed on Charles as he rummaged in his broad leather pack and extracted a half-liter bottle of wine. Pulling the cork, he held the bottle out to Resik. "Shall we drink to a free Romania, comrades?"

"By God, I will!" Resik took a swallow, then handed it to Mikel who passed it to Dimi, who paused, then grasped it as well until, four fifths empty, it returned to its owner. "To Romania," Charles repeated, "and to the vices of her patriots." As he tilted back the bottle and drained it he considered that of all the family, he alone understood the immense social value of small human vices.

A short time later he left the rest and climbed the narrow, rotting ladder to the top of the silo. He pushed open what remained of the doors and looked out at the heavy snow. The storm raged, the wind blowing from the direction of the mountains, and above it he heard a louder, longer, more desolate howl . . . the part of his life that had ended. He stared at the countryside a moment longer, then descended and walked back into the dim pool of light. "Well, comrades," he said as he produced two more bottles, "no one will disturb us tonight. Shall we forget the war for a while?"

"Then perhaps you will tell us what it is like to serve the Mountain Lords," Aden said. "I have heard . . ."

As he spoke, Charles was extracting the remaining treasure in his sack. Seeing the crossbow, Mikel began a warning, "If you are caught with that . . ."

"You carry guns that, when used, reveal your location. I carry this, which is silent, and, in my hands, swift." Charles had been twirling an arrow as he spoke; now he let it fly, to land on a beam on the other side of the barn.

"I could not see you load or shoot," Dimi said in sudden understanding, then looked down at the straw and crossed himself. The others stiffened, suddenly alert, as if an enemy soldier had fallen into their midst.

Resik glanced at Hunter, then repeated the gesture he'd used earlier, laying a hand on Charles's shoulder. Charles stared at each of the men, making sure he met each man's eyes before he spoke. "I am no devil, and none of you should fear me. We share the same country and the same goal and there will be no shortage of victims to meet my needs among the soldiers we will kill together . . . each in our own way."

Aden stared at their new ally, his fear slowly turning to wonder. "The legends are true," he whispered.

"They're true," Charles replied, and sent another arrow flying to split the first.

As Charles answered the questions that followed, he exuded such charm that even Dimi forgot his fear. Only Hunter sat apart, meditating on the words that had formed in his mind. —What I say makes no difference. Death has them in her net. Perhaps we shall share their fate.—

Dear Lord! Why did he sound so hopeful?

Chapter Eighteen

I

BUT IT DID not seem that Hunter's group was doomed; indeed, their successes had never been so great. They downed miles of phone lines, blew up two bridges, and, when explosives or supplies ran low, Charles left them and traveled by night into the nearest town, returning before dawn with their shopping list complete and enough money to provide them with months of bribes.

Later their radio gave out and Charles stopped an army truck, freezing the driver and men inside with the power of his mind. Hunter's men killed all but one. Charles claimed the last for his own needs, dragging the soldier into the cab, slowly draining the life from his body while Hunter rummaged through the cargo, picking the best equipment he could find.

When he had no need of life or blood, Charles killed in a human manner, mechanical and quick, never looking at his victims' eyes or into their souls. He followed orders perfectly, his response—"I can"—becoming the affirmation that ensured their success. At last the day came when, after a long meditation on a simple maneuver, Charles responded with "I cannot" and was left behind.

The others nearly died that night, running away from an ambush with a dozen soldiers in close pursuit. Bullets were hitting the ground around them when an arrow whizzed overhead, followed by a scream. A second German fell, a third, and the soldiers scattered in disorderly retreat, later claiming an attack by at least twenty.

"My instincts have never betrayed me," Charles said. "Perhaps you will listen to them now."

In response to their success their actions grew bolder, and they made the railroad line between Budapest and Cluf their special target. Charles used darkness to move close to a country station, stealing the army schedule from the unwitting attendant's mind.

They waited for the night a supply train was due. Aden, Mikel, and Resik set the charges on one side of the railway bridge while Hunter and Charles sat on the other and listened for the approaching train.

"It's early," Hunter said when they heard it.

Charles hissed, a sign of danger.

"What is it?"

"I told Aden the train comes . . . but there is something wrong—no, not dangerous. . . . It isn't a supply train."

"Troop?" Hunter asked hopefully.

"Prisoners!"

Hunter swore, then went on as if this information made no difference. "Three engines. We can't lose this! Force the engineer."

Charles closed his eyes, his face tight with concentration. Though they saw the explosion, the crew stared straight ahead and drove the train at full throttle over the edge.

The valley wasn't deep but it didn't have to be. The train's own weight destroyed it, cars twisted and crushed by the next ones in line. Hunter ran to the place where the valley fell away. Below him fires flared, children cried, a woman screamed. Hunter heard another, more terrible scream and looked back at Charles. In the growing light rising from the valley, Hunter saw him on his knees, his long arms folded over his stomach, swaying, shrieking. His mind had been open, trapping the engineer's, and had felt the man die, then the rest. One death was a banquet, ten gluttony. But the tidal wave of misery that had flowed over him had left him blind and shaken.

Hunter took a step toward him, then halted as Charles stood, his arms rigid at his sides, the fingers curled, ready to destroy the first life he touched. Shots cracked in the valley, and Hunter spun and saw Resik lumbering down the opposite side. "Karl!" Hunter screamed. "Karl, no!"

A second shot ricocheted off the rocks to Resik's right. Before he understood what was happening, Hunter saw a figure push past him, Charles leaping into the valley, landing on the back of the soldier, who was trying to force his failing eyes to take aim at Resik. He died in Charles's arms, as did another and another until only the victims remained.

Charles scanned the wreck and saw Resik pulling open the doors of the boxcars, calling into each, "Get out. There will be a fire. Run!" Blank, shocked faces looked up at Resik. The few who obeyed huddled close to the cars . . . the conquered waiting for the conquerers to return and claim them.

Charles heard a rumble in the distance and called to Resik, "The supply train's coming. Run!"

But Resik did not hear him. He stared into a tilted boxcar, deaf and paralyzed by the sight of small corpses, tangled with the living bodies of Gypsy children. He pulled out four, who stood with eyes round and hungry but dry, as if they knew tears would make no difference.—Run!— Charles warned Resik again, but small pale hands were held up to him and he swore one oath after another as he began pulling them free. With no time to argue, Charles dragged him away from the wreck. The supply train fell atop the rest, the gasoline it carried igniting in one lethal blast that consumed the wounded and the dying and the dead. Resik's bellow of rage was lost in the roar of the fire, and he fell from Charles's arms to the ground, sobbing, his fingers clutching earth and stones.

As Resik calmed, his breathing grew uneven and Charles saw the blood glistening on the man's leather jacket. He did not need to touch the wound to gauge its depth or to taste the blood to know what had been hit. The bubbling of the blood flowing slowly from it told him Resik had at best a day of life left him. Charles piled up dirt to support Resik's head and shoulders and, Resik's breathing had steadied, said, "I'll get the others."

"No! I don't want them here crying over me. Only you. In the time left me I want to tell you why I have fought with Hunter."

Charles began to shake his head, then felt the strength of

the old man's need. He crossed his legs and held Resik's hand. "Go on," he said.

Resik squeezed his hand and began. "My wife and I married late, and many years passed before our only child, Ilse, was born. Ilse was small, always smaller than her friends, and frail. We lived in Bicas. I worked in a plant that, even before the pact was signed between Romania and Germany, had switched from the making of machine tools to the manufacture of small arms.

"Within a month of the signing of the pact our town filled with German and Austrian soldiers; enlisted men, career officers, and the SS. We were supposed to be allies, but they treated us like a conquered people.

"On the Saturday before Christmas I took Ilse shopping to buy a present for her mother. I met some friends from the factory and sent Ilse to the park with their children while we went into a tavern across from it for a mug of beer. Soon afterward we heard a woman screaming outside. We all ran out, thinking perhaps an accident had occurred. She was hysterical. 'Soldiers,' she said, 'soldiers have stolen my daughter.'

"I remember looking for Ilse, and when I did not see her, I thought how fortunate that she had not heard this sordid tale, for I thought, as did everyone, that this woman was referring to an older child and that the men meant to rape her, then let her go. Someone must have said as much, for the woman shrieked, 'What do you mean, she's only seven years old! Little children. They took her and two other little children!'

"The effect on the bystanders was horrible. So many had children playing in that park. We all ran through the park searching for them. My friends found their boys cowering in a stand of bushes. One was old enough to be ashamed that he had not fought. 'There were so many,' he said. 'They took Ilse away.'

"I left my friends waiting in case the soldiers returned and went to the police station and told my story to an officer I knew slightly. He said he would try to help, but he never looked at me and I knew there was nothing he could do.

"I returned home, told my wife what had happened, then left her crying and went everywhere . . . to the park, to the

place where the German army was headquartered, to the
mayor, then back to the police. Later I did what I hoped those
more powerful would do for me—I went to the SS. They were
suprisingly polite, showing me to a small office, bringing me
coffee, then locking the office door. I sat there for three hours,
until, long after the train pulled out of the nearby depot and
I understood, they let me go.

"In the morning I began following that train, stopping in
small towns and asking, 'Where have the Germans taken the
children?' The trail was littered with grieving parents who
could give me no answer, but gradually a pattern emerged."

Resik stopped speaking long enough to grope in an inside
pocket, pull out a picture, and hand it to Charles. "She is
blond, you see. All the children were fair, like little German
children. They were being saved for the Reich.

"At last I began hearing rumors that led me to a destination . . . a big old house on a secluded street in a small town
in Hungary. I waited outside until a young woman came out.
She was dressed all in black, her hair pinned up under a
veil. She looked like a nun and I thought she might be merciful. When she rounded the corner, I approached her and
she shook her head, as if she did not understand what I asked.
I begged. I fell to my knees and grabbed her wrist as I begged,
thinking that if she did not tell me what I had to know, I
would kill her. It was almost dark and she looked around
fearfully, then grabbed my shoulders, telling me loudly to
calm myself. 'Her name,' she whispered, 'what is her name?'

"I replied in the same quick, soft tone. She thought a
moment, then shook her head. 'We didn't keep her. The authorities questioned her size and the color of her eyes. I'm
sorry. They sent her away. I'm sorry.'

" 'Where?' I whispered. 'Where?' but she only shook her
head again and backed away. I must have been the first parent
ever to approach her, because when I let go of her wrist, she
ran. I returned the next evening, hoping perhaps that the
woman would come and tell me more news, but instead the
Germans arrested me and took me to a station where I was
questioned. I told the truth, and a day later my interrogator
suggested I enlist in the Romanian army if I wanted to stay
out of prison. I did as he suggested, signed a paper, and,
under guard, boarded a train to Bucharest. When it reached

its destination, I walked off the platform and kept on walking.
I met Gygory a week later.''

Resik began to cry . . . huge, loud sobs that drained the
last hours from his life. ''They're supposed to be our allies,
may the devil burn their souls—and they didn't even send her
home.''

Charles sat with his head tilted, his expression flat and
unreadable. ''Why did you want to tell me this?''

''Because you can find her . . . please.''

This had been Resik's demeanor when he had begged that
young woman for news, and time, Charles saw, had not dulled
his grief. *If I leave here now,* Charles thought, *I can forget
this war and my place in it and every death I have caused
for the days I go on.* But, like the prisoners on the railway
train, he had no place to go.

''I can't find her, Karl Resik, not unless we are near her.''

''But you know. Your kind always knows.''

A score of memories made Charles shudder. ''About our
own, Karl Resik, as you know about yours.''

What do you mean? Resik wanted to ask, but instead he
looked into Charles's eyes and saw through his perfect memory the empty stares of the Gypsy children in the boxcar. Six
years old and always frail. How long would Ilse have survived? Would he have wanted her to survive?

Charles said, gripping his friend's hand, watching silent
tears of grief roll down those ruddy cheeks and disappear into
Resik's thick beard.

If I leave here now . . .

Charles shook his head in self-denial. He couldn't follow
Hunter's orders, not after thought, but he could hunt as he
had once hunted men—silently and alone. He gripped Resik's
shoulders. ''Do you understand what I require?'' he asked.

Resik nodded. ''Why do you wish to share this pain?''

''Because I wish to share your cause. Give me your grief,
Karl Resik. Make me human and I will seek vengeance for
you.''

Resik coughed and swore. ''It hurts,'' he said.

''If there is a God, Karl Resik, Ilse will be waiting for
you.''

''Maybe we get what we expect. That's enough. Now?''

Charles raised Resik's head. As he lowered his own, their

cheeks brushed and he tasted the salt of the man's sweat and tears as he searched for the best vein and bit through.

Later Hunter and the others found Resik's body. They saw the wound and the marks on the neck and the peace in the dead man's expression and understood. Though they watched for him for days after they'd given up hope, Charles did not return.

Charles traveled only by night, and his targets were the labor camps, the railways, the guards with the death's-heads on the lapels. Romanians would find the bloodless corpses in the snow, cross themselves, report the death to the authorities, and slyly smile at the expected reaction. The farmers had no interest in politics. To them the Nazis, like the Russians, were foreigners and invaders, and a Mountain Lord returned to the Plains of Alfold to defend them.

When rumors and the corpses became impossible to ignore, Colonel Haller, commander of the Gestapo in western Romania, sent for the only expert he dared trust with this problem: Cristof Baivie. And though an hour with the Swiss doctor left Haller vaguely unsettled, he had no choice but to promise full cooperation with the doctor's strange pursuits.

II

The sound of high-pitched music woke Kurt and he stood slowly, a hand against the stone to brace himself. When he was able, he walked unsteadily down the dark corridor, climbing the narrow steps to the tower.

The clouds were low that afternoon, hanging in the air around the keep so that the world seemed to end at its walls, and even the sounds of the pan flute were muffled by the damp.

The player sat cross-legged on the battlement. His back was to Kurt and Kurt stood silently listening to the song rise and fall, break away, then return to melodies almost familiar. Wagner . . . Kurt was sure he heard strains of Wagner, and even that brief reminder of home made his eyes wet with tears. The player laid down the short pipes, picking up a lower-pitched one, and began another selection, a sonata by Schubert. Unbearable! Kurt was turning to leave when, with no pause in the playing, the musician's thoughts flowed into his mind with the song.

—I play this for you.—

"Then say so! Speak the words."

The music stopped and Charles turned and faced him. "I played for you," he said.

"Thank you," Kurt whispered.

Charles might have reminded Kurt of their last meeting, but he paused to look at the young German, and any amusement he might have taken from this encounter twisted into pity. Kurt's face had a sickly yellow tone, the pants he once had been unable to button were now held up with a crude leather belt. He approached Charles with reluctant awe, like a primitive approaching a demanding demon. Charles put down his flute. "Do you wish to speak to me?" he asked gently.

"I . . . I wish to speak to someone. To . . . speak."

"Francis cares for you?" Only a slight rise in tone at the end implied it was a question.

"Cared," Kurt said bitterly. "He saved my life, and then, when he had given me health, he took it and whatever else he wished. He even made me enjoy it. He's skilled that way, and who am I to refuse him anything? When the day came that I knew if he used me again I would die and not care, he stopped coming. It's been weeks, and he does not speak or even seem to notice my presence."

"How do you live?"

"I found a store of wine and the frozen carcass of a goat. I roasted some, then made soup with the rest. I keep a fire beneath it, so it does not spoil. There may be better ways to preserve it, but I don't know them."

"You wish my help, then?"

"I wish nothing. I only came because the music was beautiful." Kurt turned and shuffled slowly down the stairs.

Charles listened to the footsteps recede, the soft closing of Kurt's door, then picked up his flute and played a quicker song, a song the Gypsies had played centuries ago, that they still played softly in those stinking hovels in which they were penned, that they hummed to themselves as they stood in line waiting to cough out their lives in the death chambers of the Reich. He couldn't save them all, saw little use in saving any, and the riddle was that, yes, even before he'd promised vengeance to a dying, broken man, he had cared.

But he had brought Kurt here, had made him a promise, too, and he could not turn his back on the misery for which he was responsible. Though Charles had returned for a few days of solitude, he found instead one more cause. From that misty afternoon, his life was ordered by both his vows.

Charles would leave the mountain for weeks at a time, returning with blood crusted on his hands and in his hair, his eyes blank, shocked by his own savagery. But always he remembered to bring sacks of flour, potatoes, cheese, and fruit. He would drop these outside the keep, then run free under the stars until the memories of what he had done and seen blurred and faded in the peace of the present. Then Charles would return to his father's house, seeking out his prisoner, his only human friend. He taught Kurt to play the pipes, to use a crossbow for hunting, to carve, and to paint. On the canvas he saw true talent and the love Kurt had for these barren peaks.

As for Kurt, the days Charles was gone were long and hollow, their emptiness something he could only try to understand. One night, the first night Kurt had seen him in a month, Charles sat cross-legged beside the fire in Kurt's room, telling old Romanian legends. Kurt sat beside him, eating bread and cheese, looking so anxious that Charles halted midsentence, his silent question brushing the edges of Kurt's mind.

In response Kurt rested a hand over Charles's, and though it shook when Charles looked at him, he did not pull it away. "Don't," Charles said, as if Kurt's touch wounded him. "No matter what you do, I will leave again."

"That's not important." Kurt hesitated, then added, "You wear sadness like people wear clothes. I thought that if I touched you, that if you understood that to me what you are and do makes no difference, I would be helping you."

"Everyone I have ever loved has died," Charles confessed. The words were strained, forced from him, and, once spoken, ignored. As he buried his face in Kurt's hair he thought briefly of Hunter and felt only regret.

Chapter Nineteen

France
June 1941

I

PARIS WAS A diseased whore disguised as a lady, doling out gayly wrapped packages of pleasure and death. Most German officers loved a Paris assignment. It offered them a chance to rest and to sample the easy delights in its *boîtes* and brothels. But to the unlucky few, it meted out unexpected ends from guns, knives, clubs, and fists, the sentence delivered with an apparent lack of bias by an organized resistance. For Eric Ruthinedt, whose day-to-day duties had always been near the fronts and who, in the hours before a battle, would labor frantically to acquire the stoic bearing that so well hid his fear, the capricious terror of Paris was hell.

His requests for a transfer back to active duty in Hungary were repeatedly denied. Resigned, he settled into his Spartan quarters, carried out his administrative duties with meticulous efficiency, and took the small pills his doctor had ordered to hold back the waking dreams and the sleeping nightmares. Few officers knew him, save through odd tales exaggerated with each telling and, at functions where they were forced to meet him, would answer his quick acknowledgments with ones more fleeting and move away, leaving him alone in a corner, nursing a cognac or glass of wine. They thought he had a wartime plague, he knew; they thought him mad. After a few weeks he didn't go out at all.

One evening an intelligence officer visited him. Herman Roessler made it clear to Ruthinedt that he held a colonel's rank but he dressed in civilian clothes and insisted Ruthinedt relax and speak as if they were equals. Roessler had wisely brought a bottle of brandy, from which he poured his confused host a number of generous drinks before requesting Ruthinedt repeat his story. Roessler's disbelief must have been noticeable, for Ruthinedt concluded by asking, "Have you read the reports from that area? Our airfield was bombed by our own men. A platoon disappeared on a mountain. Planes driven by expert pilots crashed for no reason. And they say, 'He is mad, don't listen to him' and so you do not."

"What I believe is unimportant. I have come to tell you that Colonel Haller has begun an investigation into the very problems you mentioned. He has sent a doctor from Hungary to question you."

"Ah, another of those. He will listen, take notes. Then, when I have gone, he will laugh and maybe you will stay and laugh with him."

Roessler shook his head in apparent sympathy, and in response to that small encouragement Ruthinedt added in a lifeless tone, "I saw a creature use its mind to destroy armed men, and I could not raise a hand to save them. I wanted to run, instead I fell to my knees and begged for my life. I have been broken and I will never be whole again. I am alive and I curse my luck."

Roessler filled the glasses, holding one out in a deliberate gesture of camaraderie. "Whatever you saw was real to you, Eric. I promise I will not laugh."

Neither did Cristof Baivie. He met with Ruthinedt and Roessler in Roessler's office, sitting at Roessler's desk, taking notes as Ruthinedt spoke. After he heard the entire story he began asking the questions Ruthinedt had always longed to answer: how the attacker was dressed; the color of his eyes and hair; and how the words had seemed when they flowed into his mind. After an hour Ruthinedt interrupted with, "You believe me, don't you?"

Baivie laughed, a sound loud and coarse, the kind of laughter heard in a tavern filled with factory workers on a Saturday night. He leaned forward over the desk separating them so that his face was only inches from the lieutenant's. Ruthinedt had a sudden urge to pull back when he noticed some quality to this thin-lipped cadaverous man that was uncomfortably similar to the one on the mountain. Lust. That same sadistic hunger. "Of course I believe you. I know all the legends, and I know that the being you faced was old and that there was no defense."

"He looked so young," Ruthinedt protested.

"But he is ancient, Lieutenant, and he does not age. I came to you because this creature is important to my research. I am studying longevity. There are many in high places with uncomfortable consciences, and now, thanks to the strange reports in Romania, I have unlimited means. I wish to capture a Mountain Lord."

"For what purpose?" Roessler asked.

"To study it, to learn to use its power, to force it to unlock the secret of immortality. Consider time, Lieutenant. Consider seeing empires rise and fall. Consider the ultimate triumph: never to know death. But we must find a young one, you see, for only they can be captured. The old ones have a special power that warns them of danger."

"But how will you know which one is young?" Roessler interjected, disturbed by the sudden fantastic turn of the conversation.

"Ah! That's the trick, you see. Grab the wrong one . . ." He ran two curled fingers across his throat and laughed again. "So we must know which to take before we move."

"Where will we find them?" Ruthinedt asked with obvious fatalism.

"In Romania, in Hungary, or so I hear." He patted his forehead. "I have my own special sense and I will find the one I must have. Come, do not look so doleful, Lieutenant. You wanted to go east, did you not? And"—he paused to make his next words more meaningful—"you wish vengeance, and I think you will have it."

"Demented," Roessler concluded as they walked back to their quarters, then noticed his companion's anger. "You misunderstand. I mean Baivie and the work he does. Did you see the greed in his eyes when he spoke of eternity?"

"I did," Ruthinedt replied, "but I wait to pass judgment on his sanity until I read the file he left with us. Did you learn anything about him?"

"Nothing except that he has lived in Cluf for the last three years. If the situation is as serious now as when you were there, it's no wonder. Colonel Haller is growing desperate.''

As they passed the guards on watch outside the officers' barracks, Ruthinedt suggested they share a late supper while studying the file.

Roessler declined. ''Tomorrow is soon enough. Tonight I've been invited to a party.'' Roessler took pity on the man walking beside him and asked, ''Why not come with me? The hostess is a charming woman. She won't mind another guest.''

''Is she French?''

Roessler replied first with a lewd chuckle, then said, ''Only in the best ways.''

Ruthinedt began to say no, then abruptly changed his mind. Tonight he dared not remain alone.

Even in darkness the Austra château seemed bathed in sunlight. Classic long before the revival, its pale stones were arranged in magnificent simplicity atop a rise of well-manicured gardens and plush green lawns a few miles south of Paris. The house had seen the dawn and dusk of kings and dictators and citizen despots with the same impartiality. No standard had flown there save once, during the heat of the revolution, when an angry mob smashed the cupids' faces adorning the intricate brass locks on the oak doors and rushed up the stairs to hang their standard from the second-floor balcony, sing the ''Marseillaise'' and uneasily depart.

Elizabeth Austra upheld the family neutrality with irresistible good humor. ''One parent was Czech, the other Austrian. I was raised in France and am a citizen of Portugal. My politics are impossible,'' she declared when pressed to make a political statement and would immediately change the subject. Men who tired of war were charmed by her insouciance, her blithe belief that, come what may, her château, her gardens, the music, and the laughter would endure.

She was not stingy with her favors, nor was she wanton. She had taken three lovers since her arrival early in the year; two had been flyers, the third Roessler's superior. One had died of a stroke, the others shot down by the British, and Elizabeth's socials now overflowed with officers, each hoping she would turn her bewitching eyes in his direction.

Ruthinedt found her features disturbing, and as they were
introduced, she instinctively grinned and laughed at something another guest had said, exposing small, even human
teeth. Upon learning he was lately from the eastern front, she
ignored him, apparently preferring to concentrate her charm
on an intelligence officer recently stationed in Bordeaux.

Ruthinedt helped himself to a drink and stood alone near
the foyer doors. The string quartet playing in the salon broke
off. Distracted by a spattering of applause, Ruthinedt turned
in time to see Robert Austra step up on the small stage and
seat himself at the piano. For a moment Ruthinedt denied his
eyes and memory, then panicked. He searched out Roessler,
pulling his companion rudely away from a group he had
joined, dragging him through the wide doors into the empty
garden. He whispered, "The one at the piano! He's one of
them!"

"Elizabeth's cousin?"

"Yes."

Roessler responded with flinty silence, then started back
to the doors.

Ruthinedt grabbed his arm. "Wait! If Baivie was correct,
that one will know I told you, and I will die, perhaps both
of us. Please, I would like to return to Paris! If you will not
believe me, at least have the courtesy to take me back."

Roessler studied the lieutenant, once more amazed at how
persuasively this man's delusions controlled him. One hour,
after all, was not important, and the party would last all night.
"Come on. We'll walk around the house to my car."

Before he returned to the château, Roessler paused to scan
the file Baivie had given him. Soon after he began, he
pounded on Ruthinedt's door and the two sat together and
studied the fantastic.

It began with an odd assortment of statements from Ro-
manians living close to the Vardo range, much of it legend
yet all similar. "The one I saw met this description. So does
Robert Austra, you see." Ruthinedt studied another account.
"Listen to this! It's a report from a doctor practicing near the
Varda Pass." He began to read.

"I was seeing my last patient of the morning when
the man arrived. He was fair-complected and incredibly

tall and wore a knee-length cape over dark leather pants. He told me there had been an accident and a young man had fallen on the mountain. The symptoms he gave were similar to those of a ruptured spleen, but when I explained the man must be moved to a hospital, he only shook his head.

" 'Come,' he ordered and, though I wished to tell him I had others to see after lunch, I followed him.

"Outside there was no conveyance. The snow fell steadily, the sky was dark, and I did not know how he had arrived. 'We'll use your sled,' he told me, and we went to the stable and had it readied.

"During the journey I attempted to speak and found myself unable to do so and strangely unconcerned by this, as if I traveled in a dream. Eventually the road narrowed to a path and we left the horses in a copse of trees and continued on foot.

"I remembered nothing until I stood in a small, overly warm room looking down at a sandy-haired man in his late teens, who appeared in shock. I examined him and saw that my original assumption had been correct.

"Remember the young man I said had been captured?" Ruthinedt asked.

"I remember."

Ruthinedt's voice grew more confident as he continued.

" 'You will operate here,' the man told me. I recall looking at him, too stunned to disagree. 'He will die if you do not operate. Begin.'

"I did as he asked. We had no anesthetic, but he never woke, and when it was over, I'd done as good a job as in an operating room, perhaps better, as I took great care to see there would be no complications.

"I remember nothing of the journey to that room or back to my home. The following day I might have not even remembered had I not noticed the surgical supplies missing from my bag. Late that morning eight people came to me, all complaining of a vague malaise, all with marks on their hands that may have been caused by a needle. Every one had type AB blood."

They continued reading the file, paying special attention to the description given by an old woman who had once met a Mountain Lord. When they'd finished, Roessler commented, "There have been major security leaks in this area. I believe we should return to the Austra château . . . no, not to go inside but to observe. We'll take horses. They're quiet and we can slip away more easily."

The house appeared nearly empty, only one Mercedes still parked at the front door. Sometime later its owner departed, the two following at a distance along the bridle path. When the car pulled over, they reined in their mounts and slipped into the brush. They crept close enough to see two men move beside the car and hear the officer begin listing the bombing schedule for the following day. "Traitor!" Roessler whispered.

"He may have no choice," Ruthinedt replied.

The German officer concluded with words that proved Ruthinedt had been correct. "I am being transferred to Belgium. You have orders to kill me."

One *maquisard* pulled his knife, using it so expertly that the blood spurting from the victim's neck never touched his fingers. By the time the German had fallen, the two Frenchmen had disappeared into the trees.

"Will we report this?" Ruthinedt asked as they returned their mounts to the stables and walked toward the barracks.

"Only to Baivie. Well, Eric, I think you may have found your Mountain Lords." He returned to his companion's quarters and reread sections of the report dealing with mental power. "A family of telepaths! Think of the possibilities. If they are few, as these reports say, they must value one another a great deal. Consider holding one as hostage and forcing the rest to work for us, Moulin and the rest falling into our hands with one crook of a feminine finger."

"Baivie wants to study one."

"So long as the one we take is not killed, I don't care what Baivie does with it. Besides, a clinic with bars is as good as a prison, is it not, maybe better, for clinics are small and private and easily moved." He paused, contemplating a course of action. "But we must be certain we have not made a mistake. The Austra family has friends in high places, and a rash move would mean more than a transfer. I have been where they would send us. Eric, we must be cautious. Besides, an investigation will help us find their young, will it not? Tomorrow I'll arrange to have you transferred to my staff and we'll begin our work at once.''

II

The questions came too fast, and Linda Bradley knew her answers must seem evasive. Nonetheless, she told the truth and stuck to it during the hour the young Germans questioned her.

The shorter of the two men pointed to the recent letters, spread out on her uncle's library table. ''You are certain this is Ernst Bradley's handwriting?''

''If it is a forgery, it is expertly done.''

''So you are not sure.''

''Not entirely, no,'' she admitted.

''And you have no idea where he might be now?''

''I don't.'' She added defensively, ''In his profession that is not so unusual.''

''When did you see your uncle last?''

''In March 1939, in this house.''

''You never saw him later in Chaves?''

''No, that is . . . no.''

''Explain your hesitation, Fräulein.''

''I dreamed I saw him in Stephen Austra's house. It was a vivid dream.''

''You had never seen Stephen Austra's home except in that dream?''

''Never.'' She provided what details she could still remember from the dream.

''Did anything else unusual happen that night?''

''Only that I was at a party and had too much to drink.'' She toyed with the folds of her skirt. ''I do remember making love to a young man and taking a bath afterward.''

''Had you and the man been lovers before?''

''Not lovers, but yes, we had made love once.''

''And was this similar?''

''Yes, except . . . except I somehow bruised my lip on the cast on his leg.'' She broke off, giggling uneasily. ''You said to mention anything odd, and I suppose this could be included: You see, he was not the sort to be, ah, experimental.''

''He was inexperienced?''

''Yes. And not the type to be taught.''

The German made a sudden point of studying his notes, underscoring the section concerning Linda's dream. ''Is there anyone else in Lisbon who might be able to give us more information on the Austra family?''

''Heinrich Schoofs. He is one of Elizabeth Austra's lovers.''

''One of?''

''She's notorious,'' Linda said with disgust.

''Do you know if he ever visited the family estates in Chaves?''

''He has.''

''Excellent, Fräulein!'' For the first time there was animation in the German's voice. He reached into the briefcase he carried and pulled out a bottle of German Moselle. ''No gift would be adequate for the help you have given us, but perhaps we could drink to the Reich together?''

''If you like,'' she said, and went to get the glasses. Looking back to ask a question, she detected the regret in his expression and the blood left her face.

III

Their questions were an outrage! Schoofs told them so directly, and when the two cold-eyed young Germans could give no reasonable explanation of why they needed his information, he ordered them to leave. Anticipating their protest, he pulled a gun from his desk drawer as a reminder that for the moment he held the advantage.

Once he had locked the door behind them, Schoofs paced

through the house, then dressed quickly, deciding to walk the block to the Bradleys' and pay a call on Linda before meeting Samuelson for dinner. Though the men hadn't mentioned her name, he guessed that they had seen her first.

When repeated ringings of her bell brought no response, he tried the door and found it unlocked. He moved cautiously through the lower rooms and, finding nothing out of place, went upstairs and into the main bedroom. Linda lay facedown on the bed. He called her name but she did not move.

His eyes scanned the room and the open door as he rested his fingers on her neck and searched for a pulse. They came away bloody. He rolled her over and saw the purple-edged slash of a wire across her neck. There were notes from her uncle on the floor beside the bed, and as he reached down to pick them up a floorboard creaked. He swung around too late.

The best interrogation methods were the simple ones. No need to leave marks on a victim when something as gentle as a gloved hand would do. For an hour Schoofs was allowed his next breath of air only if he had said something of value in letting out the one before it. More than once he'd been certain he'd died.

Afterward Schoofs survived only because he had the good fortune to roll off Linda's bed. The hard landing jarred him back to consciousness, and the pure air near the floor cleared his head. He heard a soft hiss and smelled the gas. Raising his body as high as the ropes on his hands and feet would allow, he saw a lit candle in the far corner. The gas grew thicker, the blood pounding in his ears as he forced himself toward the flame. He might have burned through the ropes, but he dared not risk a fire and blew out the candle instead, then extinguished the glowing wick with his tongue.

He remembered Elizabeth's laughter, how she had held him through that long night after he'd learned that his oldest son had been killed in the Battle of Britain. He pictured her ragged, starving, the light beaten from her eyes, and rage spurred him on. He would warn Samuelson, he would survive at least that long, and, if fate were merciful, long enough to hold her again.

The bedroom door appeared locked and he did not waste

precious time trying it. Instead he worked his way toward the
heater beneath the window and managed to angle himself so
his hands could partially close the valve. Catching his breath,
he inched himself up and managed to balance uneasily on the
window ledge. He intended to lean backward only far enough
to break the glass but lost his balance and fell through it, the
sharp edges slicing into his neck and back.

Samuelson sat in the Café Lagos savoring a fine Havana,
the first of the box of cigars Rachel had sent him for his
birthday. He had three more in his pocket, which he planned
to give to Schoofs, knowing how much the German agent
appreciated such luxury. He'd begun to signal for a second
drink when he glimpsed the time on the café's wall clock.

Schoofs's punctuality had the precision of a Swiss watch.
The town could be invaded and leveled, but if Schoofs were
still alive, he would arrive at the Café Lagos, or what was
left of it, at the agreed upon time and expect the one he met
to do the same. Samuelson left the café immediately, walking
the few blocks to Schoofs's home. When his knocking brought
no response, he started back toward the café until, passing
the Bradley house, he noticed its door ajar.

He stuck his head inside. "Linda!" he called, then
"Schoofs!" and thought he heard his name cried faintly from
the side of the house. When he reached the narrow walkway,
no one was there, but as he turned to go, blood spattered his
hand and he looked down and saw the puddle on the stones.
Above him, Schoofs's head and shoulders dangled over the
window ledge, blood dripping from his face and hair.

Samuelson ran back inside, running up the stairs two and
three at a time. He broke the lock on the bedroom door, then
carried Schoofs to the fresher air downstairs. In the same
room in which Bradley had plotted Stephen's murder, Schoofs
forced his last words. "Elizabeth . . . They wanted to know
about the houses . . . and Elizabeth. They wanted to know what
it was like . . . to love Elizabeth."

Long before Blackwell could have arranged her escape,
Elizabeth followed her own self-preserving instincts. She left
Paris in the company of a recuperating German flyer. After
deserting him in Vichy, France, she crossed the border into

Spain with her steamer and two crates of modern Italian pottery. She arrived in Lisbon in time for Schoofs's funeral, sitting beside Paul Stoddard in the front pew of the church, looking shocked and, other mourners agreed, unusually sedate. For nights afterward she and George Samuelson searched Lisbon, but the assassins had vanished.

IV

New York
September 1941

Thelma Reger had just sat down to dinner when someone knocked on her door. She opened it to the length of its thick security chain and peered out at a middle-aged man in a business suit.

The man slipped his card through the crack. *Urban Anderson,* she read as he explained, "Private Investigator, ma'am."

"What do you want with me?"

"I'd like to ask you a few questions regarding your work."

Thelma only stared, as if trying to memorize his singularly forgettable face.

"My client is prepared to pay." To emphasize this he pulled ten dollars from his pocket and slipped it in to her, moving back a step so she could slam the door if she wished. The gesture of trust worked and the door opened.

They sat at her peeling oak table and he insisted she eat before they talked. She brought him coffee, then tried to hold her hands steady as she stabbed at the pieces of fried liver, but she was certain the detective noticed that they shook. They always shook, and it was only a matter of time before somebody at work noticed and she would be moved. But if they separated her from her babies, she'd quit and live on her small saving. After forty years of babies she'd have nothing to do with sickness and dying.

"You are an obstetrical nurse at St. Joseph's?"

She nearly laughed at the term. He couldn't be from the

hospital! "I'm not a nurse. I take care of the babies. I've been in the same department for thirty-five years," she answered proudly.

"It's good to see someone else who enjoys her job." They laughed together and he asked, "Have you cared for many sets of triplets?"

"Twelve. And three sets of quads. Litters, we call 'em."

Anderson laughed again, an ingratiating laugh. "I am trying to obtain information on one set of triplets . . . Ann, Simon, and Laurence. Their parents were Charles and Claudia Austra."

"How old are they?"

"Twenty-eight."

Her look of recognition was immediately veiled by a self-protective distrust. "We ain't supposed to talk about patients." When Anderson did not push her, she asked, "What do you want to know?"

"Only that they were born in this country rather than in Europe. The Department of Immigration is questioning their citizenship, and the doctor who delivered them is dead."

"Of course they was born at St. Joe's! You say you work for them?"

"Yes, handsome people." He gave her a description he'd been given.

"They must look like their parents, then. Funny people. We broke every hospital rule for them."

"Really?"

"Indecent, the man was, but you had to sympathize when you saw how devoted he was to his wife. She wasn't supposed to live, and he refused to leave her or let us take her to the delivery room. She had the three in a private room with only the doctor attending. And the woman's screams! The whole building heard them. I tell you, the staff was jumping."

"How was the children's health?"

"They were small but strong. They held their heads up right away . . . and such pretty things with those serious dark eyes and hair. You knew they'd be tall just like their parents, all arms and legs they were." Now that Thelma had begun, she chatted on happily. "You hardly ever know what happens to them once they leave unless they get famous. So what are they doing now that they're grown?"

"The three are in Europe working in the family firm."

Thelma looked away suddenly to hide the expression on her face. This man couldn't have been sent by them or he'd know there was only two. She'd read about the ship in the paper and a doctor had confirmed it. Oh, girl, you've been had. There were knives in her kitchen drawer. Sharp ones. She stood.

"Is something wrong?"

"I was just thinking how Europe ain't the most healthy place to be nowadays." She picked up their cups and walked toward the kitchen. The man was fast. Her hands just grazed the counter as she fell.

V

Normandy
December 1941

In a secluded cottage near the coast Cristof Baivie displayed the restraints to Ruthinedt. "Will they be strong enough?" he asked.

Ruthinedt picked up the steel handcuffs and jerked on the chain. "The one I saw could snap this."

"And the others?"

"I don't know, but it is not the locks that concern me. It will try to use us. If it gets loose, we will all die." Baivie laughed and Ruthinedt flared, saying, "You must take me seriously or we will fail!"

"I do, my useful friend. This is only delight at how fortunate I am to find someone so knowledgeable and so cautious. You assure our success, Eric. I could not ask for a finer ally."

Praise pushed Ruthinedt to greater candor. "I cannot face one of them alone. Someone else must go."

"Of course, Eric. You give the orders, you know the plans. Of course, someone else must go. But when the time comes and the prisoner is brought to you, you must be certain. Look, then, into those unforgettable eyes and think only of hate and vengeance and pain. Let it know who is the master and who is slave. Show no mercy and it will break for us like any animal.''

In that instant all Ruthinedt's doubts about Baivie vanished. In that instant he loved the man.

Part

Three

LAURENCE AUSTRA

Chapter Twenty

Banlin, Ireland
December 21, 1941

I

THE GERMAN SUB surfaced at dawn in the choppy waters off the southern Irish coast, signaled its arrival to contacts on shore, and submerged once more. Its presence was noted by three old Banlin fishermen, who saw no reason to interrupt their livelihood to inform the town.

Later that same morning Laurence shook Emma awake. The two avoided the bustle in the kitchen, slipping out the front door into the misty air. Their boots left tracks on the silvery hoarfrost as they climbed the hill on which the fir trees grew.

"Do we have to kill the tree, Laurie?" Emma asked.

"If the ground wasn't frozen we might dig it up, but they usually die, anyway. Now pick the one you want, Em, and let's get it home."

"But I don't want to choose any tree, not if it's going to die," Emma insisted. "Couldn't we have a yule log or drape the house in mistletoe like the old Druids?"

"The Alpha Christmas party always has a tree, Em, and I doubt the children coming tomorrow would understand if their gifts were laid before a pile of vines. Besides, where would we put the decorations you and Tad have been making?"

"Around the front door?" He shook his head so seriously that she laughed. "All right, take . . . this tree!" If fir trees could ever be said to droop, this one did, and it was bare of needles on the top few branches, half the rest of it hard and brown.

"Bad, bad luck, Em. We must find the thickest and strongest, and then, if you like, on the twelfth night you and I will take it outside and set it afire and chant a prayer to the spirits of the woods and waters to claim its soul and let it be reborn."

She stopped dead in her tracks and gaped up at him. "You know such a prayer?"

"Scraps of one," he lied, "and between us we're certain to embellish it into something quiet powerful, don't you think?"

Emma looked at him strangely and made a sly pretense of searching for a different selection. "If the tree is reborn, perhaps one day my little sister will choose a different tree with the same soul." She spoke matter-of-factly, only a sidelong glance at Laurence's reaction betraying the importance of what she had said.

"Little sister?"

"I heard you tell Mother. Tell me how you know, please."

When the time for honesty came, it would be important that he not lie to her now. "It's a trick. If you don't tell anyone and wait a little while, your mother and I will explain and let you share an adult secret, all right?"

"When?"

He studied her a moment. She hadn't said a word, even to her brother, and he remembered Alec had been even younger than Emma when he'd been told. "At Christmas." *When my uncle is here*, he thought, *and if it is too soon, the mistake can be corrected.*

Emma wanted to beg to be told now but instead tried to be adult and sensible, pointing to the biggest tree she had seen. "That one. Oh, look!" she exclaimed when they got nearer, "It's got a bird's nest."

"That's especially good luck, but we must be careful when we take down the tree or the nest will fall and all our New Year's hopes will tumble with it. Now you hold it while I chop." He whistled the call of an English sparrow and began to work.

"Why did you begin with a birdcall?" Emma asked.

"To appease the mother who built this nest, of course. Careful, careful . . . that's it! Good fortune for another year."

He handed Emma the ax and began to lay the tree down when Emma cried, "The nest!"

Laurence pulled the tree up just in time. "I take back my whistle, you shoddy bird," he said with mock severity, and, holding the tree upright, he began to walk home, Em following with the ax resting on her shoulder. "What carol shall we sing first?" Laurence asked her, and in a moment "The Twelve Days of Christmas" rose in the clear, chilly air, he singing the even numbers and she the odd.

Blackwell pulled back one of the heavy drapes and watched the pair on the hill from the privacy of Ann's bedroom window. Ann padded up behind him, pressing her body against his and running her hands over his bare chest. "It's early, Harry, come back to bed."

"After last night I'm amazed I'm awake at all." He leaned back and kissed her forehead. "Look at them. I suppose it's no wonder I think of Laurence as much younger than you."

She followed his line of vision. "They're decorating the old house. I wish you could stay for all the holidays."

"I've made family commitments, and this is not a time in which one breaks them." He stared at Laurence, commenting absently after a moment, "He's much happier than he used to be." He felt Ann shudder and turned to face her, looking puzzled and sad as he asked, "Is what he does so different than you and me?"

Her hands cradled his face. "I call you lover, not husband, and you have no children who think of me as their mother." She walked back to bed and stretched out on the emerald comforter, her ivory skin patterned by the light from the window beside it.

"Do you believe I was wrong to arrange the annulment Laurence requested?"

"No. It is not his role that troubles me, but rather that he believes it. I wonder how lonely he will be when he loses them."

No worse than any other's loss, Blackwell thought as he looked at her.

Her magnificent eyes saddened and she held out her arms. When he sat beside her, she said, "Tonight is a special night for us, Harry. Go back tomorrow, please?"

"The solstice?"

She nodded. "Tonight in Chaves the family will gather, a bonfire will be lit, minds will link and memories will form so perfectly that you can smell and touch them. It is enchantment without a spell, a merging that gives us the strength to stand alone in your world. Three years have passed since Laurie's gone and this year I did not go, either. Though our minds are not strong, Laurie and I have decided to hold our own small celebration. Kathleen will be there, and we want you to stay as well. Please, Harry, share tonight with us."

He realized that more than affection prompted her request, but even affection would have been enough. "Of course, but I must tell others that I'm staying. Are you free to drive into Banlin with me?"

"On the last workday before holiday closing! I should be home by five but Laurie has a late appointment. In any case, we can't begin until the house is quiet."

"And when will your day start?"

"Later, much later."

At times such as these he wished he were immortal or, better, that time itself would grind to a halt and he could go on loving her forever. Had he known how soon he would lose her, he would have held her longer, loved her better, but he held back a part of himself, anticipating the night that would never come.

The foyer of the old house smelled of Christmas, the scent of pine mingling with the aromas of cinnamon and anise and orange rind as the pastries baked for the next day's feast. Laurence placed the tree in the wooden stand he'd hidden in the closet and went into the kitchen, where Kathleen and Maura, one of Blackwell's security force, formed cookies on the baking sheets. Laurence kissed Kathleen and admonished gently, "The next few days will be exhausting enough without tiring yourself now."

"I've never been fragile. And what has you up so early this morning?"

"Come and look." He took her hand and pulled her into the foyer.

"Oh, it's beautiful!" she exclaimed when she saw the tree. "Now we can decorate it this afternoon."

"Oversee Em and Tad. No standing on ladders, please?"

She patted her stomach. "I suppose I am a bit off-balance. All right, Laurie, but I'm only agreeing because it's what I planned to do, anyway. If I can't look beautiful on Sunday when your uncle comes, I can at least look healthy."

She spoke with deceptive cheer, and no amount of reassurance could silence her fear. But Stephen would be genuinely kind to her, then privately vent his wrath on Laurence. He'd take the pain of it, for he deserved it.

He drew her into the tiny Victorian parlor and sat beside her in front of the fire. "So tell me how yesterday's sale went."

"Well over the goal. Even though the funds were only to aid the Catholic widows and orphans of Ulster, it was good to see Banlin support the war effort." She laughed. "After the sale Mary Gallagher suggested we donate the extra monies to the IRA. The sale's planners are actually considering the matter. Only in Ireland!"

"But Mary is right. It is wise to appease both sides."

"I should also tell you there were tongues wagging about Ann and her Mr. Harris." She fingered her plain gold wedding band, never more thankful for the sham. "Later I was asked directly why Alpha employs so many British when there's fine Irish lads in need of work. Thank God they're Catholic and Harry's grounds keeper Irish."

"And raised in these parts. Cullen and Jake are boyhood friends."

"Speaking of Jake, did he ever find you?"

"He did."

At the sound of distant thunder she raised her shawl higher on her shoulders. "Do you think Harry's precautions are necessary?"

"My uncle believes it, and there are only five miles of open country from here to the sea," he replied evasively. After the murders in Lisbon he wished they were all in Chaves. Even with the extra aid the protection seemed less than adequate.

"Em and Tad think of their drills as a game and have found the most amazing number of places to hide in the old wings. Someone would have to burn the house—" She stopped in mid-sentence and managed a wan smile. "That's silly, isn't it?"

"Don't worry about the man you saw yesterday."

She rested her hand on top of his. "I have no defenses against you, do I?"

"And a good thing, Colleen," he said, using her nickname, "or you'd keep too much to yourself. No, Jake told me the man was asking about Ann and Harry, not you and I. I'll pass the worry on, but now I had best change and drive to work." She began to stand and he shook his head. "I'll have Emma bring you some tea and breakfast." He arranged a coverlet over her legs and kissed her cheek and stopped in the doorway, some instinctive sense of self-preservation telling him to record every detail of the scene.

II

Eight batches of cookies had been baked and stored; the Christmas tree stood on the tile floor in the foyer, resplendent in glass icicles and painted wood ornaments; and brightly colored ribbon decorated the banister of the winding staircase. Kathleen called a halt to the activity and sent the children outside.

"Would you like anything, Mrs. Austra?" Maura asked.

Kathleen laughed. "We needn't be so formal when we're alone."

"Then we make mistakes when we're not, or so they told me."

"True. Then no, Maura, except not to be disturbed." She rubbed the small of her back. "It's been too long a morning and I need a longer nap."

"Shall I wake you in a few hours?"

"No, Laurie can when he gets home. We have plans tonight."

"Would you like me to run a—"

"No!" Kathleen turned white and faltered. "That is—I—" She gave the older woman an unexpected hug. "I don't know how I'd manage without your help. I'm sorry."

"I take no offense, Mrs. Austra. Have a good rest."

Upstairs, Kathleen untied the drawstring waist of her plain green work dress and stretched out on the bed. The baby moved, and she wondered if she'd been hit by her foot or hand. She and Laurie were arguing over names, like any couple. Like any couple. It seemed such a comforting thought that she smiled as she feel asleep.

In the barn Emma saddled Henna, then Tad's placid pony, Lafitte, named after the American pirate. They had just mounted when they heard someone approaching the house at a gallop and rode out to see Jake Finnerty dismounting. "Cullen!" he bellowed, then noticed the two. "Is Cullen here?"

Emma pointed to the barn, and Jake started as they heard the sound of an automobile coming up the drive. "Get inside the house," Jake told the children. "Find your mother and Maura. All of you, hide!"

They did as he asked while Jake raced toward the barn, falling in a line of gunfire halfway through its door. "Cullen!" he called out once more, then lay still.

When he heard the gunfire, Cullen retreated to the tack room, removed his weapon from its hiding place, and pulled open the shutter. The maneuver came too late. Three of the five men were inside the house, the other two standing guard outside the door. Uncertain what to do, he waited.

Kathleen heard Emma's call, and before she could rise, the girl rushed into her room. "Someone's—" As shots were exchanged outside, they both screamed.

"Tad?"

"Hiding. I . . . oh, no!"

They both whirled as guns were fired downstairs. "Keep to the wall and go to your brother."

"But—"

"Go!" Emma ran out the door and found herself halted by the barrel of a revolver pressed against her chest and a powerful hand gripping her shoulder.

"Come out or I'll shoot her!" the man called to Kathleen in heavily accented English.

Kathleen raised her handgun and walked out the door. On

the tile floor below lay Maura, blood seeping from the wounds
in her chest, one of her attackers dead beside her. Without
moving his weapon from Emma's chest, the German said,
"My orders are to take you alive. What I do to your child
depends on you. Put down your gun and she will not be
harmed."

A long glance passed between mother and daughter, then
Kathleen nodded. "Go join your brother," she told the girl.

Her eyes never left the man's as Emma obeyed. Only when
the doors to the old wing were shut and locked did she lower
her hand, let the weapon fall from her fingers, and walk
slowly down the stairs, seeing only each polished wood step
and the tile on the floor. Someone wrapped Maura's shawl
around her, and she stored that fact with all the rest in some
private place from which she could recall it later and mourn.

Cullen had dragged Jake into the barn and crouched behind
the car, prepared to fire when the door opened. The first one
to step through it was Kathleen, with a gun at her back.
"Come out," someone called to Cullen. "We have what we
want. Come out." When there was no response, the German
holding Kathleen ordered, "Tell him to obey."

She didn't even shake her head. "Tell him," the man repeated as she tried to decide what course to take.

Love won. "They need me alive, Cullen. Shoot me."

For a moment all motion stopped, then the leader thrust
himself in front of Kathleen, firing at Cullen as he took the
shot intended for her. Both men fell, but only the German
got back to his feet and walked unsteadily to where Cullen
lay clutching his revolver, trying to find the strength to push
himself up and use it. The German rested his foot on Cullen's
back and, with no change in his callous expression, fired at
the nape of the Irishman's neck.

"Shall I burn the house and barn?" a soldier asked in
German.

"No. The smoke would be noticed. Shoot the horses instead, and make sure the other stable hand is dead."

Kathleen didn't attempt to understand their exchange. Instead she closed her eyes and thought of Laurence. "I will
never desert you or your children," he had told her once.

Now she prayed a hopeless, impossible prayer; she prayed that he had lied.

The leader gave new orders and two men returned to the house. Kathleen had understood only one word. *Kinder,* the man had said, *kinder.* Kathleen screamed, "No!" and tried to break his hold, kicking and sobbing. "No. You promised. No!"

The German soldiers separated in the old wing, moving quickly from room to room, searching under draped furniture and in empty closets. At last one heard an abruptly cut-off sob and flung open a large cupboard to see Emma hugging her brother, her hand over his mouth. Tears leaked from her eyes as she screwed them shut and shielded Tad with her body. "Shhh," the sailor whispered, then raised his gun and fired.

At the sound of the shots Kathleen fainted.

In the barn a German aimed his handgun at Little Mary's month-old foal and found he couldn't shoot. Children, pregnant women, penned animals . . . what sort of a war was this?

"Are you through?" his partner called from the other end of the barn.

"Yes."

"Did you find the one we wounded?"

"He's dead. Let's go."

As they drove, the men did not look at each other or at the woman who sat between them, as still and silent as the rocks that looked out at the stormy sea.

Chapter Twenty-one

I

HARRY BLACKWELL WOULD have started back to Alpha, but a shawl of fine Irish lace displayed in a shop window caught his eye. The owner was out—for how long the sign did not specify—and he stopped at Finnerty's for a beer and something to eat while he waited. "Englishmen!" An old fisherman spat out the word like an obscenity. Blackwell buttered his bread and pretended he had not heard.

"Enjoy being away from the war for a while, do you, English?" another asked.

"Bangor's not been touched," Blackwell said, trying to put as much distance between himself and the Crown as possible.

"Welsh, are ye, Mr. Harris? Why, that's practically Irish, isn't it, Brian? Who knows, maybe someday ye'll even want to settle here—that is, if the girl will make an honest man of ye."

Blackwell's knuckles grew white around the stone mug he'd been given. "Pay them no mind," Brian Finnerty muttered. "They have the immunity of age and you're not the only one who suffers from it."

Blackwell shrugged. "Is your brother about?"

Brian appeared troubled. "Jake took the sea road and rode toward Alpha early this afternoon."

"Horses, no doubt."

Brian shook his head and led him to a table near the back of the inn. "Last night while the church sale was going on, someone came in asking about you and Ann. Wanted to know

232

if you were at Alpha and how long you'd be staying. He was a sly one. Jake answered before he even knew a question'd been asked. As soon as he saw what he'd done, he rode up to see Laurie. That would have been late last night.''

"Do you know the man's name?"

"No, but I've seen him before. He has a long, jagged scar here." He drew a line across his temple. "Jake's been keeping an eye on him, and when he left this afternoon, Jake followed him and hasn't come back since."

"Thank you, Brian. I think I'll skip dinner and take the same route back."

At the bar the two old fishermen stood on either side of a younger man. "Ah, Aaron, it was a pretty thing. Long and gray like a whale shimmering in the morning light."

Blackwell turned back from the door. "Are you speaking of a submarine?" he asked.

"A U-boat, English. It came up. It went down."

"Where?"

"Five, six miles east."

And Ann walked home from Alpha every night, her route just a few miles north of where the sub had been sighted. Blackwell drove toward Alpha at a suicidal speed.

II

Only Laurence and his secretary still worked at Alpha, getting out the final correspondence before the fortnight closing. When every small detail had been handled, Laurence suggested she go home. "I shouldn't leave if you have visitors coming," she reminded him, cleaning off her desk while they waited.

She was filing papers away when the two men arrived. One made a pretense of paging through a magazine while the other approached her. She could not place the accent, which troubled her, nor did she like the way he swaggered as he walked into Laurence's office.

Laurence stood to greet his visitor, his tone polite as always as he studied the sinister triumph emanating from this man. The door had not yet closed behind his secretary when his mind moved out, catching the reason for this visit. His expression altered to one so painful that Mary Burke, turning to ask a routine question, looked at him with concern. "Is something wrong, sir?"

"No," Laurence said, feigning weariness, "just so much to do and it's already after six."

Even after they were alone Laurence remained standing, wondering what means he had to fight this unexpected move against him. His caged expression caused the visitor to smile. "I am Otto Schivuld, and I was told you would know my message before I spoke it, yet let me say the words so there is not confusion. Two of my countrymen have your wife waiting with them in a cove south of here. Two more are outside with a radio. Unless we leave here within five minutes with you restrained and blindfolded, she will be shot. If we do not arrive in that cove within half an hour, she will be shot."

"And if I do as you ask?"

"I have orders to release her. She and the child she carries will not be harmed."

Laurence's response was to lock eyes with Schivuld, probing the German's intent so painfully that Schivuld winced.

"Believe me, Herr Austra, we would not have risked so much had we intended to try to kill you." The precise words, the absence of any weapon, and what he glimpsed of the German's thoughts told Laurence he spoke the truth.

"In times of crisis, trust your instincts," Stephen had written; but Laurence's instincts had to be wrong because they told him to slam this too smug man against the wall, then kill the others as well. Yet he was not to be harmed, nor was Kathleen. As he considered his alternatives the German commented, "The British children are dead and the driver of the car is holding the radio. One small word and your wife dies as well. You do not have the time to stop him. Accept it, Herr Austra. Your destiny lies in Germany."

"Very well." As if it were an afterthought, Laurence added, "My only exit is through the outside office. I do not wish my secretary to be harmed."

"Dismiss her."

Laurence pressed the intercom. "You may go home now, Miss Burke," he said.

Mary Burke packed her purse and nodded to the man in the waiting room. She walked to the back of the building, and hoping the men would not wonder why a secretary drove such luxury, she turned Laurence's Delange out the Alpha gates and down the road leading to the Austra estates. An excellent secretary and a Blackwell appointee, Mrs. Mary Burke had been given the warning.

"Turn around, Herr Austra." Schivuld's tone was polite, but the thoughts behind it were cold and barbaric. Though Laurence had decided not to resist, he was thankful the man worked quickly, shackling his wrists behind his back with a figure eight of half-inch metal. Similarly heavy cuffs were attached to his ankles, these with enough of a chain between them that Laurence could walk with an unnaturally short gait. "I was told you have remarkably lethal feet," Schivuld commented as he covered Laurence's eyes with a thick blindfold.

—Ann!— Laurence's panic forced his power to its limit, but Ann was miles away, walking toward home, and there was no reply.

In his short life Laurence had never been this helpless. A new facet of his nature rose to dominate . . . a desire for vengeance, so cold that all other emotions grew brittle and shattered. It gripped his soul so subtly, his expression never changed, but the men who walked on either side of him sensed it and pushed him forward too quickly so that he stumbled and would have fallen had they not caught and dragged him into the backseat of the waiting car.

The driver's mind showed him the way, and in an emotionless fashion Laurence called to his own. —We go west, south . . . under the Shenena bridge. Please, Mary, please, find someone . . . family . . . family.— He heard the rushing of water against the rocks, a familiar sound, a familiar turnoff. —Ann! Rose Bay!— Then with all the force he could drain from the three minds near him: —Ann! Rose Bay!—

The windows rolled down, his escorts were suddenly in need of air. Cold metal pressed against his thigh. "I will make your journey extremely painful if you do that again," Schivuld said.

* * *

As the car stopped, Laurence sensed Kathleen's presence
. . . the quiet fear, the concern for him, and, when she saw
what they had done, the regret that he could be forced to such
weakness for her sake. She stood on the short pier the fishermen sometimes used, staring over the water at the distant
German submarine. He detected the edge of something thick
and metallic at her feet, something she would not contemplate, the same way she tried to ignore the guns aimed at
both of them. Her calm was a negation.

His mind embraced her. His eyes were the eyes of the
guard beside her, and he marveled at how her auburn hair
could become so perfectly copper in the setting sun. —I love
you— he said, only because he knew at last that love could
be his own emotion, real and true.

Kathleen flung her guards a defiant look, then walked stiff-
legged with fear to where he stood and, standing on tiptoe,
kissed him a final good-bye. "No," he whispered, "their orders
are that you shall live . . . and me, what can they do to me?"

A boat bobbed beside the pier, and now a second one
pulled up behind it and a man stepped ashore . . . lieutenant's
bars, the lightning insignia, the unquestioning respect. He
reeked of triumph, and Laurence knew this was the one on
whom he would take vengeance. He swallowed the rage and
its taste sustained him.

The lieutenant came forward, standing in front of Laurence, grabbing his chin tightly with one hand while the fingers of the other were forced between his lips, running back
along the edges of his teeth. When his blindfold was ripped
off, Laurence squinted from the light of the setting sun, then
looked into his captor's eyes and saw recognition . . . not a
name but an unconquerable fear. As the blindfold was re-
placed, Laurence felt the man's hands shake.

"You have done well," the lieutenant said to Schivuld.
"Finish this."

Laurence was pushed sideways, lifted and lowered, his elbows brushing the sides of a metal box. His mind sought the
lieutenant's and he saw how easily he had been betrayed.
Orders could be changed; promises could be broken. Panic,
impossible to control, seized him and he began to tremble as
a thick steel collar closed around his neck. There was a sound,
a low and desperate cry surrounding him, coming like a sur-

prise from his throat, bouncing off the sides of his tiny cell
and from the lid as it closed down over him. He barely heard
the padlocks slide shut or felt the slow motion of the box or
detected the light footsteps running swiftly toward them until
Ann demanded, ''Release him!''

Schivuld was merely puzzled by his desire to obey. Guns
were pointed at Ann, and the men moving the box continued
to slide it onto the little boat. Ann dared not strike, certain
the box would fall and sink and she would not have the
strength to retrieve it. Then she would feel Laurie drown, as
Simon had drowned, and she would go mad with grief.

''Go!'' the lieutenant ordered. The boat pulled away, but
the thoughts of their captive moved faster, showing Ann how
he had been betrayed.

Ruthinedt debated his best course. If he took these women
as prisoners, there would be trouble, particularly with the
sister. He looked at Kathleen, huge with child, tears glistening on her cheeks. Animals, he thought. Animals, both of
them!

Ann caught his decision before he voiced it. —Run!— she
told Kathleen. —I can hold them. Run!—

But Kathleen remained on the dock, staring after the small
boat pulling away from them.

—Go! You carry his child. Run!—

Kathleen forced her eyes away from the sea. Not daring to
look at anything but her destination, Kathleen dashed toward
the gully on the far side of the road, the child throwing her
off-balance. Resolve forced her to hold an impossible pace,
and she got farther than she had ever expected—thanks to
Ann.

Ann could not paralyze but her attraction could divert, and
knowing this, her eyes, huge and exotic, moved from man to
man, promising pleasure and passion and, ultimately, the
consummation that was herself. Only great need could arouse
such seductive power, and as it grew, she felt first like a
whore, then a huge cat, too beautiful not to touch and lethal
when stroked. She smiled as she drew them closer to her,
flinging back thoughts as obscene visions. —That, why, that's
simple . . . of course, I can move just so . . . here, I like

that, here. . . . No, kill me later; pleasure first . . . the dock,
the water . . . look at me . . .—

Had the cause not been so desperate, she might have
laughed at the strength of her power. Like the plate balancer
from the Birn fair, she kept them spinning by touching them
one after the other. As they stood, charmed by her presence,
she slipped off her shoes and her hands moved to unfasten
the zipper of her straight shirt. At all times she was aware of
how far Kathleen had run. Once the woman had taken cover,
she would strike.

She had longed to kill once before, and though she had
been held back, the strength rising in her was welcomed as
a familiar friend. Begin with the lieutenant, she thought. He
gives the orders. Once he is gone, destroy the others, and
then there is the second boat and Laurie.

She directed all her powers to Ruthinedt, her lips slightly
parted, her body posed at its most sensual. "My skirt. The
zipper is broken. Will you help?"

Her voice was music, playing a familiar melody in an al-
luring new way. Ruthinedt forgot his mission and moved toward her. She was beautiful . . . such incredible eyes, such
fair skin, like . . . like the one who had devoured the soldier
on the mountain!

Dread freed him. "Shoot them," he ordered, and stepped
sideways into the boat. Instructing it to follow the other, he
turned his head away, staring only at the waiting submarine.

Although they were being deserted, the men reacted automatically. Two bullets hit Kathleen's back. Three more hit
Ann as she ripped off the confining skirt. Those were the
only shots fired.

Ignoring her wounds, Ann's fingers closed around Schivuld's throat. In the instant before he died, he heard two cries
. . . Ann's shriek of rage and, from the farthest boat, a lower,
more sorrowful note that might have been thought instead of
sound . . . the howl of a wild creature caged and in pain.

Ann's frenzy did not allow for precision, and after a few
quick thrusts she stood alone, looking at that small speck
speeding away with her brother, the second boat closer but
still too far. She never could have caught up with it, even if
she had somehow found the courage to jump from the pier
into the thick black waves. —Laurence!— she screamed, then

—Harry!— Stumbling from loss of blood, she turned and ran to the place where Kathleen lay, one hand protecting her belly, concerned even now with a child who had such a tenuous chance of ever knowing life.

Ann sank down beside Kathleen, turning her over and cradling her head. Kathleen looked silently up at her, only a sob revealing her agony. "Your children are waiting for you," Ann whispered.

Dead. Kathleen mouthed the word. She could not speak.

"They're with Mary Burke at home. I saw them."

It seemed Kathleen smiled. —You'll watch them? You'll take care of them?—

For her brother's sake Ann promised.

—And this child. Do you think . . . ?—

"I don't know." Fear poured over Ann, an avalanche sweeping away mercy. She wanted to drop the woman and run.

"If it is one of you?" Kathleen persisted, speaking now, her need giving her impossible strength.

"I don't know what to do!"

"I do. Watch my mind, like Laurie watched." Kathleen struggled to hold the thoughts through her pain . . . to show Ann how to tie off the cord and cut it and clear the lungs. —Take my little girl, please.— She forced her eyes to remain open, to beg one last time. —Please . . .—

—I will try.—

Kathleen slumped against her. Ann lifted the loose maternity shift, moving aside the undergarments, beginning with no instruments save her nails. They were enough.

Ann sensed her own weaknesses, her growing need, but she could take nothing from Kathleen until the delivery was over, and then it was too late for the mother. As for the child, she was pathetically human and her birthing had come far too soon.

Ann labored only by instinct, forcing air into lungs that could not use it, hearing a strong new heart pound wildly, then begin to fail. While she held the dying child close to her, her body began its relentless demand, an unfamiliar need, the brutal reality of hunger rising omnipotent to devour any decency. With a last act of will Ann kissed the child's bloody cheek and turned its head away from hers.

* * *

Harry neared Alpha when he felt Ann's call—all its panic, all its pain. He sped south, the picture of the pier and soldiers taking shape in his mind. So many . . . and the guns!

He drove as close as he dared, then abandoned the car and ran. When he reached the pier, he found nothing but bodies ripped apart, as if a grenade had exploded among them. "Ann," he called, and listened for a reply, hearing only waves pounding against the silence.

He called her name louder and detected the low, breathless moan rising from the other side of the roadway. He walked cautiously toward the sound, then ran when he saw Ann kneeling, swaying back and forth, clutching something to her chest. Before her, her face nearly unrecognizable in its final agony, lay Kathleen.

"Ann," he said, and repeated softly, "Ann." She looked up, her eyes wild and unfocused, and he saw the blood on her hands and face and in her hair. "Are you all right?" he asked.

In response she held out the infant, its head at the impossible angle only newborns or the dead can achieve, a huge hole in its throat. "I am now," she said, her voice shaking with dry sobs.

Horrified, he backed up a step, his hand flying to his neck, to the mark of their passion. And though he only mouthed the words, she heard them as clearly as if he had screamed them. "You damned animal!"

She lowered her head back to the infant and the keening began once more—a hollow, broken sound as she mourned the dead and the lost.

Blackwell could not look at her, so he walked back to the dock and studied the bodies instead. She had done this . . . the one he loved had done this! He turned when he sensed her standing behind him, seeing her from a new perspective, aware now of the complete measure of her power and of whose blood covered her clothing. In response she ripped the shoulder of her blouse away, exposing wounds already healing, wounds dangerously close to her heart. What she forced him to understand made no difference. He would never touch her willingly again.

—But you will touch me one last time. I need you in a way

I never have before.— In response to her still ravenous hunger he became a captive holding his jailer, comforting his tormentor as she showed him too vividly the tragedy that had occurred here.

—I have never killed before. I have never craved life so mercilessly before. . . . I survive . . . *szekorny* . . . *szekorny* . . . *szekorny* . . .—

When she had feasted on his rage and his grief and he lay among the corpses, flushed and weak and shamed by his fear, Ann stood beside him and stared at the dark water. —Go to Stephen. Tell him . . . that vengeance is in his hands.—

Chapter Twenty-two

Chaves, Portugal
December 22, 1941

I

ON THE MORNING after the abduction, Hermann Roessler arrived at the Austra offices and all his apprehension vanished. Whatever else the Austras might be, they were far from the barbaric creatures Eric had described. As Elizabeth, and now these surroundings proved, these were a cultured, civilized people. Once he explained that he held the upper hand, they would concede.

The spice-toned windows cast an illusion of warmth, but after an hour the feeling vanished and Roessler hunched down in his chair, holding his arms close to his body and shivering. Someone was to meet him here, the guard outside had said, but no one had come.

At last he felt the draft from the door swinging open and turned to face a woman. Her dark hair cascaded down her back, an Empire dress of steel gray draped from one shoulder. Her long arms and shoulders were bare, as if she did not mind the cold outside. "I am Rachel. You are to follow me," she said, and led him through a narrow tunnel into the furnace level of the glasshouse.

"I don't believe you understand," he said as they entered the stifling room in which the pots were dried.

"Perfectly," she replied, and locked him in.

The heat grew intense and Roessler's head began to pound with a frightening chant . . . no food, no water, a fortnight shutdown. By the time men returned, he'd be dead. He beat his fists against the door. He screamed, "I am here to discuss Laurence Austra!"

—We negotiate for his life?—

"Yes!"

Someone laughed in his mind—sinister, sadistic—and he knew why Eric had broken.

A day passed. More. He lay prone, dry lips pressed against the crack beneath the door as he fought for every breath of air.

—Shall we speak of his release?—

"Too late," Roessler mumbled. "Ship's gone."

—Ship?—

"Porto. There'll be repercussions." And if they'd asked, he could have answered honestly that he didn't know what those might be. He didn't know anything save the signal and the beach three miles south of Espino. He should have been there hours ago. Days ago. Certain he was dying, he closed his eyes. He slept. He had been in that hot, cramped cell two hours.

—Michael, Marilyn, David! Get ready to leave! Rachel, call Elizabeth in Lisbon. She and George must meet us in Porto. We board that boat when it rises tonight!—

But the sub did not stop to retrieve Roessler. Neither the captain nor Ruthinedt had any knowledge of a rendezvous. Instead, obeying Baivie's instructions, it slipped south of Lisbon for one final assault on the Austra family.

II

Paul lay on the soft wool carpet in Elizabeth's living room, watching the setting sun move across the glass vines and sky and alter the patterns of the gray stone floor. He'd left his own reception early, pleading exhaustion and hobbling to his car with more pronounced a limp than was needed. Perhaps it was the size of his twelfth home commission in Lisbon or the owner's traditional furnishings, but the house seemed too large and cold. No, this one was better. Even after seeing two scores of buildings rise, this was still the best he'd done.

He poured a glass of wine and moved outside. He sat in a

shaded corner of the terrace and looked out at the tranquil sea, thinking how far he'd come since Boston.

Stephen had been right about war slowing their orders, but it did not influence Spain and Portugal. Elizabeth's enthusiasm started an avalanche, and the work had begun when the studio was still under Savatier. Later it became Savatier and Stoddard then, just Stoddard . . . Stoddard . . . Stoddard.

Magazines interviewed him; photographers snapped his picture when he went to inspect his work. If recognition truly demanded sacrifice, then he deserved to be third-rate at best, but he knew the old proverb wasn't true. The Austras had taken all the years he would have struggled and made them years of creativity instead. He raised his glass to the evening sky and saluted Stephen and Elizabeth and all the rest he had come to love as kin.

A car drove up; doors opened and closed. Elizabeth, dressed in a gown the color of the evening sea, arrived with Samuelson. She sat beside Paul, resting a hand on his knee as she spoke. "You left so early. Are you in pain?"

"A little, but my ego aches more. Too many compliments, the real and the polite, have distended it terribly."

"You are something I never thought to meet, a genius with humility. As to the compliments, all but two were genuine, and those given by tasteless swine. But let us not speak of your latest triumph. Instead tell me if you like my new pottery."

"I do. So much color against the white walls is dramatic."

"Like an assortment of hard candies in a milk-glass dish, *oui*?"

"Elizabeth!"

"Tais-toi! Do not feed *me* polite lies . . . and there is no reason to be embarrassed, when it was precisely the effect I had hoped to achieve, *mon ami.*"

Paul's response was drowned by Samuelson's laughter and the ringing of the phone. As Elizabeth went to answer it, Paul stared wistfully at her back, wishing *mon ami* was not merely a pleasant affectation . . . but a word she meant only for him.

Trapped by both of them, Samuelson thought. He'd developed admiration for young Stoddard . . . for how well he'd survived those days of imprisonment with Stephen, how stoically he'd borne the pain as they'd driven into Lisbon, and, perhaps most important, how attached Stephen had become to him. Of one thing Samuelson was certain: There was no greater judge of human worth than his employer.

"A game, George?" Paul asked, pointing to the cribbage board.

"Not now." Samuelson walked over to the stone ledge and looked down at the bay without really seeing it.

"I seem to be asking this of everyone recently, but what is it that's troubling you?"

"I keep waiting for you to ask the obvious."

"Ask about what?"

"Rachel and I."

"I wouldn't have inquired, but if you're volunteering . . ." Paul said with a grin.

"Volunteering a warning," Samuelson began gruffly, then returned to the table and sat across from Paul. "After I resigned from naval intelligence I went to live out my youthful dreams at sea. The ocean fell short of my expectations and I drydocked in Lisbon. A friend suggested I try for a job at AustraGlass. Six months later I discovered Rachel . . . that same dowdy Rachel who works every day in the glasshouse. I wasn't attracted by that damn Austra magnetism—I don't even think I've ever felt it—but by her efficiency, her intelligence, and her aristocratic poise. One evening after work she invited me to her home on the mountain, offered me tea, and said she was going to change into fresh clothing. When she came back, I gawked at her like a youth about to experience his first carnal act. And if you inquired, I would say she has been worth everything I've given up for her. But I'd already lived half a life. I'd buried a wife and had two boys in boarding school. Do you understand?"

"But you have each other."

"And whenever I pass a mirror, I see every line and wonder if she is only waiting for me to know it's over before she tells me good-bye."

"I've seen how she looks at you. She loves you."

"You fool! Their closest word for love is an inflection of *take*." Samuelson exhaled audibly and poured himself a glass of wine. "Maybe you're right. Then that's worse, for it will be me who makes the logical decision." He continued, his face a dark profile against the sky. "Stephen stocks the woods around the Chavez estate so he can have the pleasure of a good chase. Rachel sometimes joins him now, and I can't help but wonder what else they do together in those dark hours while we mortals sleep. Yes, she's been worth it, but yes, now I pay."

The silence following Samuelson's revelation was broken only by the sound of the sea. Paul looked toward the horizon, and a dark shape in the bay caught his attention. He walked to the terrace wall and pointed. "George, do you see that?"

Samuelson looked first with curiosity, then with alarm. A U-boat in Portuguese waters? He had climbed to the upper terrace to get a better view when Elizabeth rushed from the house.

"The call was from Rachel. She had terrible news. Laurence—"

Samuelson's bellow cut her off. "Run! That ship's going to fire." He was halfway down the outside stairs when a portion of the terrace wall was blasted away. Elizabeth ducked as stones and glass flew around her then pulled Paul to her, slid sideways a few steps, and fell backward down the long drop to the sea.

The same gnawing damp, the same long arms wrapped around him. Paul began to whisper a name, then stopped and opened his eyes and looked in wonder at the tones of blue and green swirling across the walls of the sea cave. The space whistled like wind trapped in chambered seashells, and, seemingly from a distance, he heard another explosion, followed by Elizabeth's muffled cry. "They've destroyed the house. Oh, Paul, I'm so sorry."

She moved away from him and he saw that her dress was ripped at the shoulder, wet from their swim and stained with his blood and her own. In the light her skin seemed more pale and her eyes and hair shone blue-black. She appeared so thoroughly miserable that he asked, "Is George all right?"

"Hurt but safe. I have more than one back door."

"Good. Houses can be rebuilt."

"Please, Paul."

He smiled bitterly. "For my own silly pride, let me keep

up the false front. You can go to George, if you like. I can wait until the tide turns.''

"There's an inside exit that will let us out safely inland. But before we use it, there is something we must do.'' She rested her head on Paul's shoulder and quickly told him of Laurence's abduction. "He's in the U-boat. We must see him.''

He knew what she meant to do; he abhorred it, and though it took effort not to slide away from her, he said nothing.

"We have so little time," she whispered, and, pulling him to her, kissed him with an intensity that drew out all his desire. It flowed between them . . . growing, building until they could contain it no longer. They broke free and walked the narrow metal halls.

Paul trembled at what he saw and felt . . . the tiny room behind a locked door, the steel coffin with only one small vent. They brushed Laurence's mind, and it seemed to Paul that Laurence winced at being called back from his dreams.

Afterward they prowled the boat, finding at last the one who had taken Laurence captive. In the engine room where he conferred with the captain, Ruthinedt's face turned white and he swallowed a scream. "You fools!'' he whispered. "I can't release him. I don't have the key.'' He turned his attention back to the captain. "Bring the cliff down, then pull out,'' he ordered in a taut whisper.

In that last moment before they retreated, Elizabeth sent the threat. —Someday you will face him. Someday you will die.—

The cave whirled around Paul as they pulled back too quickly. He was dragged deeper into the labyrinth as, behind him, the air roared and the light fell away.

III

Stephen waited for Blackwell at the edge of the Austra airstrip, the dust raised by the propellers swirling around his feet. There Blackwell relayed what others had told him, end-

ing with what he had seen on the dock. He could not separate
his disgust from the memory or avoid one small step back as
Stephen clenched his fists and sucked in his breath, as if
trying to conceal sudden pain or rage.

"What happened to the German contact in Banlin?" Stephen asked.

"Timothy Ryan is dead. I killed him," Blackwell replied.
Coldly. Deliberately. Painfully. When he'd finished, Blackwell only regretted that he couldn't wake the man up and kill
him again. He was no more civilized than this family, no
better at all.

"Vengeance cleanses," Stephen replied, as if this were a
family maxim and Blackwell knew this last thought had been
noted with the rest. He wanted to apologize, but the hypoc-
risy of it held him back.

"Our agreement stands, yes?"

"I will not break it."

"That is what matters now. As for Ann, blame fate, not
yourself or her."

Though the words were terse, they seemed consoling, but
Blackwell saw no way to hide the uneasiness he felt as he
walked a few yards behind Stephen up the hill to the Austra
estates. Nor could he conceal the moment when, rounding a
bend on the narrow, tree-lined path, he brushed against Stephen's arm and recoiled with a sudden surge of fear. In his
profession and as a man, he had failed this family.

They entered a rustic house of circular design, large open
beams radiating from the center, where a stone fireplace
warmed the main room. As he approached the hearth Blackwell finally admitted exhaustion and sank down in a chair. A
quick, sad smile brushed Stephen's face and Blackwell knew
he was remembering the night they'd first met.

"Paul's house is the only one heated during the Christmas
shutdown. I'm sure he won't object to your using it for a few
hours. Get some sleep, Harry. We'll talk when George ar-
rives from Lisbon."

As soon as Stephen departed, Blackwell sought the bed.
He noticed the candelabrum on the night table, three candles
burned down to the holder and a fourth halfway, as if the
room's occupant kept one lit because he was afraid to sleep

in the dark. If it had been night, Blackwell might have done the same.

He slept, tossing with terrifying, breathtaking dreams.

Sometime between midnight and dawn, Rachel woke him and he followed her to Stephen's office. He sat in a chair in front of the desk while Rachel stood beside the only exit. Roessler had been placed in a chair beside Blackwell. The German's shirt was stuck to his body and his pants were clay-stained, yet he still exuded an air of confidence, as if he were prepared to forgive his brief imprisonment when an accord was reached. If he felt any concern about the presence of a British Intelligence agent, he did not mention it. Instead he explained why he had come.

When Roessler had finished, Stephen walked around his desk and stood in front of Roessler's chair. "You arranged to have my nephew delivered into the hands of a madman and a coward, and you come to me and say that if I cooperate with you, he will not be killed?"

"I will assure it," Roessler replied.

"You can assure nothing. The boat was never told to claim you in Espino. You have been played for a fool, Hermann Roessler."

"There will be reprisals if I am not released," Roessler said coldly.

"Will there?" Stephen crouched in front of Roessler, his long fingers curling around the German's wrists. "Tell me, who else knows the nature of my family?"

Though Roessler refused to answer, Stephen laughed. "So it has been kept a secret. That's something in our favor, yes?" Roessler stared past Stephen, meditating belatedly on a picture on the wall. "Look at me when I speak to you, German." Though Roessler winced, his eyes did not move.

Blackwell watched Stephen's facade fall, the long rear teeth brushing the edges of his lower lip as he spoke, his voice flat and hard with rage, his eyes . . . well, like Roessler, Blackwell did not look at his eyes. "Where is my nephew being taken? Where!"

Roessler stared at the top of Stephen's desk, trying to see his captor's reflection in the polished cherry wood.

Stephen's fingers tightened and Roessler screamed. "Look at me when I speak to you, German."

Roessler did, panting with the effort of fighting off the swift, painful invasion of his mind.

"I see that you don't know," Stephen said as he moved away from Roessler. He turned to Blackwell, as if the German had already ceased to exist. "Our agreement will not be altered, Harry."

"And your nephew?"

"We discussed this last night at the family gathering. We will do nothing."

After the slaughter of Alpha, Stephen could say this. "I could make some arrangements," Blackwell began tentatively.

"And risk our secrecy in the process? No, if Laurence chose this captivity, he can destroy his captors."

"I would attempt to release him myself, if you would go with me."

"We do nothing!"

Cowardice was the last trait Blackwell had expected to see in this ally. "Then I will make my own arrangements," he said.

"This is a family matter. You will stay out of it, yes?"

That final yes bored into Blackwell, begging him to echo it. He gripped the arms of his chair and thought of the carnage at Alpha, of all the late-night suppers he'd shared with Kathleen, of Laurence and his music. Laurence had played no part in this espionage, yet he was the one suffering for it, and if he had one tenth the mental power of his uncle, his captivity was as much a danger as a tragedy. Blackwell started to protest as the office doors were thrust open and a young man pushed his way past Rachel.

Though he limped, the man swaggered with that indelible Teutonic blend of bluster and dignity. "I am from the embassy in Lisbon," he said in flawless German. "I have come to demand the release of Hermann Roessler." He continued, making it clear the embassy had known of Roessler's visit, and when no immediate response came from Stephen, he slammed his cane hard on Stephen's desk, leaving a long narrow dent in the polished wood.

"I hadn't expected this," Stephen said with sad surprise.

"I cannot allow Roessler to leave here, but you may claim his body, if you wish."

"What . . . what?" The man faltered, then quickly recovered. "A German officer on a diplomatic mission!" The threats that followed were very real.

"Sit down," Stephen ordered with apparent weariness, then asked, "Harry, what do you recommend we do?"

"Speak of this in private!" Blackwell snapped, then recalled where he'd seen this young man before. This was the American, playing a German role in front of a German officer . . . and succeeding! Roessler reformed his composure instantly, certain he had won this battle, waiting confidently for the negotiations to continue.

"Leave us," Stephen ordered, and crouched in front of Roessler.

As Paul walked past him Roessler gripped his arm. "What! You would let him kill me?"

Paul glanced sadly back at Stephen, then forward to where Elizabeth stood watching him from the lobby, pulled his arm free, and left without a word.

As Blackwell followed Rachel from the room Roessler's memories flowed into him. His face turned white and he gripped Rachel's arm as if they were not strangers, as if they were friends, as outrage turned to horror. He walked beside her to a sofa beneath one of the magnificent wine-colored windows, burying his face in his hands as Roessler's past unfolded. Blackwell had heard rumors of Nazi atrocities, but to be shown the full savagery of the Reich with such vivid indifference ripped him deeper than what he'd seen last night on that narrow wooden dock. What chance did the world stand against such insanity? For an instant he saw Britain die.

When there was nothing left to take, the darkness slammed down around him and he found himself staring through tears into Rachel's sad, dark, dry eyes.

Paul had taken the chair beside him, and Elizabeth sat at Paul's feet, her head resting on his thighs. Paul stared straight ahead, as if he were looking at something Blackwell could not see or pulling some strength from deep inside himself. "I will do it," he said, absently running a hand over Elizabeth's hair.

* * *

Stephen joined them and fell into a chair, his eyes glazed, his expression one of loathing. "When you are through, burn it," he said to Rachel, and nodding, she left them. "Rachel raised Laurie as her own child," he explained to Blackwell after she'd gone. "She is owed this life. What information I acquired will, as always, be given to you."

"And after all you learned, do you still think we should do nothing?" Blackwell asked, not gently.

"*We* would fall."

"But we may not," Elizabeth said, regaining some of her usual buoyancy as she conveyed the information she and Paul had learned. "We must be in Vannes in two days. Paul will go with me. It would be helpful if he had the necessary identification should we be detained."

"Harry, can papers be had so quickly?" Stephen asked.

"Yes, but of greater importance is whether or not the effort can work."

"We know where they are landing. Two go in, three come out." Elizabeth explained. "I am safe in France. Robert has no objections to the flying if it is done at night. Paul . . ." She shrugged, the gesture meaning more than it revealed. "Paul is willing to take the risk, and if I were stopped, a German presence would be helpful. That is enough reason to take him, *oui*?"

"You'll still need a pilot," Blackwell said, then spoke to Paul. "You have no training in espionage. How do you expect to get by?"

"That act was for you," Paul countered. "How many of your agents could have done as well?"

"If you're caught, you'll die. If you're lucky, they'll kill you quickly. Do you understand?"

"I do," Paul said, surprised at how evenly he answered.

Blackwell's objections made Stephen waver. Sensing this, Elizabeth moved to a place at his side, squeezing his shoulder. "He must go," she insisted in a sharp whisper.

If Stephen replied, only Elizabeth heard him. In a moment the two left the room and closed the doors behind them.

Blackwell used the time to talk to Paul. As he did, he decided the young man was ill suited for espionage . . . too idealistic, a potential martyr . . . and he wished there was time to prepare him better. Nonetheless he said, "I'm pleased you and Elizabeth will help. Stephen has refused to do so."

"If I walked through a wall, how would you feel if I blamed you for not following me?" Blackwell looked puzzled and Paul continued. "Stephen isn't able to rescue Laurence. His limits are as simple as that."

"And so he's going to ignore what happened to Laurence?"

"Stephen believes that if Laurence had seen death in his future, he would not have been able to leave with those men."

"Does your faith in them run as deep?"

"I've had to learn it." Paul described his three days in the D'Oscuro dungeon, from the rats to the slaughter. As he did, Blackwell began to see there was more self-preservation in this young man than was evident at first glance. "My faith is this," Paul concluded. "I intend to stay as close to Elizabeth as possible."

Chapter Twenty-three

I

THE AIRCRAFT TRAVELED high, Blackwell killing the engine when Robert sensed the need for stealth. Paul attempted to convince himself that nothing that followed could be as terrifying as the ride to Brittany and that final painful moment when Blackwell swooped down on a field and without fully stopping, dropped Elizabeth and him off and rose again into the night. In twenty-four hours the plane would return and they would have either succeeded or failed.

Elizabeth needed no new identification. Paul's was nearly flawless. He had been wounded in the invasion of Holland and, no longer able to serve the Reich in a military capacity, worked as a war correspondent for a little-known publication in Frankfurt. Only a face-to-face meeting with his editor would reveal that this Franz Wustoff was an impostor, the real one killed by the Resistance only a week before. They wore dark clothing and good walking shoes and carried a great deal of currency, both German and French. The closest thing Paul had to weapons were his cane and the woman beside him.

They traveled by moonlight the few miles to an abandoned fisherman's cottage and hid in a nearby stand of trees. Elizabeth moved her mind through the house, then pointed down at the sea at the U-boat, barely visible in the mist.

"We're on time!" Paul exclaimed.

Elizabeth shook her head. "They've come and gone. Nothing lives on that boat or in the cabin. Come, let us go inside and see if dead men can be made to speak." Her voice sounded detached, as if this failure were merely a brief setback.

The treachery was obvious from the moment they entered the cabin . . . food and half-empty glasses of wine and cognac on the splintered wood table, the smell of vomit but no sign of blood. There had been no struggle here, only betrayal and, they discovered, revenge, for clutched in the hand of one of the victims was a scrap of paper, and on it the scrawled words 'Cluf, Romania.'

"So it is true," Elizabeth whispered. "The jailer is mad." As they traveled back to the airstrip she described the power of the Old One, who lived atop the peaks a mere twenty miles from Baivie's destination. "Baivie is like a sorcerer seeking an incantation that can only destroy its user."

"Will Laurence be able to call so far?"

"No. Even Stephen barely has that reach. But the British have agents behind the Eastern lines. Blackwell can find someone to carry the message into the Varda." She smiled, and in spite of her neatly clipped and capped rear teeth, it was as predatory an expression as Paul had ever seen. "Yes, Laurie will be pleased with how it ends when Frn'cs comes for him."

When, not if. Elizabeth's faith was concrete and innocent, and Paul said nothing to break it as they walked the miles back to the airstrip. The took shelter at dawn in a bombed-out chapel, and that evening they stopped in a copse of trees near the airstrip to wait.

The weather changed, the temperature dropping as the wind rose. A storm attacked and was gone. They sat for hours after Blackwell and Robert were due, listening for the drone of the engine. At sunrise they heard it. The plane circled over them and Paul caught a thought soft from its distance —The Germans have seen us. Tomorrow at the same time.—

The plane swung and lifted, the gray metal glistening in the morning sun and two Me-109s moved in for the kill. Robert's plane had no guns, but Blackwell's skill kept them out of the lines of fire long enough for Robert to use his mental power to send one pilot spinning toward the ground. Blackwell veered right to avoid a crash, and the second German pilot strafed the side of their plane.

Elizabeth gripped Paul's arm. Their minds soared united,

and captured the German in the heat of his triumph. It would be over in a moment. The German tried to rise but fell instead, his senses blurred, the sky and earth transposed.

Perhaps Blackwell had been wounded, or perhaps he did not expect the German's suicidal move, but as he dipped and headed for the open sea the Me-109 hit him in the midsection, the two planes falling together, their crash turning a moment later into dense, oily smoke and rolling flames.

Paul hobbled after Elizabeth. He saw Blackwell's body, the German pilot's legs, then Robert's hand, coated with burning oil, reaching through the fire, clawing the ground. He lived, pulling himself to safety though his skin cracked and his blood glistened in the brilliance of the rising winter sun.

Elizabeth waded into the edge of the fire and pulled her brother free. She seemed in shock, unable to do anything but hold him, whispering something softly to him in her own language. Paul beat the flames from her skirt, then placed his wrist over Roberts's charred lips, trusting Elizabeth to pull him away when the time of hard need ended. He felt Robert try to bite down, then his jaw went slack. Paul might have ripped at his wrist himself, but all sounds, all thoughts, all motion ceased as Elizabeth bowed her head and said goodbye. Paul watched the grief and rage building in Elizabeth's clenched hands, her pressed lips. Finally it broke free in a wail so anguished, it seemed to echo from the south and west, and he knew that every one of the family, from Chaves to Ireland to the tiny prison traveling through France, had felt Robert die. The sound of her grief ended as quickly as it had begun, then Elizabeth lifted her brother and threw him into the blaze. "I will be back," she whispered, and looked at Paul. "We leave no traces," she said, her eyes all the sadder for their lack of tears.

They traveled until Elizabeth decided it would be safe to stop, then rested and agreed their best course would be to leave France on their own. "We'll go to Paris and stay at the château," Elizabeth suggested. "From there I can make arrangements for us to leave. Now I think we must find a safe place to hide from the painful day, *oui*?"

Paul knew of one, close and excellent.

II

This Christmas Day the Dutiel farm was deserted. On the table in the kitchen sat a cast-iron pot filled with moldy stew, a basket of stale rolls, and a pitcher of curdled milk. Paul scavenged food while Elizabeth filled a large jug with water. They decided it was best to hide, and climbed the narrow ladder to the security of Philippe's tiny room in the loft.

Even before Elizabeth sensed the tragedy, Paul separated the familiar stench from the healthy scents of straw and offal. He stepped back while Elizabeth pushed open the door. Philippe lay on his plain iron bed, an old bandage on his arm caked with dried blood and pus. A pair of flies defied the cold to circle him, and in the corners small feet rustled in hasty retreat. But Philippe was not dead, for when Paul called his name and rushed to his side, his lips moved.

Elizabeth drew Paul away. As she had done with him on the way from D'Oscuro, she ripped off the soiled cloth that covered the wound. Frowning, she sent Paul for soap and clean rags, then set to work. Though Philippe moaned with pain, he was never conscious, and for the first time Paul was thankful he could not speak to his friend.

While working, Elizabeth discovered a half dozen letters beneath Philippe's pillow. One had been addressed to Mark McCray but Mark's name had been crossed out and Paul's substituted. Paul sat on the floor beneath the small window, reading the tragic words aloud.

Paul,
   I know it sounds trite, but if you read this, I am dead. It is right I tell my story first to you, not Mark, for it was you who begged me to stay at AustraGlass. I wanted to listen but I knew that if I did, I could never face my father again. So I returned to Brittany and enlisted in the French army, as my father had in the last great war. Such a fine, fast defeat . . . so unlike the slaughter of the last . . . and I thanked God when we surrendered.
   Such a relief to be home again. For a few months the Germans treated us well. There were privations, but after all, we French had seen war before. Then my father

began pushing me to join the Resistance. I had been a fool to think I could be neutral. I had forgotten what he was like. Yet I managed to refuse and stayed home to tend the cows and prune the vines and watch the planes fly overhead on their bombing runs to London. One day my father disappeared, and I knew he had left us to follow his beliefs.

Months passed and we heard nothing until the day the Germans came, carrying proof that they had captured my father. They offered to bargain. I would spy for them and they would let him live. They were so certain I would agree, they did not care that my mother sat beside me, her face pale from sorrow and rage. I refused for her sake, but later, in private, I agreed.

Unbelievable, yes, but so easy. I thought of my family and their little farm as a grassy knoll surrounded by a forest filled with wild beasts, one no better than the other, and my duty was clear. Still, I admit that the night I betrayed my company, less than half were present.

The Germans shot them on the spot, one by one, and their eyes accused me. I forced myself to watch, playing the role of traitor perfectly. It was the only role left me, you see. When the executions had ended, a truck pulled up carrying my father's corpse. He had chosen suicide, the Germans told me, rather than to be released and have to kill his son.

I can hardly remember my rage. I attacked one of the soldiers, beating him like a madman until another shot me. They brought me home and left me lying beside my father's body on the grass in front of the house. My mother brought me here to hide me from the Resistance, then went for a doctor and has not returned.

How could I have ever believed I could exist in the midst of war and take no side? And still it seems so right that all I wish to do is return to my old place in the glasshouse, create beautiful things, and forget.

Give Mark this letter if he returns—I say if because Brittany is littered with the bodies of English flyers, then kiss some pretty lady all over and think of me.

Poor, poor peaceful creature," Elizabeth said sadly. "I will not lie and say I am hopeful. He needs a doctor, *mon ami*."

No local doctor would risk his life to treat a traitor. "Then it's hopeless, isn't it?"

Elizabeth shook her head and pointed to the letter. "He gave us a way to save him."

"Elizabeth!"

"His last wish is clear, Paul. Let's do what we can to grant it."

At dusk she traveled to the nearest town and arranged transport to Paris. During the long truck ride Paul held Philippe's hand while Elizabeth sat beside the hired driver, laughing, purring, enticing as ever in her perfect act.

In Elizabeth's absence the guest rooms of the Austra château had been occupied by German officers . . . the most expedient means of keeping the rest of the Bosch rabble at bay. By evening her guests had assembled in the larger drawing room to welcome back the lady of the house.

She looked magnificent in her brilliant red silk dress. Her hair glowed in the candlelight, the gems on her fingers sparkling as her hands helped to weave her story. Her trip through Brittany became high adventure: the brave young Frenchman defying the fanatic Resistance . . . Franz Wustoff, the German correspondent who had found him then flagged down her auto and begged for aid.

No! She grew too dramatic! Someone would see through the lies. As distinctly as if she stood beside him whispering in his ear, Paul heard her lilting words. —They are licking my fingers, young fool. Play your part half as well!—

"Listen to her!" a German officer said, startling Paul. "No one will dare lecture her on the danger, but if the French had found her, half the officers in Paris would be mourning tonight."

"And I," Paul said, then added with a quick laugh, "But would a true Frenchman slit such a pretty throat."

The German chuckled. "Maybe afterward. What made you save the one upstairs?"

"I read the letter and decided there might be a good story

in it, if he lives to tell it all.'' When the officer inquired about
Philippe's condition, Paul only shrugged. "I'm not his doctor. I only hope he wakes before I must go." The German
asked the logical question, and Paul learned a great deal about
traveling through the combat zones.

The party was winding down when Paul pleaded weariness
and stiffly climbed the stairs, slipping into the sickroom to
sit beside his unconscious friend.

Paul dozed, and when he woke, he saw Philippe watching
him, bewilderment visible through the pain on his face.

"You read my letter?"

"Yes. I'm sorry, but we had to call a surgeon."

Philippe managed a wry, fleeting smile. "So I noticed.
What irony. If I live, I can say I lost an arm in the war."

"Guilt is a luxury of the living."

Philippe hesitated, then asked, "Did you see my mother?"
Paul shook his head.

"Where am I now?"

Paul told him. "Elizabeth will see you get to Chaves."

It occurred to Philippe that Paris was not safe for an American. "Why did you come here?" he asked.

"I am looking for someone," Paul answered honestly.

"Will you keep looking?"

Paul thought of Linda and the debt he owed the Austra
family. "I must," he replied. "I share the blame for his
being lost."

His decision came that quickly. Acceptance came harder.

Long after the house had fallen silent, Paul lay awake in a
guest-room bed. He stared up at the blue chintz canopy, seeking a way to tell Elizabeth good-bye. He finally decided to
avoid her altogether, leave a note, and catch the morning
train. He found paper and pen in a writing desk in the corner
of the room and began his farewell. The words were hard to
find, and the dim, gas-fueled sconces shed just enough light
to make writing possible. Concentrating on his letter, Paul
did not realize Elizabeth had joined him until she placed a
delicate hand over the paper.

"Don't stop me from doing this," he said, knowing how
easily she could.

''No, Paul, I will not stop you, but there are things you must have. In your closet is a good German-made suit and hat and a few shirts that will fit you. I also have a typewriter and a case, and something else.'' She handed him an envelope containing a draft of an article Wustoff had been carrying when he'd been killed. ''Be darling, *mon ami*. Write your stories and send them back and no one will question who you are.''

''You knew! You always knew I would go on alone, didn't you?''

She shook her head, genuinely stricken. ''No. I asked Blackwell for every scrap of information he had because I sensed you would need it. But believe me, Paul, when I tell you I thought we would be only in Brittany rescuing Laurie together.''

''And then?''

''Then I knelt beside the body of my brother and I understood. Someone must go. Yes, I could leave here with you, but I cannot.'' She rested her hands on his shoulders and said candidly, ''I have made intelligence officers my . . . *affaire d'amour*. If you wish to put it that way. If I were recognized, my presence could destroy you. And if I leave the job I have pledged to do, all the family's plans, perhaps their entire future, would become as painful as it has for Laurie. What is Laurie's captivity compared to that?''

Laurie's death! He wanted to scream, to demand that she face that truth. But she couldn't, he had to remind himself, not even after the pain of Robert's convenient pyre, not even if another wrenching surprise shot through her again. Elizabeth moved closer to him and he backed away, keeping the distance between them, as if the space would conceal his thoughts. She looked down, scanning the letter on the table.

''You have written too strong a farewell for someone who will be coming back.''

''Will I?''

She rested her hands on his shoulders. ''Imbecile, what did you think I came here to tell you?''

Her mind touched his in an intimacy greater than bodies and years could ever achieve. He tried to think of some words to make her go, but nothing came to him except an unformed plea for help and understanding. With a quick, fierce shudder his shell broke and all the doubt and dread poured out of him. He pulled her to him, crushing her against his chest, saying in a forced, broken whisper, "Holy God, Elizabeth! I've never been so frightened!"

—I share it . . . beloved.—

He shuddered again, but what she destroyed now was the barrier of his reserve. She lifted her head and he kissed her, for the first time freely admitting the passion he had felt since he had seen her walking through Stephen's ordered dreams.

Yes, he feared losing himself in her . . . but the fear of dying without ever knowing her was far, far worse.

Then she was kissing him again, and the past and future vanished into now . . . her lips yielding, then demanding, fitting his as if they were one body. Her hands undid the buttons of his robe, sliding over his chest, leaving a warmth in their wake.

She turned and he fumbled with the buttons down the back of her dress, every brush of his hands against her skin sending another tremor of passion through him. In a moment the red silk fell in a colorful pile at her feet, then a black slip followed and there was nothing separating them except a few inches of air that seemed charged, pulling him like a magnet toward her. He fought it, holding back so he could look at her.

The dim gaslight turned her skin pale gold, long legs rising into a narrow band of pubic hair, sparse as a young girl's, accenting rather than concealing the sex beneath it. Her arms hung straight down, the painted tips of her fingers brushing the outsides of her knees. The pale pink of her nipples darkened and hardened, and he looked at them as if his thoughts could really touch her. She lowered her head and looked up at him coyly, her dark eyes flashing beneath their winged brows, her short hair falling forward, brushing the hollows of her cheeks.

Did any of the officers she used ever see her like this? No, they could not, or they would know in an instant that they held something rare and precious in their arms.

She answered his thoughts. —Only you see me as I am, beloved. And when this war is over, there will be only you.—

He felt a shadow, some hint of grief buried deep within her, and sensed she was thinking that caring could only end in some inevitable good-bye.

For a moment their natures formed a wall between them, but she raised her arms and slowly spun full circle. "Best of all, I am a woman—and you, beloved, a man." She moved so quickly that his eyes could not follow her, and she plucked the robe from his back to land beside her gown on the black tile floor. Then she did something so strange and so natural, lifting him up, carrying him to bed as easily as if he were a tiny child. She kicked off the covers and stretched out beside him.

Paul rolled up on an elbow and laid a palm against her cheek, touching her softly, as if she were as delicate as she seemed. He felt younger than his age, more innocent, and he wished he had waited for her. She pulled him down and he buried his face in her hair, breathing in its forest-scent, enhanced rather than hidden by the perfume she wore. Then there was only her . . . her hands and her lips and her mind . . . and neither one woman or a thousand could steal any passion away from this.

Long after he thought he could not hold back, that it would be over, she was still gripping him with her mind, as her long legs had wrapped around his hips, holding him high and tight and motionless within her. He struggled, trying to break free, grabbing for her arms so he could pull her down and kiss her. She raised him instead, pulling up his head and shoulders with one arm wrapped around his back. He felt her hand brush the side of his neck, a stab of pain, her lips covering the wound. He closed his eyes, almost seeing his passion swirling inside him, like light through smoke leaking slowly through the spot her lips touched.

He could not make a sound. For a moment he could not even move. And because he loved her, he would give her this . . . as much as she demanded, his life if she demanded it, his soul.

She slowly unwound her legs, and he pounded against her, a man against a woman. In the moment of release she kissed him, and he tasted his blood on her lips and tongue, felt their final cries of passion merging and echoing together in the private silence of his mind.

At dawn he carefully pulled himself from her arms, packed a single bag, and caught the morning train. Much later she woke and saw a new note sitting on the desk. "I would go even if I did not love you," it read.

She crushed it in her hand and looked out the window, east toward the destruction of one more war. "You will come back," she whispered, as if her belief were a charm that could protect him.

Later she went downstairs and found an officer wolfing down breakfast in the dining room. "Fräulein!" he said, and laughed and clapped his hands.

For a moment her instincts failed her. She had to remember to smile.

Chapter Twenty-four

I

DURING THE LONG journey from Ireland to Romania, Ruthinedt relinquished his guard of the metal casket only for sleep. Though he hid it well, every unexpected creak of the ship or the train made his heart pound, and he tried not to think of that future when he would open the box and, like Pandora, face his nightmare again.

No attempt was made to give their prisoner even water, but no sound came from that casket, nor any motion, as if the creature inside had willed itself dead. A consoling notion, yet Ruthinedt knew it was untrue, for no smell of death—indeed, no scent at all—could be detected. When he slept, Ruthinedt would dream vivid, happy dreams of woods and fields and music, the laughter of children and the comfort of the woman's arms. And when he woke, the ghost of the woman hung before him and he knew he was compelled to mourn, though he had killed her and did not care.

Reality also troubled him. An official questioned them at one of their stops in Germany, inquiring about the where-abouts of Herman Roessler, later another asked if they knew anything concerning the poisoning of the sailors in Vannes.

"Resistance?" Baivie suggested sadly. Ruthinedt, who knew nothing but suspected a great deal, said he was inclined to agree.

Baivie's house stood on a residential street close to the Cluf rail depot. It sat back from the road behind a high stone wall and huge iron gates. It seemed a madman had built it. Wings jutted out at odd angles, gables and towers rose where only a roof rightfully should be. As they entered it Baivie explained that the bottom floors were occupied by German intelligence, with only the attic reserved for Baivie's quarters and his laboratory. As had become his usual practice, Ruthinedt hid his relief. There would be aid if needed, and men, so he would not be alone.

The soldiers who had come with Colonel Haller to meet them at the station hoisted the heavy metal box and, with much open swearing, maneuvered it up the winding main staircase, then the narrower ones that led to Baivie's laboratory. If Haller minded their lack of discipline, he made no mention of it. Outside the door the soldiers were forced to pause and mumbled impatiently while Baivie unlocked the three padlocks, slid back the bars, and pushed open the heavy metal door.

Baivie entered first, followed by Ruthinedt and Haller. Like the rest of the building, the bars on the laboratory windows made it resemble a small prison. The lab had none of the order of the lower rooms, and any charm the old room might have held was obliterated by the clutter, the dust-coated lab tables, the old furniture and the dingy yellow light that leaked through the filthy, narrow windows. The only modern items were an X-ray machine taking up most of one corner, vials and microscopes in a glass-doored cabinet beside the window, and a massive lab table cluttered with papers. With a sweep of his arm Baivie cleared its top so the soldiers would have a place to set the casket.

Noticing Ruthinedt's disgust at the filth, Haller said disdainfully to Baivie, "We have our own equipment, Doctor, and no use for yours. Had you left me the keys, I would have seen that your rooms were cleaned in your absence." As if he had no interest in Baivie's treasure, Haller left, ordering the guards to remain with them.

When the locks of the casket were undone, Ruthinedt stood stiffly beside Baivie. Like the other soldiers ringing the room, he had his gun drawn, but only he took the danger seriously. The others joked as the lid was raised and the sides lowered. But when their captive lay exposed on the thick metal slab, they became completely silent.

In spite of their ignorance the soldiers stared in fascination as the blindfold was removed and Baivie ran his fingers over the face . . . hard, alabaster pale. When he got no response, Baivie grew suddenly distressed, hands groping frantically for a pulse.

"You collect statues now, Herr Baivie?" The sergeant sneered, turning on his heel and stalking from the room. He requested no permission, as if Ruthinedt did not outrank him.

Ruthinedt stared down at the creature. Perhaps his dread had been for nothing. Perhaps death came pure to these monsters. Ruthinedt's thoughts grew absurd in their triumph and he imagined Baivie standing this one in the corner of his filthy lab until he tired of it. Then Ruthinedt would take it to his quarters and display it—his David, his Apollo—and find relief in its stony presence. *This is my nightmare . . . not so terrible; just look at it, not so terrible at all.*

The rest of the soldiers were leaving now, jeering laughter in the hall. Ruthinedt joined them for a moment, taking the cigarette the sergeant offered. "He's no different from the ones who send our orders. Did you ever hear Göring speak?" The sergeant shrugged and let the matter drop when Ruthinedt did not answer.

The sergeant went away, and Ruthinedt leaned against the door until the ash reached his fingers, then stubbed out the butt and rejoined Baivie.

The doctor sat at his desk, hands covering his face, seemingly lost in thought. Ruthinedt moved close to the captive and looked down at it. Now that he was unobserved, Ruthinedt dared to brush a shaking hand across the dark, curly hair, lightly over the eyelids, over the lips that did not so much part as yield. He put a finger inside the dry mouth, running it over the needle-thin lip of one rear tooth.

He pulled back, his finger bleeding, a streak of red staining the creature's lower lip. Even now . . . even now. His hand swung hard across the prisoner's face. "Wake up, damn you!" he bellowed. "Wake up!"

Nothing . . . nothing except Baivie pulling him away. "Is he dead?" Ruthinedt asked in a hoarse, hopeful whisper.

"No . . . no, not at all."

Ruthinedt shook his head in denial and placed an extra step between himself and that table.

"He is like one of those insects that roll into tight balls when you frighten them. But if you hold them in your hand and wait long enough, they unroll." As he spoke, Baivie made a fist and slowly opened it palm up, then closed it again more tightly. "Their shells make them hard to crush, but unrolled they are vulnerable, you see."

Baivie moved a bulky machine beside the table and fumbled in a cupboard, pulling out metal plates. "There are ways to make him unroll, but while he is so still, I will take the X rays." He placed the first plate beneath Laurence's head, lowering the machine to the correct height. A low hum droned in the room as he switched it on.

A flush rose on that pale skin, gone as quickly as it came. Baivie removed the plate, pushing away the second Ruthinedt offered, increasing the radiation, hitting the switch again.

The flush lasted longer this time, and the creature's fingers curled into hard fists. "Move back," Baivie warned, and lowering his machine another few inches, he hit the switch.

A shriek rocked the room, a sound so loud and high that it seemed to pierce Ruthinedt's eardrums and pound beneath his eyes. His arms covered the sides of his head but he could not block out the pain. Fire! His face was in flames. He spun and looked into a mirror and saw the same ruddy complexion as always, no difference save in his expression of puzzled agony.

"And I thought I would have to try something as barbaric as sunshine, my young lord," Baivie was purring as Ruthinedt rushed from the room.

Ruthinedt placed a hand against the wall to steady himself, not looking up when the sergeant rushed back. "What was that?"

Ruthinedt laughed, and only with difficulty could he stop long enough to say, "The statue . . . the statue woke."

II

During the day the Germans headquartered in Baivie's house and practiced their techniques for obtaining information with endless precision. Citizens knew what atrocities went on inside it, and they would stare bleakly from outside the gates or spit on the sidewalk as they walked past. The interrogators could have moved prisoners in and out at night, or closed and shuttered the windows to hide the cries, but Ruthinedt guessed that they sought this publicity, this reputation for pain. Yet, as had happened in France, instead of fear, oppression only made rebellion grow and the rooms below Baivie's were very busy.

On some afternoons Ruthinedt would walk through the streets, seeking escape from the misery of that house but finding only a different kind of sadness. Thin-legged children standing in lines beside their mothers, waiting to buy food until the shops closed and they went home hungry. The hasty transactions in back rooms and alley that he tried to avoid noticing. The old. The wounded. The beggars. All shivering, all too drained to face the cold Romanian winter. Why had he never seen these small tragedies before? Perhaps he did now, he decided, because this was humanity, and these people, for all their cultural disparity, were his kind.

Sometimes he would stand at the depot and watch supply trains roll east. The offensive had been tremendous until winter declared a truce neither side had the stamina to disobey. In spite of the hardships at the front, Ruthinedt wished he were going there, wished he could once again lead young men into battles and through the harder waitings between them.

Once he had thought how easy it would be to go, but he never tried until the evening he watched the train filled with people roll slowly past him, hands reaching through the grates, eyes barely seen in the dimming light, pleading for nothing but some small sign that there was a reason to hope. On the end of the platform a young Romanian soldier ran a finger across his throat. Whether he meant honesty or malice Ruthinedt did not know, but the gesture disgusted him. That night, when he attempted to write a formal request for a transfer and could not put the words to paper, he learned the truth: The creature in Baivie's lab would not let him go.

Though it remained motionless, it now gave terse, direct responses to questions if it was addressed by name. Baivie was meticulous about its care, seeing that it was bathed daily and covered with a blanket, though Ruthinedt suspected it had no need for warmth and no particular feelings of modesty. Ruthinedt wondered how it ate until the night he discovered master and slave together, Baivie on his knees, its face pressed against his shoulder.

"Strange," Baivie said to him afterward, "like no feeling I have ever had. Not unpleasant, just the opposite, and I can pull away anytime I wish, you see."

"It's safe, I suppose," Ruthinedt said cautiously, hiding his dreadful certainty that the doctor was mad.

And if Baivie was mad, what of himself? Ruthinedt considered this often as he spent hours in the lab, pouring over Baivie's data. He no longer feared the captive. There was no way it could break the thick metal collar on its neck and the shackles on its hands and feet. All had been welded to the heavy metal table. Still he would not look at it for to do so brought a different kind of horror, that of seeing and sharing utter despair.

Gone was the flashing beauty of those eyes. Dull and glazed, they stared at nothing. The pale skin had grown sallow, the mouth slack, the cheeks sunk in, and what it thought, Ruthinedt did not dare to guess.

"It will die, Cristof," he said one afternoon as they sat in Baivie's library. "It is dying already."

Baivie looked up from the book he was reading. "He cannot even conceive of his death. That is our power over him. We can do anything, you see."

"And what have you discovered?" Ruthinedt asked reluctantly.

"You read the reports, don't you?"

"Yes, but what do you think is most important?"

"The child you did not bring me."

"It could not have been his!"

"It was!" Baivie rushed to the lab and came back with

recent local interviews and the results of the previous day's work. "Here, this section! Legend states that if his blood is mixed with that of a human female, he may father a child by her. And look, his blood will mix with any human type. We are so lucky the young one is a male. Soon I shall begin to create a new race, an immortal race possessing the innate power to rule."

Ruthinedt, who had on more than one occasion coldly ordered surrendering soldiers shot, felt ill.

When Baivie had retired, Ruthinedt went to the lab and stood close to the door, his back to the one on the table. "Do you know I did you a favor in killing her?" he began, and relayed what Baivie had told him. "What do you think he would have done to her and the child? Would it have been any less than he has done to you?"

He felt it then, the hint of a plea, the desire to make the expected request. But it did not ask to be freed; instead tears came to Ruthinedt's eyes, and he fled the lab, running down the hall to his room. "Colleen—" he whispered, and his voice broke.

The next day a workman installed a plate of two-inch glass between Baivie's laboratory and library and covered it with bars. Baivie carefully inspected the work, then ordered an extra, heavier, bar and lock added to the doors connecting the two work rooms. Ruthinedt followed the doctor into the lab, asking with a hint of panic, "Are you going to let it loose?"

"No. No, of course not. I but do this to make certain we can't get in. Haller has sneered long enough. Tonight I will show him the power of my beast."

Though he wished to be anywhere but in that lab, Ruthinedt forced himself to remain beside Baivie as the doctor explained his procedure to Haller. A prisoner was brought in, a boy of perhaps fourteen, who would be shot if Baivie's experiment failed. He was shirtless, his hands tied behind his back. The soldiers pushed him into a seat, then left him shivering with cold and fright, staring in panic at the equipment around him, as if the lights, the machines, the tubes, the scalpels, and the needles were the threat to him, not the pale, still body strapped to the table.

Ruthinedt looked sadly at the victim, wondering what crime had been so terrible that he should pay with his life. He was unaware that Baivie spoke to him until the knife was pressed into his hand.

". . . to kill him," Baivie was saying.

Ruthinedt looked from Haller to Baivie, then blankly at the weapon.

"Clean cuts heal too quickly. We must damage him so his body is forced to demand life. Though you won't succeed in killing him, I want you to try, Eric, so you will know he is no different from the one you saw." Baivie nodded as he said, urging again, "Try."

Why doesn't it look away! Why doesn't it close its eyes! Why doesn't it beg? Anything, anything to make this easier. But it watched Ruthinedt take the knife with silent, pathetic innocence, as if it did not comprehend what was done to it here, had never known real evil or pain.

"Try."

Ruthinedt raised the knife, holding it in both hands above the pale, lean body. He thrust down but his hands stopped, then hung suspended a foot above its stomach, as if he had struck a wall of unset concrete that had solidified with his hands inside it.

In what seemed a maternal gesture, Baivie gently pushed his prisoner's head sideways and bent over so their faces were only inches apart. "We will do this, Laurence Austra," he whispered, then said to Ruthinedt, "Try now."

He could move! Ruthinedt buried the knife in its stomach and three screams filled the room . . . the creature's penetrating shriek of agony, the prisoner's cry of fear, and his own as he felt the horrible pain course through his insides like a bloody flux. He ran to the outside door, finding it locked, fled to the library, and in the glass saw a hint of his reflection, his face spattered with the alien blood. In the lab Baivie stabbed down over and over, and over and over the creature screamed—and Ruthinedt screamed with it.

"He will die, anyway, my young lord," Baivie said softly, and he and Haller joined Ruthinedt in the library, padlocking the door behind them. To enter the laboratory they would have to leave by the outside doors, go downstairs, and request the key from the sergeant who had been given it.

Ruthinedt leaned against the glass, still weak from pain that had vanished as quickly as it had appeared. In the lab, blood dripped to the floor, forming small, expanding pools. "Will your precautions be enough?" Ruthinedt asked.

"Of course. Many times I have wished to free him, and always I leave and the compulsion vanishes. Young ones do not have the mental strength."

Young ones. But the creature seemed old now . . . far older than the boy walking slowly toward the table. Ruthinedt watched with reluctant fascination as the drama unfolded on the other side of the glass.

He must not kill! All his carefully woven plans would fall apart if he let the beast in him rise and kill! But Baivie, that insane creature he could not touch, was watching, making restraint impossible. Without turning his head he sensed the presence of the boy, his exact position in the room. His control faded and he clenched his fists and tried to think.

The boy walked slowly to the table, speaking a language Laurence did not know. As Laurence forced himself to remain conscious, his body trembled and the bleeding intensified.

The boy knew Laurence should be dead. "What are you?" he whispered with awe.

Laurence used the old word, and the boy retreated in panic, pounding his body against the locked door. That bewitching scent of fear filled the room and Laurence began to weaken. —Come here!— he ordered, but the boy only stood, shaking with panic. Laurence was too weak to summon without words, so he repeated the mental order in German and in French, with no better result. At last he trusted the only ally he had, and Ruthinedt, his hands pressed against the glass, whispered the Romanian command.

When the boy stood close to him, Laurence continued. —You must help me. Turn around. Raise your arms so I can reach them.—

Still trembling, the boy obeyed. Rope! Yes, luck was with him. He bit it through.

* * *

Baivie swore and pounded an angry fist against the glass.
"The fool! Does he think that child can free him?"

Ruthinedt hid his loathing, thinking he could afford the
pity he felt for victim and killer.

"What is he doing now!" Baivie exclaimed as the boy
picked up the blanket and covered the form on the table, the
near edge brushing the floor. Baivie's mouth twitched, and
he pawed Ruthinedt's arm as if expecting an answer.
"What?"

But Ruthinedt did not take his eyes off the drama before
him, conspiring with the two to thwart this madness.

—Yes, yes! Find what you need and come to me.—

The boy circled the lab, picking up equipment, putting it
down, making certain his back was always to the observers.
Afterward, he knelt on the far side of the table, where he
would be hidden from view. There was motion under the
blanket, then nothing for a half hour until the boy stretched
out beside the captive, covering both of them, resting his
cheek against Laurence's shoulder.

"Now he's caught," Baivie exclaimed, the tip of his tongue
brushing the corner of his upper lip. "Watch them now, Colonel. You will see!"

Ruthinedt watched as carefully as Haller but for a different
reason. He'd seen the beast and it had not looked like this.

When there had been no motion for some time, Baivie sent
for the key, and the lab was opened. Four armed guards
waited outside as Haller pulled off the blanket and looked
down at the half-healed wounds on Baivie's captive, at the
boy, pale but alive. On the edge of the table sat a basin, a
stained towel, a cup, and on the floor beneath it only untidy
smears marked the place where the bloody puddles had
formed.

They had won! Ruthinedt shared the brief thrill of triumph
as he stared at the two . . . the boy glaring up at him, the
captive impassive as always. Ruthinedt would have laughed
had the officers not been in the room. The colonel and Baivie
argued about the victim until Haller unexpectedly agreed.
"The prisoner killed an officer. I don't care how he dies. But
tomorrow this thing will begin its work for us or I'll shoot it
myself. Do you understand?"

Baivie nodded and called to the guards, "Come inside. Strap the boy down."

Though the conversation was in German, the boy understood enough that he tried to bolt, guards catching him just outside the door, dragging him back and tying him to a second table. "It would have been more merciful had you killed him, my young lord," Baivie said, when the four were alone.

A sudden vivid image of Baivie's plans came to Ruthinedt and he excused himself and took a long walk through the streets, but no matter how far he traveled, he heard the screams. Twice he thought he saw the insolent sergeant following him, but perhaps it was chance or his eyes playing tricks. He wasn't valuable, after all; there was no reason to watch him.

Hours later he returned to the lab, and though the body was gone, the blood-soaked linens on the table remained. The creature had refused to kill. Now it would survive on the blood of the dead.

—And more. Look.—

Ruthinedt opened the icebox and saw the neat bottles of blood, six half-pints, two others marked with yellow tape, and a vial of white, cloudy liquid marbled with blood. Ruthinedt walked to the table and saw the new wounds on the captive's wrists, a bloodstain midway down the fresh sheet, and the shame in those dark eyes. Though it had taken a knife to do it, Baivie had won and Ruthinedt felt all the sorrow of the defeat. He ran a finger along the inside of the thick metal collar that banded its neck. "If I help you escape, Laurence Austra, will you kill me?"

The creature that had been Laurence Austra closed its eyes and turned its head away.

That night Ruthinedt had a vivid dream of traveling through the quiet halls to the storage room, where he lifted a narrow hacksaw blade from a toolbox. When he woke, he remembered enough of the dream that the scrape on his finger troubled him. It might have been caused by the rough edges of his metal bed or by something he had done the day before and not remembered, but alarmed, he searched his room and found nothing hidden there.

He waited until Baivie left for his usual evening walk then

went to the lowest level, a basement remodeled to hold a dozen cinder-block cells, two interrogation rooms, and a large guardroom, where the soldiers on duty could sit and talk while the prisoners slept. He came down the back stairs, sharing a few quick jokes with the guards stationed at the far end of the narrow cell block, until the sound of feminine laughter startled him. He looked quizzically at the corporal, who pointed to the lit guardroom at the other end of the corridor. "Baivie's arrivals. Go and meet them."

"German?" Ruthinedt asked, incredulous.

"Married to Russians, or rather they were until the assault on Kiev."

There was another burst of laughter. "They seem to be making the best of captivity," Ruthinedt commented with disgust.

"Special treatment for our own. They're pretty. Go and meet them."

"I will soon enough. Good night." He began to walk upstairs, but on the first-floor landing he turned into the storage room instead. The toolboxes were closed, the room's arrangement nothing like in his dream. As he turned to leave, he saw an ax beside the door. A plan began to come to him, an escape from this misery, and he slipped the ax beneath his coat. If that thing on Baivie's table could survive decapitation, nothing could kill it.

It was sleeping when he placed the ax behind the laboratory bookshelf. He relaxed long enough to pour himself a double shot of the brandy Baivie kept in his desk, thinking it fitting to celebrate this planned betrayal from the doctor's store.

Chapter Twenty-five

I

ON THE RAILS from Paris to Bucharest, Paul kept the shades pulled in his compartment. He did not wish to see the trains that passed them filled with the wounded and the doomed and, mean but no less real, recall how close he might be to joining them. The journey was marred by frequent stops, and had he not discovered so many willing assistants, Paul never would have completed it at all.

His alias became his most valued asset. Though the magazine he represented was not well known, officers and petty government officials vied for his attention, hoping to be quoted in the series of articles he said he would be writing on the Eastern Front. When he was detained for a week in a village near Linz while his credentials were checked, he wrote a glowing account of the town. He made special mention of the mayor and the chief of police, then asked them both to read the article and suggest any additions. His audacity won his release from the private cell to the mayor's custody, and he was treated like a visiting general while the verification—a "usual procedure," he was assured—was expedited.

Only fatalism allowed him to sleep at night, and then fitfully, until his papers—stamped and signed—were apologetically returned to him, along with an irate letter from his editor in Hanover. Apparently Franz Wustoff had been something of a maverick, his sudden disappearance and resurfacing not at all unusual. Paul was ordered to keep the proper vouchers and send an article immediately. He mailed

the story on Linz. It ran in the next issue, and when a copy
of the magazine fell into Samuelson's hands, he took the encouraging news to Chaves.

On the final leg of Paul's journey a heavy snowfall halted
all trains, and rather than wait for the tracks to be cleared,
Paul traveled the last thirty miles in a horse-drawn sleigh.
The Romanian farmer was as taciturn as Samuelson had been
at their first meeting, though more accommodating for the six
hundred liu he'd been promised.

As they approached Cluf, Paul studied the eastern
peaks, wondering which of them he had to climb. They
looked menacing—sheer and gray—and he rubbed his stiff,
aching knees and wondered how he would be able to scale
it when the time came. He tried to ask the mountains'
names, but the farmer only shook his head in feigned confusion and looked at Paul with the hard, suspicious eyes
of a forced ally.

But Paul didn't need the information. When the road to the
pass came into view, he discovered it had been fastened to
his memory like a familiar street. If he hadn't acquired some
confidence, he would have asked to go immediately to the
small village nearest it, but it was late in the day and he
needed rest and food. Where there were no Germans, Franz
Wustoff would find no friends.

In Cluf, Paul rented an unheated attic room for a price that
could only be termed extortion. He stretched out and slept
until the storm woke him. The wind whistled around the eaves
and the snow and sleet beat on the windowpanes. Paul did
not need to go to the window to know the truth. Though his
destination had been mere hours away earlier, it might be
days before he could reach it. He buried his face in the warm
feather quilt and shivered.

The next morning Paul decided to take a walk and see the
town. Its center was dominated by a train station, now teeming
with disgruntled, stranded passengers. Behind a barbed-wire
enclosure, prisoners from the stalled train huddled around coal
burners, parents at the fence begging bread from passersby.

Most of the pedestrians avoided going too close to the
makeshift stockade, but there was a score of boys who

had split into two groups, one diverting the guards by
shouting anti-German slogans while the other kept a sharp
eye out and quietly passed bread to the outstretched palms.
The guards, furious when they saw how they'd been duped,
fired a round over the boys' heads and the gang broke and
ran.

Paul began to turn away, wishing it would not be so dangerous for him to help, when he glimpsed a man approach
the fence and begin asking questions of the prisoners inside.
Two guards ordered him away and, when he didn't move,
approached him with drawn guns. Paul waited for the sad,
inevitable conclusion to this drama, but unexpectedly the man
pulled back the flaps of his coat. Paul could see only the
sleeve of the man's uniform. The guards saw more, backing
off and saluting.

"Who is in command?" the officer asked in a voice loud
enough for Paul to hear.

"I am, sir," the sergeant said. "Lieutenant Hanson is north
of town with the prisoners who are clearing the roads. The
captain went to Arad for supplies."

The lieutenant waved a hand back at the stockade. "These
people will be laborers for the Reich. Dead workers have no
value, Sergeant. See that they are given some soup."

As the officer waited for the orders to be passed, he
noticed Paul watching him. Paul left the scene with as
much haste as he dared, disappearing into a nearby restaurant where he ordered corn biscuits and gravy. He'd just
begun eating when the officer entered and asked to join
him. "Of course," Paul said, falling naturally into his
Wustoff role.

"You saw what I did for those people?"

"Yes."

"Do you approve?"

Paul shook his head. "An act of kindness is a welcome
change in this war."

"I wasn't being kind. I was preventing a riot," the lieutenant responded coldly. "Did you serve?"

Paul replied with his usual story.

"Wounded in action? Most soldiers would be thankful if
they could go home, not that home is so pleasant now. So
you're covering the war?"

"Yes."

"You are far from the front."

"With these legs I'm not a very useful combat reporter, so I get the human-interest stories: how our allies support us, that sort of thing."

"You saw how these support us. I warn you, watch over your shoulder."

Paul thanked him for the advice and, as he had observed Samuelson do on many occasions, offered to buy drinks.

The officer responded with a swift, uneasy smile and pulled up a chair. He waited until the innkeeper brought the mugs to ask Paul's name, then gave his own.

Eric Ruthinedt! One of the two people Paul least wanted to meet! He tried to remain calm and hoped his expression had not betrayed him. Apparently his act worked because Ruthinedt asked, "So what brings you here?"

"My editor." Hoping Ruthinedt could not hear how fast his heart was beating, Paul tapped his forehead and raised his eyes to the ceiling. "He heard a story about some local legend. He thought there might be a story in it."

"Legend?" the lieutenant asked with obvious interest.

"Vampires or something. He thought it might make entertaining reading."

"Nothing entertaining about the loss of over forty men and three airplanes."

"I . . . I'm sorry," Paul said with sincere surprise. "I wasn't told of that."

"I wouldn't expect you to be. Do you believe in legends?" Ruthinedt asked.

"Three airplanes?"

"No, they were not shot down."

"What do you think happened?" Paul asked cautiously.

"I believe the stories, Herr Wustoff. Talk to the Romanians here. They like to frighten us with details."

Ruthinedt changed the subject and later suggested they meet for dinner. Paul, who had already admitted he knew no one in the town, couldn't think of a reason to refuse.

The snow fell sporadically over the next few days. During that time Paul saw much of Ruthinedt. In the beginning he thought the lieutenant was suspicious of him, but Ruthinedt asked no questions to trick him into revealing his true identity or his mission. Actually Ruthinedt said very little, seeming content to share a table with him, taking turns buying drinks or coffee, as if they were old, close friends. They spoke of Germany before the war, of favorite towns and old memories. Often Paul had to remind himself that this lonely, graying man was the villain who had ordered the slaughter at Alpha.

Paul went about his work as if it were his, interviewing soldiers and talking with townsfolk. When two corporals laughingly told him he often sat across from the very fountain of information he sought, Paul knew he must speak to the lieutenant or risk raising the man's suspicions.

Ruthinedt did not deny his knowledge. Instead he requested anonymity, then returned with Paul to his attic room. He sat stiffly on Paul's bed and told his story as if it had happened to someone else, softening no details, not even the extent of his own terror. Afterward he spoke of Baivie, his horror at the doctor's insane experiments, and his own belief that he was now kept in Cluf against his will.

Ruthinedt was his enemy; nonetheless, Paul felt a deep sympathy for all the torment he had endured. "Why didn't you mention this sooner?" Paul asked.

"You said it yourself; it's an impossible tale. I intended to tell you my part in it after you heard others speak of it. I thought perhaps you might believe me then."

"I see," Paul replied. "Does Haller believe it?"

"He's seen too much to doubt the creature's power, but he has kept its presence a secret. Considering what happened to me, I think he's being wise."

Because he knew Wustoff would have done this, Paul asked, "Would it be possible for me to interview Baivie?"

"He won't talk to you, and you would be in danger if he knew I had done so." Paul looked alarmed and Ruthinedt quickly added, "Don't worry. I told him about you the night we met. I promised to tell you lies so you would not guess the truth. But you know the truth and you will print it, won't you?"

"Of course," Paul replied, then asked, "Could I see Laurence Austra?"

"Impossible. That room is guarded."

"What will happen to him?"

"I will kill it," Ruthinedt said simply. "I've made my plans. All I need is a moment. Baivie may have guessed my intent but not my resolve, or I would not be free to walk these streets."

"But if he is really valuable . . . ." Paul began.

"It isn't, but they think it is. That's one of its tricks. If you want proof of what I say, you need only consider our failures in this district. Look at the town. These people should hate the Russians, but they are ready to fight beside the invaders. We used to catch the major saboteurs . . . now we apprehend the petty thieves while the real traitors go free. And then there's Baivie's women. He'd anticipated trouble getting them to conceive, but every one is pregnant. Baivie is as puffed up as if these were his own children. Of course they're not, but they're not that thing's, either. No, they're going to look like the guards no matter whose blood and semen has been pumped into their mothers. Oh, I tell you, it plays its tricks."

"But you said yourself: Young ones do not have great power."

"It doesn't . . . but it has time to be persistent. Things will get better here once it's dead."

Ruthinedt began to reach for his coat and Paul grabbed his arm. "Eric, when you kill it, you will be committing suicide."

Ruthinedt stared at Paul, his eyes empty of everything but resolve. "I died months ago. I died on that mountain."

Paul did not sleep that night. At dawn he left by the back door and went straight to the stables. Though the owner refused to allow his horses to travel through such deep snow, he was not above selling one and renting out a small sleigh. Every cent Paul had went into the arrangement, and he thought only of the progress he was making and not at all about how he'd return to Chaves when he was through. The weather was finer than he'd expected. Absorbed in the comforting thought that his mission would soon be over, he did not notice the soldier that had followed him, eavesdropped on his conversation in the stable, then run back to his commander as quickly as the city streets would allow.

* * *

A half mile before he would have to abandon his sled, Paul heard an army truck bearing down on him. He pulled over, intending to let it pass. When it came closer, Paul saw Ruthinedt sitting beside the driver, two other men in the back, pointing rifles at him.

Had Eric been alone, Paul affably would have said he was going to get a better look at the mountain. But Eric was not alone, and even if Haller and Baivie did not know the truth, the lie would be enough to destroy him. Paul veered off the road, making a direct line for the footpath, hoping the horse could take him where the truck could not go.

Fifty yards. A hundred. Ruthinedt called out a warning, the officer beside him a threat. Paul shouted something back, an inane plea for a writer's privilege. As he did, a runner slammed into a rock and snapped. The flight was over. He would fall and they would catch him unless . . . unless . . .

"*Frn'cs. N'vas tsu!*" The Austra cry for help climbed the mountainside, the inflections muffled by the snow and wind. "*Es . . . su!*"

No help came. Paul waited for the soldiers to reach him, certain no charade could save him now but determined to try. Ruthinedt reached him first and Paul mumbled, "Is this concern, Eric, or has Baivie learned the truth?"

Ruthinedt did not reply until the soldiers stood behind Paul. Then, without a word, his boot shot out, catching Paul in the stomach. Paul doubled forward and would have fallen had the soldiers not grabbed his arms and dragged him into the waiting truck.

II

Kurt stood in the tower of the keep, studying Paul's capture through a pair of stolen binoculars, then ran down the stairs to the room where Charles slept. Early morning was the wrong time to wake him, and Kurt's hand shook as he touched

Charles's shoulder, hardly able to rouse him from his deep, dawn lethargy.

When he did, Charles jumped to his feet, his eyes fully black, filled with ancient horrible dreams. He gripped Kurt's upper arms painfully and Kurt fought down his fear. Francis, in one of his rare verbal moods, had told Kurt that Charles's dreams were a sign of illness and Kurt must never fight off an attack. "Please . . . please, wake up!" Kurt whispered.

Charles shuddered, closed his eyes, and, with effort, discarded the past, confusion softening to recognition. He looked down at his hands and abruptly let Kurt go. "Did I hurt you?" he asked.

"No, but please. There are soldiers. They chased a man in a sleigh. They dragged him away from the path."

Charles's expression grew flinty. "For that you—"

"I would have ignored him but he called something in your language. I'm sure of it."

"Could you understand it?"

Kurt shook his head.

"No matter. Some of the old words are known." Charles brushed the fine dusting of snow from Kurt's hair and tossed another log onto the fire. "It's cold. You should not have been in the tower."

"I only have a cough," Kurt mumbled.

"Drugs were hard to come by last time. They'll be impossible to find now." Charles lay back on the bed, sliding over so there was room for two. "When you're well, we'll go hunting."

"The soldiers . . ." Kurt began.

"Shall I go into Cluf and ask the Gestapo what they wanted?"

"No!" Kurt said with such alarm that Charles laughed. Kurt hated the times when Charles was away, watching for him, sensing him even from a distance. Kurt wondered if Charles's power surpassed even his father's. If so, it was a darker power, born of the savage deaths he saw and gave on the plains below and some strange private misery. Since the last time Charles had returned, wearing an expression of such anguish that even Francis had relented and asked him to stay, Kurt's worst fear was that Charles would leave again and never come back. He pressed tightly against Charles, as if his body and his life could hold Charles there.

"No, I won't go to Cluf, but I am leaving tonight." He felt Kurt shudder and pulled him closer, his lips brushing the back of Kurt's neck. "Don't worry. I'll be back. I am condemned to that."

Chapter Twenty-six

I

A CELL DOOR closed, a lock clicked into place, and darkness—the same pain-filled darkness Paul remembered so vividly—squeezed all remaining strength from him. He lay against concrete floor and moaned.

A man spoke softly, apparently trying not to startle him. Nonetheless, Paul drew in his breath, a sound as loud as a scream in this silent darkness. He had thought he was alone.

When he was able, Paul replied in German in the same low tone, "I don't understand you."

The man hesitated, then tried the comment in English. "Fortunately there are no rats." When Paul responded with a halfhearted chuckle, the man asked, "So they've resorted to preying on their own?"

Paul adopted a heavy German accent. "It's all a mistake. My name is Franz Wustoff and I am a correspondent. I assume you are American?"

"Gregory Hunter. And yes, I'm from the States. That's one fact the bastards've learned. What brings you here?"

"The wrong story." Paul shuddered again, some of the panic returning to his voice.

"Must have been one hell of an exposé. How bad are you hurt?"

"I . . . I'm not, not really. It's just that I can't see and I . . . I'm sorry—" Paul's voice broke. He found it impossible to continue.

"No, don't apologize. Here, take my hand." Hunter held

out his arm and snapped his fingers until Paul's closed over them.

The touch reassured him, and eventually Paul's breathing steadied. "Thank you. It seems that in the last few years I've spent too many hours in dark, cramped cells."

"A hazard of some professions."

"Not of mine."

"Oh? Have you been questioned?"

"Yes . . . that is, no. Not the way I think you mean. You see, I was collecting information about—"

"No! No details. You don't know me and I sure as hell don't know you. You understand?"

"Yes."

"Good." Hunter slid closer to him. "Now tell me the date and how the war is going."

"It is the sixteenth of February and winter has won every battle." Paul began backtracking. When he described November's battle at Stalingrad, Hunter finally showed some recognition. Paul continued until a narrow slot in the door opened and metal bowls were slipped through. Hunter used the brief, dim light to pass one to Paul.

There were no utensils, so Paul dipped his fingers in the mush and tasted it. "What is it?"

"Better than yesterday. Now eat it. They may come for your plate at any time."

"I'm not hungry."

"Don't be a fool. They may not feed us tomorrow."

Paul ate, gagging on every lump. He'd nearly finished when the tiny door slid open. Hunter jerked the plate from his hand and passed it through. No sooner had the guard moved on than the door opened again.

"Franz?" Ruthinedt whispered.

"Yes!"

"Haller searched your room. He found your notes and burned them. There were so few. Did you send your story?" When Paul refused to answer, Ruthinedt added, "Do you think I'd be free to help you if I'd shown you any mercy today?"

"I sent the first installment," Paul lied, then asked hesitantly, "What are their plans for me?"

"I don't know, but soon they'll have no reason to hold

you. I didn't tell them you called out before they arrested you, but for your own sake, when you're released, forget your story—forget everything you learned.''

No reason to hold him! Paul answered as calmly as he could, ''The publisher decides what to print.''

''Then it's settled. Haller wired your paper. They won't dare refuse. Take these.'' Ruthinedt dropped a pack of cigarettes and some matches into Paul's hands. ''I'll come again. I promise.''

After the lieutenant had gone, Paul lit a match and, for the first time, saw the bruises and burns on Hunter's body and the blood that caked his shirt. He wanted to scream for Ruthinedt, for Baivie, for anyone who might come and save him, but the panic would be useless.

''Convenient of your friend to slip you a light.'' Hunter's mocking grin opened the cut on his lip. ''But we all have our jobs to do.''

''Do you think that's why they put me here?''

''They did the same to me, threw me into a cell with a man fresh from questioning. I listened to him moan for so long that I was thankful when he died.'' Hunter looked away and muttered, ''Damn Nazis.''

When the match burned out, Paul didn't light a second. It seemed easier to avoid speaking in the dark.

''You Party?'' Hunter eventually asked.

''Correspondents have to be.''

''They'll beat the hell out of you if you give them an answer like that.''

''If a lie is better, I'll try to sound more patriotic.'' Though Paul had attempted to be flippant, his hands shook as he lit another match. He passed the pack to Hunter. ''I don't smoke. Would you like them?''

''Another minute and I would have pounced on them. What in the—?'' Hunter pulled four thick candles out of the pack before he found a cigarette.

''I once told Eric that I hated the dark. I'm surprised he remembered,'' Paul said, astonished again by the contrasts in the man.

They lit a candle and Paul studied his cell. There were no beds or blankets, no toilet except for a hole in the floor to the left of their cell door. It was built of cinder blocks, in dimensions wider but lower than D'Oscuro, so it would be impossible to stand. No, Paul wouldn't have to listen to Stephen pacing in a place like this. On the other hand, he couldn't pace, either. A few days here and he'd need crutches. Two weeks and he wouldn't be able to walk at all. He flexed his legs a few times and considered other ways of keeping his knees limber.

The two men sat facing each other, Hunter giving details of prison life, heavily spiked with gallows humor. Paul often noticed Hunter eyeing him warily, but that, after all, was to be expected. They talked until they heard footsteps in the hall and pinched out their tiny light just before the trays were passed in.

After the meal Hunter nodded into an uneasy sleep, shivering often from cold and pain and, Paul suspected, the beginnings of a fever. Paul, who was still dressed for his winter climb, slipped off his outer jacket and laid it over the sleeping man, then positioned himself so the side of his stiff leg rested against Hunter's back. Hunter's warmth alleviated some of the ache, and Paul managed to sleep as well.

When he woke and lit his candle, Paul saw Hunter sitting in the corner, wearing an expression of bewildered suspicion, his hands deep in the pockets of Paul's coat. "I want you to do me a favor," Hunter said abruptly. "My father's name is Emerson Hunter and my family lives in Des Moines, Iowa. If you survive this war, would you write and tell them I died? It would be easier on them if they knew."

"Are you so certain they're going to kill you?"

"I'm to have one final questioning. If I don't cooperate, they say they'll kill me." Hunter laughed the way he laughed when he was alone: long and frantically. "I'm sorry," he said when he was able, "but you see, nothing is ever as bad— or as good—as you imagine."

"I don't understand."

"If you're lucky, you never will."

They talked until their next meal, sharing their impressions of the war with the strange, soft focus Hunter insisted they adopt until Paul exclaimed, "No more! Please, we're only making the misery worse."

"We're eating. There's a roof above us. My future is se-
cure."

"Shut up!"

Hunter chuckled. "You're right. War isn't a pretty dinner
topic, is it? So change it. Tell me about the most pleasant
place . . . no, I don't want to think about going anywhere.
Instead tell me about the most beautiful woman you've ever
known."

Paul finished his soup, then, nibbling on the black bread,
he began. "There is a woman who lives in a white house
overlooking the sea." Paul changed the name, of course, but
he described Elizabeth—her laughter, her beauty. Before he
finished, he grew almost confident that she had not lied for
his sake and he really would be with her soon.

"Now get down to details."

"I already have."

"Oh, hell! You've never made love to her?"

"God, no!" Paul lied.

"Why, you sound as if you're afraid of her. Does she
bite?"

"What!"

"That's a figure of speech, you German fool. I only used
it because you speak of a woman you desire but are afraid to
love, and she resembles a dream that kissed me. Aren't we a
pathetic pair?"

"You had a dream?"

"Thin mountain air," Hunter said.

"What mountain?" When Hunter didn't answer, Paul
dropped the subject. Perhaps Hunter had been forced to spy
and his hint was just a trick. "Your turn," he said instead.

"I have to start with how I met her, because it's irony,
Franz, it really is. You see, everyone who had fought with
me died, and once the Germans began fighting the Russians
I didn't know who my friends were. I tell you, the fight lost
all its meaning when the entire country became my enemy. I
would have left but I couldn't reach the border. Eventually I
took a job in Tirgu and met a woman. I was lonely and she
so apparently understanding. We got drunk together far more
than once, and I suppose I said things I'd been trying to
forget. Eventually she fell for a man in uniform, and here I
am."

"I thought we were going to discuss pleasant women?"

Hunter chuckled at the play on words. "She was more than pleasant. A real tiger in bed, and that's where we were when the Nazis came for me. The bitch liked drama, I'll grant her that."

"I'd rather hear the details of the dream."

"Dreams don't come with details, Franz." Following a wicked snort of contempt, Hunter began discussing his betrayer in elaborate, sordid detail.

One day passed. Or two. Or three. They measured time by the meals brought them, lighting candles only while they ate. Paul watched Hunter slowly fade, eating less, crying out in his sleep. Paul thought of Laurence constantly. He called to him silently and got no answer. Had there been some means of escape, Paul would have been desperate to try, but the few times he mentioned the subject to Hunter, he got only a short, grim laugh for a reply. "Don't think I haven't tried, Franz. But I must warn you that for someone who says his imprisonment is all a mistake, you are far too willing to leave without a proper discharge."

Paul never mentioned escape again.

But when he slept, he had a different kind of release. He dreamed of Elizabeth and the house that no longer stood, of Chaves and of home. At last it seemed the family had invaded his dreams, for he heard someone speaking a language he had only begun to learn. He opened his eyes and rolled up on one elbow. Hunter was mumbling words that made it clear which mountain had given him his perfect woman.

Paul shook him awake. "You were talking in your sleep," he whispered.

Hunter gripped his arm. "What did I say?"

"You spoke an odd language. Perhaps of your mountain," Paul replied, then lowered his voice and added, "I think we should risk being honest, Gregory." When Hunter didn't reply, Paul moved closer to him, dropped his accent, and went on. "Look, I know you have no reason to trust me, but there is no way you could speak that language unless one of them has trusted you. Now listen to me. I was arrested because they thought I was writing a story on the Mountain Lords.

But there was never any story. You see, I'm an American and
I came because—"

"Stop!" Hunter moved away, certain that if he stayed
within reach of Paul, he'd use what strength he had left and
kill him. "The ones who put you here were clever, Franz
Wustoff, but you are a fool. Tell them they've failed."

"You don't understand. One of them has—"

"One more word and I'll strangle you."

"You must listen—"

Hunter attacked, his hands closing around Paul's throat. "I
meant it, you son of a bitch!"

Paul's strength was no match for Hunter's rage. His legs
thrashed helplessly and he clawed at Hunter's hands as he
struggled to breathe. He'd nearly lost consciousness when his
kicks against the door brought the guards. Hunter, still swearing, was pulled off him, and while one guard blocked the
door, a second began kicking Hunter, opening old wounds
and creating new ones as Paul watched, silent with shock and
relief. When Hunter stopped moving, the guards left as
abruptly as they'd come.

Paul lit the stub of his last candle and saw that his fingers
were coated with Hunter's blood. He could do nothing for
the unconscious man, so he stared at the flame until the candle burned itself out. Then he closed his eyes and tried to
pretend it was night.

Paul used some of the water provided with the next meal
to clean Hunter's face, then ripped off one of his shirt sleeves
and soaked the cloth in the rest. He knew from experience
how terrible thirst could be, and if he could save Hunter even
a few hours of it, he'd feel less guilt about the beating his
stupidity had caused. Hunter was a doomed man, half dead
already. Even if he was an ally, what could he do?

Much later Hunter began to move. "Thank God!" Paul
whispered, and moistened Hunter's lips with the cloth until
Hunter rolled away from him.

"The act is pathetic . . . *Herr* Wustoff," Hunter said.

Paul pressed the piece of bread he'd been saving into Hunter's hand. "Did you ever consider that your killing me was
what they'd hoped for all along?"

"Then they wouldn't have come when you called, now

would they?'' Hunter retorted, and said nothing more even after Paul had finished his story. After one more meal the guards came and took Hunter away.

They handcuffed Hunter, dragged him up the stairs, and shoved him into a dimly lit room. He stumbled and fell hard against a white linoleum floor.

''Get up,'' someone ordered.

''Go to hell,'' Hunter muttered. In the beginning he'd been polite but they'd tortured him anyway. Now he hoped insolence would drive these experts too far and that they'd kill him.

But the soldiers held back, and after a while Hunter rolled over and surveyed what he could of the room—books strewn across a pair of desks, more on shelves behind them, large metal tanks that might be used for oxygen or gas, a colonel and a thin old man in a plain black suit and, last, a table. He studied the table, trying to make out what rested on it.

''Get up,'' the colonel ordered again. ''Take a good look at the last face you'll ever see.''

Hunter struggled to his feet. The man on the table was looking the other way so Hunter couldn't see the features, but the hands, the color of the hair, and the pallor of the skin were enough. Behind him someone was speaking, but Hunter didn't hear the words. In the face of this obscenity his fate held no meaning. Tears came to his eyes. He took a tentative step forward. ''Even you,'' he said in a voice so soft, it could scarcely be called a whisper.

—Yes. Even me.— The thought came dimly to Hunter's mind, as if the sender was too weak, or weary, for clear contact.

—What will happen?—

—I will kill you after I tell them what you know. If I don't, they'll kill you, anyway. It's better to die with me.—

—Then before it's over, Charles, let me . . .—

For the first time Laurence looked at Hunter, his expression revealing for one quick moment his surprise. Then, as quickly as it had come, it vanished, and Hunter shook his head and backed away as a rage, far too strong for his weakened body, flowed into him. ''No, no, no-no-no,'' he said, moaning, and crumpled into a motionless heap in the center of the room.

"How dare you play these games with me!" Laurence spat at Haller, then, sensing Haller's honest confusion, quickly added, "You turn your soldiers loose on these prisoners, then bring them to me when they're nearly dead. Do this again and I warn you, no matter what you threaten, you'll get no more help from me."

Baivie glanced at Laurence, then examined Hunter. "Your prisoner is faking," he said to Haller. "Leave him with me."

For the first time since he'd been taken, Laurence turned the full measure of his power on someone other than Ruthinedt, and with no sign that he felt the intrusion, Haller conferred with a guard, then told Baivie, "The prisoner attacked his cell mate and the guards had to use force to restrain him. We'll wait for this questioning. When he's stronger, we'll bring him back."

When Hunter dared open his eyes, he found he'd been transferred to a different, private cell. He lay on a mattress, and water and food were on the floor beside him. As he ate, he considered the day's strange revelations.

What he had experienced in that upstairs laboratory had been markedly different from his time on the mountain. No demands, no screams in his mind, only one incomprehensible hammer blow of anger. And Franz? Was he really an American or a plant put there by his jailers? There was someone who might tell him, but no matter how carefully he concentrated on the one trapped upstairs, he felt no answer. Well, he could take another beating to learn the truth. He staggered to his feet, then banged on his cell door until two guards opened it. "I have to see Haller. Franz Wustoff is an impostor."

"How do you know?" one guard demanded.

"He confessed it to me. I'll only give details to Haller. Go tell him his command is at stake."

II

Days passed before Paul was taken to Haller, days in which Paul lay alone in the dark, dreaming of one building, one perfect building, constructing it as a composer might arrange a symphony piece by piece in his mind. The guards who escorted him were courteous, handing him his cane and helping him up the stairs to Haller's office. There Haller pointed to a seat and offered brandy. Though a drink would have tasted marvelous, Paul refused thinking of the more subtle ways of acquiring information.

Haller looked amused. "I could have ordered your food drugged. That would be far less wasteful then destroying this." He filled two small brandy snifters and slid one across his desk. "Here, take it."

Paul cradled the delicate globe, feasting first on the scent before taking a tentative sip. Haller had excellent taste.

"I'd send a bottle to your cell, but I don't think it will be necessary for you to return there."

The confidence flowed back into Paul like the heat of the alcohol. He settled back in the cracked leather armchair. Haller opened the file on his desk, held up a copy of the magazine Paul represented, then opened to a photograph and handed it to Paul. "You don't look like the Franz Wustoff shown here. Would you like to tell me who you are?"

When Paul didn't answer, Haller went on. "I never would have checked your credentials so carefully, but your cell mate told me about you. Have you sent your report?"

Paul had to remember to breathe but, he was amazed to see, his hand did not shake. Since he didn't understand what Haller meant, he settled for saying nothing.

"I could have you shot as a spy," Haller purred with confidence. "I could have you stripped of your papers and sent to a labor camp. With your legs you'd last a few days at the most. Now tell me if you sent your report."

"My superiors know I am here," Paul said carefully, and noted Haller's veiled concern. He began to realize what Hunter had done for him.

"And their names?"

The man had already formed a conclusion. Amazed at how

cool he'd become, Paul replied evasively, "You don't need me to tell you that."

Haller laughed. "Well, perhaps you're right. But your refusal to answer my questions makes things convenient, does it not? I think the time has come for you to meet the creature you are so curious about. I think it will be pleased to tell me who you are."

As Paul walked through the door of Baivie's lab he thought he'd never seen one of the family so weak or so defeated. Then Laurence looked at him, his will burning into Paul's soul, and Paul knew that the defeat and the agony of his weeks of captivity had pulled Laurence from adolescence to adulthood. Here was a force equal to his captors . . . and just as cunning, for Laurence had already guessed the truth and whined fearfully to Haller, "You promised me, Colonel. You promised me no one would ever know."

"Rumors, Laurence Austra. We will stop them."

Hearing Laurie's full name, what remained of Paul's optimism vanished. No one would allow him to talk himself free, not anymore. He saw only one chance for both of them and began repeating the mental litany. —Help is mere miles away. Merge with me and we will call for Francis. . . . Help is mere . . .—

—Fool! My entire world ends at the edges of this house.—

—And there's nothing we can do?—

Laurence watched him intently, and Paul winced from the pain of his mental probing. This merging, which had nothing to do with thoughts or commands, left Paul weak, and he caught the side of Baivie's desk for support. As quickly as they touched, Laurence withdrew, saying to Haller, "This man knows too much about my power. He resists me. Let him stay here and sleep. Then his guard must fall, and I will learn what he has done. In exchange you must give him to me. Promise me that!"

Haller considered this. The man's disappearance would arouse little suspicion, especially after the stable hand had retrieved the sleigh from the flat rise leading into the Vardas. He ordered the curtains closed and a cot brought in for Paul. "See that he stays on it," Haller snapped to one guard, or-

dered two others to stand outside, turned on his heel, and
left.

Hunter expected nothing more than he received: a return
to that same plush cell with its bed and table of food and
water. Maybe they wouldn't shoot him when they'd finished
with him, Hunter thought dryly. Then again, if they guessed
the truth, they might start the execution with bullets in his
feet. No, this was not a time for false optimism.

When he heard the turning of the key in his lock, he as-
sumed the worst and lay weakly on his cot. "Back so soon?"
he croaked as the door opened. When he received no reply,
he stared through slitted eyes at his guard. What he saw made
him bounce to his feet, roused by the joy of possible escape.
The guard stood beside the door with his eyes closed, as if
he had managed to fall asleep on his feet. When Hunter
moved toward him, he did not respond.

—Can you walk?— the one upstairs asked.

—Walk? You damned beautiful beast, I can run!—

—I am Laurence. Tell *Frn'cs* that. He will come.—

The inside guards were not at their posts; the outside ones
acted as if they did not see him. Nonetheless, Hunter kept to
the shadows until his absence was discovered. Then he grew
rash and found the truck.

It allowed him an easy escape, but the sound of its engine
alerted other soldiers, who gave chase. Hunter was thankful
the sun had set, for after weeks in the dark cell, snow blindness would have been a possibility in daylight. When the road
ended, he abandoned the truck and ran, keeping to rocky
outcroppings to hide his tracks. The soldiers were less than
a quarter of a mile behind him when he started up the path.
At the third turn they caught sight of him and a round of
bullets whistled overhead. Had Hunter not been out of breath,
he would have laughed. Nothing like gunshots to get the attention of Francis, Lord of the Mountain. As if in answer, he
heard the high shriek of the great beast descending from
the peaks above. He'd succeeded! Freedom . . . then—oh,
Lord, what an ally!

Another quarter mile and his hope vanished. He stared

down the length of a rifle to the grim face of the young soldier
he thought he had killed. "You!" Hunter swore.

"Go back!" Kurt ordered. "This mountain is closed to
you."

"Let me pass."

Instead of answering, Kurt fired.

"Laurence . . . they're holding . . ." Hunter whispered as
Kurt moved in for the kill.

III

Paul had almost drifted off when he heard the commotion
outside: cries, a few shots. "What—" he began, then halted,
not daring to speak.

But his guard was at the window, peering out into the
gray evening light. The German's concern and the fleeting
triumphant expression on Laurence's face told him the truth.
Hunter had escaped. One word formed in Paul's mind.
—Prudence . . .—

Paul willed his expression to remain flat. —How long?—

—A driver left the keys in his truck . . . stupid of him,
yes?—

—Yes— Paul responded happily. Help might come within
hours if Hunter was not stopped.

—Long enough for vengeance.—

Laurence didn't look to be in any position for defense, let
alone revenge. Before Paul could press for details, Laurence
ordered, —Think of Chaves and the family. There is strength
in memory.—

Paul began with happy thoughts, then, knowing what desires drove Laurence now, he zeroed in on Roessler. When
he could visualize the past no longer, Laurence told of his
captivity, from the ship to when he had finally broken and
began to kill.

—They were so sure of themselves after they butchered the
young Romanian, and they were right to be. Though they
threatened me, I knew they did not mean it. They brought in
prisoners, one after another, who would stand stoically, their

bravery almost enough to give me strength. But they died, Baivie and Haller finding new and more horrible ways to kill them. Baivie was the more clever; afterward he would take their blood and use it to sustain me. It wasn't enough—I needed life to live—and as I felt them dying, I wanted them. And I did feel their deaths; I couldn't help it, for I had caused too many deaths not to be a part of these.—

—No!— Paul nearly mouthed the word as he thought it.

—No, not those brave patriots. But my mother. Kathleen. My daughter. I've had time to think, and that time has been my worst punishment.

—At last they brought me a young woman. Her arm had been broken and never set, her face was bloody, and she swayed on the edge of shock, but I felt a resemblance to Kathleen in her mental touch. And, like Kathleen, she had been taken because she had loved. Baivie began to tell us how she would die if I did not help them, and I felt her fear grow, then vanish, as she moved past it to some private place beyond the pain. I couldn't let them kill her, not that one. That one had to die in peace with me. I began to speak her thoughts and I don't know who was more amazed, she or Haller. She cursed me even when, knowing one or two facts would condemn others to her fate, I lied. When the questioning was over, they left her with me. She was covered with cuts and bruises, but when she stood beside me, I felt not fear or pain, only pity.

—''Yield to me,'' I told her, ''and I will lead you to death and leave you peacefully in its arms. And your bravery and your love and your life will fill me and make me strong and I will destroy them for you.''

—I used my power and stole her pain, and in the last hour of her life I gave her joy. She died with her lover's name on her lips but she never even whispered it. Not even then.

—Their mistake, Paul, was in giving me so many lives. So much nourishment leads to power. I am the equal to any of the family now, and we will act.—

—If you wait, Francis will come.—

The reply cut like ice. —I am an Austra. I save myself.—

Paul saw the library light come on, Ruthinedt's face framed in the glass. Though Paul mentally screamed for time, Laurence did not answer. Absorbed in his power, he continued with his plan.

Paul saw his guard rest his head on Baivie's desk and go to sleep. He heard a bar slide into place on the metal laboratory door, the clicking of its heavy padlock. Though he had no way of knowing, guards whose hands were acting on another's orders also locked the library door. Baivie's simple security system had sealed both rooms.

—Now we begin . . .—

Chapter Twenty-seven

ON THE LOWEST level where prisoners were kept, guards obeyed their silent orders and opened the cells. As the prisoners milled into the narrow hall their leaders weighed the odds and the battle began.

Every prisoner knew this opportunity would not come again and they fought accordingly. The soldiers retreated up the stairs, the few prisoners who had grabbed arms in close pursuit. Each fallen German added to the prisoners' arsenal, and by the time the fighting spilled onto the main floor, the sides were evenly matched.

Though shots were heard in nearby houses, no one was curious. Even the most ardent Nazi supporter had learned to ignore the sounds coming from Gestapo headquarters.

The battle seemed to take place within its own prison, for no one attempted to escape until the last soldiers on the lower floors had fallen. Then, instead of checking the upper floor, the prisoners fled silently into the night. Haller died in that battle. So did the laboratory guards who rushed downstairs to aid in the fighting, the German women, the insolent sergeant, and all the other soldiers who had watched while Baivie had tortured the man and roused the beast, who had heard the name of the prisoner strapped to the table. The only Nazis left alive were Ruthinedt and the old Swiss doctor, who was taking his evening stroll down the quiet streets of Cluf.

And one other. Inside the laboratory the guard sat with his head on Baivie's cluttered desk and slept.

"Go. Take his weapon. Then reach behind the bookcase.

You'll find an ax. Bring it here,'' Laurence ordered. When Paul slowly began to rise, keeping his eyes constantly on the soldier, Laurence's mental prod hit hard enough to shake him. —I can hold him just long enough. If he wakes before you've finished, you'll die.—

Obeying with as much speed as he was able, Paul stuck the revolver in his belt, retrieved the ax, and carried it back to the table. —Start at my neck. That must be freed first or we will fail.—

Paul glanced at Ruthinedt, his hands pressed against the glass, gloating in his triumph. "Kill him," Ruthinedt mouthed, and Paul knew the next words as plainly as if he'd heard them: ". . . and end it for all of us."

Suicide? Was that what Laurence meant to do? But he spoke of vengeance, not defeat. Could he not understand that some things were impossible, even for him? Paul looked numbly down at his ally. "The ax will only break if I try to cut through metal so thick," he protested, dreading what he expected would be the next suggestion.

But Laurence had already laid his plans, and though Ruthinedt could not remember, it had been he who had carried them out. —The collar has been weakened. Hit to my right where the metal meets the table!—

The ax fell, metal meeting metal with a deafening clang. Paul looked fearfully from the guard to Ruthinedt, but neither man stirred. —Again.—

Three more blows and still no more came to investigate. Once he'd cut the collar through, Paul used the ax handle as a lever. The other side, also weakened, began to give, and Paul managed to bend the metal back a few inches. He would have continued but Laurence moved him down to his feet. —Enough! We must be ready when the soldier wakes!—

Paul ran a finger along the inside of the cuffs. They were undamaged. "This won't cut such thick metal," he protested.

—But it will go through flesh and bone.— A hint of grim laughter. —Even mine.— Paul shook his head and backed up a step. —You were with my uncle. You know how we heal. When you are through, stay back. The guard will sustain me.—

Laurence was cold with need, as cold as Stephen had been;

perhaps he'd grown as powerful. Though Paul was already breathing fast from his last exertion, he raised the ax again.

Laurence stretched as far as he was able, giving Paul a clean shot at the thinnest part of his ankle. Days of inactivity had made Paul weak, and it took him three tries to cut through the bone. Laurence never made a sound. "How can you let me do this?" Paul whispered.

—What's a little more pain? There's been . . . so much, yes?— Though that inner voice took more effort, it sounded calm, but the soldier began to shift uneasily in his seat. Laurence was losing his hold. Paul posed above the other foot.

The blood covering his clothes and spilling off the table made Paul ill, and the illness made him weaker. Drops of sweat formed on his forehead and he swallowed convulsively, promising himself that once this was over, he would allow himself the luxury of being violently sick. Five strokes were needed, and on the last Laurence screamed. In that quick release of agony the soldier woke. He blinked, saw the carnage, and rushed Paul, halting midway, as if he'd run into a thick, transparent wall.

—My hands! Damn you, my hands!—

Paul had gone too far to stop, but he altered his angle so that he could remove only the thumb and forefinger of the left hand, just enough so Laurence could slip his hand through. Before Paul could move to the other side, the soldier rushed him. Paul swung the ax with all his strength, some last-minute command making him hit with the blunt edge, a blow that stunned but did not kill. The soldier fell.

—Now the other!—

Panicked by the attack, Paul swung too fast. His bad leg buckled and the ax missed Laurence's hand. The ax head, already weakened, glanced off the metal cuff and cracked. Paul turned and ran to the cabinet, searching for a knife, a saw, anything to finish this. As he worked, the attraction began to grow, Laurence's need rising, calling to him. Paul broke into the instrument cabinet and found scalpels and small knives but nothing large or quick enough.

Self-preservation made Paul wary. The attraction pulled at him as it had in D'Oscuro. He knew how deadly Laurence had become and it took all his will to keep from retreating and letting the worst occur. But he hadn't come this far to

fail now. Paul made a quick survey of the room. The soldier's
gun? Possible, if he could hold it steady, but he felt dangerously close to shock. As he walked toward the table he
glanced past it into the library and saw Ruthinedt draw back
and shake his head, as if coming out of a trance. Laurence
had held him frozen as long as he could. Now the lieutenant
raised his revolver and fired, making a small bull's-eye in the
thick protective glass.

A second bullet cracked it. A third made a small hole.
Ruthinedt stepped closer to it, preparing to shoot at Laurence's head. Gambling that the lieutenant would not shoot
him, Paul lunged forward and placed himself between Ruthinedt and the table. He would have been too late, but the
library door opened. Baivie stood in it, gripping his ring of
keys.

Startled, Ruthinedt swung the gun toward the doctor, but
instead of shooting, he merely backed up a step. Baivie's
watery gray eyes locked on his. Baivie narrowed the gap between them, chanting the words in as hypnotic a tone as any
Mountain Lord had ever used. "Look at him. He's still
caught. We'll have a smith forge a new collar. Look, Eric.
Do you see?"

Ruthinedt, his eyes shifting between the doctor and Laurence, began to lower the weapon. He did not notice Baivie's
hand dip into his pocket, pulling out a thin, sharp blade.
"No, no, no," the doctor went on. "Put down the gun and
everything will be all right. Just put it down."

Paul caught the flash of metal and saw Baivie's arm swing
back. "Eric!" he screamed. "Eric, look out!"

Ruthinedt automatically raised his revolver, but some last-
minute tremor ruined his aim. Baivie fell, clutching the hole
in his side, trying to stop the flow of blood.

The shot still echoed in Ruthinedt's ears when he heard
the howling rising above it, beating on the glass, running
through his mind. "—Baivie! Give me Baivie!—" Ruthinedt
swung and stared as Laurence hooked his bleeding hand under the cuff and pushed. It moved another inch, and ignoring
a wound that would have killed a human, he forced his neck
free. Laurence propped up on one elbow, the blood seeping
from the stumps of his legs and his mangled hand, staring at

Ruthinedt with eyes that had no whites, fiery with hatred as he screamed again, "—Give me Baivie!—"

Laurence was still caught by one hand, and Paul, his face ashen, seemed unable to move toward the captive. Ruthinedt looked at both of them and made his decision. If Baivie's death would save him, so be it. Ruthinedt had lost all stomach for murder. "If I give him to you, will you let me live, Laurence Austra?" he called out. Almost imperceptibly Laurence nodded.

Ruthinedt tossed the scalpel aside, grabbed the doctor by the arms, and dragged him down the hall. He dropped Baivie outside the lab door and fumbled with the ring of keys. Though Baivie was too weak for any real struggle, his hand closed around Ruthinedt's ankle. "Please, don't do this, Eric," the doctor begged, and coughed and cried out from the pain. "Please," he repeated.

"My life, Doctor. You and that creature have made a mockery of it. You'll die, anyway, die with him."

The moment Ruthinedt left the library, Paul found the will to move. He rushed to the table and reached for the gun, but Laurence shook his head and glanced toward the door. —Get back.— Laurence tried to speak the words as well but could make no sound until his throat healed. He bent his head over the hand still cuffed to the table and, with only a brief shudder of his body to show the pain, used his teeth to rip away the smallest finger below the first joint. The blood coated the cuff and helped him force the hand through.

—Stay back.— After what Paul had just seen, that soft suggestion in his mind was enough. Paul pressed himself into the narrow alcove between the desk and the window and watched Laurence roll from the table, his pale, naked body splaying onto the back of the half-conscious soldier, as if he were some huge ravenous spider, his teeth tearing at the man's neck like the starving beast he'd become.

Laurence glutted on this life until he heard the door swing open and looked up to see Ruthinedt standing in the doorway, the helpless doctor under one arm. If the blood sickened him, Ruthinedt did not show it. If the sight of Laurence freed from the table terrified him, he did not show that, either. "I've kept my bargain, Laurence Austra,'' he said, and, after a moment's hesitation, dropped Baivie in front of him.

This was everything Laurence had planned for, that one final moment when revenge would be slow and total. He dropped the unconscious soldier and crawled toward Baivie, leaving a trail of blood along the grimy floor. When he'd come within reach of his victim, he let the last of his control dissolve. Ruthinedt's eyes widened, and all the faded dignity that had impressed Paul left his face.

Ignoring the doctor, Laurence looked up at Ruthinedt. —Few people ever see the person they could have become. I have cursed you with this for the last weeks of your life. What are you now but the coward you once were?—

Ruthinedt felt the mental bonds began to wind around him, saw Laurence prepare to spring. With one insane burst of will he broke free and bolted, leaving Laurence to land half dazed on the floor where Ruthinedt had stood only a moment before.

Paul heard the locks on the lab door click shut, then the ones for the library as well. He stared at the bars on the window, wondering if Laurence could break through these or if they would be trapped here. Sooner or later soldiers would come, and when the lab door was forced open, Laurence would have trouble enough saving himself. Paul imagined how he would die as he watched Laurence, still caught in a blood-need, take the last shreds of life from the soldier.

Laurence's spread knees straddled the back of the soldier, an arm lifted his torso, the other held his head high and side-ways to keep the wide neck wound open. Throughout it all Laurence's eyes were locked with Baivie's.

The doctor sat up against the door, his breath coming in ragged gulps, his feet kicking in time with the soldier's final contractions. Paul watched, forcing himself to try to under-stand the need that drove his ally now. This was torture and murder of the most horrible kind, and yet he had heard enough from Ruthinedt and Blackwell to know that these deaths were owed. He looked at the table where Laurence had lain, at the blood still dripping from it, then focused all his concentration on a little Dresden figurine on the far side of Baivie's desk: a blond-haired girl balancing a basket of peaches under one arm, her wind-tossed skirt a perfect shade of paint-box blue.

A calm descended on him from a hope so deep, it was marred only by a brief shudder, when, finished with his first victim, Laurence's grip tightened and Paul heard the soldier's neck snap.

Baivie sat waiting. In spite of his pain and the terror he had shared, his lips turned upward with the sly hint of a smile, as if he had somehow been the winner here. When Laurence's hands, the wounds already half covered with new skin, squeezed his upper ams, his expression did not change as he whispered, ''Feed on me. Absorb my life from vengeance, and all I have done here will be a part of you and my memory will live on forever.''

Laurence recoiled, his disgust so intense that it rocked Paul. Called from his reverie, Paul shifted his position slightly so he could see Baivie's face and hear him begin to coax Laurence toward him. ''Come to me. Take me, my young lord. It's what you've desired all along. And you are still hungry, I can sense it. Come, you would not kill your ally when an enemy sits helpless before you. Come, feast on me. Let my life fill you.''

Wide-eyed, posed between flight and attack, Laurence weighed need against caution. He was young and rash in his newfound power, but his elders had trained him well. This was evil only an Old One could absorb. Though it took effort, Laurence broke their mental bond and picked the revolver up from the floor. With only a brief, cold glance and a shake of his head, he lifted it in both ravaged hands.—I will forget even your face— he declared, took careful aim at Baivie's head, and fired. The shot still rang through the room when Laurence tossed the gun aside, lowered his body to the tile floor, and closed his eyes.

Paul hadn't closed his own fast enough. He fell into Baivie's desk chair, leaned forward, and vomited, retching long after his stomach had emptied. When his body calmed, he wiped the sweat and tears from his face, pushed himself to his feet, and staggered closer to Laurence.

Though he knew the danger, he wanted to see what he could not have seen in D'Oscuro. Laurence's skin seemed paler, almost translucent, as if he were made of parchment, hollow and lit from within. He lay so still, he seemed not to breathe at all, but the wound on his neck began to close. It

was not an accelerated form of human healing for a scab
never formed. No, the wound seemed to roll in on itself, the
damaged tissue reform, the skin expand to cover the jagged
line. The hands and feet were next, skin-covered bones
thrusting out from the limbs, the tissue filling in after. An
hour passed. Two. Laurence opened his eyes and scanned the
room as if seeing it for the first time.

His gaze rested on Paul, grew sharp in its need, then softened into sadness. He padded across the room as if those
new feet had always belonged to him, pulled the brandy bottle out of Baivie's desk, and tossed it to Paul. Afterward he
stared sadly down at the notebooks, filled with Baivie's small,
precise writing, details of his nature no one should know. He
ran a finger down the side of the little statue. "I used to stare
at it and pretend I was somewhere else while I tried to escape
what Baivie did here. It's the one thing I will take when I
leave. I'll keep it with me the way Uncle does the great crystal beast my father made; a reminder of what I am."

A beautiful thought, yet Laurence did not sound happy.
Understanding the need Laurence must have to share his sorrow, Paul walked the few feet to where he stood and rested
an arm over his shoulder. Laurence stiffened, then trembled
and pressed close to Paul, pouring out all his anguish and
grief and his certainty that for all the strength he had shown,
he had failed. "I don't understand?" Paul said softly when
Laurence, composed, began to pull away.

Laurence brushed away a few specks of dried blood clinging to Paul's blue wool sweater, his long musician's hands
moving gracefully, as if they had never been less than whole.
"The thought of the agony I would inflict on Ruthinedt sustained me when there was nothing else. And when the time
came to take him, I made a foolish error . . . deliberately.
Now he is gone. He is too terrified to control and he knows
our name. I failed the family, Paul. Once again I failed
them."

Paul shook his head. "You were raised to be what you
are."

"I was raised to be something I am not," Laurence corrected, then said, as lightly as he was able, "Maybe you're
right, but the cause of my mistake doesn't make the situation
any better." He filled the lab sink and began washing the

blood from his body while Paul dug into cabinets and drawers searching for clothing. Both froze as they heard a single truck driving up to the house, a single door slamming.

Ruthinedt heard this too. He had been sitting on his bed, locked in his room, incapable of any decision, reflecting on the horror he had seen in Baivie's lab. The creature was trapped, but now someone would come and let it out and it would find him. He should escape, he knew, but he could never run far enough. Never. As he had many times over the last hour, he ran a shaking hand through his damp hair. Thoughts of suicide were bubbling inside him and he swallowed them back and tried to think.

At last an idea came to him. The Gestapo kept an arsenal in the basement. All he had to do was go down the back stairs and set a fuse before more soldiers came. The house would be destroyed and the creature with it. The prisoners had started a fire when they'd escaped, he'd tell the authorities, and no one would suspect him. No one. He slipped on a heavy winter coat and opened his door. With a fearful glance at the heavy steel locks of the lab door, he started down the hall.

At each end of the long hallway dividing Baivie's living space from his library and lab were tall bare windows. No one had thought to cover these with bars; their height made bars unnecessary. The curtains had been removed and the windows were stark and empty, lit day and night by the sun and the spotlights that shone down on the grounds. Ruthinedt heard no footsteps, only the brush of fabric against fabric and a beast—a beast he had feared since that day on the mountain—stood silhouetted against the window at the top of the main stairs. Ruthinedt's terror hit him with the force of a club across his chest. He mouthed a single word. "You!"

The silhouette altered as the form dropped to a running stance, fingers hard as talons pressed flat against the floor. Ruthinedt heard the snarl of rage, felt a mental force more horrible than any he'd experienced or imagined, felt himself trapped in an eternity of pain. —More . . .—

Ruthinedt screamed with all the terror he'd suppressed for months, turned, and ran. A claw raked his back when, with one final leap, he broke through the window and fell to the freedom of death.

Francis halted, listened. His mind was not needed, the voices were enough. He gripped the bars of Baivie's lab, pressed a foot on either side of the door, and pulled. One set of screws gave way. He pulled again, harder, and the door was forced from its hinges enough that he could slip inside. He stepped over Baivie's body: a single, sweeping glance of the room telling him all that had happened there. He studied the two young ones, his own tense and hungry, the other untouched and gripping a revolver, both ready to fight if anyone else had walked through that door.

—*St' ca'we . . .*—

He said they had won, inflected as if they were both kin! "*Nas szekornes,*" Paul replied, the words spoken perfectly for a claim of victory. Francis studied him, eyes meeting eyes. Paul had been warned about the appearance of those full black eyes, capable of draining all resolve from a man's soul, but nothing could have prepared him for the rush of pleasure that poured into him. Paul laughed—he couldn't help but laugh—and stepped aside as Francis rushed forward to gather his suddenly limp grandson into his arms.

Chapter Twenty-eight

I

FRANCIS CARRIED PAUL up the mountain. At first Paul was slung over his shoulder, so he had the best possible view of the fall he'd take if Francis slipped. Paul was never certain if it was his terror or his bulk that irritated Francis more, but he ended his ride piggyback, feeling ever more foolish for having once believed he could have scaled this path unaided. Through the long journey Laurence plodded behind them, never making a sound.

As they approached the keep, lit by the gray dawn light, Paul understood what design had inspired Stephen's modest castle, for this great structure had the same timelessness, as if these stones had stood forever, challenging God and earth to touch them. A great crack, made by lightning or ice, had rent an outer wall and had been left untended like a warrior's battle scar.

Francis dropped Paul just inside its great doors, and a slight young man dressed in leather and fur helped him to his feet, throwing a quilt over his stiff and frozen shoulders. "Kurt," he said, pointing to himself. "I have wine and a fire. Come." He spoke German slowly, accompanying the words with descriptive gestures. When Paul surprised him, introducing himself and asking to see Hunter, Kurt began chattering happily as he helped Paul down a narrow hall.

Hunter lay sleeping on a cot close to a well-tended fire in a small stone-walled room. The space was warm—at any other time Paul would have thought uncomfortably so—but now the heat soothed the pain of his stiff knees, bringing blessed re-

lief. Kurt lightly brushed Hunter's forehead, then nodded in
satisfaction. He took two pills from a tiny brass cup on the
nighttable and handed them to Paul, along with a glass of
wine. "For the pain," he whispered, and left Paul sitting on
a stool beside the bed. Paul sipped the wine slowly, wishing
he'd asked for something to eat. By the time Hunter woke,
Paul's aches had vanished, though he felt somewhat dizzy and
ravenous.

Hunter's eyes focused on Paul's face. "Franz!" he exclaimed, and grabbed Paul's hand. "Tell me everything that
happened!"

Paul gave details of the last twenty-four hours, watching
Hunter pull himself higher and higher in bed, finding strength
in satisfaction. The quilt fell from his shoulders and Paul saw
the bloodstained bandage on his side. "Did the soldiers shoot
you?" he asked.

"No, Kurt the Hun got overenthusiastic. I'm alive only
because the German soldiers thought he was the enemy. Francis ended the battle—once and forever, I suppose you could
say. I came to long enough to say a name. Since then Kurt's
been a perfect nurse."

"Is there a cook on duty too?"

Hunter glanced at the empty wine bottle beside Paul's chair,
whistled, and rang the bell at his bedside. "The nurse is the
cook and quite willing to serve. Considering how angry a
mountain lord can get, he knows he's lucky to be alive."

A quarter of an hour later their food appeared: a hearty
though somewhat bland stew of meat and potatoes in a large
clay crock; a few black rolls; and a large bar of German
chocolate. Kurt passed around smaller bowls, then went back
to the hall to retrieve a bottle of chilled French champagne
and three delicate crystal glasses. Paul shook his head, looking in complete bewilderment from Kurt to Hunter. "I don't
ask," Hunter replied with a chuckle. "I just enjoy."

"Are you the cook?" Paul asked Kurt as the three men
ate.

"I had to learn."

"Have him explain what he's doing here," Hunter suggested.

Kurt waited until they'd finished eating before beginning
his story. By the time he'd finished, Paul had all the pieces

of the tragic puzzle neatly in place except one. "There is another of the family here?" he asked.

"Sometimes one day out of thirty. Sometimes less," Kurt said sadly.

"His name?"

"Charles." Hunter and both men looked curiously at the odd expression on Paul's face. "Is something wrong?" Hunter asked.

Paul shook his head thoughtfully. Something might be very right. "Where's Laurence now?" he asked Kurt.

"He and the Old One are sleeping under the glass in the great hall. They plan on hunting tonight when Laurence is stronger. I am to join them soon. My blood will help him recover. He's a musician, isn't he? That should be interesting, I think." Kurt spoke as if he enjoyed his use. Given the circumstances of his arrival, Paul thought him remarkably resilient.

Intrigued, Paul asked, "May I come with you?"

"You may watch. I'll show you where."

He led Paul up a narrow winding staircase to the catwalk above the great hall. Below them were the family treasures in crystal, and carvings and canvases. In the center, bathed in the light of Stephen's windows, lay Laurence.

No fabric stood between his skin and that soothing golden light. He lay curled with his head resting on one bent knee, a hand reaching out, long fingers twined with his grandfather's. Francis, clad in a woven robe of blue-black darkness, lay curled around him. Paul thought them both asleep, but as Kurt left him, Francis opened his eyes and looked up at Paul.

—Is he well?— Paul thought.

—Not yet.—

Paul detected the Old One's concern. He gripped the rail and leaned forward to watch Kurt enter the hall and approach the dais. Again Paul was impressed with how confidently Kurt walked, as if nothing could harm him. When he was within arm's length, Francis held out a hand and helped him up.

Everything went calmly, it seemed; Kurt moving slowly to lie above Laurence, their heads almost touching. Paul was

reminded of the night in Chaves with Stephen, but there was
a more solemn meaning here than a sharing of blood or the
pleasure of a vision. Francis's hand brushed his grandson's
forehead, and Laurence woke, his eyes not focused, as if it
were he who dreamed. Paul wished to know . . . and the
wishing was enough.

Music fills the space; music mingled with the sound of
children and scents of orange and chamomile. There is no
piano here and no player, only lace and whitewashed floors
and a woman standing beside a peat stove boiling water for
tea. The sounds form in his mind as he sits across from her
and stares at the candlelight reflected in her hair.
    The hills roll around them, green and damp from the sea
and at the shore, one by one the whitecapped waves cover
him and cannot wash him clean.

Through the haze of the vision Paul saw Kurt, his head
back, lost in the deep, almost pleasant dream. Laurence
stirred, trying to hold back the nightmare that would come,
but Francis pushed him on.

He is small and lonely and their laughter is beautiful. There
is an organ-grinder with a monkey, and he puts a penny in
the cup and sits with his head on his knees while the old man
plays the Blue Danube Waltz. There is a metal gym in the
park with a ladder stretched high across two supports, and he
reaches up to it and begins to swing, innocent of the few
children who have stopped their play to watch him. Someone
laughs. Another calls him some name he does not understand. He swings higher, faster, aware too late that below
him the child-sounds have stopped. He hears his mother's
mental scream and it goes on and on. The water turns red, a
sweeping, deadly whirlpool of blood sucking him down and
down as he feels her die.

Kurt thrashed in his mental bonds, tears in his blind open
eyes, fighting to escape this memory. Francis held him with
hands aiding his mind until Laurence raised the young man's
shaking wrist to his lips, feasting on fear and guilt and misery.

Paul had seen enough. He took a few deep, steadying breaths and hobbled down the stairs in time to see Kurt bolt from the great hall, skirting Paul at the portal, not pausing to speak as he ran down a dark passage. Paul heard the slamming of a door.

—Go to him. Stay with him. In the morning I will speak with you.—

—As you wish— Paul responded to the Old One, and followed his directions to the young man's room.

Kurt lay across his bed, his blanket smeared with blood, shaking, unable to stop. "I can't remember what he did," he said through dry sobs. "I'm glad."

Paul stayed with Kurt for hours, telling him everything Laurence had suffered in the weeks since he'd been taken. By the time they heard Hunter's demanding bell, the young man looked far more calm. It seemed, Paul thought with a wry touch of irony, that he had a real knack for comforting the wounded.

The wind shifted north that night, bringing in a bitter cold that chilled even the walls of the warm, tiny room. The three men shared the space, Paul and Kurt sleeping before the fire, taking turns feeding it while Hunter slept the night through. Hours passed and Paul took his cane and slipped quietly from the room.

Yes, the sun had risen. He walked down the corridor to the great hall and circled it. The works on display were magnificent, but his eye was drawn more to the construction.

He studied the way the stones had been laid, how the arches were vaulted, how the long catwalk had been built into the stones. He examined the tiles beneath his feet, lifting a corner of the rug to view the expanding swirl of color that spiraled from the center to the walls. Could this have been the inspiration for the swirl of color at Lyons? He looked up at the windows. They seemed so plain, yet already the range and blend of color was evident. Given time—and, yes, Stephen had time—the artist would develop genius.

—And human stupidity.—

—Do you think so?— Paul's reply held no surprise. He'd been expecting this intrusion on his thoughts.

—Since the day that poor child walked confused and ach-

ing into Chaves, has anyone told him his mother's death and
father's abandonment were not his fault?— Paul felt Francis
moving closer and turned slowly to meet the Old One's eyes,
the insides of their black shells red with anger. He felt the
waves of guilt and sorrow and shame as Francis invaded his
mind once more.

—Here was how he felt when his lover died, when his sister
stood wounded and bleeding calling his name, when his
cousin died in a fiery blast trying to save him. Even you.
Here was how he felt when you limped into that room to
rescue him.— Francis saw that Paul had been holding his
breath to keep from screaming at the bombardment of this
mental pain, and he reached out, holding Paul steady as he
released him. —He cannot walk among men, not wounded
as he is now, and he cannot stay with me. His place is not
in my world. I need your help.—

"What can I do?"

—Nothing but help me find the one who can.—

Paul looked away, unable to hide the fear growing in him.

—Name it!—

"That what I am will be lost in you, even more than in
the rest of them."

—Fool!— Francis's hands gripped Paul's shoulders, only
the motion of the loose sleeves of his robe revealing that they
had been at his side. —Look into me and see your future.—

Paul dared not disobey. These eyes were like windows at
midnight in which Paul could only reflect but not be seen.
He saw himself in them—not older, but more mature, as if
the years had steadied, not aged, him. In a sudden burst of
will his hands moved out to rest on Francis's forearms, and
they stood motionless in the great hall as the buildings rose
around them.

Here are his dreams, his children . . . small and large,
high and sprawling, born and taking shape within the mirrors
of those eyes. He sees Chaves altered, and Lisbon and London and the skyline of New York . . . His children . . . The
one small gem he had built for her growing into atriums and
domes and steeples of churches so delicate, men marvel that
they can stand . . . His dreams, his genius, something no
creature could take or control.

They vanish in one moment, and all that remains is his

greatest creation, built of earth and steel to hold back man's final fiery tide.

And her face, loving as is has always been, pale in the light of a single candle. With all the trust of their years together, he rests an open hand against her cheek.

—When the world ends, it will be you who saves them. Save one now.—

Paul nodded. He felt himself led forward, falling onto the soft pillows of the dais as they flew.

Francis needed only Paul's confidence to aid him, and Paul gave it freely. The mountains sank and the land lay cold and dead beneath them. They spiraled out and out from the great stone keep, master and willing slave tethered only by will to their bodies, searching for one tiny point of light. They found it as they knew they would, and the light grew brighter until it shone like a beacon, souls touching, the command given: —Come home . . . come home.—

Again they soared, lost for hours in the ecstasy of flight. When the walls closed around them once more, Paul saw Francis sitting cross-legged beside him, his expression calm and thoughtful. "Will he come?" Paul asked.

—Soon.—

Exhausted by the hours they had traveled, Paul closed his eyes and slept.

Days passed. Hunter recovered and the three young men filled the great hall with shouts and laughter. Laurence joined them sometimes, but his sorrow made him seem fragile and empty, like a crystal glass waiting to be filled. He never stayed long, and often Paul wished he could say the words to heal those wounds but it must not be he who spoke them.

Days passed. Paul's confidence never waned.

Paul was present when Francis heard the call. The old one paused in mid-sentence, his eyes lost their focus, and without a word he left. Though his presence might be an intrusion, Paul had to see what he had helped to do, and he hobbled up the steps to the tower and stared out at the moonlit snow.

He saw Francis first, the tall gaunt, figure gliding down the path as if the dark cloak wrapped around him were a sail in the wind. From the shelter of a boulder beside the path a shadow rose to meet him. They stood motionless, speechless, their mental exchange evident in the way they faced each other. He sensed Laurence beside him. "You helped do this?" Laurence asked.

Paul nodded and prayed. When the summons came, Laurence did not bother with the inside stairs. Paul judged the tower height at sixty feet, a paltry jump for a mountain lord. By the time he looked up, Laurence was in his father's arms.

The father and son hunted. For days they ran free beneath the moon and stars on peaks that were reserved for creatures more surefooted than man. They slept in caves with no fire to warm them. They spoke long and cautiously about the past, and there were secrets, yes; secrets Laurence was too young to claim. But one truth was clear: The family would have gone home, anyway. His mother's death had never been his fault.

The room rose full again before Laurie returned, and when he did, he was not alone.

II

Spring came, green and flowing with icy runoffs, and beneath them men fought and died, but here, in another world, peace came early.

Charles disappeared from time to time, bringing back supplies and reports of the war, which he shared only with Hunter. At last Laurence and Paul were included. This would be their best chance to leave. Once the Russians took Romania, Paul, who could never pass for Romanian, would be trapped there.

They wore native clothes. Hunter had a revolver, Charles his bow. They traveled to the tiny depot south of Tirgu. Three days passed before an afternoon train stopped to take on passengers, and as it did, Paul pointed to an open boxcar and whispered to Charles, "Now?"

—Wait. We'll let it pull out first.—

Though Paul didn't argue, he gripped his cane and thought he'd never make it.

Charles looked sideways at him. —It's only your knees, isn't it? Not your hands or even your thighs. When the time comes to move, all you'll have to do is hold on.—

"Thank you."

—You came to save my son's life. This is hardly payment for the debt I owe.— Charles handed his bow to Laurence, and Paul slipped over Charles's back like a child. —Close your eyes, keep your knees high. I'll guide your movements."

The train rolled slowly out, gaining speed as it left the station. Paul followed Charles's orders and the wind whipped through his hair. This was not like holding on to a horse . . . there was no lumbering heaviness. It was more like soaring or riding a swing, the feet touching the ground only long enough to push them off again.

—Now!—

Paul's knees moved higher and he leaned into the jump. He felt the thud, the sudden lurch sideways, and they rolled into the back of the dusty boxcar. A second thump and Laurence landed behind them. With no added burden to unbalance him, he stayed where he landed a moment before coming back to sit beside Paul. Charles laid an affectionate hand on Laurence's shoulder and moved forward to pull Hunter up.

Hunter ran beside the train, his legs pumping furiously. But the healing weeks on the mountain had not undone the damage of months of starvation. He began to tire and lose speed. The rear engine was approaching, and rather than risk being seen and ruin the chances for the others, he rolled down into the ditch and lay flat.

Charles crawled to where Laurence sat beside Paul, wrapped his arms around his son, and kissed him. Paul did not share the exchange but he knew what had been said from the desolate expression on Laurence's face. Paul's vision blurred and he turned his head away. When he looked back, Charles had gone.

Laurence bowed his head, his chin touching his chest, his hands tight fists against his cheeks. "He told me his place was with Hunter in this tragic, stupid war."

Laurence began to shake from one more grief, and Paul could do nothing but hold him as the others surfaced. They both mourned as they lay side by side, feeling the train move south.

Epilogue

Paul Stoddard
March 1946

I

STEPHEN ASKED ME to write this because it is primarily my story. He asked that it be written to give some sense of my own feelings, a human perspective on what occurred, for those of the family who will learn this history long after I am gone.

We made it home, of course, or this would not have been written. We rode and walked and swam, and there were times I thought I'd died, but always Laurie pulled me back. I think sometimes that he only left with me so he could deliver me back to his uncle, one minor flotsam from the deluge, but by the time we traveled to Greece, then on to Europe, a friendship was forged that will last my lifetime and beyond.

Elizabeth was waiting for me with the others at Alpha, and it was only her face I saw as I stepped off the plane. She ran forward, and as I kissed her, some joy not her own flowed through her to me. She pulled back and pointed past me to where Emma and Tad were running up to Laurie, who had crouched down, his long arms spread wide to receive them.

I hadn't known he thought them dead, but it was better I never told him the truth. The happiness of that surprise cleansed more of his sorrow, and that night, as I lay beside Elizabeth in the bed Laurence had once shared with Kathleen, I heard his music rising from the room below us.

The family failed as I suppose they were destined to fail. I think sometimes of everything I saw in my journey through the Reich and the stories we heard after the war had ended, and I know that nothing one insane man had done to Laurence Austra could begin to equal the horrors that sane men inflicted on one another. No, Stephen could as easily hold back the tide as prevent the end his experts had predicted.

I waited two years before I began writing this story. I started the day after the bomb exploded over Hiroshima. Michael heard the news on the radio and all of us congregated in Stephen's office to hear the few details the Allies were providing. As I sat there watching the family listening intently, concerned not with the fate of the victims or of themselves—for they cannot conceive of an end to their lives—but with this fragile world, I understood what a small part of Earth our lonely race is.

In half a century its end will come. No need to dwell on the inevitability, only to be prepared.

II

Gregory Hunter
October 1955

I don't know how in the hell he tracked me down. One day I was sitting at my desk, tired and more than a little bored, when Grace buzzed and told me I had a visitor. "He won't give his name," she said, and I wondered why she sounded so uneasy. I wondered, that is, until I saw him standing in the doorway, looking no older than he had twelve years before.

And no more happy, though now it seemed he'd been surprised by grief rather than immersed in it for months. "I want you to tell me what happened to my father after I'd gone," he blurted. I admit I got a minor rush of pleasure in how uneasy he sounded.

"Then close the door and sit down, Laurence Austra," I replied. If he felt any surprise at my knowing his family name, he didn't show it.

I spoke for hours, telling him how we fought in those months of chaos, not for one side or the other but for the people trapped between them. I told him about the refugees

who took shelter in the foothills of the Vardas, protected only
by the minds of the great and ancient lords above them.

I spared nothing, not even the darkness I sensed growing
in his father, as if each death he had caused pulled from deep
inside him some savage, ancient strength. I told him how we
would sleep close together, his father's hand always resting
on me, my human presence somehow holding back that darkness inside him.

"One night in the shelter of the keep I dreamed I was the
enemy. It was a terrible, vivid dream, one I had called up
many times before, but this time I woke with your father's
hands around my throat.

"He looked right at me, but I knew he saw an enemy's
face. It would have been fatal to fight, so I called his name
softly, calling it mentally when his hands tightened and I
couldn't speak, and the part of him I knew took control and
released me. He lay shaking beside me. I wanted to tell him
we should call it quits, but the next evening we went back to
the destruction. His disease—I suppose you could call it that—
grew worse, until it seemed my choices were to die from an
enemy bullet or at my ally's hands. Each time we returned to
our lonely, private war, I would swear this would be the last.
Then I hear news of some new atrocity and forget that vow.
I thought about how the war was destroying your father. I
think he did, too, but we never talked about it."

"And afterward? What happened after the war was over?"

"Your father kept his promise and we took Kurt home. We
had heard of the destruction of Hamburg, of course, but no
one told us that Bremen had been so damaged. There was
nothing standing to mark Kurt's street but a few intact sections of brickwork, a solitary pillar, and a small piece of
twisted iron. He'd dreamed so long of home and family, and
now he found that both were ashes.

"There were three British soldiers nearby. Their backs were
to us and they were laughing at something one had said. Kurt
focused all his hate on them. He wasn't armed, but when he
screamed *'Mörder!'* and rushed toward them, one panicked,
raised his gun, and fired.

"We had fought together for so many months, but I had
never seen your father in a rage to equal this. He was on the
guilty soldier before I even knew what had happened. The

other two had their weapons raised, but before they could use them, I shot them.

"I remember how your father looked, blood dripping from his hands, his expression defiant as he waited to see the hate that I could never feel for him. He took a step forward into my arms and I finally understood that need he had to touch something alive when the sorrow grew too great. Then we ran."

"But did you see him later?" Laurence prompted.

I nodded. "He came back with me. He wanted to see America, he told me, but it seemed to me that he had nowhere else to go. I made him promise he'd keep in touch, and a few months after I began working for the OSS, he called me.

"We met at dusk in a New York street café. He arrived first and had claimed a table in a quiet corner. He was wearing a spotless black suit, a broad-brimmed hat shading his eyes from the setting sun. As he sipped ice water he stared at a building under construction across the street.

" 'I brought your papers,' I told him, and slipped the envelope across the table.

"He opened it and looked at me with an odd expression. 'Stuart Charles Hunter,' he read. 'You've placed too much trust in me.'

" 'It was my brother's name. He died at Normandy. I pulled some strings. They're yours and they're legal.'

" 'They'll do for a while.'

"I couldn't understand why he looked so empty, so I began to tell him, 'If you ever need a place to stay or any money—'

"He laughed. 'I make a thousand a week.'

'I smiled sheepishly. Then, thinking of the good name of my family, I asked what he did to earn it.

" 'I've found a number of callings. I paint flattering portraits of rich Connecticut matrons at a thousand a canvas. If they guessed who they're really getting, they'd gladly pay fifty times the price. Once or twice a month I play the piano in a café on Forty-seventh Street.'

"I couldn't shake the feeling that something was wrong, so I asked him outright.

" 'The sun sets and rises and sets again and I go on. I thought I wouldn't. I expected we would die together.' He spoke as if the words meant nothing, then stared once more at the building. 'What do you think of it?' he asked me.

"It must sound stupid now, but that was the first modern skyscraper in New York City and I wasn't the only one who said out loud, 'Too high, too fragile. It will never stand. But I hear the architect has quite a reputation. His picture was even on the front page of last night's paper.'

" 'Was it?'

" 'He's getting some award tonight. The owner of the building will be there with him. Should I go?'

" 'That would not be wise.'

" 'Damn it, Charles! They're your family!'

"He patted the envelope on the marble-topped table. 'My name is Hunter now. Fitting, don't you think?' I nodded, unable to argue, then followed his eyes back to the building. A construction elevator was going up its side and I saw something familiar in the build of the tall, slender man standing inside it. Charles caught the resemblance, too, and looked quickly down, his wide-brimmed hat shading his face. We sat silently for a half hour or so. Then he slipped the envelope into his suit pocket and left. I never saw him again."

Laurence stared down at the papers strewn across my desk. "Why did you come here now?" I eventually asked.

He told me a long, tragic story that has never been written. Perhaps it's just as well.